The Boggart Sourcebook

a companion volume to
The Boggart: Folklore, History, Place-names and Dialect

https://doi.org/10.47788/KZLH9484

by Simon Young

also published by University of Exeter Press

Exeter New Approaches to Legend, Folklore and Popular Belief

Series Editors:
Simon Young, University of Virginia (CET, Siena) and
Davide Ermacora, University of Turin

Exeter New Approaches to Legend, Folklore and Popular Belief provides a venue for growing scholarly interest in folklore narratives, supernatural belief systems and the communities that sustain them. Global in scope, the series encompasses milieus ranging from ancient to contemporary times and encourages empirically grounded, source-rich studies. The editors favour the broad multidisciplinary approach that has characterized the study of folklore and the supernatural, and which brings together insights from historians, folklorists, anthropologists and many other branches of the humanities and social sciences.

The Boggart Sourcebook

Texts and Memories for the Study of the British Supernatural

COMPILED AND EDITED BY
SIMON YOUNG

UNIVERSITY
of
EXETER
PRESS

First published in 2022 by
University of Exeter Press
Reed Hall, Streatham Drive
Exeter EX4 4QR, UK

www.exeterpress.co.uk

A CIP catalogue record for this book is available from the British Library.

https://doi.org/10.47788/QXUA4856

ISBN 978-1-905816-93-4 Hbk
ISBN 978-1-905816-94-1 ePub
ISBN 978-1-905816-95-8 PDF

Cover image: a boggart throws its head after an escaping pedestrian. From James Bowker's, *The Goblin Tales of Lancashire* (London: W. Swan Sonnenschein & Co., 1883), p. 136

Typeset in Perpetua 11½ point on 14 point by
Palimpsest Book Production Ltd, Falkirk, Stirlingshire

Contents

Introduction

'Boggart' is a generic term to describe the solitary supernatural creatures that terrified the English North and parts of the Midlands in Victorian (and in some cases later) times. In the process of researching and writing my recent University of Exeter Press book *The Boggart: Folklore, History and Dialect*, I built up three corpora:

(i) boggarts in ephemera (broadsides, letters, magazines and newspapers);
(ii) boggart names (boggart place-names and boggart personal names);
(iii) a contemporary boggart folklore survey (the *Boggart Census*).

In the following pages I include part of the ephemera and all of the boggart names and the boggart folklore survey, hoping that the material will be useful to others. In Part I, 'Boggart Ephemera', there is a selection of nineteenth-century boggart writing (particularly material that is difficult to find in libraries); in Part II there are 'Boggart Names' (boggart placenames and personal names); part III presents the entire *Boggart Census*. Please note that, throughout, I use the English county boundaries as they were prior to the reforms of the mid-1970s.

I dedicate this sourcebook, as I did *The Boggart*, to my elder daughter, Lisi.

Abbreviations

BC: Boggart Census (part three of the present volume)
Ch: Cheshire
De: Derbyshire
ERY: East Riding of Yorkshire
La: Lancashire
Li: Lincolnshire
Notts: Nottinghamshire
OSCh: Six-inch Ordnance Survey map of Cheshire
OSDe: Six-inch Ordnance Survey map of Derbyshire
OSLa: Six-inch Ordnance Survey map of Lancashire
OSLi: Six-inch Ordnance Survey map of Lincolnshire
OSY: Six-inch Ordnance Survey map of Yorkshire
WRY: West Riding of Yorkshire

Corpus One: Boggart Ephemera

This section gathers nineteenth-century boggart ephemera, particularly from newspapers but also from magazines, rare books and broadsides. Given the space constraints, I concentrate on material that other researchers might have trouble finding. I have typically included here actual boggart news (everything from 'boggart hunts' to children dying from boggart stories, *sic*) rather than incidental asides about boggart-lore. I have not (again for reasons of space) included the works of John Higson (valuable as they are). These are now available in *South Manchester Supernatural: The Ghosts, Fairies and Boggarts of Victorian Gorton, Lees, Newton and Saddleworth* (Pwca Ghost, Witch and Fairy Pamphlets, 2020). Nor have I included James McKay, 'The Evolution of East Lancashire Boggarts' (1888), as this can be freely downloaded on my academia.edu site.

The material is given in order of publication.

Boggart Pun

The following serio-comic scene, we are positively assured took place in the neighbouring town of Kirkham, about a fortnight since: One morning, (evening we should think) a tall, thin personage of ominous aspect, and most awfully enveloped in a long grey cloak, of the most ample folds we can imagine, advanced towards a young woman in the public street, and with a hollow voice and mysterious air, most condescendingly vouchsafed to open his sepulchral lips to her, with a question, which, from the poor woman's agitation at being addressed by the ghost-like stranger, she did not comprehend. Thinking, however, at last, that if flesh and blood at all, her grim inquirer could be no other than a six feet sybil, she plucked up resolution enough to say she did not want her 'fortin tellin'. 'I beg pardon,' returned the man, 'I am no fortune-teller, – I want' – lowering his tone again, of course, the gravest pitch – 'I want a spirit vault.' This plain question the poor girl, who had never ceased to associate boggarts and goblins with the dreadful stranger from the first moment she beheld him, directed him, with fear and trembling, to the church-yard, then turn to the right hand and he would see a monument (one just erected to the memory of E. King, Esq.) underneath which she could assure him he would find the object of his search – a spirit vault. Saying this, she darted off, leaving the thirsty gentleman in amazement at the extraordinary instructions he had received, for it seems his half-smothered inquiry had no other object than a drop of comfort from the nearest gin shop. *Preston Pilot.*

'Practical Pun', *Berkshire Chronicle* (14 October 1826), 3.

Red Boggart

On Saturday last, a considerable sensation was excited in this town in consequence of a report prevailing that a woman had cut the throat of her child and afterwards her own. From what we have been able to collect, it seems, that the person alluded to, with her child, have been for some time residing at the house of Robert Simpson, in China Lane, and the woman has been in the habit of attending a debtor in the Castle, and had passed for his wife, although her husband is still living. The woman's name is Sarah Parker, and the child's, a girl about twelve years of age, Amanda Parker, and daughter to the former, by her husband. Early on the morning in question a little girl, daughter to the person with whom they lodged, was ordered by her mother to go into the room which the two persons occupied, and fetch a clean cap out of a drawer for her; but she came running downstairs saying that there was a red 'boggart' in the room, and she durst not go in. Her mother then went upstairs, and as soon as she reached the door of the room observed the wretched creatures lying on the bed, weltering in their blood. She therefore hastened to communicate the circumstance to her neighbours, and shortly after returned with two or three of them, who accompanied her to the place, when they found the two persons in the state above described. On examining them it was discovered that the girl's throat was cut in three different places, and both hands were shockingly mangled, in attempting to save herself; and her breasts were also scratched. The woman's throat was likewise cut, and an incision made in the wind-pipe. A surgeon was immediately sent for, and the wounds had proper care taken of them. The woman resisted having her wounds dressed, and as soon as that on her throat was sewed up, she attempted to pull the stitches out again, but was prevented.

'Attempt at Murder and Suicide', *Lancaster Gazette* (19 Apr 1828), 3.

Dead Baby Boggart

[Editor's Note: a baby's body has been found at Brindle. The man who discovered it first believed that it was a 'whelp'. John Parker who apparently discovered the baby in his house thought that it was a 'boggart'.]

John Parker said that on the Tuesday previous he went up into the garret of a house in which his mother lives at Brindle, and in one corner of the room he saw something which he took to be a 'boggart'. He brought it downstairs: and immediately after laid it on the grass, near a midden stead. Towards night, on the same day, he went back to see it and it was gone! On Saturday night he went again and found it near the place where he first saw it, and he then took it up, and threw it over the hedge into the adjoining field. He believed the child to be the same as that produced at the inquest.

'Extraordinary Case', *Preston Chronicle* (21 Jul 1832), 3.

Nude Boggart

The neighbourhood of Winsford, near Middlewich, has, for the last three years, been disturbed by an apparition of rather a strange character which, in that part of the country, is termed by the country folks 'a *Boggart*.' This apparition appeared in the shape of a naked man, generally at dusk, on the road adjacent to Winsford, sometimes three or four months intervening between the appearance of this much dreaded *boggart*. At length the terror created by his appearance so much scared the female part of the community, that they dared not venture out of doors after dusk. On Saturday night, the 4th instant, between the hours of eleven and twelve, as a female servant at a beer house was washing the floor, all the family but herself being in bed, she heard a gentle tapping at the window. She lifted up her head, and, to her terror and amazement, there beheld the much dreaded '*boggart*,' standing before the window. The terrified girl uttered a scream, and fell insensible on the floor. The noise awoke the master, who ran through the back door to the front of the house, where he came in contact with the apparition: but being in no way daunted by his ghostship, he seized him, when he stated that he had merely come for a glass of ale. The individual, who had been behaving in this disgusting and extraordinary manner, turns out to be a member of the Primitive Wesleyan Chapel, in Winsford, named George Barlow. Of course, he was brought before the magistrates, who regretted that the law did not empower them to punish him further than by sending him to the tread mill for three months. He is now undergoing that punishment at the Knutsford House of Correction.

Macclesfield. 'Commitment of a Ghost to the Tread-Mill',
Leeds Times (25 Jan 1834), 3.

Boggart Assault

John Higginson, a young man was brought up under a warrant obtained against him and another person (not in custody) charged with a most serious outrage and assault upon Betty Dinsdale and her husband, in September last. Mrs. Dinsdale said that on Sunday night the 2nd of September, she was coming with her husband between Ewood Bridge and Moorgate Fold; they saw something lying in the road and her husband said, do not speak I have seen a 'boggart.' Soon after a young man jumped up from the road side in a white sheet, and stood against the barn door. Another person (the one not in custody) struck her husband several times and would make him fight. She seized hold of Higginson to keep him from her husband, for at this time the other man had him down and was punching him. Higginson at last got away from her and began punching her husband. William Cook, the watchman at Moorgate Fold, was next examined. He heard a woman screaming apparently as hard as she could 'you'll kill him, you'll kill him.' He ran to the spot as quick as he could and there he saw the defendant and the other man with Dinsdale against the dyke striking him. On his arrival they both ran away. He had a dog with him which seized one of them and they kicked it. He followed them a short distance and then turned back, he was afraid of being misused. They took Dinsdale's hat with them, and afterwards brought it to the witness and wanted him to take it to the complainant but he refused. The complainant's husband corroborated his wife's story, and said he had been confined to his bed for a month, in consequence of the injuries he had received, and been obliged to call in a medical gentleman. Mr Cort, surgeon, deposed that he found Dinsdale in bed, with several bruises on various parts of his body. His spine was much injured and he had lost the use of his limbs. He had great doubts at one time that he would not get better. Higginson said the complainant first ran at him and he slipped aside and Dinsdale fell on his face. They walked on and Dinsdale came after them and would fight, and then they struck him. The damages amounted to £7, 2s. 6d., and the defendant was ordered to retire and settled with the complainant, or they would inflict the heaviest penalty upon him which the law permitted. He was also required to find sureties.

'Serious Assault', *Blackburn Gazette* (21 Nov 1838), 3.

The Spaw Boggart

One of those singular cases commonly classed amongst the supernatural has produced a considerable sensation amongst the inhabitant of the district of Middleton and the surrounding villages. The following are a few of the particulars. In a small valley called Spaw in the township of Acrington [Alkrington] near Middleton, are three small cottages joined together, which stand on the site of a spaw or bathing place, and from which it derives its name. The families who last resided in them state to our correspondent that they have been obliged to leave them in consequence of being disturbed in the dead of night by what are vulgarly called 'boggarts', making a noise as of a person trampling up and downstairs in a heavy pair of clogs; at other times removing the chairs, fender, and other articles of furniture. Lately, one man, a collier, named Jacob Kendal, digged up in the house several yards of earth, expecting to find the bones of some murdered person, but found nothing except a fire poker and part of an old wall, supposed to be connected with the bathing place. The houses have been uninhabited, and of late hundreds of persons have been to visit the supposed haunted premises, from the neighbouring places. On Tuesday evening week, a young man, a coal-miner, named Isaac Unsworth, went himself, as if in bravado, and according to his own statement, when within a few yards of the haunted place, he knelt down, and prayed, that if there was either boggart or devil to be seen, he might see it. He then proceeded to the houses, and kicked open one of the doors, when (as he states) a girl, of apparently about three or four years of age, appeared, with a buff nankeen bonnet on, but immediately disappeared. A very tall man of forbidding aspect, also made his appearance, whence he knew not. After being offered money by the man he was thrown against the wall with great violence. He then began to offer up ejaculations. When the supposed apparition disappeared, he hastened home, a distance of about 100 yards, and told his neighbours the story above related; he was considerably excited and several persons endeavoured to reconcile him, but in vain. He went to bed, but could not rest. He rose about two o'clock in the morning, and again went in his shirt towards the haunted houses, and met the tall man about half way there, who offered him a handful of gold, as he stated, to go with him: but he again began to pray, when [the tall man] disappeared in a flash of light, with a report similar to what would have been produced by the ignition of a barrel of gunpowder!!! The young man, by some means, got home, but was for several days unable to follow his employment. He still persists in saying, that it was either a boggart or the devil. Strange as it is, all the families who have resided for the last 30 or 40 years, declared they have often been terrified by similar unearthly noises. The houses are empty, and persons are going daily to view them. Singular and ridiculous as the above may appear to philosophers, even in these enlightened times, it is believed by most in the neighbourhood, that the above houses are haunted by something, not of this world; and even to the more enlightened classes it is wrapped in a deep mystery. The parties named in the above are well known in the neighbourhood as being respectable in their calling, and can testily to the truth of the above strange account. [The editor adds] We publish the above as sent to us by our correspondent, but cannot avoid expressing a belief that some designing persons for some purpose or other, are imposing upon the 'good folks' of the neighbourhood. The age of superstition is past, and can only be revived in a rural district.

'The Spaw 'Boggart', *Bolton Chronicle* (19 Jan 1839), 3.

Since the disasters of the storm have ceased to occupy the attention of the good people in the neighbourhood of Middleton, they have found an exciting topic of conversation in a ghost story, which has been very generally circulated there, and which, we have no doubt, has just as good claims to belief as all the other stories of the same kind, that have at various times obtained currency and credence in different parts of the country. The scene of this story is an uninhabited house, not far from the Alkrington colliery, in a lone and desolate situation, and altogether as suitable a domicile as any ghost need desire to possess. It is connected with a tradition of some atrocities, ending in the murder of a child, which was said to have been buried in the cellar; and the house has, almost as a matter of course under such circumstances, had a very indifferent reputation ever since; successive occupiers having heard, or what was quite as good, imagined that they heard, during the dead of night, diverse sounds, which could not be accounted for by any natural causes. Some years ago, the house was tenanted by a man known in the neighbourhood as 'Owd Jone Whittaker,' who, it was said, became familiarized to uncommon sounds, for the most part beginning with something like the tread of a very heavy foot, and ending like the cries of a child. 'Owd Jone,' however, does not appear to have been quite so faint-hearted as some of his successors; for he, and two sisters who lived with him, withstood the supposed noises for several years without flinching. It is said that Whittaker believed that the sounds indicated the concealment of money somewhere about the premises, and he had nearly brought the building down by digging in the cellars, in the vain hope of finding the hidden treasure. Since his time, the house has been divided into three tenements, with separate doors of entrance, and has been repeatedly occupied by colliers and others, who however, after a short sojourn, have always been driven away either by strange noises or by their own fears: and the last tenants, an elderly couple, were so much terrified one night, that they fled at once from the house, and several days elapsed before they durst return for the purpose of taking away their furniture. This fact, of course, confirmed the reputation of the house, and since that time, it has been wholly untenanted; very few persons choosing even to venture near the 'boggart heawse' as it is commonly called, except in good broad daylight. Recently, however, an individual has been found adventurous enough to beard the ghost in his own territory and the particulars of the adventure, as related by or for the adventurous wight, are the subject of the narrative and discussions which we have already alluded to as being current in the neighbourhood of Middleton. The following is the substance of them: At a beer-shop in a place called Stocks, which is very near the house in question, there lodges a man named Isaac Unsworth, a collier, who, for one of his calling, is said to be a quiet orderly man, when sober. On the first night of the present year, however, as might reasonably be anticipated, he came home a little elevated with liquor; and after sitting a short time by the fire, he started up, about ten o'clock, and declared he would go to the 'boggart heawse.' In vain did his landlady try to dissuade him; go he would, and go he did. After being absent about half an hour, he returned home, in a state of great apparent terror and distress; and, as soon as he became composed, related a story of which the following are the leading particulars: On coming up to the place he 'punsed' at the first door, when it flew open, and he went in; and, having danced a step on the floor, called out: 'Ho! if there's ony one here, let him come!' Nothing, however, appeared; and he went to the second door, which, in like manner yielded to his foot, and be there in like manner, repeated his summons without effect. 'The third time', however, according to a vulgar adage, 'pays for all;' and so according to the story, Isaac Unsworth found it. On approaching the door, he found it open, and there he had no occasion at all to repeat his summons; for, as he entered the door, a little girl, having a bonnet on, with a bow of ribbon on one side, went in before him, and stood in the middle of the floor; on which, being apparently in a humour for dancing, he danced a step round her, when she suddenly disappeared. At that moment a man entered the room, as if pursuing the girl. The newcomer was of very formidable appearance, but Isaac Unsworth had had too many new-year's gifts to be frightened at trifles. As in the case of Burn's Tam o' Shanter, under circumstances not very dissimilar: The swats sae ream'd in Isaac's noddle,/ Fair play, he cared nae deil's a bodle;/ and he therefore resolutely challenged the stranger to wrestle for half a gallon of ale! The challenge was as promptly accepted; they closed, and Isaac, though he put in all he could found himself immediately lifted from his feet, and thrown with great violence against the wall where he lay stunned and senseless for several minutes. On coming to himself he beat a speedy retreat, unmolested when a voice called after him, that he must return at two o'clock, and pay his debt. This demand greatly troubled him for being a man of honour in his way, he did not like to 'levant,' as the sporting phrase is; but he had very little stomach for facing his formidable antagonist a second time. Fearing, however, that worse might come of it if he failed, he determined to keep the appointment; and, accordingly, a little before two o'clock, he sallied forth on his way to the place of meeting. Whether he duly carried with him the half-gallon of ale he had lost, or whether he meant to tender 'dry money' (which, we should imagine, would be an affront to any ghost of respectability), the story is unfortunately silent; but it records, that, on arriving at the house, he saw his old antagonist, who now seemed of gigantic stature, and who offered him a handful of money if he would try two more falls. Isaac Unsworth, however, had had quite enough in the first encounter, and very prudently declined the offer; on which the spectre, according to all ghostly etiquette, 'vanished in a flame of fire,' letting the money fall upon the ground, which Isaac did not stop to pick up, but made his way back home with all the speed he could master. Such is the story which at present occupies the attention of all the gossips in the neighbourhood of Middleton, and it is repeated in a great variety of shapes, and with embellishments according to the respective tastes of the narrators. There are, indeed, some sceptical folks who express a doubt whether Isaac Unsworth was not far too drunk to know at all what happened to him on the night in question; but these doubts have very little influence on the multitude, who accept the entire story as gospel, and the 'boggart heawse' has recently been the principal place of public resort in the neighbourhood. Some of the more knowing ones suggest that the man seen by Isaac Unsworth, was the evil one himself, and that the recent tempest was the natural result of the disturbance which Isaac Unsworth's visit had caused him; in which case undoubtedly, a very large number of persons have good reason to complain of folly and temerity.

'A Ghost Story', *Sheffield Independent* (26 Jan 1839), 6.

Earthquake Boggarts

Our Wigan correspondent says, this phenomenon [earthquake] took place in this town and neighbourhood at about five minutes to one o'clock on the morning of the 17th inst. The shock was apparently from south-west to north-east, and the vibration of the earth, which lasted for a few seconds, was more or less felt in Ince, Hindley, Aspul, and the surrounding villages. The details of alarm and fright are numerous, and tend greatly to shew the ignorance that prevails upon the subject. Some alarmed the house by raising a cry of thieves; others lay quaking in be close covered up, for fear of seeing a 'boggart,' and others equally superstitious, thought that it was sent to forewarn them of the sudden demise of their relatives, who were then lying on a bed of sickness. The effects of the shock caused some alarm in a gentleman's house, by ringing the bells, &c., but happily without doing any damage to either life or property.

'The Earthquake', *The Liverpool Mercury* (24 March 1843), 93.

Boggart Rape

Eli Salmon, aged 20, and William Palin, aged 18, were indicted for a rape on Hannah Sutton, at the parish of Wolstanton, on the 11th of July. Hannah Sutton, the prosecutrix, stated that she was the wife of William Sutton, living at Compstall Bridge, near Marple, Cheshire, and was the mother of six children. On Monday, the 10th of July, she left her home for the purpose of proceeding to the Potteries on business. She slept at Congleton in the evening, and on the following morning, at six o'clock, went to Congleton wharf on the Macclesfield canal, where she saw the two prisoners in a boat. Prosecutrix asked them if they would allow her to the Red Ball aqueduct, when one of them said, 'Captain, will you let this woman go with us?' which the other replied, 'Oh yes, we never deny any woman going with us.' She accordingly got into the boat, and when it got to the Red Bull aqueduct she wished to get out, when the prisoners said it would be better for her to go with them to the bridge near Tunstall; she consented, and the boat entered the Harecastle tunnel; the two prisoners were in the boat, and the person driving the horse took it over the tunnel. The tunnel, except at each end, was very dark. Prosecutrix was in the stem end of the boat, when the prisoner Palin came to her, and felt round her, and was proceeding to take further liberties, when she told him to leave her as she was a married woman, and had left six children at home; she further told him that she was not a common woman, and begged that he would not interfere with her. Palin then went away. The prisoner Salmon then came near to her, and said he was very sleepy, and would lie down, putting his legs upon her. Prosecutrix told him that could not do with him; that she could not bear him, and asked him to think of her children and husband. The prisoner said, 'D__n your husband, what is he more than any other man.' She was leaning with her back against the stern of the boat when the prisoner thrust her down, and shouted to the other man, who immediately came up. The prisoner Palin then lay across her breast, according to the direction of the other prisoner, who proceeded to take further liberties, and succeeded in perpetrating the offence. Salmon then held her down by laying across her breast, and Palin completed his purpose. Prosecutrix called out, upon which Salmon said that if she did not hold her peace they would put her into the water. The prisoners then went away from her for half an hour. Salmon then returned again to her, and asked her if she had heard of the 'Kitcrew Boggart,' to which she said that she had (Prosecutrix here explained what she meant by the Kitcrew Boggart, which, she said, was sort of ghost, and a thing which was heard or seen against any accident). Salmon said there was always some accident or some one killed when this 'Boggart' was heard. He again laid hold of her, when she asked him to leave her alone for God's sake or he would kill her. He again threatened to throw her into the water, when she told him that if he would spare her life and let her live, she would submit to their will. Both the prisoners the second time completed the offence, and very roughly treated her. In about three quarters of an hour afterwards the boat came out of the tunnel, and they were shortly at Tunstall bridge. Between the tunnel and the bridge she saw same men working near the canal, when she put her hand to attract their attention they did not perceive her. She got out at Tunstall bridge, before which Salmon told her she had better go to Longport; but she objected. The prisoner Palin assisted her to get out of the boat. Prosecutrix went to a house a few yards from the bridge, occupied by Joshua Shaw, and told him what had happened to her. Mr. Allen addressed the jury for the prisoners, in the course of which he remarked that he did not attempt to deny that the prisoners had connection with the prosecutrix; but the principal question for their consideration was whether there was not partial consent on the part of the woman. His Lordship summed up the case, and having pointed out the chief facts to the jury, they, after short deliberation, returned a verdict of guilty against the prisoners. Sentence deferred.

'Conviction of Two Boatmen for Rape', *Wolverhampton Chronicle and Staffordshire Advertiser* (16 Aug 1843), 4.

Fair Becca

One very cold wild winter's night, you might have seen a very old man sat in a very old chair, by a very large fire, in a large old chimney corner, in a very old fashioned room, in a very old house. Opposite him, was a very old long-settle with a black oaken back, and a very soft old fashioned cushion, which made it very comfortable to sit upon on such a very cold wild night. On this old settle sat two boys who had just finished their tasks, in preparation for the school next morning, and a young woman their sister who was working at her needle. The window blinds were down, and the shutters were closed, and they could hear the wind roar like thunder in that old chimney, and drive the rain tremendously against the shutters, and it made that little circle feel very thankful, and very happy, that they were so very comfortably sheltered from such a very uncomfortable storm without. [p. 86] 'Grandfather,' said the eldest boy, 'you promised us, when we had learned our tasks, to tell us some fairy-tale or ghost-story.' 'Tell us,' said the young woman, 'about "Fair Becca," who, when you was a young man, used frequently to be seen about your neighbourhood.' Then thus spoke the grey-headed old man: In the village in which I was born, on such a night as this many years ago, as I have heard old people tell, a young man was observed to come into an inn there. He sat down, and placing his elbows on the table, laid his head upon his hands, as if some heavy care oppressed him. Long in moody silence did he thus sit. Then, as if pierced by some sudden anguish, he would start and pace the room as if some damning thought seemed burning in his brain. Then he left the room abruptly as he'd entered. That night too, a fair but erring being left her home, to meet one in whom she had too fondly trusted. That one was this young man, and they were seen to wend their way to a lone spot, called 'Brakenhall Green': shortly after, a solitary traveller passing that way, heard a wild and fearful shriek, that rose above the raging blast. And in the morning, that young woman, who had left her [p. 87] home that night, had not returned, nor was she to be found. That morning should have been her bridal morn: and when assembled friends had come to greet her with greetings fitting such a morn, their smiles of congratulation were changed into tears of anxious grief. The bridegroom too was there, and seemed as if paralyzed by the weight of his affliction; false traitor that he was! for he too truly might have told why 'twas she was not there. The night before she met him confiding in his love. And a fitting night it was for such a deed as then was perpetrated. One unto whom she had given her young heart's first, purest, holiest offering, its early love, that fair young girl went forth to meet. And he who had promised and vowed to become her protector through life, her husband, on whom she had relied as upon truth itself, that on the coming morn, before God's throne, and upon his holy altar, he would record that vow, and seal that promise. He, her young heart's choice, became her murderer. And in the very moment, when love and happiness and hope, were perhaps lighting up her soul with bright visions of years of bliss to come, that [p. 88] ruthless destroyer, with words of love upon his tongue, and hell within his heart, led her to the brink of a deep pit, down which he hurled her headlong; and that wild fearful shriek, which was heard to ride upon the blast that stormy night, was her death-cry. And oft at midnight's solemn hour, and o'er the tempest blast, and in the hollow meanings of the winds, has that wild shriek been heard, startling the matron at her own fire-side, as well as the lonely traveller on his journey. And clothed in white, her bridal dress, around the places where her trusting confidence had been betrayed, her restless spirit was seen to wander. And often round the winter's hearth, would some old villager beguile the evening hours, with many a tale of how fair Becca has been seen to linger in some lone place, where oft with her false lover she had strayed, and listened to his tale of love. And how perhaps some wild and reckless youth has met her, and mistaking her for some village-maiden, has tried to clasp her in his arms, when that wild shriek again would rend the air, and the vision would vanish from his sight. At all times of the evening might she be seen, from the first grey twilight to the deep gloom of [p. 89] midnight. But chief the moonlight were her chosen hours, when she would wander by some bubbling brook, or 'neath the shady trees, those choice resorts where lovers love to meet and breathe their vows. And many a time, when listening maiden has been drinking in the whispered words which cheer'd her soul like sunlight with their warmth and beauty, and were reflected back, with the truthfulness of first confiding, sinless love, has the spirit of this betrayed one glided past, and a smile was seen to play around her countenance, as if she too sanctioned those holy breathings of purity and faith. But when deliberate falsehood sought to lure from virtue's paths its meditated victim, and pour into the not unwilling ears the insidious poison of the flatterer's tongue, which charms but to betray, and with his honied words, but black deceit, would tempt the yielding maiden to her ruin; that warning spirit has been seen to beckon that young being from the brink on which she stood, and when the faithless vow was on the lips, and the fire of burning passion in the veins, she would be heard to rend the air, as if in mercy sent, to startle human frailty, and preserve it from sin. I remember well, continued the old man, when [p. 90] I was about eighteen years old, about the latter end of Autumn, I was walking forth into the fields with one who has long been an angel in Heaven; one whom you never knew, but who very much resembled you Marian (addressing his grand-daughter), for she was your father's mother, she was then about your age; well, it was about the time that the soft twilight, mingling with the first rays of the moon, casts all around a sort of dreamy shadowing, creating in the heart its semblance. Hopes in that hour, founded on the existing present, throw their shadow before us into the dreamy vista of the time to come, swelling the heart to bursting with its fulness of buss then, and its anticipations of a bright future. Such was the influence that that soft twilight shed upon our souls, while hand in hand we walked silently, as if fearing to break with voice or word, the spell that held us, and on we walked, until we came to one loved trysting place, where oft we'd sat beneath an aged oak, happy in ourselves, the whole world to each other. That night scarcely a breath of air caused a rustle in the trees, and all around us looked as lovely as an angel's dwelling place. When suddenly, a mighty wind came rushing through the trees, scattering the sear leaves around us, and [p. 91] when we looked around, we saw a beauteous form like to a youthful maiden coming towards us; she seemed to glide along the air, for neither sound of falling footstep or rustling of a garment did we hear, but I remember well her face was pale as was the moonbeam in whose light she walked; she passed; and when we turned to look, the form had faded from the view. And when we after told what we had seen, 'twas said by those who knew it well, and had seen it oft before, that 'twas Fair Becca. Since then they say that she has ceased to wander on the earth, and let us hope her spirit now has rest.

E. Riley, *Juvenile tales for boys and girls: designed to amuse, instruct, and entertain those who are in the morning of life* (Halifax: William Milner, 1849).

Note that the story immediately after this one begins with the following words: 'It is a very foolish, as well as a very wrong thing, to fill the minds of children, with old women's stories about ghosts, hobgoblins, and raw-head and bloody-bones, &c.; for two reasons, in the first place, the time might be better employed in telling them some interesting story, which would have a tendency to instruct, as well as to amuse them. And in the second place, because it leaves injurious impressions on the mind, which exercise their influence upon it in after years, in opposition to both better sense, and maturer judgment. How many among us now, who have grown up to be men, when passing some lone spot, at the "witching hour" of night; which spot, we have been taught in our early youth to believe was haunted by some evil spirit, or troubled ghost, do not feel those early impressions, at times, act very powerfully upon us, and in spite of our better judgment, we feel that curdling of the blood, and that [p. 93] sensation, to use a common phrase, which makes the "hair to stand on end". Whatever of the marvellous is conveyed to the minds of youth, ought to carry along with it some instructive moral, and let the amusement or the wonder it causes, be calculated to leave some benefit behind it.'

Poltergeist Boggart

The *Westmoreland Gazette* of Saturday inserts the following singular communication: 'Much excitement has of late prevailed amongst the inhabitants of Orton and its vicinity, in consequence of some singular disturbances which have recently occurred at Cowper House, near Orton. The name of the present occupier is Mr. William Gibson, jun. who about four years ago married a daughter of Mr. John Bland, Bybeck. A year previous to his marriage, Mr. Gibson's uncle, Mr. Robert Gibson, occupied the same place, with whom his nephew lived; and, singular to relate, these unaccountable disturbances commenced on Tuesday the 17th inst, being the fifth anniversary of his uncle's death, who was found drowned near the house. Tuesday the 17th, loud knocks were heard in the house, various articles placed on the shelves fell on the floor in rapid succession, which alarmed the inmates. Wednesday, half-past eleven o'clock a.m., two children's stools, placed in the craddle [*sic*], were thrown out, and the cradle clothes thrown under the firegrate; the chairs moved on the floor of their own accord (with the exception of one, which was lately purchased in a sale), and went over with great velocity; the churn, standing on the floor, was upset; the churn works were set into the outer porch; out of which into the house is a crooked passage; the servant girl, on going out, met the churn works coming like the flight of a bird, and fell near the churn without being injured. The young girl's cries on this occasion were alarming. Tables, containing dishes, were thrown off; fenders, knives, pans, tubs, butter, and almost every other article the house contained were in wild commotion one after another. The inmates were so alarmed that they took some provisions and proceeded to Mr Robert Bousefield's, a neighbouring house, and had some tea. They returned in the evening, accompanied by Mr. Bousefield who is an upright person, and may be relied on. Similar disturbances again commenced. Mr Bousefield, being horrified, advised the family to go with him and stay all night, which was accordingly done. Next day (Thursday) the family, which consists of Mr. William Gibson, his wife, two children, and a servant girl, returned to the house, when nothing particular occurred until afternoon. Mrs. Gibson's brother, Mr. Thomas Bland, of Byebeck, paid them a visit; when about to sit down to tea, Mr. Bland placed his hat on a dining table, when it immediately took place toward the fireplace. Clothes and other articles moved about in the house; and Mr. Bland being much affrighted, thought they had better all proceed to Bybeck. They did so, and there they are at present remaining. These things were soon published, and on Saturday the 21st, a company of young men from Orton proceeded to Cowper House to ascertain the fact. The family not being there, nothing particular transpired. On Tuesday last, Mr. James Elwood, grocer, Mr. Torbuck, surgeon, Mr. Robert Wilson, jun., Mr. John Robertson, joiner, Mr. Mark Atkinson, and Mr. R. Bland, all of Orton, proceeded to Bybeck to see if the family would accompany them to Cowper House. They consented and went in order to explore this strange occurrence. They arrived at the house in order to find out the cause, but found none. But knocks were heard, their hats moved from one place to another, a large dining table moved from its place into the middle of the floor, and, as before, one thing after another was in disorder, and moved about of its own accord. What can be the precise meaning of this we are at presnt [*sic*] unable to determine. Some are of the opinion that something has been done which is very wrong, or it is a forewarning of some great evil. It is the worst when the children are in the house. As a matter of course, a love for the marvelous has induced hundreds to visit the locality, and among them have been several parties residing in Preston, one of whom has furnished the *Preston Guardian* with an account of what he himself witnessed. This gentleman spent about an hour in the 'haunted house,' on Wednesday, and was eye-witness to the rocking of a cradle and the leaping of a metal spoon from a shelf without any visible agency! This spoon is said to have formerly belonged to the Mr. Gibson who met with his death by drowning, as above stated. A few days ago the family removed to the house of a friend in the neighbourhood, thinking by that means to get rid of their unwelcome guest, but the 'ghost' followed them, and the annoyances were renewed. From this, Mrs. Gibson concludes that the disturber of their peace is 'not a spirit,' a stream having to be crossed in order to reach the abode of their friend; and a spirit, it is said, 'was never known to cross a stream.' A fireman on the railway affirms that whilst he was on the premises the other day, an invisible hand removed his cap from his head and dashed it in his face. The occurrences following were detailed to the gentleman second hand: The lid of a metal pot rolled in at the porch, and broke into four pieces, which retreated in the same mysterious manner. A chain was removed from a 'crook' over the fire, and thrown upon the ground; the chain was replaced and tied on, when a violent tugging at the string was perceived. Mr. Gibson and his servant man placed their hats in the cradle, and they were immediately thrown out in a most unaccountable manner. Two ladies were entering the house, when they encountered in the doorway a basin of water, which to their great astonishment, was performing great gyrations in the air. A minister called with the intention of exorcising the 'ghost' by prayer, but, receiving a blow on the head from something unseen, the reverend gentleman, concluding that he was an unwelcome visitor, made good his retreat. A gentleman from Kendal sat down in a chair, which, by the same mysterious agency, forthwith began to rock to and fro with such violence, that it was with difficulty he could get upon his feet again. On the first day of these extraordinary occurrences, Mrs. Gibson was completely exhausted with continually picking up the clothes which were thrown, as if by magic, from the child's cradle: as often as she restored them to their place they were again removed, until she was compelled to give up the task in despair. On another occasion, the malicious and untiring 'ghost' hurled at Mrs G. a loaf, which, striking her wrist, lacerated the skin. A few days ago a visitor put down his walking stick in a corner of the room, and took a seat on the opposite side: in a short time, the stick took to itself legs, and cleverly walked across the floor to its astonished owner. The incident most marvelous of all remains to be related. A man who, some time ago, had been caught stealing eggs from the farm premises, went the other day to see the 'boggart:' he had not long sat down before an egg came whizzing through the air from an opposite shelf, and struck him on the breast! In short, plates and dishes without number have been broken, and almost every moveable article in the house in some way or other disturbed. Our informant (says the Preston Guardian) brought with him several pieces of the broken pots as curiosities, and intended favouring us with a view of them: unfortunately, however, on referring to the place where they had been deposited, it was discovered that these relics were missing, and, notwithstanding a diligent search, they were nowhere to be found. The servant girl, though youthful, is said to have a cunning, sinister appearance; and, notwithstanding her assertions to the contrary, it is believed that she is cognizant of the agency by which results of so astonishing a nature have been accompanied.

'A Westmoreland Ghost Story', *The Bradford Observer* (17 May 1849), 7.

Boggart House Near Carnforth

Between Bolton-le-Sands and Carnforth, on the road side, is situated a house having the reputation of being haunted, and has ever, within the memory of that oft quoted personage 'the oldest inhabitant,' been known by the appellation of the 'boggart house.' Various are the conjectures respecting the manner in which this lonely dwelling received the distinction; but on one point all agree, that at some time or other it has been the theatre where some 'deed of darkness' has been enacted. That 'murder most foul' has been committed within its precincts, and that the perturbed spirit of the victim is permitted for a time to visit the 'pale glimpses of the moon, making night hideous.' Many a one, in passing this dreaded spot upon hearing the slightest sound, the faintest rustling of the leaves, has felt a curious sensation run down his back and ooze out at his toes, and not a few who had great pretensions to fearlessness when coming into immediate proximity with the 'boggart house,' have felt themselves compelled to 'whistle to bear there courage up.' Numerous are the forms in which this supernatural agent presents itself, sometimes as a headless soldier, a gigantic sheep, or monster goose. Often does his ghostship play fantastic tricks, such as only appertain to the denizens of another and unknown world, such as acting the part of an invisible glazier, taking out panes of glass and throwing them down on the floor without injury, &c. For a short time back his ghostship has been better behaved, confining himself within his own 'cerements,' and never disturbing sublunary mortals with 'things above the reaches of their souls.' However last week the 'dobby' strain made its appearance much to the terror of an inoffensive carter, who was proceeding on his way to Kendal market. This occurrence has been a rich theme during the past week for the gossip mongers at Bolton, and the neighbourhood, and has been the all-engrossing topic of conversation. The carter to which we have above alluded was on his way to Kendal market, with a load of wheat, shortly after the witching hour of night, 'when church yard yawn,' and had proceeded as far as the immediate vicinity of the 'boggart house,' when his horse suddenly stopped and appeared much frightened. On looking to ascertain the cause, he perceived as he imagined a large sheep lying in the middle of the road, to which he proceeded with the intention of applying his whip to force its removal. He struck, the blow fell upon vacancy, the supposed sheep aroused itself and as if with indignity at the insult, swelled out as the man affirms, into the size of a house [*sic*], and then giving him a look of ineffable contempt flew away in a flame of fire. The poor carter was petrified, the chattering of his teeth almost rivalled in noise the bone-playing of the celebrated 'Jubs,' his knees shook, and his legs refused to perform their office. How long he remained in this condition he is unable to state, but the fright had such an effect upon his nerves as to make him seriously unwell and he has not since recovered from the shock. Although we have no faith in these supernatural visitations, it must be admitted that the poor man, from the state he was in, had seen something which dreadfully alarmed him. Perhaps on the previous evening he had been partaking too freely of the 'barley bree,' and his heated imagination magnified the apparition.

'Ghost Story', *Lancaster Gazette* (25 Jan 1851), 5.

Boggart Poltergeist at Blackley

The peaceable and well-disposed inhabitants of the pleasant village of Blackley have been thrown into a state of considerable excitement by the alleged re-appearance of a ghost or boggart. The house where this unearthly visitor has chosen to take up its winter's residence is a very old building, adjoining the White Lion public house, occupied by a person named William Whitehead, a clogger, who has resided there for the last ten months. He states that he first heard the 'boggart' about six weeks ago, when it made noises like the cackling of a hen, or the moaning whistle on a railway; and when any of the family stood upon a certain flag in the back room, it screamed like a child. Whitehead removed the flag, and, after digging a hole several feet deep, found a cream-jug, filled with lime and bones. A village conference was assembled, and several declared that the bones were those of a human being, and that, at some period, a person had been murdered, and, of course, buried in a cream-jug. The 'boggart' is heard every night in the week, and occasionally during the day. The ancients of the place declare it is 'Old Shaw's Wife,' a woman formerly resident in the Old Hall, which stood near to the haunted building; others say its appearance it consequent upon the wickedness of some of the neighbours. On Saturday evening it made greater noise than usual, and on Sunday, Whitehead was digging nearly all day in search of the supposed spirit; the cellar steps were removed, and a very large hole nearly sixteen feet long, four feet wide, and above five feet deep, was excavated, of course without success. We advise him next to set a trap; he may catch something. The family state that a few days ago the kettle (full of boiling water) was removed from the fire to the middle of the house floor. An astrologer from Manchester, with his magic books and glasses has visited the house, and parties look through the latter to see if they could learn from whence came the spirit. An old man named George Horrox, who once resided in the dwelling, declares that on two occasions he saw a ghost in the shape of a young woman, and it occasionally made noises like the rumbling of stones. Several other give similar accounts, and they do not hesitate to say the house has been haunted for the last 85 years. The man who resides in the building shows no symptoms of fear, on the contrary, he declares he will find out what the annoyance proceeds from before he gives in; but it is in vain to tell many of the old people that it is anything but a boggart or ghost, and many families have left on that account. It is rather astonishing to see so many people in the nineteenth century running to visit a haunted dwelling, but numbers are attracted to the place, and the publicans and beersellers will not doubt reap a rich harvest from the boggart hunters. The police officer, who resides only a few yards distant and is professionally a sceptic in all matters relating to supernatural appearances, seems like to have his duties increased by this troublesome spirit.

'Extraordinary Superstition at Blackley', *Manchester Courier and Lancashire General Advertiser* (6 Nov 1852), 7.

Bannister Hall Doll

In an hour or two I began to tire with the monotony of my occupation; so I again ascended the bank, and sat contemplating the quiet scene. My thoughts gradually and unconsciously reverted back to persons and things which are now no more; memories of my childhood, suggested by the hour and the locality. Amongst other things I endeavoured to beguile away the time with repainting upon my imagination the image of the redoubtable 'boggart' or ghost, the 'Bannister Hall Doll', whose very name was once sufficient to awe into silence the most obstreperous children of the town and neighbourhood. I repeated to myself all the stories my memory retained of this headless woman, who, in search of vengeance upon her unknown murderer, wandered not only about the lanes in 'the dead of the night,' but even visited the streets of Preston, to the east of the 'Brown Friargate about the corner of Lune-street, and over which, from some, to me then well known, but now forgotten, cause, she possessed not the power to pass. This headless lady, according to the Christmas fire-side story-tellers of my youth, possessed the remarkable accomplishment of transforming herself into a large black dog, and some other animals; but still, as in her own person, the head was always wanting! She was in the habit of making strange noises, amongst which the rattling of chains often predominated. She was said to be tolerably considerate to all those who faithfully believed in her existence, and acknowledge the justice of the vengeance she sought; but she was supposed to be merciless towards all skeptics, and shook the very beds beneath them while they slept. But, alas! though the old churchyard, where some pious persons are said to have 'laid' this 'erring spirit,' 'yawned' in the darkness before my very eyes, I could conjure up, even in my enthusiastic imagination, but a very faint and terrorless shadow of this once much-dreaded phantom: the powerful exorcists, time and knowledge, had so nearly obliterated all trace of my boyish superstition.

An Enthusiast, 'Catching a Salmon', *Preston Chronicle and Lancashire Advertiser* (15 Oct 1853), 3.

Seed Hill Ghost/Boggard

During the whole of the past week the neighbourhood of Seed-hill, and in fact the whole of the 'lower region' of the town of Huddersfield, has been in a state of extraordinary excitement owing to most alarming 'noises' made in the house of Mr. Samuel Routledge, an extensive dyer, at Seed-hill. Mr. Routledge first called the attention of the police and the public to the matter last Saturday, declaring that the noises resembled the 'striking of a door or a table-top with a stick or switcher with all one's might'; that these noises were very frequent, and had frightened all his servants and even the cat from the house, and that he was thus left in awful solitude. The rumour spread rapidly, and every day since the house has been regularly besieged by crowds of people, all anxious to see and hear for themselves the marvellous doings of the ghost. On Monday, Tuesday, and Wednesday, several policemen were stationed inside the house. The ghost, however, was not to be intimidated either by the crowd or the police – 'bang, switch, bang, switch, bang, switch,' – continued at intervals to echo through the corridors and rooms of the budding. Impudent and cunning ghost! He is quite a ventriloquist; when you are seated in the dining-room, the sound appears to come from the front door; and when you are at the front door, the sound appears to proceed from the dining room. A policeman was therefore placed at each of these places, determined to catch the ghost. 'Bang, switch' echoes once more; each policeman rushes from his post to catch the fugitive; they meet in the passage, and a terrific collision takes place, each knocking the other down, and in the melee the ghost escapes! These watchings continued until Wednesday evening, when the police, fairly baffled, raised the siege, and left the ghost in undisputed possession of the fortress. The phenomenon remains a mystery, but the premises are advertised for sale by public auction on the 2nd of April, and rumour insinuates that the ghost is merely the result of some hidden galvanic wires, or some subterraneous steam pipes, and the ruse is to frighten purchasers, so that the house may be sold very cheap.

'The Seed-Hill Ghost', *Leeds Times* (24 Mar 1855), 5.

Our readers will remember that we had last week chronicle the excitement, alarms and curiosity, produced by the mysterious knockings at Seed-hill, on the premises of Mr. Samuel Routledge. The noises have continued in a most energetic and alarming style, during the past week. On Saturday last, the ghost was very boisterous and active, and continued its vagaries in order to amuse or frighten magistrates and gentlemen, connected with the world of letters. It was not contented with its usual manifestations, but took to ringing the bells violently, so that some of the inmates were much alarmed, and others puzzled and annoyed. It appears that Mr. Routledge had an idea that it was caused by some kind of air rushing in the numerous gaspipes, steam-pipes or water-pipes, in or around the dwelling. But drains and pipes were examined in vain. On the Thursday, in addition to the bells being rung, the pillows and bed clothes began to travel about the house, and altogether, suspicion seems to have fallen upon girl about eleven or twelve years old, employed as a servant or nurse. On Thursday night, the house was tolerably full of visitors attracted by curiosity, credulity, or scepticism, and after they had nearly all departed, a general search was made through the place. Mr. and Mr. Henry Brook, at length found in the kitchen indications that the noises proceeded from that quarter. Mr. Brook found behind the kitchen door a washing machine, which on being struck with a stick that stood by its side, produced the exact noise usually produced by the ghost. This hint was followed up industriously, and on examining the washing machine, it was found to be indented in all directions with the numerous blows that her ghostship had inflicted upon it. The kitchen also sadly battered from the same cause, and on further examination, nearly every door on the ground-floor of the house was found to bear these material marks of the ghost. There was no doubt as to the delinquent, and on the following morning (Friday) Mr. Routledge called the girl into a room apart, and taxed her with being the cause of all the uproar. After some denials she at length confessed, and Superintendent Thomas was sent for, to take her to the police station. She is a simple looking Irish girl, named Catherine Haley, and has been in the employ of Mr Samuel Routledge for eight or nine months. On arriving at the police-station she acknowledged that her only object was to frighten the inhabitants of the house, and that no one else knew of it but herself. After the departure of the girl another instrument was discovered. Under the pillow of a sofa close to the door of the large kitchen, was found a flat sand stone, and on examining the door it was found to have been used against the door frame that a space of three or four inches square was completely battered, the grains of sand still adhering shewing by what means the indentations had been produced. We understand that a clairvoyant was on the premises on Thursday night, and after many guesses in which quicksilver, a woman with black hair, and like unto a ministering angel, were mixed up with other stones and fancies, while at twenty minutes past seven on the Friday evening, he stated there would be a grand commotion. Whether this referred to the capture of the ghost which took place about that time, we must leave our readers to determine. It appears altogether, that Routledge and those interested in discovering the trick expected to find the solution of the mystery in approved philosophical style and not in simple and obvious human agency. Hence they overlooked the necessary precautions and gave the girl abundant opportunities for carrying on her deception while they were busy in every quarter but the right one. We had several times heard it averred, that if the family would only allow three or four policemen to have exclusive possession, they would hear no more of the ghost, and particularly they would only call to their help the two Hillhouse celebrities who caught the Birkby ghost in the shape of a 'billy-goat'. We had forgotten to say, that on Thursday night a bailiff on the premises stopped in bed as long as he dared, in consequence of finding the best clothes dragged away from above him, a trick which was like the other played by the little Irish ghost – Catherine Haley. So great a celebrity has she become that a photographer has given her a portrait, by way of adding to his gallery of portraits that of the Seed-hill ghost. As there was no charge brought against the girl, she was sent away after she had got a good fright for frightening others.

'The Capture of the Ghost', *Huddersfield and Holmfirth Examiner* (31 March 1855), 4. Note that the phrase 'Seed-Hill Boggard' was in used 'The Model Lodging-House and a Benighted Son of Bacchus', *Huddersfield Examiner* (7 Apr 1855), 5.

Boggart Attack?

On Saturday night last, as Wm. Taylor, limeburner, of Kellet, was returning home from the market in a cart, very tipsy, when near Carus farm some person or persons got up behind into the cart, and seized him by the neck. At the time he had two waistcoats on: the inner waistcoat had an inside pocket. Containing from 10 to 15 sovereigns, and a £5 note. The outer garment had a pocket in a similar place, with a purse in it, and two sovereigns. The thieves unfortunately tore open both waistcoats, and took the larger amount, but left the purse and two sovereigns. Taylor was so much the worse for drink that he cannot tell whether it was 'a man, a woman, or a boggart' that perpetrated the outrage. Supposing it to be a supernatural assailant which attacked our thirsty friend, it is said to have given him a 'terrible hard grip' in the neck. Of course he made no resistance, but after losing the money he drove on to Mr Turner's of Westfield House, and there gave information of the robbery, and instead of returning to the Office, he went home. However, after going home, he gave an account of the robbery to the proper authorities.

'Highway Robbery', *Lancaster Gazette* (26 Jan 1856), 5.

Littlemoss Boggart

On Saturday night, betwixt ten and eleven o'clock, whilst five or six lads were engaged in card-playing in an old disused brewhouse, one of them happening to turn towards the window, espied to his horror standing before it a white faced apparition, with a huge headdress of the same colour, and jingling a mass of chains. No sooner had he called the attention of his comrades to the spectre than it flew on the roof, and louder and louder 'ricked' the chains, and hurled bricks down the chimney flue. Immediately the place rung again with shouting, and screaming, and crying, and although in possession of the key, yet fear paralysed their efforts to unlock the door. At length, attracted by the infernal-like din, a youth rushed to their rescue, and afterwards accompanied them home. The two packs of cards were burned forthwith, and resolutions entered into never again to take cards in hand. It is whispered that the lad who conducted them home was no less an important personage than the ghost in *deshabille*.

'A Boggart at Littlemoss', *The Ashton Weekly Reporter* (6 Sep 1856), 3.

Debate on Boggarts

Much useful information may be acquired at discussion or debating classes when well conducted, and when the subjects of debate are judiciously chosen. It often happens that neither the one nor the other is the case. The other evening the members of the debating society in connection with the Young Men's Club met to discuss the question of apparitions, and whether there were good grounds for believing in the existence of such super-natural agencies. The discussion resulted in the wiseacres declaring, by a majority of votes, in favour of the existence of supernatural apparitions.

'Debating Societies: Belief in Boggarts', *The Preston Chronicle and Lancashire Advertiser* (24 Jan 1857), 4.

Boggart Frolics

An old woman, residing at Penwortham, met with a serious accident under very unusual circumstances, on Saturday night last. It appears that the old lady, who is upwards of sixty years of age, took it into her head, whimsically enough, to play the boggart, and with that intent actually left her house for the purpose of interrupting a young woman, who had just before departed on an errand to a public house at the bridge. The girl, however, returned without having met any interruption; but the old lady, who had gone forth in such merry mood to scare the lass, came not. After waiting anxiously till a late hour of the night, her friends thought it high time to take measures for ascertaining the cause of her absence. Accordingly they went in the direction of the road along which the girl had passed, and after a little searching about, sure enough, the poor old lady was found lying in a ditch contiguous, with one of her legs broken. She was instantly conveyed home, and it was soon explained that the fracture had been occasioned by the frolicsome old dame having witlessly leapt into the ditch with the intent before-named. Medical aid is doing remarkably well. *Manchester Mercury*.

'Singular Frolic', *The Preston Chronicle and Lancashire Advertiser* (17 Jan 1857), 3.

Whitegate-Lane Boggart

The Fylde has a variety of 'Boggarts'; the principal one has the appearance of a white calf, and frequents ancient houses and old dilapidated ruins. Whitegate-lane has hitherto boasted of having two different kinds, viz. '*Hobthurst, the Lubber Fiend*,' a friend of the cleanly dairy maid, but a desperate foe to the slovenly farmer; and the '*Headless Lady*,' who is said to carry her decapitated caput under her arm, and to keep kissing it. Last week, however, the ghost of a lately deceased female appeared to two unfortunate *whites*. The tale is thus: A Marton husband lost his wife, and after his neighbours had intererred her he, leaving his two little children alone in the house, went upon a three days' 'spree'; and, afraid to go home alone by himself, prevailed upon a jolly butcher of Blackpool to accompany him home through the lonely road of Whitegate-lane [*sic*], which extends from No. 3 Public-house, Blackpool to Great Marton. It was the witching hour of night, when lo! mid-way there stood before them the ghost of his late wife, fully developed to sight. The apparition so horrified them that the husband fell flat upon his back, kicking and screaming, and praying to the Lord to have mercy upon his soul. At length he exclaimed, 'Luthee, luthee!' and his friend the butcher, seeing the same horrid apparition, also immediately fell across his companion, where he remained till he says that he had the presence of mind to whisper, 'Be quate, mon – be quate, mon; there is a running brook near, let us cross it.' Hours and hours it took them to get to the widower's home; but his friend the butcher, refusing to enter the house, went back by a far longer route to Blackpool, in to avoid such another horrifying scene. He still keeps the resolution of not being out late at night with such a character, and the widower has deserted his children and left the locality altogether. Most people disbelieve the truth of the tale, thinking it an illusion; and an Irish servant at Blackpool positively denies the whole story, saying 'Faith an' sure, I cannot believe it, because a ghost never did or could appear after twelve o'clock at night.' Such a true story as the above is an addition to the witchcraft and other superstitious stories going the round of the public papers. The butcher, who resides at Blackpool, constantly affirms the truth of the above, and he has not yet dared to go alone in any lane after dark.

'Superstition in the Fylde: Whitegate-Lane Boggart', *The Preston Chronicle and Lancashire Advertiser* (2 May 1857), 5.

Urinating Boggart?

At the Chorley petty sessions, on Tuesday last, before Messrs. R.T. Parker, T.B. Crosse, E. Silvester, J. Eccles, and R. Sinethurst, Wm. Marsh, collier of Shevington, was charged with assaulting James Breakell, a boy about six years of age. The chief witness was the boy's sister, Mary Breakell, a girl 13 years of age, who stated that on Saturday evening last she and the boy were going to a neighbour's house, when she saw the defendant making water. Her brother thought it was a boggart, and threw a stone at him, upon which defendant seized him by both ears, lifted him up by the hair, and threw him upon the ground, and kicked him once or twice. The boy's mother said the boy came into the house with his sister in such a state that she did not think he would ever come to himself. She did not examine him to see if he had any marks upon him. The defendant said he pulled the boy's hair for throwing a stone at him, and that was all he did. The lad's father said he had served him right [the boy?]. The girl was not there. The Bench dismissed the charge with a reprimand upon payment of costs.

'Assault Upon a Child', *The Preston Chronicle and Lancashire Advertiser* (24 Dec 1858), 6.

William Marsh, of Shevington, collier, was charged with having on Sunday last assaulted James Breakell, a child about four years of age, the son of John Breakell, of Shevington. From the statement of the child's sister, Mary, who spoke with great volubility and boldness, and who said she was 13 years of age it appeared that on Sunday evening last she went with the boy to a neighbour's house, and on their way saw the defendant standing against a wall. The boy 'thought it was boggart, and clod a stone at it,' upon which the defendant seized him by both ears, and, according to the girl's story, lifted him up, and then 'smashed' him on the ground and 'purred' him once or twice. The boy's mother said the boy was brought into the house by the girl, and he was so ill she thought he would never have come to himself but she did not think to examine his person to see if there were any bruises or marks of violence on his person. The defendant admitted pulling the boy's hair, but denied doing anything further. The girl was not present, at least he did not see her. The boy's father told him he had served him right. The bench appeared to think that the matter was exaggerated, and dismissed the case on payment of costs.

'Petty Sessions Tuesday', *Bolton Chronicle* (24 Dec 1858), 8.

Boggart Excuse

For some time past the occupants of land in Halmerend have been considerably annoyed by strange cattle being turned into their fields during the night and removed early the next morning to avoid detection. Shortly before midnight on the 2nd instant, Mr. John Lawrence, a farmer, was on the look out, when he saw Sarah Madders, a female living in the neighbourhood, pass down a lane and deliberately drive a horse and a donkey into one of his grass fields. On inquiring why this was done, she said that 'there was a boggart in the lane and she durst not go further!' The woman was summoned on a charge of malicious damage, which was laid at a penny.

'A Midnight Trespasser', *Staffordshire Advertiser* (24 Dec 1859), 7.

Shallcross Mill Boggart

For the last fortnight the susceptible people of Whaley have been put into great fear by the report of there being a 'boggart' at Shallcross Mill. A large something has been seen with long ears horns tail &c which always glides and vanishes out of sight. There certainly is something to be seen, I know well the person who occupies the mill. It is the opinion of some that it only an otter; but there is not food sufficient for an otter, there are no fish. However, it is the intention of the rifle corps to assemble on Saturday night about the time of its appearance, and have a shot.

'Boggart', *Glossop Record* (4 Feb 1860), 3

To the Editor of the Record. Sir, A letter [not found] appeared in your paltry contemporary of last week, bearing the signature – 'Volunteer.' From inquiries

I have made, I am led to believe that delectable production never emanated from this locality. The shabby journal in which that effusion made its appearance, is too mean to be used as a medium of communication by any person having claim to respectability. Indeed, the only real boggart ever seen at Whaley, is a thing called the *Chronicle*; but, then, its presence is not very appalling; it is merely contemptible, and causes laughter, rather than alarm. I am, sir, your obdt. servant, Elos. Whaley, Feb. 16th, 1859.

Elos, 'The 'Boggart' at Whaley', *Glossop Record* (18 Feb 1860), 4.

The Whaley Bridge 'Boggart' has augmented into a Boggart and a half. It is hawked about the neighbourhood, at the charge of three-halfpence for a sight; and it is, indeed, great to all who see it,—as the half-penny sheet is nothing more than reprint, word for word, of the former half; not an addition of news, as is usual in a supplement, but the same matter over again. Some persons who have had the curiosity to look at the thing, say the sight of it is not worth a farthing. I am, sir, yours, etc., A True Volunteer, Feb 22nd.

A True Volunteer, 'The 'Boggart' at Whaley',
Glossop Record (25 Feb) 1860, 4.

Pit Boggart

Progression's bright rays.
(Both elves' foe. and fays',)
Have banish'd the Boggart for ever;
Which thought fit,
Near a pit,
To scare out of his wit
Each wight passing by, dull or clever.
Old, for a long time
Has pass'd since their prime.
Are many grey-headed poor creature;
Yet more old.
Twenty-fold.
Was a tale often told
Alike to both sinners and preachers.
In long by-gone times,
(An age gross crimes),
There a murder most foul was committed;
And the tale,
In our dale.

Rosy cheeks has turn'd pale,
And has been by tradition transmitted:
How Spire-Holly's Sprite,
In winter's dark night.
And oft cooling courage much vaunted,
Would appear.
Gliding near
To the man who, with fear.
Approach'd the lone place which it haunted.
The Tale may be true:
Oft, ghost-seers did view
Strange, indistinct forms very nigh,
As at night,
With affright,
By the pale moon's faint light.
They drew near that lone place, or slunk by,
And people, too, tell
What there once befell
The wild tapster of Glossop, Will Froogart,
When, one night at nine,
(Elated with wine),
He would visit the pit and the Boggart
Entreaties denying.
Friends' wishes defying,
Will left his boon revellers drinking;
And he tried,
As he eyed
The lone fields spreading wide
To cheer up his courage, by thinking
What laughter – what scorn
Would greet the return
Of the braggart
whose courage now lighten'd
And he thought
'Cheaply bought,' If he should see nought,
Would the boast be – he had not been frightened.
(to be continued)

Henry Dawson, 'Spire-Holly's Sprite',
Glossop Reporter (3 Mar 1860), 4.

Mr William Bennett, born Jan 5th, 1805, a minder at Wood's was a poet of local repute. Two of his poems, 'The Flying Serpent' and 'The Spire Holly Boggart', both founded on local incidents, were printed by J.Perry, Hall Street, Glossop. Mr Bennet's preface is as follows: 'as I neither have, nor want, nor deserve a patron, to whom with sincere respect I can dedicate the following pages, without fawning sycophancy, lying panegyrick, or servile adulation, I dedicate my work to myself'. WILLIAM BENNETT. Glossop, Oct. 17th, 1840.

The Spire Holly Boggart

This composition was as follows:

'If that is no o boggart, ther never wor non, if ther'n reetly sifted in too' Tim Bobbin.

'Twas on a dreary winter's morning, very soon,
And clouds had veiled the stars and overcast the moon,
I left my easy bed and quiet peaceful cot,
And hurried down a lane [Smithy Lane]; that often was my lot.
I took both drink and victuals for the coming day;
And in a cheery mood I bent my lonely way:
A way which timorous mortals often passed with fear,
Believing some foul murder had been committed there;
For dismal, doleful groans, some fancied they had heard,
And ghostly visions to some eyes had oft appeared.
The morn being chilly cold, I quickened my pace,
Unthinking of the lonely, dreaded, haunted place:
And as I hurried on, I heard a startling hiss;
Which caus'd me to exclaim, in sudden fear, 'What's this?'
I stopped, looked round, yet nothing could see, still
I heard a noise at hand which sounded loud and shrill!
Long I stood wondering, till the sound was lost:
Was the sound but fancy? or, was there a ghost?
Unwilling to believe the last, I checked my fears;
Thinking imagination, perhaps, deceived my ears.
Or as the morn was dark, there many things might be,
As birds, or reptiles near, which I could not see,
And whose loud chirping tokened the approach of day:
Concluding this the case, I hastened on my way.
But, dreadful to relate! I'd not gone many feet
Before the sounds again my listening ear did meet!
While I stood trembling near the dismal lonely spot,
A loud report sounds 'Pop!' I thought I had been shot.

I started – turned me around, almost as quick as thought:
And by doing, reader, found the biggest boggart out!
A bottle of well-brew'd beer I carried; which, at length,
By jogging in my pocket, needs must show its strength
By pressing past the cork, and chirping at the top:
At last the cork flew out, and boldly cried out 'Pop!'
Ah, fickle self, thought I: whither did reason roam
Whilst thou stood trembling here at what thou brought from home?
Hadst though not been abroad, where ghosts and goblins dwell,
Thou would not have been scared by what thou lovest so well:
Or hadst thou quaffed the juice of generous barleycorn,
It would have kept thy spirits up on that drear morn,
And all the spirits that Spire Holly ever bred
Before thy bold, undaunted courage would have fled.
So, when again of drink thy pocket bears a Bottle,
Remember, first, to let a drop go down thy throttle!

To amuse his hearers, the author often recited the foregoing piece in public. Previously to its being first heard, [there was?] a notion that Spire-Holly Pit was haunted. The tale, however, if it had no other merit, had the merit of banishing the Boggart; neither is the sprite now ever seen, nor the rumour believed that the pit was formerly haunted.

'A Local Poet' (n.d.)

This extract was found on this site: http://freepages.genealogy.rootsweb.ancestry.com/~glossopfamily/news.htm [accessed 14/4/2016], with this comment 'Whilst emptying cupboards, I found some fragmented cuttings saved by my Great Aunt, Violet Hambleton (1893–1983... They are from local papers but no dates or titles included.'

Moss Lane Spectre

'A ghost in Manchester! Nonsense', some of our readers will exclaim. But there is no 'nonsense' about the fact, for a ghostly form – whatever it is – has been seen on two successive evenings, and has frightened one man nearly out of his wits, while the whole neighbourhood has been disturbed in the dead of night by the ghost-seer's cries. Close to Brook's Bar runs Moss Lane, and in selecting this neighbourhood for the honour of a visit, the ghost has certainly shown some poetic taste. It appears that a portion of Moss Lane has been undermined by the bursting of a water-pipe and the roadway for a length of about two roods is now broken in, and in course of repair. The roadway has, in consequence of this, been blocked up for nearly a fortnight, and from dusk to daylight fires have been kept burning in tripod fire baskets to prevent accidents. The man who has been tending these fires during the last fortnight is a little active-footed, wiry framed, wizen-faced man, and has for many years pursued the dreary calling of a night watchman. On Thursday night a constable, passing down the lane, found the watchman busily engaged shovelling coal on to the fire basket. Nearby stood one of the closed handcarts, in which gas-men and watermen carry their tools. 'Hallo', he shouted, 'You're just the man I want.' At the same time the shovel was dropped, and he hastily scratched his head preparatory to a long 'spell.' The constable crossed the road and stood by the side of the fire basket; while the watchman, in a voice husky with fear, proceeded to tell him of the appearance of a ghost between three and four that morning. Of course, it was dressed all in white; but, unlike other ghosts, this one kept bobbing up and down in the roadway, a short distance beyond the other fire basket, while, at the same time, it kept its eyes fixed upon the watchman. After the ghost had disappeared, the alarmed 'seer' knocked up a man belonging to a brewer's yard not far off and after telling him he had seen a ghost, the two searched the whole neighbourhood, but could find no track of his ghostship. The watchman's terror had been so great that persons residing in houses a short distance from where he stood, had been aroused from sleep by a most unearthly long-drawn 'oh' which had escaped him. The constable laughed at the man's story, but told him that years ago, he had heard, a man was murdered near the spot, and his spirit never could 'settle.' The watchman repeated the word 'settle' in the greatest alarm, and taking up an old-fashioned watchman's rattle and an oak cudgel, he said he had brought those with him that night to 'nobble' the ghost with, but he thought he wouldn't try that on, but shut himself up in the cart. This the watch-man did, and the constable went on. Between twelve and one o'clock, however, the same night, while the constable was conversing with another officer at the corner of a road some distance off, both were alarmed at the sound of the watchman's rattle. They immediately ran to where he was standing, the very spot where one of the constables had seen him an hour or two previously, and where he was furiously shaking the rattle. The noise had aroused some of the inmates in the neighbouring houses, and heads were hastily thrust through open windows. The brewer's man, also startled by the rattle, had got up, and he together with the two constables, reached the spot where the watchman was standing at the same moment. The watchman was in a state of the greatest alarm, and pointing his finger up Moss Lane towards the Chorlton Road, kept on shouting, 'There it is!' 'There it is!' One of the constables stopped, looked in the direction whence the man pointed, and exclaimed, 'By gom, there it is and it's coming this way; we'd better shunt, lads.' So saying the three made a hasty movement, calling out to the watchman as they ran to 'nobble' it. But the watchman thought discretion was the better part of valour, he seized his stick, the rattle, and his breakfast can, and ran after the others as fast as his legs would carry him. He soon overtook them and was about to pass them, when they called upon him to stop. His reply was, 'No, no, my name's Hoff,' and he was quickly out of sight. More than half a mile from this he was met, still running, by a gentleman who was returning home, who called upon him to stop, but he shouted out, 'I've seen a ghost, and I can't stop.' Nor did he stop until he had reached the city. In the course of yesterday he waited upon his employer, and after telling his story, he positively refused, on any consideration, to 'watch' at the spot another night. Last evening another man was watching, and he laughed heartily as he bore testimony to the truth of our story. We have no doubt that his predecessor saw his own form reflected in the flame from the fire basket, and this gave rise to his ghost story; nevertheless, the truth of his tale is believed in by many of the more credulous residents in the neighbourhood.

'The Moss Lane Spectre', *Manchester Times* (26 Jan 1861), 5.

Sweetclough Boggart

About a dozen years ago, a man residing in one of the houses at Sweetclough, met with a sudden and premature death, and ever since, it has been affirmed by the superstitious, that his spirit is seen in the night, in the house he formerly dwelt in. Any unusual sound or appearance have been attributed to the nocturnal visitations of his apparition. A circumstance, however, occurred last Monday night, which has served in some measure to dispel the gloomy forebodings which many people had upon the subject. A little after midnight, when all seemed wrapped in the profoundest stillness, a tremendous clatter was heard at the house window. The inmates, a man and his wife, aware of the mysterious legends attached to the house were almost paralysed with fear at the strange sound they had heard. They again listened a moment in breathless suspense when the same vehement clattering was heard again. Presently, the apparition was heard to leave the window and pace steadily across the floor. Coming to the stairs it began to ascend, when to the horror and astonishment of the inmates, they could distinctly count five footsteps. In exceedingly tremulous tones, the Mistress queried, 'What ever it is?' but she failed in receiving an answer. By this time it had arrived at the top and proceeded across the chamber with a slow and measured step, the peculiar sound of five feet being clear and distinct. The man at last summoned courage to strike a match, with the intent to frighten the apparition, and at the sound, it immediately disappeared beneath the bed. Under the intensest excitement he arose and struck a light, when his eyes caught the fierce glare of a monstrous tom cat, secreted beneath the bed. With the aid of a knobstick which was fortunately at hand, he soon rid himself of his most untimely visitor. The fact was, there was a quarrel half broke, which 'Tom' finding too small to admit him, struggled with great vehemence, till he succeeded in entering, and in doing so, took the frame from the window around it's back, thus causing the singular sound of five feet. The affair has caused much merriment in the village.

'The Sweetclough Boggart Caught at Last',
Burnley Advertiser (12 July 1862), 2.

Grannie's Memories

[My grandma] answered: 'At Ashton I was under the care of the minister of the parish church, and he had an assistant, a clever man, who had been educated at Eton College, and also a young lad sent there by the Earl of Stamford and Warrington for the instruction of the girls. In truth I may say, the abilities of these tutors as scholars in education and ethics had few equals in the county; but the great mass of the people were lost and degraded in ignorance and superstition. I think there were not more than one-tenth of the people that could sign their names to the marriage register. No wonder they should be so confirmed in the horrors of witchcraft, second sightedness, and apparitions. Their silly notions, and belief in ghosts, hobgoblins, demons, and devils, were the constant torment of their minds. Ghosts were seen stalking through church-yards, three lane ends, and vacant old farmhouses. Gentlemen's mansions were haunted with frightful sights and unearthly sounds. When a poor mortal lay on his deathbed, the howlings of dogs heard, the screaming of owls on a dark night, doors opening and closing without a known cause, the cracking of whips, the whistling of the wind, these were considered to be the sure signs of death. But of all the fearful boggart places in the neighbourhood, the chief was Chamber Hill [*sic*], for if all the spirits of the infernal regions had been let loose and taken up their abode in the old hall, it could not have had a more frightful character. There once happened a very ludicrous and amusing incident at this place. It was the custom at Ashton wakes, among their other cruel sports, to have bull and bear baiting, and bear having been got for that purpose the night before the wakes, her keeper had brought her into town, and lodged her for the night in old stable; but in the course of the night bruin had managed to make her escape, and when her keeper took her breakfast in the morning, to his horror no bruin could be found. You may think what stir there was in the town; horses, dogs, and men armed with weapons were soon in pursuit of bruin, but it was a long time before any traces of her could be found. At length her footprints were traced near the old hall where all the hell of mischief were believed to be, regardless of all danger, for the thoughts of liberty so roamed in bruin's noddle, like Tam o' Shanter's fair hag, she "cared not deels obodie." There she was sure enough, stretched upon the floor, with two young cubs tugging at her teats. At the approach of man and dogs, she sprang up with terrible growl, and put to flight the whole host of men and dogs, for they came tumbling out of doors neck and heels; but her keeper being near at hand with her muzzle, she willingly allowed him to take her away. So honest bruin escaped the torments of baiting with vicious dogs, for the wanton sports of cruel man. Another ill omen was the wailings of Gabriel hounds in the spring and fall of the year. These fearful warnings once heard in the elements in the months of March and September were believed to be the sure signs of the coming resurrection. These ominous sounds were heard on dark nights, and were caused by the migratory birds on their wing to their places of destination, and their wailings were nothing than the pilots of the flock conducting them on their way. Another great terror was the ignis-fatuus, or Will-o'-the-wisp and Jack-o'-lantern. This phenomenon made its appearance very often after hot summer, about the beginning of October. The low lands at that period in this locality were very swampy, and, by the eradiation of heat from the earth coming in contact with the chilly air of the atmosphere, was the cause of igniting the electric fluid: hence the tens of thousands of sparks that were seen dancing on the surface of the earth. These were taken to be fairies or elfins under the control of witches, and that they could call them forth any time at their pleasure. Now, if the people were foolish enough to believe in these misconceptions, well may they be excused for believing in the Yorkshire padfoot and the Lancashire boggarts. But the most terrible of all the calamities to superstition was the aurora borealis, or northern light. This phenomenon generally happens in the month of March after a severe winter, and is supposed to be the electric fluid floating in the atmosphere, high above the earth. The rapid movements of the streamers are almost certain indications of that quality; and men were not wanting to play upon the fears of the ignorant by predicting the end of the world.'

An Old Native, 'Reminiscences of Ashton and Stalybridge',
The Ashton Weekly Reporter (29 Aug 1863), 3.

The Black Boggart

At the St Helen's police-court, yesterday, before Mr W. Pilkington, jun., a young woman named Ellen Clare, of Parr was charged with having, on Saturday last, decoyed two little children of Mr. Nathaniel Moxon from their father's premises, together with a little boy of Mr Wright, veterinary surgeon, each of them about four years of age. It appeared from the evidence that the prisoner enticed the children away by promising to get them some flowers. She took them from Cowley Hill to a field nearly a mile distant, and there stripped from them all their boots and a pinafore, and then left them. Fortunately, the apprentice of Mr Wrigley, butcher, was taking meat in that direction, when he saw the poor little things in a dreadful state about the loss of their boots, and he took them home. The prisoner was further charged with decoying the child of Mr John Belle, from Brook-street. This was a little girl not quite four years old, and the prisoner took her to Eccleston, and there took from them a jacket, and left her. All the articles were pawned by the prisoner at three different shops in the town. All the children, sharp, intelligent little things, were present during the inquiry, and seemed to recognize the prisoner; and Master Harold Wright, who was less frightened than the others told the prisoner that she threatened to fetch the 'black boggart' to him because he refused to give her his boots. The evidence being conclusive, the prisoner was committed to take her trial at Kirkdale.

'Child Stealing at St Helen's', *Liverpool Mercury* (22 Oct 1863), 7.

Tockholes Ghosts

Red Lee, occupied by Isaac and Sarah Smith, is a very remarkable house… This house also has its ghost stories. The last tenant used to say that 'boggarts' were often heard in the garrets. A small flag in the centre of the house is also [p. 27] pointed out on which it was said no one could ever churn, because it is bewitched. The true reason is much more likely to be that given by the present occupants – it is too narrow for any churn to stand upon.

[p. 169] The precise date of the commencement of the Independent Day School in Tockholes cannot be given, but it was about the year 1840. It began at the Higher Hill, in a small cottage there belonging to Moses Aspden, who was the first teacher. From this place it was taken to the Silk Hall room, with Moses Kershaw as teacher. The stipend being small, Mr. Kershaw, after a little while, discontinued the work, and a few of the children came to be taught by Thomas Nightingale in his shop at Top o' th' Low. The school was a second time transferred to Silk Hall, with Mr. Nightingale as teacher. On the Bethesda property coming into the hands of the chapel authorities, the vestry there was used for school purposes, and shortly after that the house at the end of the chapel, formerly the minister's manse. This house consisted of two rooms below and two above; and though not without its 'boggarts' and 'ghosts,' it had at different times been tenanted. In the days of the writer it had become very much dilapidated, the upper rooms being scarcely safe to pass over. It was taken down in 1880, having become quite ruinous, and the materials were used in the erection of the new chapel.

B. Nightingale, *History of the old Independent chapel Tockholes, near Blackburn Lancashire; or, About two centuries and a half of nonconformity in Tockholes* (London: J. Heywood, 1886).

Boggarts and Ghosts

Scarcely a nook or dark corner in a house building, or neighbourhood, in my early recollections, but had its boggart, and unruly children were frightened to school or to bed by the threat 'Th' Boggart el tak thee.' This evil spirit of the place was a sort of domestic policeman and was used to secure obedience from children, by the agency of fear, a most dangerous and demoralizing mode of dealing with young minds! Besides the household fright, some old man or old woman was used as an out-door terror. I remember well when the village postman, old Robert Smith, was used for this purpose; to avoid him, children would run in any direction, I have gone nearly a mile out of my way sooner than meet him! At length, however, I compromised the matter, and gave the old man a penny tobacco-box, on his promising that he 'would na tak me onny toime,' – and thus I got rid of one of the greatest troubles of my childhood's existence. Oh! how sad it is to think of little children being so unnaturally treated! I trust the days of Boggarts, as well as of birch rods, are passed away for ever, or are fast dying out, and that obedience from children will henceforth be won and secured entirely through the affections; obedience so won, will be found to inspire that confiding trust which will live and be cherished in the mind while memory holds a seat there. When a reflecting parent considers that imagination is the acting principle or power in young minds before reason begins her reign there, stories of Ghosts, Boggarts, and the like will, I feel assured, be expelled from every household. [...] Ghosts and apparitions had many a local *habitation* in the neighbourhood. One place near the village, called the 'FOUR LANE ENDS,' was noted for its incorporeal inhabitants. I was so impressed at the time with the truthfulness of those who stated that they had seen the spirits of departed humanity there, that whether on horseback or on foot, I always closed my eyes on passing the place; but the relators of such stories always proved too much for their establishment, for they mentioned the colour and cut of the hair, the clothing, and even the shape of the buttons of the ghosts they had seen, by which the calmer judgement of their listeners would see that the stories and sights had their origin in the fear or fancy of the narrator. A barn on the Hill Cross, then in the occupation of Mr. G. White, was considered a place where ghosts might be seen on any night in the year; the general belief in the village was, that the place was *haunted*. On opening the ground near the barn, at the time of my earliest remembrance, the remains of several human bodies were discovered very little below the surface. No doubt some foul deed and been done there, and the above-named facts are sufficient to impress on the mind the belief that the place has obtained its character from some faintly preserved tradition respecting it.

T. Brushfield J.P., 'Reminiscences of Ashford-in-the-Water, Sixty Years Ago', *The Reliquary* 6 (1865–1866), 12–16 at 14–15.

The Dongella Boggart

A story of a 'boggart' has been food for gossips for more than a week in the townships of Church and Oswaldtwistle. Rumours of a real ghost and a real 'boggart' have been passed, from one to another until some startling stories are afloat. It is impossible to give all the rumours, or any one distinctly; for, like rumours in general, they lack definiteness, but is affirmed that they are all true. The ghost is said to have appeared to the wife of a labouring man who lives at Church, whose name it is not necessary to give, as, notwithstanding all the rumours, the thing can only have a foundation in a distorted imagination. One story says that this woman is distant relation of old woman who died a short time ago, and who while she lived was reputed a witch and fortune-teller. This notorious old woman is said to have left her secrets with the present ghostseer, who, it is affirmed, had been trying to follow out the old dame's plans, and had the 'charm' broken while she was engaged over her boiling pan. Since that time she is said to have been troubled by unearthly visitations. Another story is that the ghost of the old woman comes and troubles her because she has parted with her books. About six weeks ago the woman was confined, and it was after her confinement she imparted information which has led to these rumours. A Church of England minister has been called in, and it is said has tried show the woman her infatuation, but has failed to convince her of the hallucination under which, it would appear, she labours. Of course no one who has visited the house can hear anything or see anything of the ghost. It is, however, surprising to find the large amount of credulity which the stories have received among both young and old, and especially among women. We notice this simply because the story has been made public, and because stories of witches and boggarts are still rife among some of the people in those districts. It is not above two years that an old man died, 'owd Hilly Hindle,' who was a reputed wizard, and who was shunned and feared by a great number of people who believed in his power to bewitch them, tell fortunes, and to do harm to his neighbours if he so willed. The majority and more enlightened portion of the inhabitants only smile at such stories, and are amused at the ease with which their forefathers believed accounts of such unreasonable occurrences. It is to be presumed that the old stories, which are sometimes now repeated by the aged, and which were quite common less than half a century ago, such, for instance, as 'Dongella boggart,' used to frighten children, had no more foundation in fact than the above ghost story, although there are many persons living who will tell of the 'Dongella boggart' (Dukenhalgh proper) being laid by parsons 'until olives ceased to be green and water ran uphill'.

'A Ghost Story', *Glossop Record* (9 Dec 1865), 4.

Without Shoes

I heard that there is a tradition, yet implicitly relied on, which speaks of a battle fought in 'the olden time,' somewhere in the neighbourhood of Tockholes, in the Roddlesworth valley, and stories that remains, including those of horses, have been found, which are believed to confirm it. Respecting this I may have something to say in a future paper. A superstitious reverence for the mound near Whitehall has descended to the present day. The country people speak of the place as being haunted by 'boggarts,' and children have been known to take off their clogs or shoes and walk past it barefooted, in the night time, under the influence of some such feeling.

Charles Hardwick, 'Ancient British Remains at Over Darwen', *Transactions of the Historic Society of Lancashire and Cheshire* 6 (1866), 273–278 at 277.

A Fake Preston Boggart

In the days of our grandfathers before gas-lights were introduced, the darksome nights occasioned many lonely localities to be considered the habitation of ghosts and boggarts, one of the most noted, in this neighbourhood, being a boggart, at New Hall, an old mansion that once stood in New Hall-lane, to which it gave its name. Many are the stories told by old Preston people of the freaks of this supposed unearthly visitant. Within the last week or two some fool or other has been annoying and terrifying timid people in the same neighbourhood by turning out at night, arrayed in a white sheet, and coming suddenly upon people at little frequented spots. We heard that the perpetrator of this foolish trick is known, and that should he repeat his 'boggart' freak, it is not improbable but a horsewhip may touch his 'feelings,' and teach him in future to conduct himself better.

'Another New Hall Boggart', *Preston Chronicle* (27 Jan 1866), 5.

Hagg Bank Boggart

Leaving the rest of the group, I strolled with this man (who was exceedingly civil and communicative, through the village [of Disley], passing between the pretty fountain and quaint old shoeing forge, and turning down by the Dandy Cock, the ornamental lamp of which is truly gorgeous, I noticed what he said was the Square, but to which it presented no more resemblance that it did to a circle; and in the Barracks there appeared to be an entire absence of anything in the shape of military. A little on our right as we passed the railway bridge was the 'cat-hole', to which he called my attention, so called from some fiendish act which was there perpetrated (it is said) a few years ago. It is at [p. 3] present used as a room for religious meetings. Farther on my companion pointed out to me a neat white farmhouse on the road side, and known as Hagg Bank [*sic*]. Here many years ago the celebrated Bank Hagg Boggart held its revels to the great dismay of nearly the whole neighbourhood. Its presence was indicated by a constant knocking which caused great and wide-spread alarm, and baffled the most strict investigation. Crowds of persons going to their work in the early morning were wont to wait here from fear and lack of courage to pass, until their numbers became such as to assure their courage, and enable them to pass with safety the haunted place. The nuisance became greater and greater each day, and the mystery more dark and unfathomable. A fortune teller, my companion informed me, was consulted and quieted the fears of the inmates assuring them that it had no power to injure them at all, but originated out of the hatred entertained towards them by a neighbour, and would never cease until his death which would occur at the hour of six in the morning. Time rolled past, and at the specified hour a neighbour died, and with his death the notorious Bank Boggart ceased.

Oliver Fizzwig, 'From Glossop to Disley and Thereabouts', *Glossop Record* (15 Dec 1866), 2–3.

Boggart Accident

William Johnson, of Macclesfield, labourer, said that on Wednesday week, between three and four o'clock he was in a spring cart going up towards Macclesfield, and had got as far as the bottom of the wood below Axe Edge Bar, when he saw a conveyance. He said to his mate, 'There's a horse taken boggart.' He then turned his horse off the road with his head over the gate, so as to leave the road free. At this time the conveyance was just coming through the toll-bar. It passed him at a rapid pace, and the horse 'slapped' into the wall, and all the occupants of the carriage were upset on the road.

'Fatal Carriage Accident', *Derbyshire Courier* (24 Aug 1867), 3.

Shadow Problems

Another of the odd folks of Mottram was one H., who was a coffin maker, and resided near to the old Grammar School, at the corner of the churchyard. He used to wend his way on Saturday nights through the church fields towards Hollingworth, and consequently he had to pass under the shade of the churchyard wall. On one particular Saturday night H. had visited sundry public houses in Hollingworth, and patronised each by having 'just another,' when he called at Old Mally Lyne's, who kept a shop in a red brick three-storey house near the Gun Inn, and supplied the people with anything from a bag of meal to a row of pins. He bought a peck of meal for the family porridge during the next week for all the little H.s he had left at home, and as it was a moonlight night he stayed rather longer than usual. He started off with his meal in a poke, and a load of beer in his interior. After trudging his way into the church fields, and hiccuping as he went along, he began to hold communion with himself as to what money he had, and what he should have bought for his wife and family. He felt as all must do under such circumstances – self-condemned; and he wondered how it would fare with him when he came to be screwed down in his coffin, the same as he had screwed down many of his boon companions. Upon looking towards the churchyard wall he observed a suspicious-looking object following him step by step. He did not like the thought of being dodged in that strange manner, so he boldly told the figure to be going as he was not going to be frightened at a thing like it. This had no effect, however, so H. quickened his pace, but the 'boggart' still kept up to him step by step. He told it again it might as well go, as he had lived too near the churchyard all his lifetime, and had put too many folks into coffins to be frightened so easily. Still, however, step by step the phantom, ghost, or whatever it might be, followed him, and gradually his blood ran thicker and thicker, and the cold perspiration stood upon his brow, as he measured the distance in his own mind that he had to go before reaching home. He counted the stiles, and concluded that if he commenced running he could not hold out to the end, so he thought he would try to make friends with his tormentor. For that purpose he slily put his hand into the meal bag, and pulling out a handful of its contents he threw the meal towards his unrelenting pursuer. Step by step, however, it continued to follow him, and he threw another and then another handful until all the meal was done, upon which he thought there was no other chance but to run for it, as he had got near home. He threw the bag behind him, and commenced a race for life, exclaiming, 'Thou greedy devil tak th' poke too.' When he arrived at home his poor wife had started up in a fright, and was still more alarmed when she saw the state he was in. She asked him, as he rushed through the house and straight upstairs, what was to do, but he only replied 'Lock th' dur; lock th'dur.' She obeyed his commands at once, and following him upstairs inquired what was to do, and she was surprised to find him under the bedclothes with all his clothing on. She tried to turn down the bedclothes, but every time she uncovered him he clutched the bedding and pulled it over his face exclaiming 'Lock th' dur; lock th'dur.' The next morning he was better reconciled, and told his wife what had taken place, and asked her to go and see if the poke was still in the road. She found the bag, and traced the route her terrified husband had come by the meal which lay scattered every few yards, upon which she returned home in passion and upbraided her lord and master with having given the week's meal to his own shadow.

A Native, 'Reminiscences of Mottram and its People',
The Ashton Weekly Reporter (6 Apr 1867), 6.

Boggart Games in the Churchyard

There was even a kind of rivalry who should take part in the midnight watches [to prevent criminals seizing buried bodies], and the Bulls Head, for some nights after a funeral, contained a strong force. The churchyard was perambulated in turns, and the old public house was doing good business night and day, although the Foresters who were watching were steady, industrious, middle-aged, family men, who thought no sacrifice too great if it was made for the benefit of the order to which they belonged. They left their homes and families to spend a portion of the night in protecting the remains of a departed brother, which was truly an act of a praiseworthy character. However, the last night they intended watching there was an unusually large company, and among them were several who may be briefly described, although some are still living. One was a stout, powerful man, with a long, flowing sandy beard and uncut moustache. His hair was long – neatly plaited – and above it he generally wore a drab broad-brimmed hat. Some readers may think it answers the description of a Johanna, and they are correct, for he was one. Another was a slim, pale faced man, with high shoulders and high cheek bones. He had a stooping gait and half closed hands swinging by his side, though he was a hard-working spinner. There were two or three others who exercised considerable influence over the rest of the company, and occasionally put a stop to the hilarity of the meeting reminding them of the object which had brought them together. However, all were glad that their duty was nearly over, feeling satisfied that the body of their brother was safe, unless we except the landlord, who united the businesses of farmer, butcher, and publican, and, as such, was prepared to assist the watchers in an efficient way, for it should be understood that the law of the land was said to be such that no legal punishment for stealing a corpse had ever been devised, the legislature never having contemplated a state of society in which such wretches as 'body snatchers' could be found. The watchers had been sadly pestered with one John Lee, better known as Tank, and they made their minds to enjoy some fun at his expense. He was between thirty and forty years of age, and had a very peculiarly formed head. His hair was very stiff and uncombable, and grew nearly to his eyes. He had curiously formed face, and his walk was of stumbling, flat-footed kind. His voice was loud, and altogether he was considered not as 'square' as he should be. He would submit to any kind of chaff as long as he could get drink. Among those who occasionally went to the Bull's Head were James Dawson and James Stanney, one a painter and the other a plasterer. They were two smart young fellows, who were invariably dressed in clean white moleskin suits and linen aprons. They were present on the night in question, and having treated Tank to sundry glasses of ale, they arranged that he should take turn round the churchyard, while the rest were eating supper. Tank started off on his perilous journey, but no sooner did he leave the house than the two young men slipped away, and succeeded in getting behind a tombstone, where they lay concealed when Tank appeared. Just as he was passing they sprang up, and poor Tank, who had bragged a deal before starting, made a dead stop. He next lifted up a furze bush to his face, so that he could not see the ghosts or resurrectionists, and began retreating, exclaiming: 'I never did nobody hurt, and I hope nobody will do me none.' This he repeated until he arrived at the churchyard gate, where he faced about and ran into the Bull's Head fast as his legs would enable him, his hair, if possible, stiffer than ever. After recovering his breath he related how he had seen, two ghosts 'or boggarts,' dressed in white, spring from a grave. He was afterwards told what he had been frightened at, when he maintained that he neither cared 'for ghosts nor body snatchers,' but nothing could ever induce him to walk round the churchyard again after dark. The company enjoyed the fun, and it has often formed the subject of a light tale to the many dark and gloomy incidents connected with the reign of the midnight robbers.

'The Midnight Robbers Being Reminiscences of Stalybridge and Mottram', *Ashton Weekly Reporter* (30 Jan 1869), 7

Burnley-Lane Head Supernatural

What I remember of the following localities, hamlets, and farmsteads I have often thought of putting in print, and I now hasten to do so. I well remember Burnley-lane Head 36 years ago. It was then a straggling hamlet, a row of houses built with every variety of shape and frontage. Handloom weaving was its staple industry. The road was mended with soft, gritty stone, which in wet weather was soon converted into mire. Gutters ran down the road side, bearing on their surface soap-suds and other filthy compounds. The young men, as a class, were brutal, drunken, and profligate, while middle-aged men were notoriously addicted to cock-fighting, race-running, night-poaching, and the like. The Methodists had opened a place of worship, which served the double purpose of a chapel and school. I went on one occasion with Henry Wilkinson, of Trawden, a local preacher gifted with considerable powers of eloquence. It was Sunday evening, and, as many of the houses seemed well-lighted with candles, Henry thought he would, have a lively congregation, but he had to begin the evening service with six persons. His text was, 'Come all ye that are weary,' but he had not proceeded far before a strange fluttering noise was heard in the chimney, and presently something having wings dropped upon the fire in the grate, and a scream, as if emanating from a scorched fiend, filled the room; the soot fell in quantities and floated through the room. The congregation, believing that something supernatural had occurred, dispersed, and Henry Wilkinson (after ascertaining that some mischievous person had climbed onto the roof of the building and thrown a farmer's goose down the chimney) turned his steps homeward, over one of the most rugged roads in England, contemplating with sad and silent disgust the miserable failure of his mission to Burnley-lane Head. The Cunliffes, after selling Hollins to the Hammertons, about 1720, removed to Wycollar Hall, a mansion remarkable for the beauty of its architecture and the costliness of its internal ornamentation. It was situated on the banks of the Wycollar, and had a Hall, another ancient ancestral mansion, for its neighbour. The floors of the chambers were made of black oak, polished with wax. It was erroneously said of the last of the Cunliffes that in his ire he killed his lady, and that her gore stained the floor, and percolating the crevices found its way to the ground floor. This is a palpable falsehood. The flooring being so perfect that nothing could ooze through it. The owner of Wycollar Hall was passionately fond of cock fighting, and when he was too ill to leave his room ordered the birds to be fought in his presence he being raised up on the bed for the purpose of enjoying deadly strife and if any marks of blood were found on the flooring it would be that of fowls, and not human gore. The usual addenda that the hall was haunted, that the form of the lady besmeared with blood was sometimes seen on dark nights passing in and out of the mansion, &c, were and are steadfastly believed in. The ancient hall has been pulled down, and in its sight a weaving shed has been erected. The legends of Worsthorn and the district are curious, if not extensive. At the time I speak of there was a common belief in the existence of boggarts, brownies, and fairies. The derivation of Brownside is from 'brownie' – the place being frequented by brownies. The ford at Brownside was alleged to be their favourite resort. The bridge that now crosses the stream there was erected in 1829. A woman named Stanworth, who lived at Bottin, assured me that on the occasion of fetching the doctor to her father from Burnley, after midnight, she saw a brownie sitting behind a hedge and taking it quite coolly. It was in size equal to a man, but devoid of clothing. At the bottom of the great meadow at Rowley there was a sheltered and sunny spot between the wood and the river Brun, that was held to be the happy hunting ground of the fairies. Shreds and patches of their dresses, but of the tiniest kind, were said have been found. Even fairy smoking-pipes were said to have been seen strewn about the ground. A 'wise man' named Stanworth, lived at Bottin, and obliged his friends and relatives by discovering the whereabouts of lost or stolen property. A woman who had lost her pocket [*sic*], containing money, on returning from Burnley market, was alleged to have recovered possession of the lost treasure through Stanworth consulting his conjuring glass, a circumstance that caused his fame to spread far and wide. Rowley, it was said, received visits from one of its ancient residents, who, attired in the ball costume of Queen Elizabeth's reign, was frequently seen beyond midnight. A joiner named William Chaffer averred that, while employed making a coffin in one of the barns, where he had been working all night, he received a silent but unmistakable visit from the personage referred to. Another man, who fetched milk from the farm, frequently avowed that he had been stopped from going in a certain direction by some invisible agency. An uncle of mine often assured me that he had repeatedly seen supernatural visitors, but such sights never excited any or apprehension in his mind. He also assured me that was gifted with 'second sight,' and that he had a fore-knowledge of the death of any member of the family. He could relate with marvellous exactness the circumstances attendant upon the 'laying' of the Rowley boggart; how, prayer and supplication at the confluence of two streams near Rowley – at Netherwood Bridge and at the Water Meetings, a little lower down the stream – the treaty with the boggart never again to emerge from spirit-land had been ratified by placing a sort of headstone on the ground, as a seal and sign-manual of the ceremonial... I have no wish to ridicule the mistaken notions of these who believed in the reality of ghosts or apparitions, because, from a vivid recollection of the cardinal virtues that many of those persons possessed, I sometimes draw an unfavourable comparison between the unforgotten dead and these who sometimes talk so glibly about 'civilisation,' 'advancement,' 'excelsior,' &o. James Heaton, *Preston Guardian*.

James Heaton, 'Stray Notes by the Wayside: The Environs of Burnley', *Burnley Advertiser* (13 Feb 1869), 3.

Boggart Bike

A gentleman who is well known in Bacup, encouraged by the success of his performances on musical instruments, determined in an evil hour to try his hand on a velocipede, with what luck we will now relate. Having occasion to travel weekly the barren moorland road between Bacup and Todmorden, and wishing for some more easy means of performing the journey than walking, he purchased a two-wheeled velocipede in Liverpool, and started on his trial trip. On the level road he managed to get along easily enough, but had some difficulty ascending the hill, and no sooner had he gained its summit than he had to commence the descent. At first the velocipede appeared a great success, requiring little or no exertion, only that he should steer straight. The road becoming steeper, the velocipede gradually but surely increased its speed, and began to bound over the loose stones with an anything but comfortable jolt, and presently the disheartening fact dawned upon the adventurous velocipedist that he had lost all command over his two-wheeler. Still his presence of mind does not seem to have deserted him, and whatever fate awaited him, he prepared himself to brave the worst. His first thought was to spring into the first soft place in the road that presented itself, but he soon discovered that slipping off the vehicle was no easy matter. He therefore determined to keep his seat, and, fixing his hat firmly over his brow, on he went as fast as the vehicle could carry him. Presently a new object of terror startled him, and that was lest he should run over one of the many things that might be in the road, or what would be still more disastrous, come into collision with some approaching vehicle, but helter-skelter went the velocipede, its exciting occupant all the while calling out, 'Police! Stop me! Fire!' &c., to the no little astonishment of the natives of the district. Happening to approach a turn in the road somewhat suddenly, the machine upset, the rider being shot out of his seat like a rocket and left sprawling in the mud. It is not very likely that he will again soon ride abroad, but if he does 'may we be there to see'. It is said that workmen are now busy building velocipedes in Bacup for their own private use; but with the fate of the unhappy professor of music before their eyes, we shall be very much astonished if they venture on the same road.

'A Velocipede Taking "Boggart"', *The Ashton Weekly Reporter* (1 May 1869), 2.

Death by Boggart (and Boy)

At Ashton-under-Lyne, Ellen Macnamara, four and a half years old, died at 18 Swift's Yard, Tatton Street, on Saturday afternoon last. Between eight and nine o'clock on Friday night she was in the house of a neighbour. The neighbour's son, a boy seven or eight years of age, frightened the deceased by telling her that there were 'boggarts' in the coal hole. The fright affected the child very seriously; she was seized with vomiting fits, and during the night became insensible, and a few hours afterwards died.

'A Child Frightened to Death by "Boggarts"', *The Dundee Courier and Argus* (9 Feb 1871), 4.

Mr F. Price coroner held an inquest on Tuesday morning, at the Talbot Inn, Stamford-street, upon the body of Ellen Macnamara, five years of age, who died from the effects of being frightened by a lad named Harlow, on the 3rd instant.—Matthew Macnamara said: I am an out-door labourer, and live at 18 Swift's-yard, Tatton-street. The deceased, Ellen Macnamara, was a child, and was five years of age. Previous to Friday last she was in good health, but in the evening I was told that she had been frightened, though her mother said that she looked pale in the afternoon. Just before we were going to have our supper, between eight and nine o'clock, Mrs. Harlow came into our house, and, addressing my daughter, asked her if she would come and rock the cradle whilst she went on an errand, and she went with her. About a quarter of an hour afterwards I sent my other daughter, who is about eight years of age, to take her sister's place whilst she had her supper. When she got to the door she ran back, and told me that Ellen was crying, through Edward frightening her. I went to the house, knowing that the child was easily frightened, and found her crying, but rocking the cradle still, though trembling. I took my daughter home, and she said that the lad told her that there was a boggart in the coal-hole, or something of that sort. After pacifying her she got her supper, and went to bed, apparently all right. During the night she vomited several times, and in the morning, about eight or nine o'clock, my wife took some tea upstairs for her, but on her raising her up found her motionless. I was in bed in the same room, and heard the mother speaking to her, but as she could receive no answer from her I carried her down stairs. In a short time she vomited whilst in the cradle, and about twelve o'clock I went to the relieving officer for an order. Upon receiving it I went to the doctor, but he was bad with the rheumatic, and gave me two powders saying that if it grew worse I had to see him again. I gave the child one of the powders but she got worse during the afternoon and died about half-past four. The doctor called to visit her the next morning but she was dead. In reply to Mr Heaton, the foreman of the jury, witness stated that the boy who frightened her was between seven and eight years of age. A juror thought the buildings wanted looking after, and the houses cleansed, in order that the atmosphere might be rendered more pure. Another juror: Don't you think Mr Coroner that the doctor ought to have seen the girl. The coroner:

Yes, if he had been told that the case was an urgent one; but he was also affected with the rheumatic. Witness: I told him that the child was very ill, but he said if it was worse by five o' clock I had to go for him. I went in the afternoon, but he was out. Ann Gee said: I live at Delamere-street, and about half-past twelve Saturday I was asked to go and see the child, when I said that it was 'strucken with death'. The father was in the house, and had been for the doctor. I stayed in the house some little time, and then went home. About five minutes to four I went again, and found that the child was dying, and it died whilst I was there. The father did not go a second time for the doctor until after the child's death. A juror thought it strange that Dr. Galt could not attend the child when Macnamara went for him, but could go to another case. Macnamara was re-called, and, in answer to the coroner, said that the child was not dead when he went a second time for the doctor, but it was on his return home. The jury returned a verdict that the child died from the effects of the fright. The foreman and one of the jury expressed their opinion that parish doctors did not appear to attend to the cases they ought. The Coroner said they could not state whether Dr. Galt was in fault or not, because he was absent and therefore not able to explain the case; though no doubt, had he been told that the matter was urgent, he would have attended earlier. From his (the coroner's) experience in those matters, that class of people often sent for the doctor when the cases were of little importance, and no doubt medical men got somewhat indifferent on account of it.

'Death of a Girl from Fright', *Ashton Weekly Reporter* (11 Feb 1871), 4.

Boggart Renown

To the Editor of the Preston Chronicle. Sir, That may be so, but it does not therefore follow that Weeton can boast of the most tremendous boggart? No, sir. That advantage belongs to Mowbrick. Other places may have boggarts possessing various qualities entitling them to notoriety in one form or other, but for being dreaded, for working mischief, and for all evil, the Mowbrick boggart licks them all put together. Why, sir, it is said that the Mowbrick boggart by way of making a mockery of all religion, would actually go to church like a pious Christian just as if he were the most conscientious character in the whole district. No boggart like the Mowbrick boggart. You think what a dreadful aspect the Mowbrick boggart must have worn, when it is said his costume was a big hat about two yards high with a feather in it, and with a pair of spurs on something like a couple of scythes, and a sword by his side of awful proportion. Whoever once saw the Mowbrick boggart, you may be sure had no wish for a second familiar séance. Yours, &c., ANTIQUARIAN.

'Boggart Renown', *Preston Chronicle* (26 Aug 1871), 6.

Boggart at Large

During the past week or two the inhabitants of Kirkham and the neighbourhood have been (at least it is reported) visited by a strange character, which many have defined as a 'boggart.' This odd being is said to be travelling about in the following parts of the country, namely – Kirkham, Westby, Wren Green, Treales, Clifton, Newton, &c., and is of high stature and dressed at one time as a man clad in a cloak or a shawl; and at another time wholly as a woman. Many persons are led to doubt the authenticity of the 'boggart' or the 'man in woman's clothing;' whilst others affirm that they have both seen and conversed with 'Margaret Henry,' as this undefined being is sometimes called. We have not heard of any depredations being committed by the 'boggart.' Save sometimes strange knocking at doors and window shutters at night time and in the early morning. The farmers in the different parts of the country above described have, for the last few weeks, had the gratification of knowing where to find their servants of an evening; for, instead of going prowling about the country as they have done, they have gone straight off to be in good time and hid their whole bodies beneath the blankets, under the impression that they were 'safer in bed than abroad,' at least so long as the 'boggart' is allowed to be at large.

'Boggart at Large', *Preston Chronicle* (23 Dec 1871), 5.

The Copp Boggart

The general belief is that as knowledge is increased, superstition with all its concomitants will decrease, and when a good school is established in a district, previously infested with boggarts, ghosts, or witches, they will speedily disappear. Such may be the rule but there are exceptions. 'In the neighbourhood of Great Eccleston a good school has, within a year or two, been erected, and is now conducted by an efficient master, who has under his care near 100 pupils. And it is much to be desired that as they attain the age of manhood, the rising generation with their accumulated knowledge, will manfully battle with the Copp Lane Boggart, and manfully lay it in the Copp gutter 'for aye,' or 'while water runs down the hill,' the usual time for putting such ghostly visitants to rest. 'The Copp Boggart' is one of very ancient date-perhaps anterior to the time when the Druidical priesthood performed their mystic rites in sacred groves, or ere Sir Lancelot sought the 'Sangrel' and formerly was in great repute. Numbers after having had ocular demonstration of its existence had their nerves so dreadfully shattered, that a considerable time has elapsed ere they were again at peace. After about half a century, in which the unquiet spirit has thought fit to keep within its den, or what is more likely, been confined there, for now-a-days spirits have vagaries [...] rumour speaks loudly that it has again broken forth, or pandemonium has been permitted to disgorge one or more of its occupants to 're-visit the glimpses of the moon,' and to the terrible consternation of the night-walkers has within a few weeks back, re-appeared with all the customary shapes and forms which demons are permitted to take, namely, a headless woman, a white lady, a donkey-like beast, and a terrific dog with a white neck and a tail similar to a sheaf of corn curled up all over its shoulders. One of the noted carding confraternity residing within a few miles of Elswick, formerly a jobber, and now about the age allotted to man, was returning the other night from a regular carding house, not so very far from Little Eccleston, where penny lant is the never changing role, and on approaching Copp Gutter, about 400 yards from his own home, he was astonished to behold an 'uncommon sight.' As a pack of cards are said to be the D-l's books, and the jobber being no common manipulator with them, his Satanic Majesty probably thought him a 'foeman worthy of his steel,' and was patiently waiting with cards, table, candle and chair ready; but the jobber, who has never before met an opponent whom he feared to encounter at either whist or penny lant, and whom neither wind nor wave could force from his game, at once turned tail to Lucifer, and left the Son of the Morning, chuckling with delight, and grinning and gibbering with bloodless jaws at the cowardice of his wished for opponent; but jobber skedaddled with all the breath at his command, back again about three miles to the house he had left, when, lo, 'with chattering teeth, he stood, and stiffened hair,/ And looked a bloodless image of despair'. Two bacchanals from the same village also encountered the ghost upon another night; but some hours earlier than disembodied spirits are allowed to exhibit themselves to mortal kin, 'And ee'r the last red light the farewell of day,/ From the rock anon the river was passing away'. This time it was in the form of the Demon Dog of Peel Castle, but the result was not so disastrous, and it probably disappeared in a flash of fire. Again a bucolic individual from the neighbourhood of Roseacre, encountered the restless shade in the semblance of a well dressed lady, gliding before him in silks, rattling with beads, and wearing three flounces to a brown coloured dress, moving a certain distance before him, stopping when he stopped. 'Her form no shadow cast,/ Her footfall made no sound.' It disappeared in the Boggart Cave at Copp Gutter. We have not heard if the said bucolic is blessed with a female partner, but if not we fear his happiness is far distant if everything in the form of woman make him as dirty as Copp Boggart did; but we hear that he is partially in order again, for on Sunday night last he was at Great Ecleston, and had again the same dreaded gate to go. We have not heard whether he had any further adventure. 'Jackathon,' a devoted worshipper of Bacchus declares there are only two things of which he is in mortal dread, namely, Copp Boggart, and a policeman when he is slew'd. Correspondent.

'The Copp Boggart', *Preston Chronicle* (21 Dec 1872), 3.

A Balloon Mistaken for a 'Boggart'

The other day, two balloons were sent up from J.S. Anderson's, cabinet maker, Fishergate, in honour of one of the apprentices being 'out of his time.' Attached to each was a note requesting the finder to send word where they alighted. A few days afterwards Mr. Anderson received a reply from a person residing in Mawdesley, stating that he had met with one of the balloons in a meadow between Burscough and Mawdesley. With respect to the other, the writer says that he had met with a young man of the district who had found it; the following being the said young fellow's account of the discovery: 'As I was going,' says he, 'down back lanes, last night, I was frightened, for just as I turned at the side of Glover's Pit I saw something white, and it kept rising up and then going again; sometimes it seemed a big thing, and then very little. My hair fair stood up, and when I got past, didn't I run home, and when I told our folks, my father said it was nothing; but I said it was; so at least we agreed to go with a lantern, and see what the boggart was; and when we had got each of us a great big cudgel, we went; but I was not so keen of getting so near. When we had got 20 to 30 yards off the pit, the white thing began to lift up, and my father said that he did not know what to think about it: but after a while we got a bit nearer, and I felt a little bit bolder with having company, so at last we got close to the pit, with our cudgels ready. Then we got it out, and found that it was nothing but a lot of wire and paper, but it did look like a boggart, and if we had not gone that night and found what it was, I dare not have come that way to work in the morning.

'A Balloon Mistaken for a Boggart', *The Preston Chronicle and Lancashire Advertiser* (22 Feb 1873), 5.

Fair Becca Again

Yorkshire, of all the Northern counties, has ever been noted for the superstitious character of its inhabitants. Anything which has a tendency to the mysterious – anything, in fact, which defies their efforts to unravel, is always regarded with awe by the rustic people. Numberless are the supernatural appearances which are believed to haunt the lonely districts of Yorkshire – 'Guytrashes,' with cloven feet and eyes large as saucers; Will-o'-the-Wisps, fairies, boggarts, and other unearthly entities of every description. Greece and Rome had their rural as well as classical deities, and it is not hard to recognize, in the uncouth creature of Yorkshire superstition, the fawns and nymphs, the satyrs and other rural deities so well known in the mythology of the Hellenes and the Latines. Pluto, the grim lord of Hades, is not so changed but we see his image in the modern descriptions of Satan, with his horns and hoofs and blackness. We still speak of the River of Death we all must cross, and in many parts of Yorkshire the eyes of the dead are weighted with coins, which *may* be a relic of that ancient custom – the payment of Charon's fee. To the curious inquirer the comparative mythology here only hinted at will form a fruitful field, and I shall be glad to see the subject more fully discussed in the columns of the Observer. Another phase of the superstitious character of the rustic population is their ready belief in ghost stories. Scores of these are related by the firesides of rural Yorkshire. Old halls of retired abodes are always described as ghost-haunted. Should a murder or a suicide occur in village, hall, or hamlet, the place is accordingly invested with the spirit of the deceased. Many a time have I listened to these legendary stories, told with graphic power by some gray-haired old dame, who has seemed to my youthful imagination to be in some weird way connected with the tale she was telling. Nearly every village in the rural districts can boast of some uncanny occurrence having taken place at some time or other, the date being often too remote for recollection. A few of these legends, such as are related of some old hall or given as the origin of the various municipal insignia, are perpetuated in the local histories, but there are others more or less authentic which are rapidly passing from remembrance. Seeing your correspondent's query (No. 6), I will give to the best of my ability this ghost story or legend, once popularly believed in by the inhabitants of the village in which I live. Mr. Milner did publish in a book of 'Juvenile Tales' a version of the legend, from which I shall quote hereafter. A work by Mr Sowerby has also been published, which I have not been able to see. The following is, however, the substance of what I have gathered from the villagers themselves: On the sunny slopes of Hollingwood there lived in olden times a young maiden named Rebecca. She was a farmer's daughter, and lovely 'As eyes could wish to see,' having passed her girlhood in the healthful duties of rustic life, up in the morn to drive the cows afield, and seeking her couch as the sun was 'westering ov'r the dell.' No wonder then that her cheeks vied with the rose in their richness of colour: that her eyes shone brightly, and that her step was as light as the bounding fawn. The villagers, seeing her beauty, with one consent gave her the appellation of 'Fair Rebecca,' the title by which her memory has lived to this day. Time passed away and Rebecca came to know the meaning of love. At the neighbouring farmstead of Bracken Hall lived the youth on whom she had fixed her affections – the young William. He had been her companion in childhood, and now, seeing her growing loveliness, had begun to pay her a lover's attentions. Alas! for Rebecca, he was a very loose-principled young man, and, listening favourably to his suit, the result was – her ruin. Time passed on, and Rebecca was expecting marriage. Like Mary, the Maid of the Inn, 'she loved,' but young William had *not* 'settled the day' when she should be happy for life. He had no such intention. Having, in the meantime, formed an attachment with another girl, he always contrived to put the marriage off on some pretext or another, till, seeing he would have to marry her or bring disgrace upon her, the heartless villain formed the diabolical resolution to murder the innocent, confiding girl. So – as the legend tells – he rode over one fine morning to her homestead. A sack of meal had newly arrived from the mill, and Rebecca was in the act of tasting the contents. Dismounting, he told her to array herself in bridal apparel, as he intended taking her to the kirk to be married. Rebecca delightedly obeyed, and was soon equipped, when they rode away, she mounting behind him on the double saddle (the fashion of the period). He then put his plan into execution. Near a lonely lane they had to traverse were some old disused pits; and, riding to one of the most remote, he told his companion to prepare for death, as he was going to throw her down. Rebecca pleaded for mercy, but he, disregarding her entreaties, galloped round the pit, and tried to throw her off the horse; but she, clinging to him desperately, he had to ride round three times ere he could effect his purpose, his victim shrieking at every attempt. The third time he succeeded in flinging her into the pit. When the deed was accomplished, the murderer seems to have suffered the pangs of conscience. In the work before mentioned, a writer puts these words into the mouth of an old man, 'On such a night as this, many years ago, as I have heard old people tell, a young man was observed to come into an inn there. He sat down, and placing his elbow on the table, laid his head upon is hands, as if some heavy care oppressed him. Long in moody silence did he thus sit. Then, as if pierced with some sudden anguish, he would start and pace the room as if some damning thought seemed burning his brain. Then he left the room abruptly as he entered.' Returning home, his strange looks attracted the notice of some members of the family, who asked him what he had been doing, and what was the matter with him. He answered evasively that he ailed nothing, had done nothing at all, &c. But on their persisting in their inquiries, he swore a dreadful oath, wishing that if harm had come to any one through him his horse might rot in its stall, and that he would never more rise from his bed. His wish was fulfilled. He took to his bed and never left it again alive, while his horse died in its stable of the rot. Thus signally did Providence interpose to punish the sin he had committed. Before he died he made a full confession of his crime, and the corpse of Rebecca was found, fearfully mangled, at the bottom of the pit. To such a sad end did this fair, unfortunate maiden come. Since then, they say, the spirit of the murdered girl has haunted the place. For many years, say the villagers, she inevitably appeared, or her thrice-repeated shriek was heard, whenever a death was about to take place. Whether 'Spirits of the loved and lost' are enabled to make themselves apparent to bodily sight, or whether, at such times folks see only like Hamlet, with the 'mind's eye,' is not for me here to discuss; but there are people living who profess to have seen this ghost, and the claim of whose testimony to respect is undeniable.

Great Horton. Jesse Mitchell. 'Fair Becca', *Bradford Observer* (21 Mar 1874), 7.

Looking for Becca

'Ah,' said an old friend to us, 'I have known this churchyard fifty-seven years. I had to come through it when I was seven years old, on my way to work at Fawcett Holme Mill. That was before the time of the Factory Acts. We used to work in shifts, and my turn then was to toil in the mill until eleven on Saturday night, and go to work again at one o' clock on Monday morning, so as just to miss Sunday. In those days we could see up to Horton, and many a night have looked out of the windows of the mill to try and see "Fair Becca," the Horton boggart, but she never appeared.'

'Churchyard Stories', *Leeds Times* (4 August 1877), 2.

Jingling Annice and False Boggarts

With all their progress and their politics, the weavers were steeped in superstition; believed devoutly in 'boggarts' and 'signs of death;' and some of them had seen 'jingling Annice,' a female figure in white, without head, dragging a chain. Peggy Corless almost sent me into a fit with her real experiences. 'I were sitting,' she said, 'one night with Mary, the housemaid, in the kitchen (it were afore I were wed), and master and missus were out, and nobody were in the house but Mary and me; and all at once, I heard a foot on the stairs, and I said to Mary, 'that's John Butcher's foot;' and two year after John Butcher died, and that were a sign.' I shuddered at the thought of Peggy hearing my foot on the stairs; nobody likes to die, old or young. I know Betsy Walker at eighty fell ill, and could no longer, as she said, 'keep scratting afoot;' so her son, thinking her time was come, sent for the minister, to help her to make a good end. The worthy man talked with her, prayed with her, and exhorted her to repent of her sins, and depicted the joys and blessings of the next world to the penitent sinner, and was feeling comfortably satisfied at the frame of mind into which he had brought her, when he was somewhat taken aback by the invalid's calling out, 'It's all very well, Mr. S., but Old England for me!' I never did see a real ghost, but I saw something very like one once. Grandpapa's maid-servant, Betsy, a fine young woman, full of fun, wrapped herself in a white tablecloth, made a torch of brown paper and pitch, lighted it, and glided slowly through the plantation in front of a row of cottages. Presently little Ann Hollows came out, and flew back like a shot, with: 'Oh, mother, mother! I've seen a sperrit, I've seen a sperrit.' The alarm spread; all the neighbourhood was roused; they all saw it; but nobody dare go to it. At length, Joseph Grindrod, plucking up a spirit, said, in a voice much louder than the occasion required, 'I'll see what it is; I'll know whether it is a ghost or not' and was moving slowly towards the shrubbery, when Betsy, who heard all, trod out her torch, slid off the tablecloth, gathered it under her apron, and disappeared, to the mystification of the wondering group, who, if any of them are living now, will still have firm faith in the 'white sperrit' that arose and vanished in the Hill-farm shrubbery.

Louisa Potter, *Lancashire memories*
(Macmillian and Co: London 1879), 99–100.

Ranscliff Boggart

Half a century ago or a little over, there was scarcely a cottage in the district but what had its tokens and supernatural visitors of some kind. It was in Ranscliff that the famous Kidcrew boggart chiefly took up its quarters, and was for years the terror and dread of the hamlet. Sometimes this ghostly invader of the quiet of the village would meet the collier as he travelled the lonely hills, or made his way along the old deep lanes that winded through the valley. On other occasions there would appear a light, and be seen dancing and flickering through the marshy dales. And the dread which this unearthly light, as it was supposed to be, inspired was something horrible. It was even known to come at night and sing in the dales in imitation of a nightingale, and hundreds of colliers with affrighted faces gathered to the spot to listen to the strange bird. To them, at least, such appearances or noises had this serious aspect, that they never were seen or heard only as predicting some accident or fatality of some kind, the occurrence of which their mission seemed to forewarn and prepare that this visitation of the token or boggart always threw the village into the greatest state of melancholy and alarm. It was to them a sure sign that some cottage or cottages were to be made desolate by the destroying hand of violent death in the mines. One principal cause for the origin of this village phantom, was the cutting of the canal tunnel under the hill. Just imagine the effect which this dark subterranean passage over two miles in length, would have on the minds of the colliers and boatmen, when in 1777 it was finished. It soon became associated with all kinds of sights and sounds, perfectly natural, but to the rude people who used it, and those of the neighbourhood, not at all to be understood in that way, after the completion of the tunnel, one of the coalmines at Ranscliff Hill was made to communicate by means of footrill, with the canal, falling into about a quarter of a mile from its mouth. It was this particular footrill that the boggart first made itself known to the people of the village. So alarmed did the colliers become on what was supposed to its first appearance, that there was great difficulty in getting them to work, and on the least unusual noise occurring, or let one of their number report that he had seen something, and work was once suspended for the day, and sometimes for a longer period. And then the news went round to every cottage household, with the usual results, that the boggart had been seen. Many are the tales told as to the origin of this village phantom, all of them differing in detail, but all in the fact of the phantom itself. And perhaps no village or hamlet in England was ever more completely possessed, or more fully believed in a goblin than did the one in question. But then it must be remembered that at the end of the last century Ranscliff was very exceptional, and many things might be urged in apology. The peculiarity of the district, the mining operations, and most of all the want of educational facilities. There was not a church nor a school in the locality; the nearest church was Lawton, in Cheshire. Sunday had no influence here, for frequently, when trade was good, it was passed in working the mines, the same as any other day. And to the boatmen of the canal, their work never stopped on any day whatever. Every day alike, their boats, full or empty, were passing under the tunnel. A part of the inhabitants of Ranscliff were made of this latter class of people, who had cottages in the villages, and lived in them near the mouth of the tunnel, when they could find time to leave their boats, which was indeed but seldom. Such a class as these were not likely to add much to the respectability or enlightenment of the hamlet. On the contrary, they were a set of men to whom all sorts of crimes were attributed, and who were believed to be capable of any deed, no matter how shocking villainous. The tale the origin of the which found the most general belief was that one of the boatmen, while under the tunnel, quarrelled with his wife, and, for some provoking words which the woman used, cut her head off. Afterwards, to conceal the murder, he dragged the body into the colliery working, which we have already referred to as communicating with the canal tunnel. The most horrible form, therefore, which the phantom assumed was that headless woman, and, unaccountable as it may seem, though robbed of this upper and essential part the body, she was able to utter that peculiar noise dreadful to the ears of boatmen and miners. But, as we have said, the spectre did not confine itself to the colliery workings, the tunnel where the deed was done. It appeared in every part of the village, the dale, the road, or the cottage. Nor was the terror confined to the village, it spread over the whole of the Potteries in one direction, and over parts of Cheshire in another. This strange spectre, as well as terrifying the colliers, appeared at lone farm houses in the vicinity and haunted the barns and the out-buildings, frightening the stable and the plough-boy out of their wits. it was made the means of effecting robberies Round Ranscliff and Ravensdale was once famous for rabbit preserves, and the boggart was always found to have surprising appetite for these four-legged creatures and it was pretty well understood that such dainty and tender flesh agreed very well with the ghostly stomach of the spectre. Gamekeepers are susceptible to fear as well as other men, and would rather have met the most desperate gang of poachers than have encountered this headless woman, or would any noise rather than that which the phantom was supposed to make. Thinking to obtain some information of definite and reliable character of this spectre, which for over sixty years had been the terror of the district, we on one occasion made up to the keeper to make inquiries. He was tall man, over middle age, dressed in a snuff-coloured velvet jacket, dark corduroy trousers with gaiters, and big hat. His face looked solemn enough to have been communicating with the spectre all his life. But perhaps melancholy is the most natural expression of a gamekeeper's face. For a moment he looked very earnest after our question had been put, and did not speak. At last he said: 'Yen see where the break in the tunnel takes place. (This was the railway tunnel referred to.) Just that part a few years ago abounded with rabbits, and we had orders to take strict care of them, and mind the poachers. Well, one night I was out, and about one o'clock heard a strange cry that sounded like the cry of woman, and seemed to die away under the tunnel mouth. I went at once to the spot, thinking that something had happened; but when I got to the place there was not the slightest sign of woman or man, nor not a living thing near except myself; and that is all I ever heard or saw.' Such are the traditions around Ranscliff, although the story of the once famous Kidcrew boggart is remembered now by few, and its terror has departed from the village.

'Up and Down the Country: Ranscliff', *Staffordshire Sentinel and Commercial and General Advertiser* (6 Dec 1879), 7.

Bounding Boggarts Fall

An accident of an alarming character and attended with somewhat serious results occurred on Monday evening at the Theatre Royal, Churchgate, Bolton during a performance of the popular pantomime, Little Bo-Peep. One of the scenes represents a dark, lonely cavern, where Bo-peep, is assailed by two 'bounding boggarts', these being represented by Messrs. G. Francis and Matthewson, the former of whom also plays the part of the harlequin, and the latter that of clown in the concluding portion of the pantomime. In the centre of the stage is a 'vampire' trap, by means of which the 'bounding boggarts' appear and disappear with considerable rapidity, the feat being also performed by Mr. J. F. Elston, the manager, who in the character of 'Simple Simon' comes to the rescue of Bo-peep. It seems that about nine o'clock this part of the programme was being enacted in the normal way. Several exits and entrances had been made in demon-like fashion and the last disappearance was then commenced. Two or three feet below the stage a kind of mattress resting on the place of boarding is supported by means of ropes, upon which the performers alight in their descent from the stage. Mr. Francis was the first to go through the trap, and one of the ropes having broken, he was precipitated into what is known as the 'well,' a distance of some 18 or 20 feet. He was immediately followed by Mr. Matthewson, who fell upon his predecessor; Mr Elliston disappeared next, and, of course, alighted in his turn upon the other two gentlemen who had not had time to recover their position. A short delay naturally arose in continuing the performance, but although the audience, which was pretty numerous, guessed that something was wrong, it was only those behind the scenes who for the time knew the actual state of affairs. Mr. Francis was found to have sustained a severe spinal injury, and was scarcely able to move; Mr. Elliston had seriously injured his ankle; whilst Mr. Matthewson had been bruised and a little shaken. Mr. Mackintosh, surgeon, was sent for, but, as he was indisposed, the services of Mr. Smith, surgeon of Folds-road, were obtained, that gentleman arriving at the theatre as quickly as possible. Mr. Elliston, supposing himself to be not much hurt, essayed to continue his humorous part, but he was obliged to desist, and subsequently he and Mr. Francis were conveyed to their respective homes in cabs. Mr. Matthewson did not appear much worse for the accident, and will not be prevented from resuming his calling; but it is doubtful whether either Mr. Elliston or Mr. Francis will be able to do anything for a night or two. One of the stage carpenters was slightly injured about the head by the fall of the mattress, he being at the time in charge of the apparatus for working the 'star' trap by means of which the artistes ascend from below on to the stage, Messrs. Elliston and Francis are under Mr. Smith's care, and are progressing very favourably toward recovery.

'Alarming Accident at Bolton Theatre Royal', *Manchester Courier and Lancashire General Advertiser* (25 Feb 1880), 5.

Boggart Hunting at Tyldesley

The belief in ghosts and hobgoblins was supposed no longer to prevail, but recent occurrences at Tyldesley go to show this to be a mistaken idea. Several evenings and an apparition made its appearance in a rather secluded place known as Langley Platt. The ghost always appeared after darkness had set in, and played some rather fantastic tricks, and though many attempts have been made to capture it, they have hitherto failed. Scores of colliers and others have been parading the district armed with sticks and bludgeons, and one of the colliers has fired several shots at the latest arrival from spiritland. The more nervous portion of the inhabitants have been greatly excited by the ghostly apparition.

'"Boggart" Hunting at Tyldesley', *The Manchester Evening News* (19 Sep 1881), 2.

Owl Boggart

A few evenings ago as the vicar of an interesting Cheshire rural parish on the banks of the Dee was conducting evening service in his church, on the occasion of a week-day celebration, he being a regular observer of fasts and festivals, there was a somewhat thin congregation his auditory being only two, one young gentleman a student for holy orders and the other an old member of the flock. All went on as usual until the service was somewhat advanced, when the nerves of the few present were somewhat disturbed by a strange hooting, which proceeded from somewhere in the sacred edifice. The church being somewhat dimly lighted nothing could be seen to indicate whence the sounds proceeded, and it being repeated two or three times some uneasiness began to be displayed. At length one of the party alarmed at the situation, which was not rendered more pleasant by associations of the past, so many graves being about and there being the memories of as many generations of departed parishioners – began to sidle towards the doorway, on reaching which he took to his heels, running through the churchyard, in doing which, he knocked down to the fellow's dismay, a youngster who wouldn't get out of the way. Service being stopped and an examination taking place, it was found that the unintentional cause of the alarm was an owl that had taken up its quarters in the lofty rafters of the church where it had issued its moanings without any disposition to disturb the worshippers. The member of the congregation who had taken so harried a departure had safely arrived at home with no worse result than disturbed nerves, and he was waited on in the course of the evening with an explanation of the innocent cause of alarm. It was some time, however, before he recovered from his fright, but ultimately assured of all being right, he, like the others joined in a laugh at the adventure.

'A Boggart in a Church', *Cheshire Observer* (10 Feb 1883), 4.

Sir, My species from time immemorial have always sought their mates about February 14, and I would do the same, but how can I with a quiet mind? The high wind yesterday brought a sheet of your usually sensible paper to the top of an elm tree where I was sitting, and there I see you speak of an owl who frequents an old church in a certain Cheshire village on the Dee as a 'Boggart'. I don't know whether you mean me, but I think you must. Dear sir, what is a Boggart? My mind is sorely disturbed at having a name applied to me which I don't understand, and which does not exist in the dictionary. But as to me disturbing the congregation during service in our church, why, sir, your silly correspondent must know as little about owls as I do about the Liberal Caucus, for no Cheshire owl (I am not in a position to report upon Lancashire or Irish birds) ever degraded himself by hooting in the presence of devout worshippers. The truth is I lodged in that church tower long before most of them were born, and with the exception of the boys who throw stones at me, and those who go 'flight' shooting at night, I love them all and do absolutely no harm to anybody, and sometimes a great deal of good. But sir, I do not think our parishioners and lodgers are aware of one of my customs, namely, that I keep a list of all those who attend church and of those who stay away, and if anybody calls me 'Boggart' again I'll publish it, and then the people will know clearly enough who did not write that stupid paragraph. With obedient hooting, I remain yours truly.

The Deeside Owl, 'A Hoot from the Deeside Owl: Hoot! Hoot!! Hoot!!!: to the editor of the Cheshire Observer', *Cheshire Observer* (17 Feb 1883), 2.

A Boggart at Worsthorne?

Sir, The good people of Worsthorne have been recently disturbed from their usual placid condition by the strange appearance in their midst of one of those unearthly visitants from the regions of darkness or elsewhere commonly called 'boggarts.' And as such beings are not very frequently seen now-a-days it will perhaps be refreshing to your readers to find that the superstitions which were once so prevalent in this part of Lancashire are not yet totally forgotten by the people of this enlightened village. A short time ago a very worthy resident departed this life, and as it has been alleged that some of his actions during his career were not altogether what some people expected, they presumed he would not be able to rest in his new abode, but would be obliged to revisit this earthly sphere at unseasonable hours of the night in human shape to disturb the people residing in and about his late home. One person who saw this 'appearance' was a woman about fifty years of age, who had been staying up with a sick person. When she was going into her house about midnight she saw a big man about the door, and for fear ran across the street for a person to go with her into the house. The man was in bed, but rose up at once, wondering what was amiss, and went with her, but he could not see anything. Another person who saw this so-called boggart was one evening walking along with her mother-in-law to the shop, who drew her attention to the boggart, then in the form of a man. The mother seemed to treat the affair as a matter of course, and said she knew perfectly well that it was the ghost of the deceased person mentioned above. Two others saw it in the form of a big black dog, which by and bye [*sic*] changed into the form of a calf and then disappeared. One of the individuals immediately afterwards fainted through terror. A big burly man who lives opposite the place where the boggart appears dare not for his life put his head out of the door after the shades of night have fallen upon the village, and many more will not pass by that part of the village after dark for any consideration. One would have thought that in these times of the Forster and Mundella codes of education that people even in this place would not have allowed such absurd fancies to take possession of their brain; but so deeply rooted is the belief in ghosts and goblins in the minds of country people that probably another generation will have to pass away before the belief in them is totally eradicated from their minds. Yours, &c., A VILLAGER.

A VILLAGER., 'A Boggart at Worsthorne', *Burnley Express and Advertiser* (26 May 1883), 7.

Same Boggart Different Form

Can you do with a ghost story this week, Mr Editor? The good people in the neighbourhood of Coddington and Stretton have been much exercised in their minds of late by the fact that they have had a ghost lodging amongst them, and several of them have seen it! As far as Rambler can learn, a young farmer was the first to make the acquaintance of the interesting visitor on the road between Stretton and Barton. The young farmer avows that he had not proceeded far along the road in this intensely rural locality, ere he was conscious that he had a companion – a very tall woman, clad all in white! Of course, the sight put him in a state of high nervous excitement. It was some time before Rambler could get him to describe the appearance of his interesting companion. But at last he did so 'Aw sid the owd dame!' he said. 'She wur a big tall ooman, all in white! She walked asoide uv me fur some yards, but she didn't speak. Then she left me and went through a gate. She went reet through wi'out opening the gate. The aw knowed that aw'd seed a boggart, or a goblin or a troll, or summat o' th' sort. Aw wur that frightened that aw run reet back to Barton for somebody to go home wi' me. Aw wouldna see her again for anything,' continued he, and from his manner he was very much in earnest. The young fellow has been considerably chaffed in consequence, but he still adheres persistently to his text. But he is not the only person who has seen the phantom, for an evening or two later another man was walking along the same road, when he too became conscious of the presence of a companion. This time it was in the form of a man, of gigantic size, again in white (of course). The strange visitant struck terror into the heart of the countryman and as he watched it his hair stood on end. But the ghost was evidently well behaved, albeit not very communicative, for it did not speak, and the country-man saw it at last turn off from the road and pass into a field (again without opening the gate). The next person who was favoured with an interview with it was a young gardener. He says it appeared to him as he was going to his work before six o'clock one morning. (Now Rambler does not like to question this gentleman's veracity, but he has never heard of a ghost being abroad at such unreasonable hours before, but of course there is no accounting for their vagaries.) However, the mind of the youthful gardener was almost unhinged in consequence. But the strangest story of all is told by a coachman in the locality. He avers that he was driving his employer's carriage on the road between Stretton and Tilston, when he saw a strange kind of vehicle coming along, drawn by a couple of horses. 'No sooner had they met,' says he, 'than the stranger vanished into thin air!' These are samples of the stories that are agitating the minds of the good people in this locality, and in telling Rambler about it they say they wouldn't object so much if the 'boggart' would keep itself respectable, but to appear first as a woman, then as a man, and then in some other fantastic form, such conduct is extraordinary. They'd rather have no ghost at all, than have such a disreputable one, they say.

Rambler, 'Out and About Chester', *The Cheshire Observer* (13 Mar 1886), 2.

The Boggarts of Pudsey

Let us imagine ourselves in Pudsey as it was sixty, or even fifty, years ago, on a dark and stormy winter's night, sitting by some fireside, with or without the dim light of a candle; a few neighbours – men, women, and children – sitting together. The children both dread and like to hear what are called 'boggard tales.' They ask the older people to tell them some tale they have heard before, or a new one. The pitch darkness outside, and the comparative darkness within, and the howling moaning winds, and perhaps heavy raindrops pattering against the window panes, cause everyone's imagination to be in full vigour, ready to drink in the weird stories. Every eye and ear is centred on the narrator. One tells of dreams he or she had before a certain death or deaths took place, which all came true; another remembers a dream about a wedding which proved to be a sign of a funeral in the family. Some have had the nightmare, which they call 'bitch dowter' (probably the result of a deranged digestion), when they saw a woman they knew well, as fair as ever they saw anyone in their life, standing over them with a dagger or 'whittle' (carving knife), threatening to murder them, whilst they could not stir hand or foot, being held spell-bound by this Pudsey woman, who was a witch, or at least had power from the devil to do mischief by her ill-wishes. They tell of ghosts they have seen, or that have been seen by someone they know, or knew; or else been seen by someone who told it to another well-known by a friend of theirs. Then they tell of well-known ghosts that have visited well-known neighbourhoods from time immemorial, and been seen by scores of people, though they may not remember any single person who ever saw them; but it is well known by all, especially the old people. They tell of seeing the padfoot, or 'guy tresh,' the 'white rabbit,' of hearing the 'night whistler,' the 'dead watch'; of heavy feet going up and down steps of chambers or cellars; or of hearing something like a pack of wool rolling about on chamber floors or steps; of hearing knocks, cracks, thumps, moans, groans, shrieks, or sighs and sobs, and all kinds of unearthly noises. The time arrives when many of them have to go home. Those who are timid dare not go alone after listening to the many doleful tales. The most courageous have to go with the others, whilst some stay till they are fetched by some of the family. They hurry along in the wind, rain, and darkness, hardly knowing how they get home; probably they see some object which in their morbid state of mind they could swear was a boggard of some sort. That night some of them dare not go to bed alone, or if compelled to go, wrap themselves overhead in the bedclothes, almost frightened to death. At last they doze off, and have horrible dreams, which are additional proof that some evil spirits have been influencing them through the night. Both young and old have their lives made miserable by these most horrible superstitions. At this time all those who deny the existence of boggards are called infidels and atheists. The Bible even is referred to as a proof of the truth of witchcraft; also the great John Wesley's *Journal*, as well as what are considered every day facts of experience with regard to ghosts and apparitions. A large majority of all you talk to believe more or less in boggards of one sort or another. One person we knew well, fifty-five years ago, was in the habit of seeing the 'pad-foot' on almost any dark night, in all kinds of shapes, forms, and sizes, from a pack of wool, to a bull, bear, ass, calf, dog or rabbit. There was generally heard a rattling of chains, and in every form could be seen large eyes like tea saucers. If two persons were together, and one only could see and the other not, by taking hold of hands both saw it. This same young man got drunk at times, though in every other respect he was a decent, conscientious person, and very exceptional in his education, being a good reader, writer, and arithmetician for that time. As for drinking, it was not looked upon as being such an enormous crime then, especially in a young man. One dark night, as he came down Tyersal Lane, a woman walked beside him, having a white cap on, bound round with a black ribbon, and had on also a bedgown dress. He was convinced that it was his mother, who was a well-known Methodist at a time and place when being one meant much more than it does now; but she had died when this young man was only a few weeks old. This made such an impression on his mind that though not sober then, he was by the time he got home. He joined the Methodists, and afterwards became a local preacher. This affair was looked upon, both by the young man himself and others not only as a direct interposition of Divine Providence, but as a proof of the existence of apparitions. There seems in this case to have been some utility in the superstition. If a dog was seen to bark looking up in the air, or to howl, it was a sure sign of speedy death, either of persons in the neighbourhood or some of their relations. There were local ghosts, and there were more cosmopolitan ghosts. All of them had been seen or heard either by persons then living or by truthful persons who, though dead, had told their experience to others. There were several at Jumble's Well; also at Green Top, where it was said a parlour had a flag stone stained with blood, and though the flag had been taken up and replaced, the blood stain struck out in the new one. It was said that once upon a time a horrid murder had been committed there, and this stain was to be a perpetual sign. There were ghosts at Greenside, and haunted houses in Fartown. Ghosts in Bankhouse lane, Bankhouse, and Bailey Gallows, and both children and many upgrown people would try not to pass those places in the dark, or increase their speed if they did, whilst their hearts beat louder. There were boggards at Littlemoor [p. 51] Lowtown, and Boggard Lane; and about the old Chapel and the Church, after the dead were buried there, the locality near was believed to swarm. In fact, at that time spirits were either seen or expected to be seen whenever anyone's death occurred, and the neighbourhood for a time after was a terrible terror to many. Satan, or the devil, was often seen in various forms on his errands of temptation and deception. He appeared to one man who was very devout; but this was at Drighlington, though often told at Pudsey by persons who lived at the former place at the time, and who knew the pious man. One day he was fretting about his clothes being so ragged, and wondering how he would be able to get new ones, as he found it hard to get sufficient food; when all at once a person with the appearance of a gentleman presented himself and offered him lots of gold. The poor man suspected his benefactor, and looking down at the gentleman's feet, saw that he had a 'cloven foot,' which it was said was caused when the devil was thrown out of heaven to the nether regions. The poor man immediately said, 'Satan, I defy thee'; whereupon the gentleman instantly vanished, leaving a strong smell of sulphur behind, which was a certain proof of his identity. In whatever form Satan appeared, he had this cloven foot, and when he made his exit left a strong smell of brimstone behind him. It was a common practice of parents when their little ones were naughty to tell them there was a black boggard up the chimney, or coming down to fetch them; also for them to make noises in secret, or knocks, said to be 'Tom knocker,' to intimate the presence of boggards; or to shut up their children in cellars and other dark places for the black boggards to take them. No one can tell the sufferings from fright experienced by thousands of little ones under the impression that they were going to be fetched by some ugly monster or malicious ghost. It is possible that some remnants of this worse than barbarous custom may still be practised by some parents; if so, they little know the dangerous effects and the demoralising influence of such, as it is a species of falsehood which their children, sooner or later, will discover, when less reliance will be placed on their parents' words, after finding out how they have been imposed upon by bogus boggards. Then there were lucky and unlucky days, persons, places, actions, and dreams. It was thought to be a proof of future good luck for a man with dark hair to enter one's house first on Christmas or New Year's Day; and for any kind of man rather than a woman. Bad luck to take a light or allow one to be taken out during Christmas time. Bad luck to spill salt; and so it was when that article cost so much owing to the heavy tax on it. One of the most important articles in the literature of that day was a 'dream book' explaining their meaning, and giving interpretations. There was no end to people's infatuation on the subject of dreams. To dream of fruit out of season meant grief out of reason, etc. Young women who ate the first egg of a pullet before going to bed would dream of their future husbands; and on Shrove Tuesday, called pancake day, young people would turn their pancake and run to the door to see their partners for life. Fortune telling was very common, and many still living can tell startling stories about what they were told by fortune tellers, or planet rulers, as astrologers were called, who described their future husbands just as well as if they had known them. Persons are now liable to be prosecuted for following such a profession. If we consider the dense and widespread ignorance of the people in past times, together with the dark lamp-less streets and lanes, the very little light even in the houses, we may easily see what a flourishing time boggards would have; for objects not clearly seen would assume all kinds of shapes, in accordance with persons' disordered imaginations. A little lime on a wall, the top of a wall being uneven, would be a ghost. To people sitting in darkness round a low fire, listening to the wind outside, the least noise would sound louder. A moaning wind would sound to some as it did to the person with a bad conscience mentioned in Miss Bronte's *Wuthering Heights*, when it was heard to say in a most plaintive and suppliant tone, 'Let me in; Let me in.' We have known persons who were somewhat sceptical about ghosts and boggards detect some imposition, and find that a candle had been carried across the floor of a house, and had shone through the crevice of a window shutter, or door lockhole, and flitted to and fro in the street as the candle was moved, and this had been thought a genuine ghost. We have seen this effect produced frequently on a dark night. The fact is, people were generally too much afraid to examine and test the matter properly; they were so full of their infatuation that their imaginations coined boggards wholesale. How is it then that there are fewer boggards now than sixty years ago? In the first place, knowledge has been spread abroad. Such men as Chambers have scattered cheap publications broadcast through the land. Their miscellaneous tracts were unequalled by anything in publishing ever known before. One we well remember on 'Spectral Illusions' was just the right kind of thing to kill boggards and boggard tales, showing how people were liable to be mistaken and imposed upon – especially those whose vision was defective, etc. Then science generally made itself known, and even Professor Pepper's Ghost has helped to extinguish the last remnants of the superstition, for then it became impossible to distinguish the genuine from the manufactured. But above all, the cheapening of books, and especially of newspapers, by the abolition of the tax on paper and stamp duty. Still more than all perhaps by the introduction into the villages of gas for the houses and streets, so that people could see objects more clearly, and were not so easily deceived. Gas was stationary, and not moved about the house like a candle; so that mimic ghosts could not be made in the old fashion. In dark weather gas made it lighter than day. We remember when a certain person who had looms in his chamber first lighted up with gas – in mid-winter – the change from candles to gas was so surprising that he exclaimed, 'No more day leet for me!' We ourselves were always rather skeptical when a boy about some of the boggards, and had the boldness to make some of them out as being natural objects. We often asked how it was that they only came at night, when they could not be seen clearly. Some strong believers in ghosts seemed to be amazed at our exposing some of their favourite boggards, as if they had rather they had been real than spurious. Another most serious and mischievous superstition, everywhere prevalent, was the belief that when any child died, it was the will of the Lord that it should be so. Sanitary science was at that time very little known or understood, and the few who had studied the matter and made themselves acquainted with the laws of life, health, and disease, – he spoke of the possibility of preventing many of the deaths both of children and upgrown people, – were called 'Infidels.' Now it is easy to see that so long as people had the idea that the mortality of a town or country was just what it was intended to be by Heaven, they would be apt to make less exertion to save life, lest they should be opposing the intentions of Providence. What do we see today. Strange, but most welcome difference. Our most orthodox papers and books, written by persons the most devout, talk about the large number of deaths annually which might be prevented, and which it is our duty to prevent. Officers of Health can tell us nearly the exact number of deaths that will take place under the present sanitary conditions and with the same habits of the people in the United Kingdom during the next twelve months. People still believe in Providence, but it is a more reliable one, more rational; one that can be depended upon – not fickle and variable, one thing to-day and another tomorrow, snatching a child here and another there without any apparent reason or cause. Providence now is seen to have fixed methods; so that by people studying its arrangements and conforming thereto, health, life, and happiness can be enjoyed. Society is now influenced more by facts of art and science than dreams, random luck, tales of planet rulers, fortune tellers by palmistry, or a capricious Providence. Local Boards insist upon proper ventilation, drainage, and the avoidance of other disease breeding nuisances. The law now steps in and prevents people selling what they like, building such dwellings as they like, making the interest of the many of more importance than the whim or self-interest of the few. Property has now its duties as well as its rights. And after all, sanitary science is in its infancy, scores of thousands of lives being sacrificed each year. Notwithstanding all the progress made during the last sixty years. Which is incalculable, our children's grand-children will probably wonder at our ignorance, with all our boasting. One thing is certain – that progress during the next fifty years will be greater than during the last hundred, having so many more facilities now than before to effect it.

Joseph Lawson, *Letters to the young on progress in Pudsey during the last sixty years* (Stanningley: J.W. Lawson, 1887), 48–54.

A False Boggart on the Edges of Cheshire

A sweet little account has just reached me from a friend in whose bona-fides I have every reason to place implicit confidence, of the exploits of a certain gentleman who has lately graced the peaceful villages of Burton and Lavister with his presence. Here is a career that was certainly a distinguished and peculiar one, so 'distinguished' that he is said to have been the talk of the neighbourhood for the past three weeks, and he has gained a wide reputation. The career he mapped out for himself, and in which he tried to shine, bordered on the supernatural. He tried to make the people of that intensely rural district believe that he belonged to another world. To aid him in this project he arrayed himself in a white sheet, and thus equipped he would wander about the lanes and by-ways of the locality after dark, and the good people whom he met were considerably scared by his strange appearance. Passers by were unable to extract even an intelligible word from the ghostly visitor to allay their fears, and the only sound he muttered was wierd [*sic*] and unearthly groan. Consequently all who saw him found themselves in a state of high nervous excitement at the thought of having been in the presence of a ghost, boggart, boogy, bogey, goblin, or whatever they called it, and the ghostly visitant (he was far too good for this world, after causing so much consternation here) kindly kept the game alive and continued his orgies for about three weeks. The simple minded villagers who had seen him declared with a shudder that 'They would na' for anything see him again.' Now, sir, you don't meet a ghost every day, and when you *do* meet one it opens up an extraordinary field for investigation. So thought the good people of Barton and Lavister. They accordingly determined to investigate the matter. (I am free to confess, with some amount of diffidence at first). And the next time the 'ghost' shewed himself his brilliant career came to a sudden end. No sooner had the white-robed one put in an appearance than he was 'caught' – not by a donkey cart this time, Mr Editor, but by a dog, who seized him in the rear. Great Jove! how he howled! He winced like a galled jade. Now there is peace once once [*sic*] at Burton and Lavister. (Oh, Hamlet, Hamlet, friend of my youth, how could'st thou?).

'Rambler', 'Out and About Chester', *The Cheshire Observer* (5 Feb 1887), 2.

Three in a Bed

Incredulous people may and will smile, Mr. Editor, when I tell you that in some parts of the lovely county of Cheshire there is a lingering suspicion and belief in goblins, or bogies, or boggarts. But it is a fact, sir. And some districts if there is one word more particularly hateful to the villagers than another it is the word 'boggart.' A little time ago an aged couple, living in an intensely rural locality, were favoured with a visit from the boggart. They had a neighbour whom they treated as a personal friend. The aged couple used to execute commissions for this neighbour, who in course of time removed to another residence. Here she was taken ill, and the kind-hearted couple went to see her. At this visit she is said to have requested them to transact some private business for her. This business they faithfully performed, and shortly afterwards the woman departed this life. Now for the boggart story, sir. It has been related unto me that one night the aged couple had retired to rest when they were suddenly aroused. 'There's a boggart or bogey in the room,' exclaimed the old man, in a state of high nervous excitement. 'Aa feel it creepin' over th' foot o' bed. She wur a queer owd ooman, wi' her skin a' dried oop!' His wife also appeared to be sensible of the proximity of the boggart, and the terror of the old couple was so real that there was no more sleep that night. A night or two afterwards they had another opportunity of a further acquaintance with the boggart, for it again presented itself. The old couple were once more plunged into the same state of terror in consequence. And a few night later the boggart paid a third visit, and sought a closer acquaintance with its flesh-and-blood friends. But this time the 'flesh-and-blood' thought they had had about enough of such visits. They determined therefore to ask for an explanation, and demand to know its business. 'In the name of all that is Holy, what dost thou require?' said the old man, 'Is there anything that has been left undone?' (This he said thinking that these nocturnal visits must have some reference to their deceased neighbour.) There was, however, no response, and the old gentleman in telling Rambler about it and asking his opinion seemed firmly to believe that by making this 'stand' against the boggart, or whatever it was, he had broken the spell, for the mysterious visits were not repeated. But in the village the people firmly believe that the bogey, or boggart, or troll, or goblin, or whatever it was, was real, and are quite ready to quote numberless instances reaching far away down the vista of time of others who have been favoured by similar visits. And from their earnestness in acquainting Rambler of the fact they evidently think that the subject is uncommonly fascinating and well worth investigating.

Rambler, 'Out and About Chester', *The Cheshire Observer* (4 June 1887), 2.

The Dunkenhalgh Boggart

Many people who are moderately acquainted with the legends and traditions of Ribblesdale, and with the folk-lore of this country-side of Lancashire, may have heard of the 'Dunkenhalgh Boggart.' I well remember hearing it spoken of when I quite a youngster as 'The Dunklaw Ghaist' and sometimes as 'The Woman that sits on the Bridge in a winding-sheet every Christmas eve.' Now I cannot say that I ever heard anyone say that had seen this boggart or 'ghaist', but I can vouch for the fact of having heard one or two say that their grandmothers had seen it with their own eyes, and that I considered quite sufficient to satisfy any reasonable curiosity. I will remember with what superstitious dread I passed over that ghost-haunted bridge when I had occasion to go that way from Church Kirk to the Holt Mill in Rishton. Even in broad daylight I instinctively cast furtive and fearful glances about me when passing the scene supposed to be visited at this season of the year by this unlaid and restless 'ghaist'; and I could not have ventured to cross that old stone bridge which spans the deep ravine through which the river Hyndburn rushes, for love or money, after dark, and hardly for deal life, at 'the witching hour of night,' when all the orthodox ghosts are permitted to 'walk'. Often have I improvised blood-curdling stories of unearthly apparitions to a huddling and shuddering group of schoolfellows, round the hearth where the Yule-log was fitfully blazing and flickering, making eerie shadows move in the glamorous and illusive light. Often has a lurid and tragic imagination given me the 'uncanny creeps' as well as put a cold spell upon my horrified audience. It is only recently, comparatively speaking, that I have learnt the history and mystery of 'The Dunklaw Boggart.' Being somewhat interested in the legends of the district, I have succeeded, by diligently cultivating the acquaintance of one or two types of 'the oldest inhabitant' of Rishton and Church Kirk, in gathering something like an authentic account of who and what this boggart was, and still is, although it, or she, has not been seen very frequently of late years. Dunkernhalgh, or Dunklaw, as locally pronounced, was, in our great-grandsires says, a grand estate. The park was of vast extent, and herds of deer bounded over its undulating slopes and copses. The old mansion, which was the seat of the lordly Petres, of ancient pedigree, was a Gothic pile of magnificent proportions, and it stood nearly on the same site as the present more modern one. At that period there was a young French lady, known to the country people as Lucette, living at the Hall as a *governante* of some of the young scions of the lineage. Lucette was remarkably handsome and lovely withal. That she was a Catholic goes without saying, but she was a pious and devoted one, and she led the singing in the Matins and vespers in the family chapel pertaining to the mansion. But a fine dashing sprig of nobility, related to the family, and who was a military officer of high rank besides, came to spend the Christmas at Dunklaw. The gay cavalier soon fell in ardent love with the sweet Lucette, and quickly found a way to woo her. Although she at first repelled him, he, nothing daunted, pressed his suit all the more fervently, and ultimately, by means of those seductive arts so well understood by gallants of his cloth, he succeeded in securing his affections. Her unsuspecting heart yielded to his blandishments. Let it be sufficient to know that she fell a victim to the wicked wiles of this noble villain who never intended to win her for a wife. Alas! poor Lucette!...

The arch-deceiver rode away when he had accomplished the ruin of the fair governante to who he promised to write and soon return – promises as false as the lips that uttered them. Poor Lucette realized her condition all too soon, and she knew that Dunklaw Hall was no place for her. Home to France! Ah! She could die, but never go there. She confessed her sin and sorrow to the chaplain, and none but he and herself knew her sad secret. Often did she wander about in the gloaming through the glades, where her recreant lover had led her. Often by the river side, where the rows of beeches are growing still, though the Hyndburn is no longer the pellucid stream it was in those days of yore. In the bark of one of those might trees her seducer had cut a monogram of his initials, entwined with her own in the centre of a heart; and it is said the device may be traced upon the tree to this day. All I can say is that scores of initials are to be found cut upon those historic trees, and poor Lucette's may be amongst the number. However, to that particular tree, as the story goes, she was wont to repair in the twilight and sing to herself a mournful melody. Her reason fled at last, and her poor heart broke, and one dark, stormy night, she wandered up to the bridge under which the swollen river was rushing in a roaring torrent. The pangs of maternity came upon her, and in a delirium of wild frenzy she threw herself over the parapet into the tumultuous waters below. Her body was never found, being probably carried away to the sea. Such was the fate of poor Lucette, whose ghost has haunted the scene of her unfortunate love for some generations past, according to local tradition. But it is always at Christmastide when she walks the part, that being the season when she met the spoiler of her innocence and peace. I have heard old Aunt Ailse at Tewit Nook relate the pathetic story of the wronged Lucette while tears have trickled down her cheeks; and Uncle Silas says it is a veritable fact that the heart which is cut in the tree bleeds real red blood every Christmas Eve, and that the chapel bell of the old hall tolls at the same time, though chapel and bell are both in the limbo of the past. Old Robin o' Giles, of Harwood Cliff, is also a rare living repository of local legendary lore, and I have his veracious version of the story, with several additional incidents. He says Lucette's child was born and had a separate existence before she threw herself into the torrent with it. The water left the child – which, by the way, was a boy – upon the doorstep of the old mill-house, which stood where Holt Mill stands now. He was rescued by the old miller himself, and brought up by his wife as one of her own, and he made his way in the world. It was noticed when he stripped that he had the shape of a blood-red heart upon his breast – a natal mark, which had foster-mother had kept a secret. Some years ago, when the old bridge was being repaired, a shawl-pin, with a head formed of a cornelian in the shape of a heart, was found in the interstices of one of the buttresses – a fact which is supposed to verify the suicide of the hapless lady. Old Robin's version possesses the merit of poetic justice; it contains a fact of retribution. The noble libertine who brought Lucette to her tragic fate was shot through the heart in a duel with his victim's brother, who, though the inscrutable medium of a vision, or physical revelation, had received intelligence of the affair and come over from France to avenge her memory. Such is the brief history of Dunklaw Boggart or 'Ghaist' as the old gossips used to call the alleged spirit of Lucette which haunted that locality in the ante-railway days of our fathers' fathers. I once inquired of old Robin o' Giles' if he had ever seen the boggart, or if he knew anybody who had. 'Nay', said he, 'aw connot say 'at aw've fairly sin id, but aw've thowt aw hed, an' aw've just bin as weel freeten'd as iv aw'd sin id ever sooa.' 'How came that about, Robin?' 'Well, aw'll tell tha. Id wer th' neet as eawr Dick were born, and thad'll be forty-five yer sin this Kesmas. My owd woman wer a bit younger then no hoo is neaw tha knows, an' ho wer hevin' childer middlin' fast. Hoo started o being confined ov eawr Dick lat on ith Kesmas eve, an' awd to beawnse eatw o' bet in a hurry an' slip into my duds an' off as hard as aw could lik to th' Alleytroydes for Doctor Bradley. We were livin' at Tottleworth at thad time, sooa th' gainest way for me to goos wer by th' Howt Mill an' Dunkley Park an' Church Kirk. To tell t' Truth awd as life o' gooan another road, but tha sees awd th' grinnelstooan o' my back as they say, when one's runnin' an arrand o' thad sort. Well aw peyl'd on beawt tryin' to think mich abeawt th' boggart whal aw geet to th' owd stooan brig an' theer aw coom to a full stop aw'll assure ta. Aw never geet sich a shock o freetning afoor nor never sin, an' aw hooap aw never shall. Aw wer stricken as stiff as a statue! Aw see'd whod aw felt sure wer th'ghaist for sartin!' 'And really what was it Robin?' 'Id wer summat sat deawn upon th' brig don't in a white sheet, summat like a shreawd. In a bit aw yerd a voice say "Come on, mon!" Id duddent seawnd mich like th' voice of a female sperit aw thowt, but aw duddent speyk back, for aw couldn't just thad minute. In a bit id co'd eawt agean, "Coem on, on. What the dule art stannin theer for?" "By gum," Aw sed to misel, "aw know thad voice", an aw stutter'd eawt, "Is thad Alick o' Reead?" "Aye, sure id it," he said, "What art afeard on?" "Awm feard o' nowt neaw, so long as it's nobbut thee," aw sed. He axt ma where aw wer gooin at that time o' th neet, an aw towd him. He'd yerd somebody coming on behint him, an he set hissel deawn whal aw goot up to him, but id duddent happen to strike him as th' white blanket he had lappe'd reawn him wer likely to freeten a body into fits. Tha mun understand Alick wer a block-printer at th' Oakenshaw, an he lived at Church Kirk. He'd been werkin lat that neet to finish his job affoar Kesmas day. He wer tekin th' new blanket whoam for th' wife to bind. Block printers use to cover their printin' tables wi't blankets when they printed patterns on calico. He thowt he must as well throw id o'er his showders to keep him warm. A varra sensible thing to do, for id were a cowd neet, though my job wer rather a warm un. Heawever th' doctor landed just i' th' nick o' time, an' eawr Dick coom into th' world just i' time for his Kesmas pot.'

Aker-Whitt, 'The Dunkenhalgh Boggart', *Blackburn Standard* (21 Dec 1889), 3.

Ab' O' Ned's 'Witchins'

'I' my young days,' said old Ab o' Ned's, knocking the ashes out of his long clay pipe, 'everybody i' eawr country side believt i' boggarts an' witches, an' uncanny things o' that sooart.' I pricked my ears at this, for I was always delighted if I could get Ab' o' Ned's – properly Abraham Stansfield – his father had been called Edward – talking about his 'young days,' and as the rain still poured down – I had taken shelter at the little farmhouse which he occupied – I was all the more pleased when a chance remark of mine brought forth the above observation. 'Did you believe in them?' I asked, determined to draw him out. 'Well, aw reckon aw did,' he said. 'Aw don't know at aw'd moor wit nor other folk. But aw think vary likely it were clemmin' an' darkness 'at used to mak' folk see boggarts sometimes, for there were no gas in those days, an' workin' folk were ill plagued then – they known nought neaw! – to get summat to ate, an' a two-three clooas to their backs. An' we didn't oft see sich a thing as a newspaper – they were sixpence an' eightpence a-piece! – an' we'd no eddication to tell us th' reason o' things, an' so when things went wrang wi' us, it were vary yeasy an' natural like to lay it on a witch.'

Sarah Selina Hamer, 'Ab' O' Ned's "Witchins"', *The Manchester Weekly Times*, 12 Dec 1890, 3.

Th' Gatley Shouter

I've another bit o' news as has happened since last Wakes time to tell you; dun you know they'n laid th' Gatley shouter at last, they an for sure. Th' Gatley shouter, you know, was a spectre or boggut that shouted at folk from among the tombs in Northen churchyard, and along th' Carr Lane to Gatley. Mony folk and childer specially were plaguey feart on him, so much so that they daresner go that way after dark, and this new parson at Northen has played the hangment with the ghoses; he's laid em all over th' countryside, but he couldner lay th' Gatley shouter. However, it's gotten done at last, and I'll tell thee how. There was once a man of the name of Barrow at Cross Acre, an he were very fond o' money, a regular ould skinflint; he'd have fleyed two fleas for one hide, an he griped an screwed ony road to get hold of ony money, an he stuck to all as he could get. Well, at last he deed, an ould Nick soon got him, an he warmt him, he did rarely, for he mit be heard moaning, 'Milk short o' measure, butter short o' weight, oh, dear, oh, dear;' then he'd cry out as old Scrat fettled him up a bit. Well, he couldner rest in his grave in Northen churchyard, but mit be heard moaning and crying all th' way to Gatley and back, and folk were plaguey feart; so th' parson got everyone as could read with their bibles, and them as couldn't read but knew their prayers were to keep on praying as hard as ever they could pray, an one neet at full moon they spread emselves aw over th' countryside from Northen to Gatley, and they kept drawing nigher in a circle, so as th' shouter couldn't pass them, an at last they'd gotten him in a corner of th' churchyard by the lane side and th' rectory garden, where there's a yew tree, an there they pinned him in; an th' parson whips out a bit of chalk and draws a holy circle round th' place, and all th' folk join hands and read their bibles out loud as hard as they can read, an t'others gabble desperately at their prayers, an th' parson sings an shouts an hops about an bangs th' book, an th' poor devil moans and groans, an jabbers an chunners, but they fair bet him, an smothert him wi prayer, an th' devil was druv out o' him, an now he let's him abide, an th' Gatley shouter's fairly laid.

Fletcher Moss, *Didisburye in the '45* (Manchester: Cornish 1891), 33–34.

Boggart Scares Horse?

Between one and two o'clock on Sunday afternoon, John Sawyer, coachman of Ellel Grange, was proceeding from there to Lancaster in a light dogcart to fetch Dr. Hall to the Grange, and was passing a gipsy encampment near the Boggart House, when the horse shied and the trap ran against a telegraph pole. The vehicle was overturned and smashed and Sawyer was thrown out and seriously hurt in the back. A messenger was sent from Scotforth to fetch Dr. Hall, and the coachman was removed to the Grange. From inquiries made on Tuesday we learn that Sawyers [*sic*] is progressing very favourably.

'Serious Accident to a Coachman', *Lancaster Gazette* (3 Jun 1891), 2.

Tramps as Boggarts

Talking of Noton's Barn, near Bakewell, the superstitious hold the idea that there is a 'boggart' there – a boggart is a ghost. I like investigating ghosts. Subsequently to being informed of this ghost story I decided if I heard anything at night as I was passing, to investigate matters. I did so the other night. I heard a slight noise, but my blood did not run cold. I climbed over the wall and entered the barn, and there were a couple of tramps. 'We're doing no harm, sir,' said one, thinking I was Sergeant Oliver, and, as it was raining hard, after sheltering myself, I left the 'ghosts' alone in their glory. So ye fearful, take heart.

'Gleanings in the Peak', *Derbyshire Times and Chesterfield Herald* (12 Nov 1892), 8.

Chips of Lancashire Boggarts

Some Typical Examples of Lancashire Boggarts. It is pretty generally known that the greater part of the county palatine of Lancashire – particularly the north-east and east portions of what is often termed the 'witches' county' – which in olden times comprised the southern portion of the ancient kingdom of Northumbria, is peculiarly rich in what has been aptly termed 'boggart lore' – the Lancashire boggart so called, being a near relative of the northern English and Scottish bogle. And in a county which was supposed to be so prolific of witches in the olden time as Lancashire – as witness the remarkable trials of the Pendle Forest Witches in the sixteenth century, already recorded in the columns of the Express – it is but natural to suppose that, at a period when general ignorance was so dense, that boggarts, fairies, and other 'unchancy' sprites were as 'numerous as the leaves of Vallumbrosa,' and especially in such wild and secluded parts of the county as Pendle Forest, the Forest of Rossendale, Cliviger, and the other 'forests' in the district, all, in ancient times, comprised within the wide-extended boundaries of the great forest of Blackburnshire. In this part of the country, especially within the boundaries of the forests of Pendle and Rossendale, despite the advances of King Cotton, and the influx of population and more enlightenment, many ancient customs and superstitions have not yet entirely fallen into desuetude. The boggart is still a quotable institution, though it may not be generally believed in. In some comparatively secluded districts in the North – East [*sic*] and eastern parts of the county, amidst the higher moorlands, where the aborigines, the 'natives' still, more or less, cling to the manners and customs of their forefathers, many yet not dimly believe in these supernatural visitants. In proof of this it may be mentioned that the yet popular name for the common fern is 'boggart meat,' or 'meyt' in the vernacular folk-speech. It will thus be seen – the boasted civilization and enlightenment of the rapidly ebbing nineteenth century not withstanding – that a lingering belief, in Lancashire at least, yet more or less prevails; though witches and fairies, except in very rare instances, have long since 'paled their ineffectual fires,' before the so-called march of intellect. The Supposed Virtues of Fern Seed – Vernacularly 'Boggart Meyt'. The supposed virtues of fern seed, gathered in lonely spots, with gruesome incantations, on St. John's Even, was supposed to render the possessor, of either sex, invisible at will and was also believed to act as a potent love charm. On the Cliviger border a comical story is yet told of how a venturesome swain was almost frightened out of his wits by some companions who waylaid him in a lonely place on the mystic eve, and where he had gone to gather fern seed for amatory purposes, and under the usual conditions of mystery and incantation. The chief hoaxer was a young butcher, who encased himself in a bullock's hide and horns; busily engaged in working the 'charm' – or rather the 'oracle' – he was suddenly confronted with a frightful figure – horns and tail complete. Though the frightened fellow at once 'made tracks,' he nearly died from fright. This affair occurred many years ago, but the principal hoaxer, who was nearly the cause of the death of the hoaxed one, died within the past ten years, and at a great age, having been for nearly half a century an upland farmer on the Cliviger border. And this tricksy knight of the cleaver was, in his young days, himself the victim of a similar hoax. The gathering of fern seed, of course *solus*, on St John's Eve is quite a venerable superstition. The custom was well-known in Shakespeare's day, and in one of his plays he makes one of his elvish characters say: - 'I have the fern-seed; I walk invisible.' Demons or Boggarts Interfering with the Building of Churches. The traditions attached to the building, or rather the sites, of various churches in Lancashire, as well as in other parts of the country, are certainly curious; and in mostly all cases a supernatural pig is the central figure in the legends – as, for example, Roby's hair-raising 'yarn' of the 'Demon Pigs.' Let us take, for instance, three local cases in point. As the old story goes, the old church of St. Chad's, Rochdale, was originally intended to be built at the bottom of the valley, on the banks of the Roach, near the site on which stands the present Town Hall. The builders commenced operations in the valley, but every morning it was found that what progress was made by the workmen during the day had been mysteriously over-thrown during the night, and that the stones and other building materials had been conveyed to the top of the hill where the church now stand. On a watch being set to ascertain how the building material had been removed each night, it was found, pace the legend that a monstrous pig – supernatural of course – had demolished the partially erected walls, and had removed the stones to the top of the hill where the church was finally built, and where the same or its successor, now stands. In olden times, when seeming pigs set up as amateur architects, their practical hints were seldom neglected. At Winwick, in South Lanarkshire, there is a similar story, in which a pig objected to the site fixed upon for the church. And in this case the 'voice' of the spectral pig, while removing the stones to another site, is supposed to have been the origin of the name of 'Winwick.' At Newchurch-in-Rossendale, as the tradition runs, another mysterious piggy, and in a similar way, indicated the spot where St. Nicholas's Church was built some centuries ago, in the reign of Henry the Seventh, the present writer thinks. The church was actually commenced at Mitchelfield Nook, but every night, after the workmen has ceased their labours, a mysterious pig, it was found, demolished the partially built-up walls, and removed the material to where St. Nicholas's Church now stands. And in this case also the 'protesting' and critical member of the porcine family had its way. It may be here observed that, before St. Nicholas's Church, at Newchurch in Rossendale was built, the nearest church available for the few and scattered foresters of Rossendale, who peopled the various 'booths' of the Forest, was Clitheroe Parish Church, more than a dozen miles away. On the occasions of funerals, baptisms, and marriages, or when the foresters wished to attend divine service at the nearest church, Clitheroe had to be visited, and by hilly and bad roads both in summer and winter. The Rossendale foresters, in petitioning the King that a church should be erected in their own boundaries, pleaded their difficulties in being compelled to go as far as Clitheroe when they required to attend church. Local Version of the German Wild Hunts-Man Superstition. – 'Gabriel's Rachets.' The Wild Huntsman, or Spectre Huntsman superstition, which occupies so conspicuous a place in the folk-lore of Germany, is by no means peculiar to the latter country; and Cliviger, and the adjacent districts have their own version of this weird figment, handed down to us, no doubt, by our earliest German ancestors. On the authority of the late Mr. Wilkinson, of Burnley, we are told that on the mystic night of Halloween (All Souls' Night) the Spectral Huntsman, under the local name of 'Gabriel's Ratchets' (ratchet being the old English term for a hound), appears with his fierce spectral dogs, and, on the mystic night, hunts 'with loud hollow and horn,' a milk white doe round the Eagle's Crag, in the picturesque Gorge of Cliviger – a place for ages intimately associated with local superstitions. 'Gabriel's Ratchets' are supposed to be heard yelping when flying through the air, and especially during the dark nights of autumn and winter, and are supposed to predict death or misfortune to all who are unlucky enough to hear the mouthings of the imaginary hounds. But this once popular superstition is by no means peculiar to the Cliviger Valley and the surrounding districts. The presumed Spectral Hounds, like the 'Gabriel's Rachets' of Cliviger and district are believed to be heard, and always nocturnally, in many parts of the country, both far inland and on the sea coasts. The Cornish fishermen when plying their calling, often hear the dreaded hounds, which the Cornish folk term the 'Seven Whistlers,' and the superstitious fishermen are always certain that there unwelcome sounds surely betoken ill-luck to them, if not disaster. But naturalists and other seasoned observers have long made it known to us that the dread yelpings, heard high in the air at nights, are simply the notes of passing birds during the regular spring and autumn migrations of our winged wanderers – whether the notes are known as in Cliviger, as 'Gabriel's Rachets,' the 'Seven Whistlers,' as on the Cornish sea coasts, or by other names. Or latter day inconoclasts have long knocked, and tolerably satisfactorily, this old superstitious figment on the head.

Henry Kerr, 'Typical 'Chips' of Lancashire Boggart Lore: No. 1' *Burnley Express* (23 Dec 1893), 3.

A Chimney Boggart

Mr Felden, senior, the farmer occupant of Law Clough – who was also a hand-loom cotton weaver, like many others of his class in the days when the present rapidly ebbing century was younger by nearly eighty years – hearing the stifled cries of his daughter in the kitchen below at once sprang out of bed and boldly confronted the burglars, who were then coming up the stairs. 'Owd Jim' hastily seized on one of his weaving implements – his 'drying iron' and at once offered battle to the masked burglars, who loudly threatened to take the lives of all in the house if any resistance were offered. Stout 'Owd Jim' undeterred by the sanguinary threats of the more free than welcome visitants, laid about him with his 'drying iron' with a will, and inflicted sundry ugly wounds on Heyworth and his eldest son, Roger, the youngest son, George, remaining downstairs, to keep watch over the terrified young woman, who fully expected that the whole family would be murdered. The old man was gallantly struggling with his assailants at the head of the stairs, when his handy weapon broke. Thereupon the father and eldest son pounced on him, overpowered him, and bound him securely to the bedstead with a rope. 'Owd Jim's' son, young Fielden, while his father was defending his hearth and home so stoutly, managed to escape by smarming up inside the bedroom chimney, and descending by the low roof ran off to the nearest neighbours. He was, however, in such a sable condition, after his hurried exit by the chimney, that the alarmed neighbours were at first inclined to believe that their frightened and incoherent midnight visitor was either a burglar, a boggart, or something else equally 'uncanny' or dangerous.

Henry Kerr, 'Sheepstealers, Highwaymen and Burglars in Cliviger early in the present century', *Burnley Express* (10 Feb 1894), 2.

The Starling Bridge Boggart

A desire to prove whether this boggart, which is reputed to have been seen of late in the romantic neighbourhood between Hurst Green and Ribchester, has any visible or real existence led two young weavers, of Ribchester, named

John and Richard Walton, into trouble the other night. There had been festivities in the prettily-situated village adjoining the well-known Roman Catholic College, and the two young men returning home at a late hour, along with one or two others, became decidedly lively, John intimating his fixed intention to cross the fields to fight and conquer the Starling Bridge boggart. He was, however, prevented from carrying into effect his daring (?) proposal, a limb of the law interposing owing to John disturbing the country for half a mile around. Not only was the Ribchester bravado subjected to this indignity, but he was called upon to pay 5 s. and costs on a charge of being drunk and disorderly, while George, who seems to have restricted the use of his vocal powers to admonitions of his brother to forego his rashly-conceived enterprise, was allowed to go free.

'The Starling Bridge Boggart', *Blackburn Standard* (2 Jun 1894), 3.

Back O' Th' Hill Boggart

This shadow, 'tis said, was an old man's sprite,
Who haunted by day and who haunted by night,
When the night was a 'fury,' or peacefully still,
This much bothered house, at the 'Back of the hill,'
Not alone did he compass with dread Mr. Clark,
By twitching the bed-clothes and leaving him stark,
(An action at once either cruel or queer,
Depends which fair season was nursed by the year).
But, shade of his brethren! Who quite unicorn,
Impale 'Opposition' with tortures sharp horn –
Unfailing to purpose, Spook tortured Clark so,
He sent in his notice, and out he did go!
Then somebody else (name quiet) undaunted,
Lived there by the sprite to be flouted and haunted,
He waited, not he, the retreat of the light,
To rattle the tables and chairs in the night,
My earnest informant, read doubt in my face,
Looked back upon time for his help in the case –
Then shut down her eyelids and shook well her head,
And more to herself, than to we folks, she said –
'I sat in that kitchen – and seeing's past doubt –
And truly I saw the things dancing about,'
Accompanied at times too by noises and groans,
Well heard, she assured me, half way to Fox Stones,

Of course, to Americanise on the spot,
They quickly determined to 'get' – and they got.
At last, alterations effecting a change,
In the chimney, I think near the old kitchen range,
Discovered by workmen, stored safe in a hole,
Was the cause of the unquiet to body and soul;
Some money by man most intricately hidden!
A soul to eternity hurriedly hidden!
Groans, rattles and shouts! (with a poke now and then).
A dumb ghost appeals for th' assistance of men!
The heir got the money, the ghost left the house,
And so 'Back o' th' Hill' is as quiet as a mouse;
But record's awake. In the lore haunted hutch,
He takes up a corner not far from 'Owd Thrutch!
A. McCandlish, Stones, Cornholme.

A. McCandlish, 'Back O' Th' Hill Boggart', *Burnley Express* (4 May 1895), 2.

Boggart Meets Magician

[p. 172] Prosaic as the district may generally appear, it is nevertheless far from lacking what is termed folk-lore. There is evidence to show that 'old women's' tales found credence in the bye-gone generations, and that bogies and goblins were supposed to haunt the woods, the churchyards, and other places usually frequented by that class of beings. Superstitions held sway and it was considered unlucky to do certain things or to omit doing others. Charms were often used in cases of sickness or to ensure the gaining of some coveted object. Fairies were believed in and fortune telling flourished.... [p. 175] The concluding story is located nearer home. In the middle of the last century there lived at Hyde a celebrated Dr. Wylde (an ancestor of the Thornelys), who bore a reputation for astrology. About 1730 a great sensation was occasioned by the report that there was a boggart in Gower Hey Wood, which made awful sounds at night. The inhabitants went in a body to ask the learned doctor to lay the spirit, and this he gladly consented to do. Noticing the direction of the sound he went in broad daylight to the spot which no one else dared approach, and there found that two branches of a tree, rubbing together with the motion of the wind, gave forth the doleful sound that had scared people from the wood. Telling no one of his discovery he quickly sawed one branch off, and then gravely announced that he had laid the spirit. Needless to say, after this, that his reputation for magic was unequalled in the neighbourhood, and for years his powers were firmly believed in.

Thomas Middleton, *Annals of Hyde and district: containing historical reminiscences of Denton, Haughton, Dukinfield, Mottram, Longdendale, Bredbury, Marple, and the neighbouring townships* (Manchester: Cartwright and Rattray 1899).

Chased Out of a House

Boggart House is situated a little to the north of Boars Den. Every Lancashire man knows what a 'boggart' is. [p. 191] I have from time to time noted down some traditions, superstitions, and folk-lore as related to me by the inhabitants of the district; these I will condense as much as possible. The traditions and superstitions which have gathered round Boars Den seem to be very similar to those associated generally with tumuli in other parts of the kingdom, the prevailing idea being that the neighbourhood is infested with spirits, boggarts, and fairies. There is a tradition that there was a battle fought at Bury Hey Wood, and another at Courage Low, and that some forty years ago, when the old pasture fields to the north of Boars Den were ploughed up, a number of badges or soldiers' buttons, of metal, were found. These are said to have been relics of a battle fought here with the Scotch. In a solitary cottage near Boars Den there lives an old man of 85, whose father lived in the same cottage all his life, and died at the age of 90. This old man tells me that in his early days he was employed as a labourer at Bury Hey Wood, in levelling the ground and planting cover for game. During the disturbance of the ground, what he called 'some implements of war' were found. He reports that these relics were taken away by Mr. Scarisbrick, of Wrightington, on whose property they were found, and who placed great value on them. My informant was under the impression that they were taken to London. A road called Robin Hood Lane runs past Boars Den. Between a certain gate and Dangerous Corner, the old man assured me [p. 192], this road is haunted by a boggart. His brother had seen it many times, and it 'went clankin' round th' field in chains'. Some two years ago, during the sickness of one of the inmates of Boggart House, the visitations of the house ghost became so frequent and terrifying, that the inhabitants finally fled in terror, and the house was empty at the time of my visit. An old labourer at Boars Den Farm, after relating some blood-curdling details of these recent ghostly visitations to Boggart House, also told me that 'sperrits' were frequently seen at Hill House Fold, an adjacent farm on the hill nearby.

William Frederick Price, 'Notes on Some of the Places, Traditions, and Folk-Lore of the Douglas Valley', *Transactions of the Historic Society of Lancashire and Cheshire* 51 (1899), 181–220 at 190–192.

Off at Boggart

An amusing incident happened one night in Manchester road. A motor car was being run to the Bull and Butcher, and back. Several men were going up by Roberts Row, when the car, on its way down, was just coming in sight at full speed. One of the men had never seen a motor car before, and he was much excited. He shouted out 'Hey up, chaps, there's a carriage off at boggart beawt horse. Get o'er that wall eawt o' th' road,' whereupon he did so, amid much laughter from the other men. (A fact.) M.H. Stotto, 21, Scarlett Street, Burnley.

M.H. Stott, 'Off at Boggart', *Burnley Express* (12 May 1900), 2.

The Dumber Boggert

It was some time ago. The date does not matter
By leaving it out will save endless chatter.
And to mention real names would be foolish, I fear.
For a tale does not lose much with some people round here.

The Hero of the story I intend to explain,
Is a Gardener who lives not a mile from Green Lane;
He would face any work that came in his way, –
Sink a drain, guide a plough, cut a stack, or make hay:
He turned out fine cabbage, and grew champion spuds,
His dahlias and asters were voted fine goods;
For the bloom of his flowers his love would prevail –
He was fond of his wife – Yes 'and fond of his Ale';
And just now and then it happened somehow,
He'd put in full time at the Buck, or the Plough,
Jig by jowl, 'good natured' and free to the core,
He would soon make a hole in his frugal got store.

Well, knowing this, his wife would oft come
And say, 'Tha great lazy yawney, art'ta coming whom';
He'd tell her to fly it, but soon he would hear: –
'A'st not go till that' goes, lets ha' thee 'art here.'
I wont [*sic*] say he was hen-pecked, still she held the rule
And would fetch him, as a child is oft taken to school,
And the neighbours around would repeat now and then,
'Who's giving owd Jimmy bell-tinker again.'

Now Jim's wife was frugal, and worked night and day –
Weeding, and bunching, and washing away;
And the gloss of her linen shone out like the sun, –
Other laundresses wondered the way it was done:
A few spiteful ones were heard to declare
'she's glazed it with handfulls of poor Jimmy's hair.'
Well, to proceed with my story – Jimmy, next day,
Would be found in his garden working away,
And chatting together, himself and his wife,
As if they had never a word in their life.
With hampers and boxes the cart they'd soon fill,
Which Tommy, their grey Nag, would drag to Shudehill.
Then Jim would return and tell of his sale
As he swallowed his baggin or the supper ale.
In their cosey arm chairs, they would gossip till ten,
She'd say 'Ah Jimmy, my lad, thar't a foo ta th' sen';
And for weeks, yes for months, he never would budge
But keep solid and sober as the proverbial judge.
But the weak and the strong oft totter – they say,
And strong ale made Jim totter one market day:
He'd loaded out heavy and had a good sale,
And the extra profits he melted in ale,
And soon his days drawings had decidedly shrunk,
Alas, poor Jim got parallatic drunk.

A boy brought the horse home, about 9 at night,
And the way Jimmy's wife stormed, filled the lad with afright, –
'Whee'r ast left you mon, tha young gawping foo,
Tell ma this minute, or I'll por ta a' two,
Spake aut, that spawn of the gawmlest pups.' –
'Why, he's asleep yon, ith Market on some Naw-Naw-Sisus bups'
'Well, get that horse put up, tha sees its ner ten,' –
'Nay, am going whoam naw, yo mun do it yer sen'.
She beded the horse down, and maledictions she swore,
If they'd acted on Jimmy his life would be o'er;
She gathered pots, pans and rowling pins, at his head to toss
And said 'she'd lee've him and go to their Salls on the Moss.

Ten struck, eleven struck, then the old church chimed twelve;
Her thoughts lost their venom, she was once more herself,
She pray'd that her old man should be sheltered from ill –
The pride of her girlhood, and her heart's treasure still.

Now Jimmy woke up from his Narcissus bed,
He'd an orange box for blanket, and a red-cabbage 'neath his head,
Being drunk when he lay down we cannot be amazed
To know that he woke up bewildered and dazed;
The first thing he missed was his watch and chain
For he'd already missed the last Bowdon train:

'Whats up, wheer am I: I know'd this ud cum -
Six long miles to Ashton – bur am guing whom.'
Shivering and shaking, down Knott Mill he strolled,
On to Old Trafford, like a lame duck he rolled,
Passed the Old Cock at Streford, and exhausted he sank
Just at the style – on the river's bank.

Now that style needs some crossing, as many can tell,
But as Jimmy crossed it, head first, it did just as well,
But the sight of the river made his old blood to freeze,
So he crawled round the bank on his hands and knees.
Foot sore, and knee sore, still muddied and drunk,
Down the dark Dumber Lane he staggered and slunk;
The night being starless, and the road winding queer,
Poor Jim seldom from the edges was clear.
Through staggering and rocking, his mind played him false,
The trees near the Ashlands seemed dancing a waltz,
For Jim at his best feared the uncanny kind,
and Warlocks and Witches found room in his mind:
For ghosts and hop-goblins he had a great dread, –
'I hope Dumber Boggert ul not see ma,' he said

Just then with one wild yell, and transfixed with afright
A most hellish object appeared to his sight, –
Two large eyes of fire, two horns long and thin, –
A face of a devil, and a sardonic grin:
Hair like the clover when weft by the wind,

And a nod that seemed saying 'I am here do you mind
O! How these orbs leered with their fiery cast,
And how Jimmy wished the danger was past:
One yell that echoed from hill side and dale,
He saw two club feet beneath a long tail.
Straight thro' the village he rushed like a shot,
O joy! He observed a light in his cot;
His pace never slackened, he pawsed not to knock
But cleared down the hinges, the door and the lock,
Under the sofa he crawled, and cried in great fear –
'If't Devil axes for ma, say a've left livin' here.'

Once more his good wife unbridled her tongue,
And the way she barged Jim is kind to call strong, –
'Wheer's tha boot, tha gawping foo; – wheer's tha hat, tha dunce,
Tha spon new un, I bought for thee last Casmus Eve twelve months?
Wheer's tha been, tha dirty scamp, till two o'clock 'ith morn?
Tha yure on end like a bed o' mint, and aw tha jacket torn,
Tha trawsers aw dirt and cracked, – to kill tha is no sin, –
Tell me, or I'll curl tha yure with this here rowling pin.'

'Ah lass, dunnot barge, it's a wonder a'm wick,
A've seen't Dumber Boggert, he's akin to owd Nick:
E'en like fiere there, lung horns and lung yure, –
Lung tail, and club feet, aw seed um, so aum sure,
Chased me up't Dumber: gradely brimstone stench,
Aw'm going to be a good mon naw, aw am for sure owd wench.[']

The wife was sorely bothered at poor old Jimmy's plight
And the plucky woman said she'd trace what caused the old man's fright:
She knocked up her next door neighbour and two lamps did obtain
And made a close inspection down the Dumber Lane, –
The first thing they came across was Jimmy's missing shoe,
A little further and his hat also came in view,
And then they saw the flaming eyes, the club feet and the hair,
For Jimmy's Boggart was nothing but – the Rector's old Brown Mare.

P. Sweeney, *The Dumber Boggart or the Misadventures of an Ashton Gardener*, Church Lane, Ashton-on-Mersey, Printed and published by D. Alexe, Merrin, Sale and Manchester

Lines on the Green Lane Boggert

If we know a man, whose head is white with age and hoary,
How we love to hear him tell a good old timeworn story,
Of dark and wild and weird romance,
Which moved the heart and makes it dance.

Some strange adventure which he saw or knew when quite a lad,
And as he tells the story, it makes his heart feel sad;
But now the storys finished, then comes what pleases most,
He finishes the evening with the story of a Ghost.

He tells of a flying Phantom, which flys from east to west,
Of lanes and haunted houses, and woods among the rest,
And speaks of white-robed figures, which appear in the dark,
But mostly ends the story, by saying 'twas done for a lark.

But the Ghost of which I wish to speak, it comes not for a lark,
But mostly when the Phantom comes, it is evening after dark.
It comes, and will not be delayed, by either door or lock,
And the time when it appears, they say, is night at 12 o'clock.

I do not wish to argue now, 'twould only waste my time,
But I'll try to tell my story in plain and simple rhyme:
Well, the Boggert that is causing the folks so much alarm,
Has taken up its residence at a place called Green Lane Farm.

It's half-a-mile from Woolpack, perhaps a little more,
Perchance a little further away from Helmshore;
However, distance matters not in what I'm going to tell,
Suffice it for present, it's a place you all know well.

They say it comes in various forms, you may think my words are wild,
And yet they say it sometimes comes in the form of a beautiful child,
With bright blue eyes and curly hair, and rosy cheeks as well,
But from whence it comes and whither it goes, my friends I cannot tell.

There's the form of a dog in which it is seen, and the form of a woman's another.

She comes and she looks with searching eyes, let's hope it is the young girl's mother,
Searching for her long lost child – If so, let's hope she'll find,
To possess her child so beautiful, will ease her motherly mind.

They say it assumes the form of a man, it sounds very strange, yes rather,
We can but hope, as we hope'd before, that now it's the young child's father,
They say it comes in at the door, like children's skip and hop,
Straight through the house and then upstairs, and out at the chimney's top.

Besides being seen, it's to be heard to sound like rustling silk,
And one has asked the question, does the Boggert ere give milk,
To tell his name, I dare not, it's not my privilege,
But the man that ask'd the question, he lives at Ewood Bridge.

It's age you want to know, well that I cannot tell,
But some folks say, for ages past, it at Green Lane Farm did dwell.
One day the farmer thought he'd try to make this Phantom shift
And not being strong enough himself, he thought he'd get a lift.

I don't know the name of the man who came, whether Jack or Bob,
But sufficient for the present, he undertook the job,
They say he talks with spirits and they think him one of their best,
And he gives it in his verdict, that a spirit cannot rest.

He tells the farmer and his wife, that what he says he'll prove
So without expense he'll undertake to make the spirit move,
He very likely tried himself to move it without bother,
However, he couldn't manage it, so he had to ask another.

So now these spiritualists tried their hands,
To see if they could move it from its ancient stand,
And some folks say, though to me it is odd
They got it away as far as clod [*sic*, corr. Clod].

But from its ancient haunt, this spirit would not sever,
For soon it landed back and became as busy as ever,
And these spiritualistic men ever since that day,
From the place called Green Lane Farm, they mind to keep away.

One night some friends, just after dark,
With boggert, thought they'd have a lark,
And the farmer joining in the fun,
He loaded his double-barrelled gun.

And they agreed if it came to a certain spot,
That one of the party should have a shot,
So they sat down and waited till the time it should come,
They were determined to see it, before they went home.

They had not waited long, when it came with a roar,
So they jumped on their feet, and made for the door,
With the hair on their heads, it was standing like wire
And the gun in their hands, were determined to fire.

But it all came to nought for no ghost could they see,
And the one with the gun, how simple looked he,
And there hasn't been one of them, e'er heard to boast,
Or tell what he thought about shooting the ghost.

Now it is pretty well known in all nature's laws,
That there's ne'er an effect, without there's a cause,
And as this effect is plain for to see,
The thing that has made it must somewhere be.

So two or three chaps, o'er to Green Lane went,
To discover this cause, where their intent,
And to search in the cellar, they all agreed,
If the farmer would find them, all they would need.

So they got a good dinner, to act as a propeller,
They marched to their work, down into the cellar,
Then into the bottom, like an unringed pig,
With a pick and a spade they began to dig.

They found plenty of dirt, and gravel and stones,
But alas! They could find no human bones,
And for fear that the bones in the dirt might be lurked,
With their hands they every spadeful searched.

As the digging proceeded each other they chaffed,
While up in the house they farmer he laughed,
Like miners they dug for nearly a yard,
But no bones could they find to act as a reward.

But at last they gave up, and with common consent
They picked up their tools, and up steps they went,
And the farmer he chuckled and laughed in good glee,
As he chaffed these hard workers, while having their tea.

And what did they think? Well one of them owns
That he'll ne'er go again a hunting for bones;
And what were their names? I'm not going to tell,
Sufficient for me they did their work well.

Now before I conclude, I just wish to state,
That the persons who have seen it, they live at Bent Gate:
And they toffy, and pies, and Eccles Cakes sell,
But the names of the persons I don't wish to tell.

And now ye men who with spirits deal,
Never try again this Ghost to steal,
For if they manage to get it away,
It is sure to be back again next day.

And ye that searched for human bones,
Amongst the gravel and the stones,
Now don't be vexed or take offence,
If I hope in the future you will learn more sense.

And you men who of your bravery boast,
Just go and try to catch this Ghost;
And if you think it will mend the fun,
Just try and shoot it with a gun.

H. – (Copyright).

H. *Lines on the Green Lane Boggert* (*c.*mid–late nineteenth century)

Corpus Two: Boggart Names

There are five parts in this section:

I) a list of boggart place-names
II) the same boggart place-names broken down into landscape types
III) the same boggart place-names broken down geographically (by county)
IV) boggart proper names from before the Great War
V) bibliography for parts I) and IV).

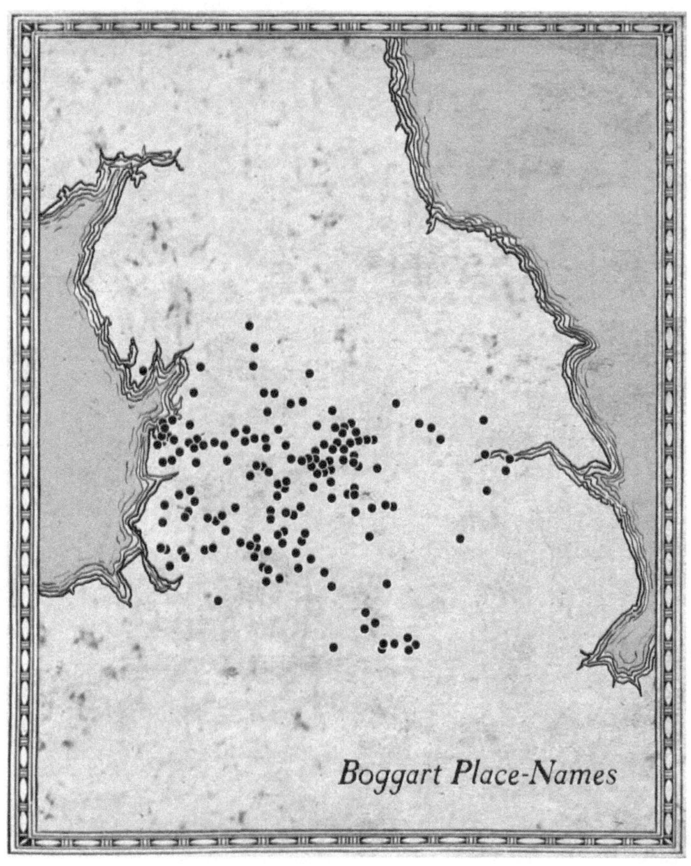

I) Boggart Place-names

Bogard Close (Nether Soothill, WRY): Smith, *Place-Names*, II, 194.
Bogard Hole Close (North Bierley, WRY): WY Archives, 68D82/14/35, 'concerning a capital messuage in North Bierley, with closes of land called the Bogard (?) Hole Close', 1705; Cavill, *Field Names*, 37 has 'Bogard Hall Close'.
Bogard Lane Close (Idle, WRY): Cavill, *Field-Names*, 37.
Bogart Brook (Whitegate, Ch): Dodgson, *Place-Names*, I, 15 referring to Pettypool Brook.
Boggard Bridge (Ovenden, WRY): 1841 Census Ovenden 2, p. 21; Mount Zion Grave Sales records 'Jonas Robinson of Boggard Bridge, Ovenden' 1849, grave 67 (mountzionhalifax.free.fr/Sales.php?MBY [accessed 30 Sep 2018]).
Boggard Close (Great Horton, WRY): 'Boggard Close, occupied by John Balme', dated to 1776 in a deed of settlement, Cudworth, *Rambles*, 88; West Yorks Archives, HOD/2/30; 'In Bowling-Lane, Part of Boggard Lane', 'Valuable freehold' (1825).
Boggard Close (Netherthong, WRY): Smith, *Place-Names*, II, 288.
Boggard Closes (Broughton, WRY): Smith, *Place-Names*, VI, 43 under 'Modern Field Names'.
Boggard Cottage (Holme upon Spalding Moor, ERY): Census 1841, Holme upon Spalding Moor 21, p. 5.
Boggard Farm (East Bierley, WRY): Parker, *Illustrated*, 278 (1904). 'In 1831 Mrs. Kay, a widow, resided at an ancient farm house situated at East Bierley, which is now called by the old inhabitants of the district the 'Boggard Farm'.'
Boggard Field (Elland, WRY): 'A CLOSE of LAND, called the *BOGGARD FIELD* in Elland', 'Yorkshire Freehold Estates' (1803); see also 'Woodman' (1816). To be associated with Boggard Hole (Greetland, WRY)?
Boggard Field (Gisburn, WRY): Smith, *Place-Names*, VI, 169; Cavill, *Field-Names*, 37.
Boggard Hall (Burringham, Li): Also known as Burgess Hall, 'In Parliament…' (1860); Cameron *et al.*, *Place-Names*, VI, 38, dates the earliest attestation to 1824.
Boggard Hole (Fence, La): 'Boggard Hole' 1633, Crossley, *Potts*, lxiii; 'Boggard Hole, Goldshaw booth', Michaelmas 1697, Property Case, DDHCL/1/28 (at http://archivecat.lancashire.gov.uk/); 'Boggard Hole' OSLa 56 (1850) (House); 'Boggart Hole House', 'Nomination of guardians' (1879); 'Boggart Hall Farm', 'A tuberculous cow' (1896).

Boggard Hole (Oldham, La): 'Hannah daughter of James Andrew of Boggart Hole', 'Giles Shaw Manuscripts – Handwritten Transcript of Oldham St. Mary Parish Registers', 1784, available on Findmypast.co.uk. 'Boggard Hole'; OSLa 97 (1848).

Boggard Hole (Peak Forest, Db): Boggart Hole, a mine just to the south-east of Peak Forest. 'Bogerd Hole' 1763, 'Boggard Hole' 1805, 'Bogardhole' 1844, Heathcote, 'History', 17, citing the Peak Forest Barmasters' Books for 1752–1856 in the Derbyshire Records Office. This is presumably the same mine as referred to by Clarke, *Supernatural*, 79.

Boggard Hole (Skipton, WRY): Smith, *Place-Names*, VI, 71.

Boggard House (Bredbury, Ch): 'Died' (1828); Dodgson, *Place-Names*, I, 111.

Boggard House (Darfield, WRY): 'A Determined Housebreaker' (1854).

Boggard House (Esholt, WRY): 'we take the road in the rear of the hall, passing the Boggard House, so named because it was some time untenanted, and the simple rustics in the neighbourhood imagined that they saw lights in the house after the death of a person named Strothers... (O)ld Strothers spirit, while visiting his old home, amused itself by playing at marbles with other wandering ghosts!', 'Round About Bradford' (1875). Smith, *Place-Names*, IV, 145; OSY 202 (1851), to the north of Esholt Hall. Census 1841 Otley 6, p. 8 'Bogard House'; 'Upper Esholt Mill to what was called Boggart Hoase [*sic*]' 'The Bradford Corporation' 1901.

Boggard House (Grassington, WRY): 'Boggard House' OS134Y (1853), on Edge Lane a half mile to the east of Grassington.

Boggard House (Halifax, WRY): WY Archives, DD/T/L/XVI/1, 'Counterpart', 'Miss Judith Murgatroyd of Willow Edge several closes at Boggard house', 1784; Smith, *Place-Names*, III, 108 gives 1797; in the 1871 Census Halifax 4397, p. 13: 'Boggart House' appears next to a 'Boggart House Farm'.

Boggard House (Midgley, WRY): Sutcliffe 'A Tour', 117–18, attestation refers to the reign of Mary and Philip in a deed; Smith, *Place-Names*, III, 133-34; 6 Feb 1657, burial of Thomas Oldfield of 'Boggard House', St Mary's Luddenden.

Boggard House (Warton in Fylde, La): 'Boggard House Field', Warton in Amounderness tithe apportionment entry, DRB/1/194 (archivecat.lancashire.gov.uk/); Wainwright, 'Field Names', 193

Boggard Houses (Greasley, Db): 1881 Census, Barford, Greasley, Enumeration District 11, p. 24.

Boggard Houses (Horsley, Db): 1881 Census, Belper, Horsley, Enumeration District 6, p. 24. Possibly the same as Boggart House (Kilburn, Db)?

Boggard Ing Farm (Huddersfield, WRY): 'Appointment of paid surveyor', 1854; Smith, *Place-Names*, II, 259 (1843); Redmonds, *Almondbury*, 39 quotes a manorial by-law: 'the footway in or over a close in Almondbury called the Upper Ing otherwise the Boggard Ing'; Ramsden Court Rolls recorded the name in 1766. David Pattern writes, pers comm, 28 Nov 2019: 'The valley near Cocking Steps is flanked on either side by ancient woodland. Even now, the area has an "uncomfortable" feel to it and I can easily imagine plenty of forgotten folklore was linked to the area. The northern wood extends towards Armitage Bridge and includes Nan Hob Spring.'

Boggard Lane (Armley, WRY): Smith, *Place-Names*, III, 213.

Boggard Lane (Baildon, WRY): 'Holden or Boggard Lane, as it is now generally called', 'Round about Bradford' (1875); 'Holden Lane… A "boggart" or ghost was at one time supposed to haunt this road, hence it is still sometimes called Boggart Lane by the older inhabitants', Baildon and Baildon, *Baildon*, I, 16; 'Boggart Lane (known as Holden Lane)', 'Fyfe Lane' (1957).

Boggard Lane (Batley, WRY): Census 1861, Batley 3401, p. 26; 'Boggart Lane' 'General News' (1871); nothing on the OS maps for the mid-nineteenth century.

Boggard Lane (Bramley, WRY): OSY 217NE (1894); 'A Freehold Dairy Farm' (1904); 'Legislation: Town and Country Planning Act 1962: The Stopping up of Highways (City and County Borough of Leeds) (No. 2) Order 1967; Location: Gamble Hill, Boggard lane, and the footpaths extending from Gamble Hill to Boggard Lane in the City and County Borough of Leeds', MT 78/306/19, WY Archives.

Boggard Lane (Cawood, WRY): 1851 OSY 206, to the north-west of the village; Smith, *Place-Names*, IV, 38.

Boggard Lane (Charlesworth, Db): OSDe 2SE (1899), to south-east of the village, off Back Lane.

Boggard Lane (Gringley, Nt): Renaming 'Queen-lane instead of Boggard-lane' 'Gringley' (1854).

Boggard Lane (Hipperholme, WRY): 'A portion of the old pack horse road between Bramley lane and Lower Winter Edge is styled Boggard Lane. It is now impassable', Turner, 'Fragments' (1869); *BC*, Hipperholme (WRY) multiple entries.

Boggard Lane (Ogden, La): 'Bogart Lane at Ogden. Just off from the visitor centre at Ogden Water Nature Reserve. The story is bogarts come out at night to cause mischief in the woodlands', *BC*, Ogden 1 (WRY).

Boggard Lane (Oughtibridge/Worrall, WRY): OSY 288 (1855), at Hagg Stones. I take this to be the reference in *BC*, Stocksbridge 1 (WRY).

Boggard Lane (Penistone, WRY): OSY 273 (1854), to SE of village; Smith, *Place-Names*, I, 338.

Boggard Lane (Pudsey, WRY): 1861 Census, Pudsey 3346, p. 12; 'Boggart Lane', 'Valuable Freehold Estates' (1870); 'There were ghosts at Greenside, Lowtown, and Boggard Lane', Lawson, *Letters*, 50-51; 'There are several substantial bridges on the railway, among which may be mentioned that … over Boggard Lane, near the Allanbrig Mill reservoir', Rayner, *History* (1887), 217; Boggard Lane 'has now a finer title for it is called Mount Pleasant Road', 'Happy Old Age' (1935).

Boggard Lane (Shelley, WRY): OSY 261 (1854), a rural route off Green House Lane.

Boggard Lane (Yeadon/Guiseley WRY): The development 'will create extra traffic on Boggart Lane that is a public footpath and lots of people use the route to walk down into Nunroyd park and into Kirk lane park' (*Report of the Chief Planning Officer, PLANS PANEL WEST, Date: 21st January 2010, Subject: PLANNING APPLICATION 09/02813/FU, 5*). *BC*, Yeadon 1 (WRY), 'There's a dirt track known locally as Boggart Lane from end of Swaine Hill Terrace off Kirk Lane Yeadon which cuts through to Queensway along the bottom of Kirk Lane Park. I grew up round there and that track was always called 'Boggart Lane'. I don't remember if there were any stories but that Lane was spooky as hell and you didn't want to warm [*sic*, walk?] there alone.'

Boggard Pit (Batley, WRY): https://www.geocaching.com/geocache/GC34Z76_white-lee-pit-the-first-of-batleys-pits?guid=03f3cce6-d13a-4060-8b25-57c51d532951, 'In 1782 records show coal being worked from the Windhill colliery (the Boggard Pit) off Upper Batley Low Lane.'

Boggard Town (Heanor, Db): 1871 Census, Heanor 3481, p. 43.

Boggard Well (Northowram, WRY): Hopkins, *Ghosts*, 114: 'Between Northowram and Queensbury was a place known as Boggard Well, later known as Bloody Tongue; according to old tales, a ghostly figure, with protruding tongue, from which blood was dripping, used to be seen running out at night!'

Boggard Wood (Dodworth, WRY): Boggard Wood on the road to the south of Ben Bank Farm, *Silkstone Valley Walks*.

Boggard Wood (Ilkley, WRY): 'The old names of fields are often very suggestive of former events and conditions. Thus we have in Ilkley township […] Boggard Wood', Collyer and Turner, *Ilkley*, 256; Smith, *Place-Names*, IV, 215.

Boggard Wood (Wakefield, WRY): WY Archives WRD1/11/Box8/34, *c.*1960.

Boggard Wood (Horsforth, WRY): 'Boggard Wood Nook, Outwood Lane', 'Horsforth' (1937).

Boggart Barn (Blackburn, La): The Roman road 'could next be traced (from Blackburn) to Revidge Boggart Barn, and Ramsgreave', 'The Roman Roads' (1850). Connected with Boggart Farm (Revidge, La)?

Boggart Barn (Chaigley, La): OSLa 46 (1847), to the west of Higher Hodder Bridge, close to the Lancs-Yorkshire border.

Boggart Barn (Preston, La): 'we used to play near "Boggart Barn", a supposed haunted building, which was then situated in a field where Fishwick-road is now built,' 'Preston Golden Weddings' (1939).

Boggart Bridge (Burnley, La): 'Stealing Eggs' (1862).

Boggart Bridge (Dendron, La): OSLa 22 (1851); Newman 'Folklore Survivals', 101: 'so called because near it during hoar frost, a human figure is sometimes outlined in the grass by the hoar frost'; *BC*, Leece 1 'Boggarts Bridge was a place we were scared about crossing in the 1960s. It was between Leece and Gleaston on the Furness Peninsula in South Cumbria. I think adults built up the story to scare children. Not sure if it's named on a map. Think it was a story passed down by mouth.'

Boggart Bridge (Ogden, WRY): OSY 215 (1852).

Boggart Bridge (Selby, WRY): OSY 221 (1851), on Selby Lane to the north of the town; Smith, *Place-Names*, IV, 34; 'To the rear is the black fen and Boggart Brigg, where Peg Fife skinned a man alive, so the natives still say. The Black Fen is the fountain and origin of the bad fiend Will-o'-the-wisp and all that is evil, and the Elf Holes, from whence the elves come tripping lightly in the moonlight, the fount of light and gladness. Thoroughly Celtic in its garmaen, its goblins, boggarts, elf holes, and spark haggs, and the curious, old-world incidents of man-skinning done at the boundary of the Liberty', Bogg, *The Old Kingdom of Elmet*, 234. Note that there is an Elf Hole Farm to the west (see the map below). *BC*, Selby 1 (WRY), 'I come from Selby in Yorkshire. There was a bridge over a stream a mile out of town called "Boggart Bridge". There were tales of people being reluctant to cross it at night or being chased home by the Boggart.'

Boggart Cave, The (Great Eccleston, La): A boggart in the form of a woman 'disappeared in the Boggart Cave at Copp Gutter', 'The Copp Boggart' (1872).

Boggart Chair (Colne, La): 'Boggard chair field', DRB/1/55 (at archivecat.lancashire.gov.uk/), Colne tithe apportionment entry, 1842 (I assume that 'Boggard Charr Meadow', Colne tithe apportionment entry, DRB/1/55 at archivecat.lancashire.gov.uk/) is the same; 'he would be willing to widen the road at Boggart Chair', 'District News' (1878); 'two cottages [...] Netherheys, in Boggart-chair, Barrowford-road', 'Building' (1881).

Boggart Church (Dent, WRY): 'Dale Head Church (in local vernacular called Boggart Church)', 'Another Peep into Dent' (1890).

Boggart Close (Snelston, Db): 'Lease and release by Charlotte Webster of Bakewell', 1826, including 'Boggart Close', D157/MT/1165-1166, http://calmview.derbyshire.gov.uk/CalmView/; Cameron, *Place-Names*, III, 603.
Boggart Closes (Leeds, WRY): 'in the Boggard Closes, in Leeds', 'To brick makers' (1787).
Boggart Clough (Lumb, La): *BC*, Lumb (La) 1, 'I've been told there's a place called Boggart Clough in the Dean area of Lumb'.
Boggart Colliery (Howden Clough, WRY): OSY 232 (1854).
Boggart Corner (Longridge, La): *BC*, Longridge 11 (La), 'My Dad and Granddad used to talk about Boggart Corner around the back lanes of Longridge. I think it was a small bridge over a brook.'
Boggart Cote (Crawshawbooth, La): 25 Feb 1776, St Mary and All Saints, baptism of Mary Lonsdale, Baptisms 1749–1783, page 130; 10 Mar 1822, St James Haslingden, burial of Alice Pickup, Burials 1813–1826, page 206, Entry 1641, 'Boggart Coat'; OSLa 72 (1849), on a hillside to the west of the Bold Venture Mill; 'and Boggart Cote, near Rawtenstall', Ditchfield, 'Legends', 93.
Boggart Croft (Goosnargh, La): Cookson, *Goosnargh* (1888), 28-29, recorded in 1814.
Boggart End (Hanging Heaton, WRY): Haley, *Real Illusions*, 6, 'My mother, Nora... was born two years after my father and three miles away in a direct line from the Home where he had been fostered on the parish... lived in Hanging Heaton though towards the fading edge of the district above the cutting. Boggart End, my mother called it.' Visited Heaton. 'Not even the old resident remembered a district called Boggart End. One old man knew the origins of the word "boggart". It was something which caused horses to shy. An invisible. But nowhere in Hanging Heaton had ever been called that.'
Boggart Farm (Barton, La): 'Barton Child' (1906); *BC*, Preston 18 (La).
Boggart Farm (Revidge, La): 'Blackburn' (1864); connected with Boggart Barn (Blackburn, La)?
Boggart Field (Ashton On Mersey, Ch): Dodgson, *Place-Names*, II, 6.
Boggart Field (Blackley, La): DRM 1/15 (at http://archivecat.lancashire.gov.uk/), Blackley tithe apportionment entry, 1844.
Boggart Field (Burtonwood, La): Tithe Maps 1836–1851, Burtonwood, Plot 415.
Boggart Fields (Howden Clough, WRY): OSY 232 (1854); Smith 1961–63, II, 181.
Boggart Footpath (Timperley, La): An Assessment of Trafford's Public Rights of Way Network Stage One of the Rights of Way Improvement

Plan for Trafford DECEMBER 2007 https://www.trafford.gov.uk/residents/transport-and-streets/roads-highways-and-pavements/docs/rights-of-way-improvement-plan-stage-1-and-2.pdf76 [accessed Dec 2019], 'Boggart Footpath, off Heyes Lane, Timperley' aka Boggart's Way, 80.

Boggart Hall (Aughton/Bickerstaffe, La): 'Forty years ago [*c.*1850, Mossock Hall, aka Moss Oak Hall] was in a very neglected state, and was surrounded with timber and old hedges. It was generally believed by the neighbours to be haunted, and was known for some time as Boggart Hall, the only inhabitant then being a farm labourer', Newstead, *Gleanings*, 19; 'Queer Tales' (1910).

Boggart Hall (Hurlston, La): *BC*, Hurlston 1 (La), 'There is a house just by Hurlston Hall that I know as "The Boggart House".'

Boggart Heawse (Middleton, La): 'A Ghost Story' (1839).

Boggart Hill (Leeds, WRY): OSY 203 (1851).

Boggart Hill (Stalmine, La): 'Boggart Hill' and 'Further Boggart Hill' DRB 1/180 (at http://archivecat.lancashire.gov.uk/) Stalmine with Staynall tithe apportionment entry, 1841. Not on mid-century OS.

Boggart Hole (Bolton, La): OSLa 87 (1850); 'Boggart Hole Cottage', 1911 Census, Bolton, Tonge, Enumeration District 2, p. 178.

Boggart Hole (Clitheroe, La): *Boggart Hole*, 'Pollution of the Ribble' (1880).

Boggart Hole (Goosnargh, La): *Boggart Hole* DRB 1/86 (at http://archivecat.lancashire.gov.uk/), Goosnargh w Newsham tithe apportionment entry, 1842; Cavill, *Field-Names*, 37 has a 'Boggart Hole, Newsham La'.

Boggart Hole (Greetland, WRY): Longbotham 1933, 70c; Smith, *Place-Names*, II, 49. To be associated with 'Boggart Field (Elland, WRY)'? Noted in Field, *Field Names*, 24.

Boggart Hole (Littleborough, La). *BC*, Littleborough 4 (La), 'My wife, aged seventy-one, born and bred in Littleborough. There was a hillside quarry in Shore Littleborough called the Boggart Hole. (1950s).' There follows on other memories of this small quarry with other names.

Boggart Hole (Mellor Moor, Db): 1881 Census, Mellor, Enumeration District 9, p. 11.

Boggart Hole (Newsham, La): Noted in Field, *Field Names*, 24, no reference. Confusion with Boggart Hall? See further 'Boggart House Farm (Newsham, La)', Wainwright, 'Field-Names', 193.

Boggart Hole (Stacksteads, La): Referred to in the historical section of the *Bacup Times* newspaper www.bacuptimes.co.uk/stacksteads.htm [accessed June 2018].

Boggart Hole Clough (Blackley, La): Plan of the Parish of Manchester in the County of Lancaster from a Survey made in 1818–1819 by William

Johnson; Wentworth 1892, 128–136; for other sources Young, 'Boggart Hole Clough'.

Boggart Holes (Chapel-le-Dale, WRY): Speight, *Chronicles*, 254.

Boggart Holes (Clapham, WRY): 'Ingleton' 1885; Speight, *Chronicles*, 180.

Boggart Holes (Higher Blackley, La): OSLa 96 (1848).

Boggart Holes (Metham, ERY): Cavill, *Field-Names*, 37.

Boggart Holes (Ribchester, La): 'Fatal Result' (1889); 'Fatal Collision' (1889).

Boggart House (Audenshaw, La): Boggart House 1848 OSLa 105, to the north of Audenshaw and to the east of Droylsden; 'from Red Hall to *Boggart House*', 'Notice' (1865). Note associated with a Boggart Lane.

Boggart House (Bollin Fee, Ch): 1841 Census, Bollin Fee 5, p. 6

Boggart House (Broughton, La): 'Bogart House' 1881 Census, Preston, Broughton, Enumeration District 18, p. 9; 'There is a Boggart House near Broughton Church' Ditchfield, 'Lancashire Legends', 93; 'a traditional route past Boggart House, to Cuddy Hill, thence through Inskip, St. Michaels, and Duncombe', John 'To the Editor' (1876).

Boggart House (Burtonwood, La): Tithe Maps 1836–1851, Burtonwood, Plot 955; 'Boggart House' OSLa108 (1849), to the south-east of Buttonwood.

Boggart House (Carnforth, La): 'Between Bolton-le-Sands and Carnforth, on the roadside, is situated a house having the reputation of being haunted, and has ever, within the memory of that oft quoted personage "the oldest inhabitant," been known by the appellation of the "boggart house"', 'Ghost Story' (1851).

Boggart House (Chesterfield, Db): 'Despite its pleasant situation the old house had an evil reputation. It was said to be haunted and after nightfall children and the timid would not pass it if they could help it. Up to recent times the house was known locally as the 'Boggart House', and local stories used to be related of the ghost of cowled figure with horrible distorted features which used to be seen in Spital Lane and near the hospital. In fact, so accepted was the story that the host at Spital House in seeing his guests off the premises, used often to say Good-night, take care of the ghost in the Lane', 'The Spital Estate' (1932).

Boggart House (Cleckheaton, WRY): Roberts, *Yorkshire*, 99 writes: 'The name 'boggart house' was famously applied to Bierley Hall near Cleckheaton sometime in the early 1800s, when the manifestations in one upstairs room of the building grew so violent that crowds of people gathered outside hoping to glimpse the phenomena.' I have been unable to find any contemporary reference to Cleckheaton as a boggart house: and Roberts gives no reference.

Boggart House (Cromford, De): Uttley, *Ambush*, 213–214.

Boggart House (Cromwell Bottom, WRY): appears to be a late-nineteenth-century house, Billingsley, *West Yorkshire*, 39. https://lowercalderlegends.wordpress.com/2010/03/15/boggart-house-southowram/ (Kai Roberts' work, accessed 20 Oct 2018).

Boggart House (Dalton, La): 'Gildsley or Boggart House Dalton nr Southport' 1911 Census, Dalton, Enumeration District 1, p. 91.

Boggart House (Galgate, La): 'A Reckless Drunkard' (1885); 'Scotforth' (1889); 'Serious Accident' (1891) details a horse bolting while 'passing a gipsy encampment near the Boggart House'. 'Some six or seven hundred yards beyond the railway bridge at Barrow Beck there is house on the west side of the road known as "Boggart["] house; a few yards further, on the opposite side of the turnpike, is a road leading to Ellel Chapel and school', 'The Brutal Murder' (1866). This description seems to correspond to Leach House on the 1848 OSLa 34.

Boggart House (Gorton, La): 'The "boggart house" now a wash cottage appertaining to Bridge House, was renowned as the locale of feeorin',' Higson, *Gorton*, 16.

Boggart House (Hayfield, Db): 'And there he saw the boggart house/ Where th' Highgate witch is seen/ By moonlight at some midnight hours,/ Dancing on Highgate green', Sandy Banks, 'Sandy Banks's Criticism' (1865). Highgate appears on the OSD5.SE (1882). *BC*, see Hayfield (Db) entries (multiple).

Boggart House (Helmshore, La): *BC*, Helmshore 1 (La), 'I was born in 1933 and lived as a child within three hundred yards of the Boggart House described in my publication.'

Boggart House (Hindley, La): OS La94 (1849) on bending Swan Lane (actually called Howler Lane 1861 on censuses; 1841 Census Hindley 10, pp. 5-6; see also *BC*, Hindley Green 1 (La) for the Boggart Houses (different?).

Boggart House (Howden Clough, WRY): 1854 OSY 232; 'Boggard Ho[use]', Smith, *Placenames*, II, 181.

Boggart House (Kettleshulme, Ch): 1871 Census, Kettleshulme 3671, p. 6; 1881 OSCh 29, to the south-east of the village; Dodgson, *Place-Names*, I, 111.

Boggart House (Kilburn, Db): 'Boggart House, Kilburn', 'Fatal' (1909). Possibly the same as Boggard Houses (Horsley, Db).

Boggart House (Kirkham, La): 1841 Census, Treals 10, p. 14.

Boggart House (Lees, La): 'One of the old dwellings acquired the name of "Boggart House", in consequence of its being haunted by a hobgoblin having the appearance of a calf, some said with a cap on its head, and others a frill round its neck', Higson, 'Boggarts and Feorin' (1869), 508.

Boggart House (Matlock, Db): 1891 Census, Wirksworth, Matlock, Enumeration District 16, p. 18.
Boggart House (Rufford, La): *BC*, Rufford 1 (La): 'My neighbour in Rufford used to refer to the house up the road as the Boggart House. He died in the 1990s.' Another user added: 'this was Field House. My dad was born there.'
Boggart House (Skelmersdale, La): *BC*, Skelmersdale 1 (La), 'where I live there was a place near the local coal mine called "The Boggart House" supposed to be haunted'; Skelmersdale 7 (La), 'When I lived in owd Skem, there was an old derelict house next to St Pauls church which all the kids christened the boggart house, there's no way you would walk past it on your own. Spooky.'
Boggart House (Strelley, Nt): 1911 Census, Strelley, Nt, Enumeration District 8, p. 65.
Boggart House (Thornton, WRY): 'that FARM HOUSE... situate at Black Car, and commonly called Boggart House', 'Estate in Thornton' (1841).
Boggart House (Wardle, La): 'Boggart House, Wardle above Syke', 'On Sale' (1915). This is not on OSLa 81 (1851), see though *BC*, Wardle 2 (La).
Boggart House (West Derby, La): 'Boggart-house, Carr Lane, West Derby', Dickinson, 'Appendix', 104 (1849-51).
Boggart House (Westhoughton/Hindley, La): 'Boggart House or Alder Lane' 1841 Census, Wigan, Hindley, Enumeration District 5, pp. 5–6; OSLa 94 (1849), to the east of Hindley and to the south of Westhoughton; 'all in the County of Lancaster, and terminating on the north-westerly side of a lane called Pungle-Lane, situated in the township Westhoughton, in the parish of Dean, in the County of Lancaster, in a field in the said township of Westhoughton, occupied by Ellen Gregory, and known by the name of Boggart Housefield', 'Manchester and Southport' (1846); 'the intended main line will cross Marsh Brook, near Boggart House' 'Lancashire and Yorkshire' (1860); 'Boggart House Farm in Sandy-Lane' 'Local Law Case' (1881); 'and another house so-named (i.e. Boggart House) near Hindley' (Ditchfield 1906, 93).
Boggart House (Whalley, La): *BC*, Blackburn 13 (La), 'There are a few farms on Whalley Old Road, which is the high road from Blackburn to Whalley. We knew one of them as the Boggatt House.'
Boggart House (Wigan, La): 'Holme House or Boggart House' 'Sale' (1836); Holme House on OSLa 93 (1849), to the north of Wigan.
Boggart House (Winwick, La): OSLa 108 (1849) to the south of Dial Post House.
Boggart House (Wrightington, La): OSLa 85 (1849); 'Conveyance of an estate called Hawetts or Boggart House in Wrightington', DDSC/129/58 (at

http://archivecat.lancashire.gov.uk/), Wrightington 1859; 'Boggart House is situated a little to the north of Boars Den… A road called Robin Hood Lane runs past Boars Den. Between a certain gate and Dangerous Corner, the old man assured me, this road is haunted by a boggart. His brother had seen it many times, and it "went clankin' round th' field in chains". Some two years ago, during the sickness of one of the inmates of Boggart House, the visitations of the house ghost became so frequent and terrifying, that the inhabitants finally fled in terror, and the house was empty at the time of my visit', Price 'Notes' (1899), 190–92; 'Boggart House Farm, High Moorlane, Wrightington', 'Wrightington' (1941); OSLa 85 (1845).

Boggart House Farm (Newsham, La): 'Boggart House Farm' (1879); 'The Ghost of John Parkinson's Farewell' (1880). Note that this does not seem to be Boggart House (Broughton, La), though they are very close and have similar names. Field, *Field Names*, 24 records a Boggart Hole, at 'Newsham La' confusion with a Boggart Hall? Field gives no reference.

Boggart House Farm (Out Rawcliffe, La): '"Boggart House" Farm, Out Rawcliffe'; 'Melancholy Suicide' (1848); 1841 Census, Out Rawcliffe 4, p. 29.

Boggart House Farm (Wetherby, WRY): 'Boggart-House Farm, situated in the Parish of Thorp-Arch, near Wetherby' 'To Be Lett' (1796); 'near Boggart House Farm, between Wetherby and Walton' 'Accidents' (1878); Smith, *Place-Names*, IV, 245 gives references from 1817 and 1843.

Boggart Land (Skelmersdale, La): *BC*, Skelmersdale 3 (La), not clear if proper name, 'It would be around the time the Skem Dev Co were building the housing estates on farm land between the old town and Ashurst beacon. The area was always described to me as Boggart land and it was not recommended to venture there after dark.'

Boggart Lane (Blackshaw Head, WRY): 'Blackshaw Parish' (1906); 'Boggart-lane-top farm', 'Latest Freak' (1907); 'The local name for the Lane is Boggart Lane. 'Boggarts' were household sprites who lurked in remote places waiting to attach themselves malevolently to hapless travellers', *Blackshawhead Packhorse Audio E-trail Script*, from Pennine Heritage.org.uk, 4 (unnumbered), undated but *c.*2010?.

Boggart Lane (Bradford, WRY): DB38/C1/page 149, WY Archives: the property of Joseph Buck and Mrs Hannah Marshall, adjoining Boggart Lane, Dead Lane, and the road from Bradford to Wakefield, Bradford (now bottom of Wakefield Road and Leeds Road), Sep 1756; 'Borough' (1835); 'there is a lane called till lately, Boggard Lane, but now it takes the title of Eastbrook Lane', 'To the Editor' (1837); 'a street meeting was held at a place known as

Boggard Lane top, in George Street in the town', 'Attempted' (1843); 'One street was called Boggard Lane and indeed it was the most appropriate name which could have been chosen', 'Public Meetings'; 'Eastbrook Lane, commonly called Boggart Lane', 'Board' (1850).

Boggart Lane (Bulwell, Nt): a level crossing 'on a footpath leading from what is known as "*Boggart-Lane*", in the Bulwell district, across the fields to Arnold', 'An Alleged Dangerous Crossing' (1899).

Boggart Lane (Didsbury, La): 'At Didsbury we had Boggart Lane until the Methodist Church was built in it, and since then the bogies have not been seen, and the lane is called Didsbury Park', Moss, *Folk-lore*, 135; OSLaCXI (1848) and OSLaCXI.se (1911).

Boggart Lane (Droylsden/Audenshaw, La): OSL105 (1848); Boggart-lane crosses Ashton New-road 'Board of Trade' (1896).

Boggart Lane (Eccleston, La): 1881 Census, Prescott, Eccleston, Enumeration District 11, p. 30.

Boggart Lane (Emley, WRY): OSY 261 (1854), Northeast of Emley, off Leisure Lane going towards Bank Wood.

Boggart Lane (Hadfield, Db): 'Mysterious Death,' 1887.

Boggart Lane (Hellifield, WRY): OS Y149 (1852).

Boggart Lane (Leigh, La): some boys 'pleaded guilty to tossing in 'Boggart-Lane', a path over the sewage farm', 'Playing Pitch and Toss' (1903).

Boggart Lane (Mytholmroyd, WRY): 'Desperate Attempt at Suicide' (1907).

Boggart Lane (Rochdale, La): OSLa 89NW (1894) crosses the railway between Rochdale and Milnrow; 'Sad Drowning' (1901); 'Anyone Trespassing' (1918); subsequently called 'Bingley Road', 'Notes and Comments' (1941).

Boggart Lane (Roxby, Li): 'and Goosey Lane, or Boggart Lane, near Roxby, in Lincolnshire, has also a spectre of the same species (Shagfoal), or had as late as the third decade of this century (i.e. 1820s)', Peacock, 'Horse', 75; 'Water or Watery-lane was called Boggart-lane from Goosey-lane to where the water crosses the road and runs eastward to form the town drain', Fowler, 'Winterton' (1920).

Boggart Lane (Sale, Ch): 'besides having a frontage to Marslands-Road abuts for a considerable distance upon Boggart-lane' 'Sales by auction' (1852); 'Moorfield Gardens' (1877).

Boggart Lane (Skelmanthorpe, WRY): 1854 OS 261, to the north of the village; Smith, *Place-Names*, II, 222.

Boggart Lane (Sowerby Bridge, WRY): 1871 Census, 4411, p. 12; OSY 230 (1908), to the south of Station Road; Smith, *Place-Names*, III, 142.

Boggart Lane (Ulleskelf, WRY): 'Ozendike Lane or Boggart Close' 'Ulleskelf'

(1844); *Boggart Lane* OSY 205 (1849), just to the west of Ossendike House; Boggard Gate Close 1845, Smith, *Place-Names*, IV, 67.

Boggart Lane (Whiston, La): 'Boggart-lane, Whiston', 'Alleged Outrage' (1893).

Boggart Lane (Wilberlee, WRY): Falconer, 'Plant Galls' (1924). *BC*, Slaithwaite 2, 'I grew up at Pole Moor by the masts and the track just below the school at Wilberlee going towards Merrydale was known as Boggart Lane. I always ran past so the Boggart couldn't get me! [Other Facebok user: 'yes that's right XXX, never liked walking past Boggart Lane in the dark on way up Heys, back in the day']… [Another Facebook user: The one just down from Wilberlee School!]'

Boggart Lathe (Keighley, WRY): 'Green Well Hobcote or Boggart Lathe', Census 1871: Keighley 4315, p. 2.

Boggart Mill (Burnley, La): 'A mill, a grist mill, takes its name from an incident of the panic times. It is called Boggart Mill. The term meant ghost. The mill was rifled one night by white-caps and nine hundred sacks of flour were baked and eaten in two days', Holden, 'The Lincoln Mark', 355.

Boggart Mill (Dinting Vale, Ch): 'He remembered that period which had been referred to when Dinting Vale Printworks was an old mill. As a lad he passed it with terror, because it was called the "boggart mill"', 'Memorial to E. Potter, Esq, M.P. Dinting' (1873).

Boggart Mine (Wirksworth, Db): Farey, *General View*, I, 328 (1811).

Boggart Oak (Selby, WRY): Broadhead, *Portrait*, 96.

Boggart Old Clough (Cronton, La): *BC*, Cronton 1 (La), 'Now, I've just spoken with hubby who is much older than me and he mentioned the name of a road or area called Boggart Old Clough. Maybe top end of Cronton/ Rainhill. I will go and do a google search lol. Actually think it was more towards Tarbock area.'

Boggart Old Clough (Rochdale, La): *BC*, Rochdale 1 (La), 'Only Boggart Old Clough in Rochdale. The family who had lived there had been so afraid of the Boggart that they had left hurriedly, never to return and the house was left to go to ruin. As a child I went there once on Halloween with some other kids and frightened ourselves to death waiting for the Boggarts to appear – which, of course, they didn't!'

Boggart Pit (Manchester, La): Griffiths and Martin, *Engineering*, 622 has a Boggart Pit, North Manchester.

Boggart Pit (Poulton, La): Moore, *A History*, 47: 'there is still a pond on Mains Lane, called "Boggart Pit".'

Boggart Pits (Treales, La). *BC*, Treales 1 (La). 'My Mum used to talk about the Boggart Pits behind Treales C. of E. school.' This seems to be a small depression.

Boggart Platt (Goosnargh, La): Cookson, *Goosnargh* (1881), 51 and 311.

Boggart Road (Hayfield, Db): *BC*, Hayfield 1 (Db): 'I seem to recall, as young children, we used to call the road to Rowarth "Boggart Road" (it's actually Shiloh Road) as I was told it, and Shiloh Farm, were haunted... Does anyone else have any recollections of calling Shiloh Road (the road down from the top of Mellor towards Rowarth) Boggart Road? Somewhere in the back of my mind we used to call it that because it was known to be haunted along there. Or, is my mind playing tricks? I'm going back over fifty years. [FB user wrote: the back lane going to the cross at Mellor is called Boggard Road]. Ah, yes, so I see. That must be where I've got it from. Thank you for putting my mind at rest. Shiloh Road is opposite the end of Bogguard Road. So many different spellings though!'

Boggart Stile (Burtonwood, La): OSLa 108 (1849), in a field to the south of Burtonwood Lodge.

Boggart Stile (Preesall, La): 'Boggart Stile Meadow', Wainwright, 'Field Names' 193 found in 1840 tithe award schedules.

Boggart Stones (Saddleworth, WRY): OSY271 (1854) on the high moors to the east of Upper Mill; 'Boggart o'th' Moss', Smith, *Place-Names*, II, 313, citing the 1843 O.S. map.

Boggart Walks (Whalley, La): 'Boggart Walks' OSLa 55 (1848), to the west of Whalley.

Boggart Wood (Allerton, WRY): OSY 216 (1852), a wooded valley just to the south of Allerton, Smith, *Place-Names*, III, 247.

Boggart Wood (Hollingworth, La): a hare 'ran by Benny Hill through Boggart Wood to Higher Fold', 'Northern Hunts' (1906).

Boggart Wood (Nether Alderley, Ch): Ch OS 36 (1882), to the south-west of Alderley Park, a tiny oval shaped wood among several fields; Dodgson, *Place-Names*, I, 97

Boggart Yate (Hambleton, La): OSLa 43 (1848), to the south of Hambleton. *BC*, Hambleton 1 (La), 'Where the Grange (house/old farm) is in Hambleton used to be called Boggart Yate/gate (in the long distant past). My Dad's family used to own it and he was born in the 1950s, but doesn't really know why it had that name'; Hambleton 2 (La), 'In the 1970s and 1980s I lived in Hambleton and there was for a while a restaurant called "Ye Old Boggery Gate". I vaguely remember older people in the area mentioning that a boggart was occasionally seen and that the gate was where he was hung.'

Boggart's Barn (Wigglesworth, WRY): *BC*, Wigglesworth 1 (WRY), 'my godmother's family in Wigglesworth had a barn now demolished situated by the road side from Wigglesworth to Long Preston and that was called Boggart's Barn. My godmother and her sister wasn't keen on going into that barn which they had to especially at hay time. The farm men had to go in the rest of the year to see to the cattle housed in there in winter etc. and they wouldn't let me go in at all. Said there was a mischievous sprite in there. They wouldn't say anything else.'

Boggart's Clough (Sabden, La): 'Here, too, met besomed witches on a dark night, for to-day we hear the name, "Boggart's Clough," when this old dell is spoken of, and sure it is lonely enough on a dark winter's night when the wind is howling and the bare branches of the trees are creaking, when every inanimate object seems as if imbued with a lifelike form, when the veriest sound casts an unpleasant eeriness upon our own subconscious minds', Kenrick, 'Tramps' (1930).

Boggart's Grave (Ogden, WRY): 'To be found along the woodland trail at Ogden Water Nature Reserve. A now fenced off, round stoned spring that unusually bubbles air as it emerges', http://www.megalithic.co.uk/article.php?sid=12207 [accessed 20 Oct 2018].

Boggart's Green (Winteringham, Li): *BC*, Winteringham 4 (Li), 'As children we used to play on a triangle of grass at the junction of two roads and called it a boggart's green. That would be in the 1940s and 1950s.'

Boggart's Inn Farm (Wirksworth, Db): 'The Like agreement to let to William Webster the house called Boggard's Inn', 1750, D/D An/Bundle 47/48417, Wigan Archives; 'Boggart's Inn Farm, near Wirksworth', 'Sad Deaths' (1893); 'Boggart's Inn, Wirksworth' 'Deaths' (1894).

Boggart's Lane (Pilling, La): *BC*, Pilling 2 (La), 'My grandparent's farmed at XXX Farm, Pilling and the road down to it (off Garstang Road) is called Boggarts Lane. As a child in the 1950s my older cousins would terrify me with stories of Boggarts as we walked past the wood.'

Boggart's Wood (Poulton, La): *BC*, Poulton 2 (La), 'Dad used to tell us about Boggart's Wood, but that could have been a nickname for Brockholes Wood (known as Tee Wood) because he used to walk through there as a child and said it was scary at night.'

Boggarts Hill (Prestbury, Ch): 1841 Census for Bosley 14, p. 8, adjacent, in the census, to 'Boggins Hill'.

Brunt Boggart Lane (Cronton, La): OSL85 (1849) records a Brunt Boggart Lane and a Brunt Boggart (house) two miles west of Cronton: it is not clear which (if either) is the original. Taylor, *Crosses*, 190 writes: 'three and a quarter miles north-east by east from Much Woolton Church we find 'Brunt Boggart,' apparently the name of a small house in Brunt Boggart Lane.' 'Brunts [*sic*] Boggart Lane' appears in the 1871 census, Tarbock 3856, p. 11

Buggard Close (Crich, Db): Cameron, *Place-Names* II, 440; the source is Tithe Apportionment of 1847 for Crich in Derbyshire (Derbyshire Record Office: D2360/3/112; plot 1238; *non vidi*).

Buggard House, The (Stretford, La): 1753, Stretford registers in Crofton, *History*, I, 160). Note that Crofton, *Stretford*, III, 73 may imply that there were two houses of this name in the township, certainly 'there was a broken down old house bearing the same ghostly name near the railway bridge at Lostock Lane. The house was inhabited by a poor man of the Hampson family, whose nickname was "Boggart John"'; OSLa 103 (1848), south-east corner on Lostock Lane.

Buggart Field (Pownall Fee, Ch): Tithe Maps 1836–1851, Pownall Fee, 487; Cavill, *Field-Names*, 37.

Buggart Field (Wilmslow, Ch): Dodgson, *Place-Names*, I, 233.

Buggart House (Walton on the Hill, La): 'Certificate regarding the road within Kirkdale from the causeway in Turnpike Road leading from Liverpool to Walton on the Hill by James Bennett's house and James Wilcock's house called Buggart House through Bootle Lane to a plot dividing Bootle and Kirkdale indicted in April 1771 is now repaired', QSB/1/1781/APR/PT2/36 (at http://archivecat.lancashire.gov.uk/), Certificate 24 Apr 1781. Same as West Derby (La)?

Higher and Lower Boggart Stones (Widdop, WRY): OSY 214 (1851); Smith, *Place-Names* III, 192.

Little Boggard House, The (Ardsley, WRY): 'Boggard House, Ardsley', 'Burglary' (1851); 'Boggart House Farm, Ardsley', 'Mence or Mense Family' (1859); 'At the village of Ardsley, near Barnsley, there is a house known to old residents as "the little boggard house", for that is the way in which they pronounce "boggart"', E.G.B., 'Battletwig' (1895). Are these actually two different houses?

Little Boggart and Big Boggart (Field) (Sale, Ch): associated with Boggart Lane (Sale, Ch) 'Sales by auction' (1852).

Nearer Buggards Croft (Irlam, La): 'the Nearer Buggards-croft and the Further Buggards-croft', 'To be sold' (1797).

Old Bogard, The (Huddersfield, WRY): Ahier, *Huddersfield*, I, 157: 'The Dives House, at one time, was known as 'The Old Bogard,' and some most weird occurrences are related by those who have lived, therein.' The Dives House stood in Dalton now part of east Huddersfield.

Old Boggard House (Leeds, WRY): '(T)he cathedral of Methodism' in the north of England', 'Ten Hours Factory Bill' (1835). 'When Methodism was introduced to Leeds, a site was desired on which to erect a chapel, and this boggart-house was a farm-house, which was supposed to be haunted and where nobody would live; but, as Mr. Wesley neither feared boggarts nor their master, he bought the house for a small sum, and John Nelson the apostle of Yorkshire... assisted to rear the chapel', 'Wesleyan Missionary Society' (1863); The story that the Old Boggard House in Leeds was so called because 'the site or premises on which it stood were supposed to be haunted by a ghost or boggard, and therefore shunned and given to Mr. Wesley, who exorcised the evil visitor by the introduction of another and better spirit'... is fabrication. The fact is that after the early Methodists had been driven from place to place by persecution... Matthew Chippendale... invited them to hold their meetings in his house. It was in a sequestered place, there being then no houses nearer than Lady Bridge, Mill-garth, Quarry-hill, and Timble Bridge.... The site of the house is called Apple-garth in the legal documents; but locally the fields about where called the Boggard Closes (Leeds, WRY), because, it is said, a ghost in white was seen to run about in them at nights, which ultimately was proved to be a white cat.' Hardcastle, 'The story that the...' (1891).

Uncertain or to be Rejected

Bog Eggs Farm (Old Town, WRY): Billingsley, *Folk Tales*, 74, misinterpreted as Boggart farm e.g. Midgley 1 (WRY)
Bogget Field (Bk): Cavill, *Field-Names*, 37.
Bogger Furlong (Ch): Cavill, *Field-Names*, 37.
Buggard (He): Minet, *Hadham Hall*, 53: 'a new common field which lay a little to the south of the angle formed by the Standon-Little Hadham, Little Hadham-Much Hadham roads, and north of Sholand. The name occurs under many forms, in 1844 it has become Bugwood and is now Buggard'.
The Boggart (Sc): MacKenzie, *Kilbarchan*, 163: 'The history of the Kirk Session's ownership and administration of Boydayard, 'The Boggard,' is interesting. It was a small farm beside the Kilbarchan Burn after it crosses the road near Easwald Bank.'

II) Boggart Place-names by Landscape Type

Here follow all boggart placenames known to the author broken down by landscape type: Buildings, 63; Lanes and Roads, 38; Fields and Meadows, 26; Dells and Valleys, 20; Copses, Woods and Forests, 8; Bridges, 6; Caves, Cliffs,

Rocks and Stones, 7; Collieries and Mines, 5; Rivers, Streams and Wells, 4; Heights, 3.

Bridges (6): **Boggard Bridge** (Ovenden, WRY); **Boggart Bridge** (Burnley, La); **Boggart Bridge** (Dendron, La); **Boggart Bridge** (Ogden, WRY); **Boggart Bridge** (Selby, WRY); **Boggart Corner** (Longridge, La).

Buildings (63): **Boggard Cottage** (Holme upon Spalding Moor, ERY); **Boggard Farm** (East Bierley, WRY); **Boggard Hall** (Burringham, Li); **Boggard House** (Bredbury, Ch); **Boggard House** (Darfield, WRY); **Boggard House** (Esholt, WRY); **Boggard House** (Grassington, WRY); **Boggard House** (Halifax, WRY); **Boggard House** (Midgley, WRY); **Boggard House** (Warton in Fylde, La); **Boggard Houses** (Greasley, Db); **Boggard Houses** (Horsley, Db); **Boggard Town** (Heanor, Db); **Boggart Barn** (Blackburn, La); **Boggart Barn** (Chaigley, La); **Boggart Barn** (Preston, La); **Boggart's Barn** (Wigglesworth, WRY); **Boggart Church** (Dent, WRY); **Boggart Croft** (Goosnargh, La); **Boggart Farm** (Barton, La); **Boggart Hall** (Aughton/Bickerstaffe, La); **Boggart Hall** (Hurlston, La); **Boggart Heawse** (Middleton, La); **Boggart House** (Audenshaw, La); **Boggart House** (Bollin Fee, Ch); **Boggart House** (Broughton, La); **Boggart House** (Burtonwood, La); **Boggart House** (Carnforth, La); **Boggart House** (Chesterfield, Db); **Boggart House** (Cleckheaton, WRY); **Boggart House** (Cromford, De); **Boggart House** (Cromwell Bottom, WRY); **Boggart House** (Dalton, La); **Boggart House** (Galgate, La); **Boggart House** (Gorton, La); **Boggart House** (Hayfield, Db); **Boggart House** (Helmshore, La); **Boggart House** (Hindley, La); **Boggart House** (Howden Clough, WRY); **Boggart House** (Kettleshulme, Ch); **Boggart House** (Kilburn, Db); **Boggart House** (Kirkham, La); **Boggart House** (Lees, La); **Boggart House** (Matlock, Db); **Boggart House** (Whalley, La); **Boggart House** (Rufford, La); **Boggart House** (Skelmersdale, La); **Boggart House** (Strelley, Nt); **Boggart House** (Wardle, La); **Boggart House** (West Derby, La); **Boggart House** (Westhoughton/Hindley, La); **Boggart House** (Wigan, La); **Boggart House** (Winwick, La); **Boggart House** (Wrightington, La); **Boggart House Farm** (Newsham, La); **Boggart House Farm** (Out Rawcliffe, La); **Boggart House Farm** (Wetherby, WRY); **Boggart Mill** (Burnley, La); **Boggart Mill** (Dinting Vale, Ch); **Boggart's Inn Farm** (Wirksworth, Db); **Buggard House, The** (Stretford, La); **Buggart House** (Walton on the Hill, La); **Little Boggard House, The** (Ardsley, WRY); **Old Bogard, The** (Huddersfield, WRY); **Old Boggard House** (Leeds, WRY).

Caves, Cliffs, Rocks and Stones (7): **Boggart Cave, The** (Great Eccleston, La); **Boggart Chair** (Colne, La); **Boggart Hole** (Littleborough, La); **Boggart Holes** (Chapel-le-Dale, WRY); **Boggart Holes** (Clapham, WRY); **Boggart Stones** (Saddleworth, WRY); **Higher and Lower Boggart Stones** (Widdop, WRY).

Collieries and Mines (5): **Boggard Hole** (Peak Forest, Db); **Boggard Pit** (Batley, WRY); **Boggart Pit** (Manchester, La); **Boggart Colliery** (Howden Clough, WRY); **Boggart Mine** (Wirksworth, Db).

Copses, Woods and Forests (8): **Boggart Oak** (Selby, WRY); **Boggard Wood** (Dodworth, WRY); **Boggard Wood** (Horsforth, WRY); **Boggard Wood** (Ilkley, WRY); **Boggart Wood** (Allerton, WRY); **Boggart Wood** (Hollingworth, La); **Boggart Wood** (Nether Alderley, Ch); **Boggard Wood** (Wakefield, WRY); **Boggart's Wood** (Poulton, La).

Dells and Valleys (20): **Bogard Hole Close** (North Bierley, WRY); **Boggard Hole** (Fence, La); **Boggard Hole** (Oldham, La); **Boggard Hole** (Skipton, WRY); **Boggart Clough** (Lumb, La); **Boggart Hole** (Bolton, La); **Boggart Hole** (Clitheroe, La); **Boggart Hole** (Goosnargh, La); **Boggart Hole** (Greetland, WRY); **Boggart Hole** (Mellor Moor, Db); **Boggart Hole** (Newsham, La); **Boggart Hole** (Stacksteads, La); **Boggart Hole Clough** (Blackley, La); **Boggart Holes** (Higher Blackley, La); **Boggart Holes** (Metham, ERY); **Boggart Holes** (Ribchester, La); **Boggart Old Clough** (Cronton, La); **Boggart Old Clough** (Rochdale, La); **Boggart Pits** (Treales, La). **Boggart's Clough** (Sabden, La).

Fields and Meadows (26): **Bogard Close** (Nether Soothill, WRY); **Boggard Close** (Great Horton, WRY); **Boggard Close** (Netherthong, WRY); **Boggard Closes** (Broughton, WRY); **Boggard Field** (Elland, WRY); **Boggard Field** (Gisburn, WRY); **Boggart Close** (Snelston, Db); **Boggart Closes** (Leeds, WRY); **Boggart Cote** (Crawshawbooth, La); **Boggart Field** (Ashton On Mersey, Ch); **Boggart Field** (Blackley, La); **Boggart Field** (Burtonwood, La); **Boggart Fields** (Howden Clough, WRY); **Boggart's Green** (Winteringham, Li); **Boggart Land** (Skelmersdale, La); **Boggart Lathe** (Keighley, WRY); **Boggart Platt** (Goosnargh, La); **Boggart Stile** (Preesall, La); **Boggart Stile** (Burtonwood, La); **Boggart Yate** (Hambleton, La); **Buggard Close** (Crich, Db); **Buggart Field** (Pownall Fee, Ch); **Buggart Field** (Wilmslow, Ch); **Little Boggart [Field]** (Sale, Ch); **Nearer Buggards Croft** (Irlam, La) **Boggard Ing Farm** (Huddersfield, WRY).

Heights (3): **Boggart Hill** (Leeds, WRY); **Boggart Hill** (Stalmine, La); **Boggarts Hill** (Prestbury, Ch).

Lanes and Roads (38): **Bogard Lane Close** (Idle, WRY); **Boggard Lane** (Armley, WRY); **Boggard Lane** (Baildon, WRY); **Boggard Lane** (Batley, WRY); **Boggard Lane** (Bramley, WRY); **Boggard Lane** (Cawood, WRY); **Boggard Lane** (Charlesworth, Db); **Boggard Lane** (Gringley, Nt); **Boggard Lane** (Hipperholme, WRY); **Boggard Lane** (Oughtibridge/Worrall, WRY); **Boggard Lane** (Penistone, WRY); **Boggard Lane** (Pudsey, WRY); **Boggard Lane** (Shelley, WRY); **Boggard Lane** (Yeadon/Guiseley WRY); **Boggart Footpath** (Timperley, La); **Boggart Lane** (Blackshaw Head, WRY); **Boggart Lane** (Bradford, WRY); **Boggart Lane** (Bulwell, Nt); **Boggart Lane** (Didsbury, La); **Boggart Lane** (Droylsden/Audenshaw, La); **Boggart Lane** (Eccleston, La); **Boggart Lane** (Emley, WRY); **Boggart Lane** (Hadfield, Db); **Boggart Lane** (Hellifield, WRY); **Boggart Lane** (Leigh, La); **Boggart Lane** (Mytholmroyd, WRY); **Boggard Lane** (Ogden, La); **Boggart's Lane** (Pilling, La); **Boggart Lane** (Rochdale, La); **Boggart Lane** (Roxby, Li); **Boggart Lane** (Sale, Ch); **Boggart Lane (**Skelmanthorpe, WRY); **Boggart Lane** (Sowerby Bridge, WRY); **Boggart Lane** (Ulleskelf, WRY); **Boggart Lane** (Whiston, La); **Boggart Lane** (Wilberlee, WRY); **Boggart Road** (Hayfield, Db); **Boggart Walks** (Whalley, La).

Rivers, Streams, Wells: **Bogart Brook** (Whitegate, Ch); **Boggart Pit** (Poulton, La); **Boggard Well** (Northowram, WRY); **Boggart's Grave** (Ogden, WRY).

III) Boggart Place-names by County

Here the boggart placenames are broken down by county: Lancashire 79; West Riding 65; Derbyshire 16; Cheshire 13, Lincolnshire 3; Nottinghamshire 3; East Riding 2

Cheshire (13): **Boggart Field** (Ashton upon Mersey, Ch); **Boggart House** (Bollin Fee, Ch); **Boggard House** (Bredbury, Ch); **Boggart Mill** (Dinting Vale, Ch); **Boggart House** (Kettleshulme, Ch); **Boggart Wood** (Nether Alderley, Ch); **Buggart Field** (Pownall Fee, Ch); **Boggarts Hill** (Prestbury, Ch); **Little Boggart and Big [Field]** (Sale, Ch); **Boggart Lane** (Sale, Ch); **Bogart Brook** (Whitegate, Ch); **Buggart Field** (Wilmslow, Ch).

Derbyshire (16): **Boggard Lane** (Charlesworth, Db); **Boggart House** (Chesterfield, Db); **Buggard Close** (Crich, Db); **Boggart House** (Cromford, De); **Boggard Houses** (Greasley, Db); **Boggart Lane** (Hadfield, Db); **Boggart Road** (Hayfield, Db); **Boggart House** (Hayfield, Db); **Boggard Town** (Heanor, Db); **Boggard Houses** (Horsley, Db); **Boggart House** (Kilburn, Db); **Boggart House** (Matlock, Db); **Boggard Hole** (Peak Forest, Db); **Boggart Hole** (Mellor Moor, Db); **Boggart Close** (Snelston, Db); **Boggart's Inn Farm** (Wirksworth, Db); **Boggart Mine** (Wirksworth, Db).

East Riding (2) **Boggard Cottage** (Holme upon Spalding Moor, ERY); **Boggart Holes** (Metham, ERY).

Lancashire (79): **Boggart House**; (Audenshaw, La); **Boggart Hall** (Aughton/Bickerstaffe, La); **Boggart Farm** (Barton, La); **Boggart Barn** (Blackburn, La); **Boggart Field** (Blackley, La); **Boggart Hole Clough** (Blackley, La); **Boggart Hole** (Bolton, La); **Boggart House** (Broughton, La); **Boggart Bridge** (Burnley, La); **Boggart Mill** (Burnley, La); **Boggart Field** (Burtonwood, La); **Boggart House** (Burtonwood, La); **Boggart Stile** (Burtonwood, La); **Boggart House**(Carnforth, La); **Boggart Barn** (Chaigley, La); **Boggart Hole** (Clitheroe, La); **Boggart Chair** (Colne, La); **Boggart Cote** (Crawshawbooth, La); **Boggart Old Clough** (Cronton, La); **Boggart House** (Dalton, La); **Boggart Bridge** (Dendron, La); **Boggart Lane** (Didsbury, La); **Boggart Lane** (Droylsden/Audenshaw, La); **Boggart Lane** (Eccleston, La); **Boggard Hole** (Fence, La); **Boggart House** (Galgate, La); **Boggart Croft** (Goosnargh, La); **Boggart Hole** (Goosnargh, La); **Boggart Platt** (Goosnargh, La); **Boggart House** (Gorton, La); **Boggart Cave, The** (Great Eccleston, La); **Boggart Yate** (Hambleton, La); **Boggart House** (Helmshore, La); **Boggart Holes** (Higher Blackley, La); **Boggart House** (Hindley, La); **Boggart Wood** (Hollingworth, La); **Boggart Hall** (Hurlston, La); **Nearer Buggards Croft** (Irlam, La); **Boggart House** (Kirkham, La); **Boggart House** (Lees, La); **Boggart Lane** (Leigh, La); **Boggart Hole** (Littleborough, La); **Boggart Corner** (Longridge, La); **Boggart Clough** (Lumb, La); **Boggart Pit** (Manchester, La); **Boggart Heawse** (Middleton, La); **Boggart Hole** (Newsham, La); **Boggart House Farm** (Newsham, La); **Boggard Lane** (Ogden, La); **Boggard Hole** (Oldham, La); **Boggart House Farm** (Out Rawcliffe, La); **Boggart's Lane** (Pilling, La); **Boggart Pit** (Poulton, La); **Boggart's Wood** (Poulton, La); **Boggart Stile** (Preesall, La); **Boggart Barn** (Preston, La); **Boggart Holes** (Ribchester, La); **Boggart Lane** (Rochdale, La); **Boggart Old Clough**

(Rochdale, La); **Boggart House** (Rufford, La); **Boggart's Clough** (Sabden, La); **Boggart House** (Skelmersdale, La); **Boggart Land** (Skelmersdale, La); **Boggart Hole** (Stacksteads, La); **Boggart Hill** (Stalmine, La); **Buggard House, The** (Stretford, La); **Boggart Footpath** (Timperley, La); **Boggart Pits** (Treales, La). **Buggart House** (Walton on the Hill, La); **Boggart House** (Wardle, La); **Boggard House** (Warton in Fylde, La); **Boggart House** (West Derby, La); **Boggart House** (Westhoughton/Hindley, La); **Boggart House** (Whalley, La); **Boggart Walks** (Whalley, La); **Boggart Lane** (Whiston, La); **Boggart House** (Wigan, La); **Boggart House** (Winwick, La); **Boggart House** (Wrightington, La).

Lincolnshire (3): **Boggard Hall** (Burringham, Li) **Boggart Lane** (Roxby, Li); **Boggart's Green** (Winteringham, Li).

Notts (3): **Boggart Lane** (Bulwell, Nt); **Boggard Lane** (Gringley, Nt); **Boggart House** (Strelley, Nt).

West Riding (65): **Boggart Wood** (Allerton, WRY); **Little Boggard House, The** (Ardsley, WRY); **Boggard Lane** (Armley, WRY); **Boggard Lane** (Baildon, WRY); **Boggard Lane** (Batley, WRY); **Boggard Pit** (Batley, WRY); **Boggart Lane** (Blackshaw Head, WRY); **Boggart Lane** (Bradford, WRY); **Boggard Lane** (Bramley, WRY); **Boggard Closes** (Broughton, WRY); **Boggard Lane** (Cawood, WRY); **Boggart Holes** (Chapel-le-Dale, WRY); **Boggart Holes** (Clapham, WRY); **Boggart House** (Cleckheaton, WRY); **Boggart House** (Cromwell Bottom, WRY); **Boggard House** (Darfield, WRY); **Boggart Church** (Dent, WRY); **Boggard Wood** (Dodworth, WRY); **Boggard Farm** (East Bierley, WRY); **Boggard Field** (Elland, WRY); **Boggart Lane** (Emley, WRY); **Boggard House** (Esholt, WRY); **Boggard Field** (Gisburn, WRY); **Boggard House** (Grassington, WRY); **Boggard Close** (Great Horton, WRY); **Boggart Hole** (Greetland, WRY); **Boggard House** (Halifax, WRY); **Boggart Lane** (Hellifield, WRY); **Boggard Lane** (Hipperholme, WRY); **Boggard Wood**† (Horsforth, WRY); **Boggart Colliery** (Howden Clough, WRY); **Boggart Fields** (Howden Clough, WRY); **Boggart House** (Howden Clough, WRY); **Boggard Ing Farm** (Huddersfield, WRY); **Old Bogard, The** (Huddersfield, WRY); **Bogard Lane Close** (Idle, WRY); **Boggard Wood** (Ilkley, WRY); **Boggart Lathe** (Keighley, WRY); **Boggart Closes** (Leeds, WRY); **Boggart Hill** (Leeds, WRY); **Old Boggard House** (Leeds, WRY); **Boggard House** (Midgley, WRY); **Boggart Lane** (Mytholmroyd, WRY); **Bogard Close**

(Nether Soothill, WRY); **Boggard Close** (Netherthong, WRY); **Bogard Hole Close** (North Bierley, WRY); **Boggard Well** (Northowram, WRY); **Boggard Lane** (Penistone, WRY); **Boggart's Grave** (Ogden, WRY); **Boggart Bridge** (Ogden, WRY); **Boggard Lane** (Oughtibridge/Worrall, WRY); **Boggard Bridge** (Ovenden, WRY); **Boggard Lane** (Pudsey, WRY); **Boggart Stones** (Saddleworth, WRY); **Boggart Bridge** (Selby, WRY); Boggart Oak (Selby, WRY); **Boggard Lane** (Shelley, WRY); **Boggart Lane** (Skelmanthorpe, WRY); **Boggard Hole** (Skipton, WRY); **Boggart Lane** (Sowerby Bridge, WRY); **Boggart Lane** (Ulleskelf, WRY); **Boggard Wood** (Wakefield, WRY); **Boggart House Farm** (Wetherby, WRY); **Higher and Lower Boggart Stones** (Widdop, WRY); **Boggart's Barn** (Wigglesworth, WRY); **Boggart Lane** (Wilberlee, WRY); **Boggard Lane** (Yeadon/Guiseley WRY).

IV) Boggart Proper Names

Prior to the twentieth century there were many 'public bogies': spirits known and talked about by entire communities. For example, parts of Preston were haunted by a headless woman who sometimes turned into a headless dog. This boggart was known as 'Bannister Hall Doll'. Around Windermere Lake there walked the spirit of a dead monk, called the 'Crier of Claife', a terrifying creature who was heard more often than seen. At Lowther in Westmorland a bogie rode in a coach through the countryside. He skinned horses, and was eventually laid by the local clergy. The folk near Lowther referred to this monster as 'the Auld Lord'. All three names – 'Bannister Hall Doll', 'the Crier of Claife', and 'the Auld Lord' – are examples of supernatural personal names. I have gathered together here all examples (known to me) of personal names which included the word 'boggart' from before the Great War.

Accrington (La, Dunkenhalgh Boggart): Aker-Whitt, 'The Dunkenhalgh Boggart'.
Alton (De, Barberry Gutter Boggart): Wigfull, 'Alton'.
Ashton-on-Mersey (La, Dumber Boggert): Sweeney, *Dumber Boggart*.
Austwick (WRY, Boggart of Cave Ha): Hughes 'Acoustic Vases', 81–82.
Bamford (De, Lumb Boggart): Evans, *Bradwell*, 44–45.
Blackley (La, Boggart of Boggart Hole Clough): Milner, *Country Pleasures*, 263–264.
Blackpool (La, Whitegate-Lane Boggart): 'Superstition in the Fylde' (1857).

Bradford (WRY, Low Well Boggard): Fieldhouse, *Bradford*, 33.
Burnley (La, Back O' Th' Hill Boggart'): McCandlish, 'Back O' Th' Hill Boggart'.
Bury (La, Freetown Boggart): 'The 'Freetown Pie' (1862).
Chapel Le Dale (WRY, Hurtle Pot Boggart): West, *A Guide*, 256.
Clayton (La, Clayton Hall Boggart): Higson, *Droylsden*, 69.
Clitheroe (La, Well Hall Boggart): Clarke, *Clitheroe*, 59 [second run of page-numbers].
East Bierley (WRY, Bierley Boggard): Parker, *Illustrated*, 278.
Eyam (De, Eyam Boggart): 'The Miner and the Ghost' (1887).
Eccleston (La, Copp Boggart): 'The Copp Boggart' (1872).
Fewston (WRY, Bosky Dyke Boggart): Parkinson, *Yorkshire legends*; 131–133.
Flixton (La, Gamershaw Boggart): Crofton, *Stretford*, III, 73–74.
Glossop (De, Bank Hagg Boggart): Fizzwig, 'From Glossop' (1866).
Gorton (La, Nell Parlour Boggart): Higson, *Gorton*, 16.
Hayfield (De, Gorse Bridge Boggart): 'Hayfield' (1869).
Helmshore (La, Green Lane Boggart): H., *Green Lane Boggart*.
Heywood (La, Grislehurst Boggart): Waugh, *Sketches*, 225–228.
Horton (WRY, Horton Boggart): Fieldhouse, *Bradford*, 86–89.
Kidsgrove (Sta, Kidsgrove Boggart): Leese, *Kidsgrove*.
Middleton (La, the Spaw Boggart): 'Spaw Boggart'.
Mowbrick (La, Mowbrick Boggart): Antiquarian 'Boggart Renown'.
Ramsbottom (La, Crowlum Boggart): Elliot, *The country,* 47.
Preesall (La, boggart of Hackensall hall): Thornber, *Blackpool*, 332.
Preston (La, New Hall boggart): 'Death' (1867).
Ribchester (La, Starling Bridge Boggart): 'The Starling Bridge Boggart' (1894).
Rochdale (La, Clegg Ho' Boggart): Harland and Wilkinson, *Legends*, 11–12.
Samlesbury (La, the Boggart of Samlesbury Hall): McKay, *East*, 9.
Wakefield (WRY, Boggard of Longar Hede): Forster, 'Dear Sir'.
Wibsey (WRY, the Wibsey Boggard): Fieldhouse, *Bradford*, 89.
Worsthorne (La, Holden Boggart): Young, 'Holden'.
Wycollar (La, boggart of Wycollar Hall): McKay, *East*, 9.

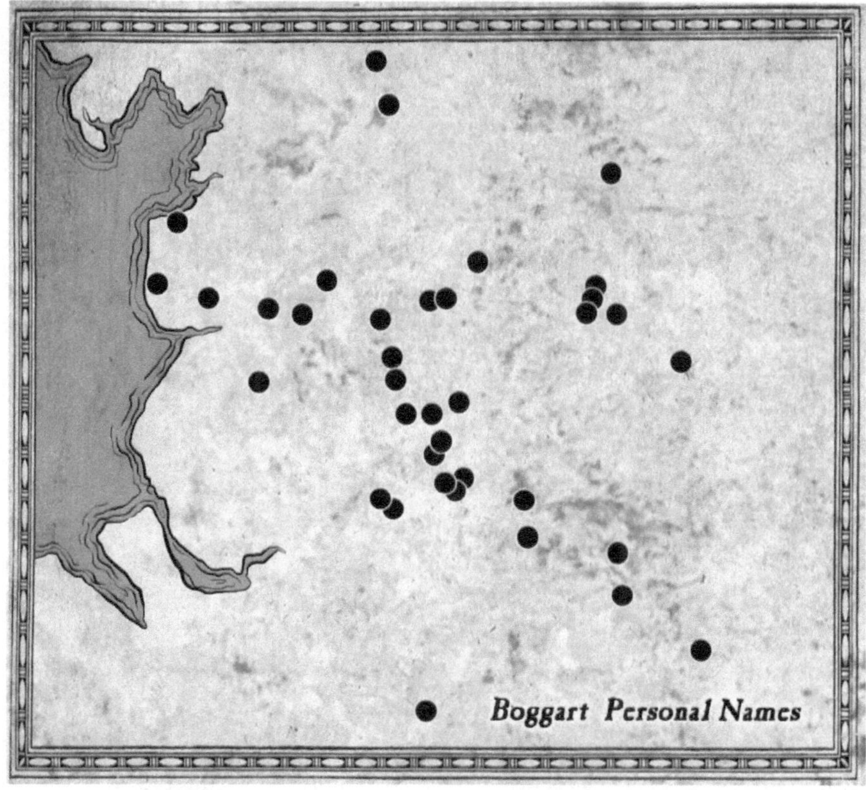

V) Bibliography

'A Determined Housebreaker', *Leeds Intelligencer* (12 Aug 1854), 7

'A Freehold Dairy Farm', *Leeds Mercury* (16 Apr 1904), 2

'A Ghost Story', *Sheffield Independent* (26 Jan 1839), 6

'A Reckless Drunkard', *Lancaster Gazette* (24 Jun 1885), 2

'A tuberculous cow', *Manchester Courier* (5 Dec 1896), 9

'Accidents and Incidents', *Leeds Times* (9 Nov 1878), 5

Ahier, Philip, *The Legends and Traditions of Huddersfield and its District* (Huddersfield: Advertiser, 1940–1945), 2 vols

Aker-Whitt, 'The Dunkenhalgh Boggart', *Blackburn Standard* (21 December 1889), 3

'Alleged Outrage of an Old Woman', *Blackburn Standard* (1 Jul 1893), 7

'An Alleged Dangerous Crossing', *Nottingham Evening Post* (6 Mar 1899), 2

'Another Peep into Dent', *Blackburn Standard* (7 Jun 1890), 2

ANTIQUARIAN, 'Boggart Renown', *Preston Chronicle* (26 Aug 1871), 6

'Anyone Trespassing', *Rochdale Observer* (11 May 1918), 1

'Appointment of paid surveyor', *Huddersfield Chronicle* (1 Apr 1854), 5
'Attempted Pocket Picking', *Bradford Observer* (10 Aug 1843), 5
Baildon, W.P. and F. J. Baildon, *Baildon and the Baildons: A History of a Yorkshire Manor and Family* (Bradford: St Catherine Press: 1912–1927), 3 vols
'Barton Child Suffocated by His Brother', *Preston Herald* (13 Jan 1906), 2
Billingsley, John *Folk Tales from Calderdale: Place legends and lore from the Calder Valley* (Mytholmroyd: Northern Earth, 2007)
Billingsley, John *West Yorkshire Folk Tales* (Stroud: History Press, 2010)
'Blackburn County Court', *Blackburn Standard* (23 Mar 1864), 3
'Blackshaw Parish Council', *Todmorden Advertiser* (12 Jul 1906), 4
'Board of Surveyors', *Bradford Observer* (18 Apr 1850), 6
'Board of Trade', *Manchester Courier* (21 Nov 1896), 11
Bogg, Edmund *The old kingdom of Elmet: York and the Ainsty district; a descriptive sketch of the history, antiquities, legendary lore, picturesque feature, and rare architecture* (London, J. Heywood: 1902)
'Boggart House Farm', *Preston Chronicle* (1 Nov 1879), 6
'Borough of Bradford', *Bradford Observer* (6 Aug 1835), 2–3
Broadhead, Ivan E. *Portrait of the Yorkshire Ouse* (London: Hale, 1982)
'Building and Sanitary Committee', *Burnley Gazette* (29 Oct 1881), 7
'Burglary', *Sheffield Independent* (6 Sep 1851), 5
Cameron, K. *The Place-Names of Derbyshire* (Cambridge: CUP, 1959), 3 vols
Cameron, K., J. Field and J. Insley, *The Place-Names of Lincolnshire* (Cambridge: CUP, 1985–2010), 7 vols
Cavill, Paul *A New Dictionary of English Field-Names* (Nottingham: English Place-Name Society, 2018)
Clarke, David *Supernatural Peak District* (London: Robert Hale, 2000)
Collyer, R., and J.H. Turner, *Ilkley Ancient and Modern* (Otley: William Walker, 1885)
Cookson, R. *Goosnargh, Past and Present* (Preston: H. Oakey, 1888)
Crofton, H.T. *A History of the Ancient Chapel of Stretford in Manchester Parish* (Manchester: Chetham Society, 1899–1903), 3 vols
Crossley, James (ed.), *Potts' Discovery of Witches In the County of Lancaster* (Manchester: Chetham Society, 1845)
Cudworth, William *Rambles Round Horton: Historical, Topographical and Descriptive* (Bradford: T. Brear and Co, 1886)
'Death of Mr John Gornall', *Preston Chronicle* (16 Mar 1867), 5
'Deaths', *Derbyshire Times* (10 Feb 1894), 5
'Desperate Attempt at Suicide', *Todmorden Advertiser* (16 Aug 1907), 2
Dickinson, Joseph 'Appendix: The Flora of Liverpool' [separate pagination],

Proceedings of the Literary and Philosophical Society of Liverpool 6 (1849–1851), 1–166

'Died', *Manchester Courier* (8 Nov 1828), 3

'District news: Colne', *Burnley Advertiser* (10 Aug 1878), 8

Ditchfield, P.H. 'Lancashire Legends', Henry Fishwick and P.H. Ditchfield, *Memorials of old Lancashire* (London: Bemrose, 1909), 2 vols, I, 90–106

Dodgson, J.McN., *The Place-Names of Cheshire*, 7 vols (Cambridge: CUP, 1970–1997)

E.G.B., '"Battletwig", "Landlady", "Boggart"', *Notes and Queries* 8 (1895), 85, https://doi.org/10.1093/nq/s8-VIII.188.85d

Elliot, William Hume *The country and church of the Cheeryble brothers* (Selkirk: G.Lewis and Son, 1893)

'Estate in Thornton', *Leeds Mercury* (24 Jul 1841), 2

Evans, Seth *Bradwell, ancient and modern: history of the parish and incidents in the Hope Valley & District: being collections and recollections in a Peakland village* (Bradwell?: privately printed, 1912)

Falconer, William 'Plant Galls of the Huddersfield District', *The Naturalist* 808 (1924), 151–156

Farey, John *General view of the agriculture and minerals of Derbyshire* (London, 1811–17), 3 vols

'Fatal Colliery Accident at Kilburn', *Derby Telegraph* (22 Dec), 3

'Fatal collision at Darwen', *Blackburn Standard* (2 Nov 1889), 7

'Fatal result of an accident at Darwen', *Lancashire Evening Post* (28 Oct 1889), 3

Field, John *English Field Names: A Dictionary* (Newton Abbot: David and Charles, 1972)

Fieldhouse, Harry *Old Bradford* (Bradford: P. Lund, 1889)

Fizzwig, Oliver 'From Glossop to Disley and Thereabouts', *Glossop Record* (15 Dec 1866), 2–3

Forster, Rev. B. 'Dear Sir', *Illustrations of the Literary History of the Eighteenth Century*, ed. By John Nichols (London: Nichols and Son, 1817–31), 6 vols, V, 308-309

Fowler, J. T. Canon 'Winterton Old Streets' Names', *Hull Daily Mail* (18 Aug 1920), 6

'Ghost Story', *Lancaster Gazette* (25 Jan 1851), 5

Griffiths, J.S. and C.J. Martin, *Engineering Geology and Geomorphology of Glaciated and Periglaciated* (London: Geological Society, 2017)

Gringley', *Stamford Mercury* (4 Aug 1854), 2

H. *Lines on the Green Lane Boggert* (Np: Np., Nd)

Haley, Russell *Real Illusions* (New York: New Directions, 1981)

'Happy Old Age', *Yorkshire Evening Post* (12 Dec 1935), 12

Hardcastle, C.D. 'The story that the...', *Leeds Mercury* (21 Mar 1891), 24

Harland, John and Thomas Turner Wilkinson, *Lancashire Legends, Traditions, Pageants, Sports &c* (London: George Routledge and Sons, 1873)

'Hayfield', *Glossop-dale Chronicle* (4 Dec 1869), 3

Heathcote, C., 'A History and Gazetteer of the Mines in the Liberty of Peak Forest, Derbyshire: 1605–1878', *Mining History* 14 (2001), 1-28

Higson, John 'Boggarts and Feorin', *Notes and Queries* 4 (1869, 4th), 508–509, https://doi.org/10.1093/nq/s4-IV.102.508

Higson, John *Historical and Descriptive Notices of Droylsden: Past and Present* (Manchester: Beresford & Souther, 1859)

Higson, John *The Gorton Historical Recorder* (Droylsden: privately printed, 1852?)

Holden, James Edmund 'The Lincoln Mark', *The Chautauquan* 45 (1906), 352–357

Holden, James Edmund 'The Lincoln Mark', The Chautauquan: Organ of the Chautauqua Literary and Scientific Circle (1907), 354–355

Hopkins, R. Thurston *Ghosts Over England* (London: Meridian Books, 1953)

Horsforth', *Yorkshire Evening Post* (25 Jun 1937), 4

Hughes, T. McKenny 'Acoustic Vases in Churches Traced Back to the Theatres and Oracles of Greece', *Cambridge Antiquarian Society* 67 (1915), 63–90

'In parliament...', *Stamford Mercury* (23 Nov 1860), 6

'Ingleton as a summer resort', *Leeds Mercury* (30 Mar 1885), 3

John, 'To the Editor', *Preston Chronicle* (8 Jul 1876), 6

Judd, Denis *Alison Uttley: The Life of a Country Child, 1884–1976: The Authorised Biography* (London: Joseph, 1986)

Kenrick, Eddie 'Tramps in Ribbleland: The Sabden Valley', *Burnley Express* (14 Jun 1930), 10

'Lancashire and Yorkshire Railway', *Bradford Observer* (22 Nov 1860), 7

'Latest Freak', *Todmorden and District News* (12 Jul 1907), 5

Lawson, Joseph *Letters to the young on progress in Pudsey during the last sixty years* (Stanningley: J.W. Lawson, 1887)

'Leese, Philip R. *The Kidsgrove Boggart and the Black Dog* (Stafford: Staffordshire Libraries, 1989)

'Local Law Case', *Manchester Courier* (11 Mar), 8

Longbotham, A.T. 'Lambert House, Elland', *Halifax Antiquarian Society* 33 (1933), 48–70c

MacKenzie, Robert Dunbar *Kilbarchan; a parish history* (Paisley: Kilbarchan, 1902)

Manchester and Southport Railway', *Leeds Intelligencer* (28 Nov 1846), 3

McKay, James *The Evolution of East Lancashire Boggarts* (Digitally published 2016 [1888]), https://www.academia.edu/28026366/McKay_The_Evolution_of_East_Lancashire_Boggarts

'Melancholy Suicide', *Preston Chronicle* (10 Jun 1848), 4

'Members Talk', *Shipley Times* (9 Oct 1957), 3

'Memorial to E. Potter Esq.', *Hyde and Glossop Weekly News* (13 Dec 1873), 4

'Mence or Mense Family', *Notes and Queries 8* (1859, 2nd), 117, https://doi.org/10.1093/nq/s2-VIII.188.117c

Milner, George *Country Pleasures: The Chronicle of a Year Chiefly in a Garden* (Boston: Robert Brothers 1881)

Minet, William *Hadham Hall and the manor of Bawdes alias Hadham Parva in the county of Hertfordshire* (NP: 1914)

Moore, Nick *A History of Blackpool, the Fylde, and South Wyre* (NP: 2019)

'Moorfield Gardens', *Manchester Courier* (30 Jun 1877), 8

Moss, Fletcher *Folk-lore, old customs and tales of my neighbours* (Didsbury: privately printed, 1898)

'Mysterious Death of a Child', *Manchester Courier* (26 Feb 1887), 14

Newman, L.F. and E.M. Wilson, 'Folklore Survivals in the Southern 'Lake Counties' and in Essex: A Comparison and Contrast', *Folklore* 63 (1952), 91–104, https://doi.org/10.1080/0015587X.1952.9718106

Newstead, G. Coulthard *Gleanings towards the annals of Aughton, near Ormskirk* (Liverpool: C. & H. Ratcliffe, 1893)

Nomination of guardians', *Burnley Advertiser* (29 Mar 1879), 8

'Northern hunts', *Lancashire Evening Post* (19 Nov 1906), 19

'Notes and Comments', *Rochdale Observer* (5 Feb 1941), 2

'Notice is Hereby Given', *Sheffield Daily Telegraph* (22 Nov), 1

'On Sale', *Rochdale Observer* (27 Mar 1915), 3

Parker, James *Illustrated Rambles from Hipperholme to Tong* (Bradford: Lund, 1904)

Parkinson, Thomas *Yorkshire Legends and Traditions* (London: E. Stock 1888)

Peacock, Mabel 'The Horse in Relation to Water-Lore', *Antiquary* 33 (1897), 72–76

'Playing Pitch and Toss', *Bolton Evening News* (10 Sep 1903), 3

'Pollution of the Ribble', *Manchester Courier* (9 Jul 1880), 8

'Preston Golden Weddings', *Lancashire Evening Press* (27 Dec 1939), 5

Price, William Frederick 'Notes on Some of the Places, Traditions, and Folk-Lore of the Douglas Valley', *Transactions of the Historic Society of Lancashire and Cheshire* 51 (1899), 181–220

'Public Meetings of Rate Payers on Municipal Affairs', *Bradford Observer* (7 Dec 1843), 6–7

'Queer Tales: Legends of Ormskirk', *Aberdeen Evening Express* (16 Sep 1910), 4

Rayner, S., *The History and Antiquities of Pudsey* (London: Longmans, Green and Co, 1887)

Redmonds, George *Almondbury: Places and Place-names* (Huddersfield 1983)

Roberts, Kai *The Folklore of Yorkshire* (Stroud: History Press, 2013)

'Round About Bradford', *Bradford Observer* (23 Dec 1875), 7 [William Cudworth, published a year later in book form]

'Sad Death of a Girl', *Derby Mercury* (18 Oct 1893), 3

'Sad Drowning Case at Rochdale', *Manchester Evening News* (3 Aug 1901), 5

'Sale of a Valuable Freehold Estate', *Preston Chronicle*, 28 May 1836, 1

'Sales by auction', *Manchester Courier* (3 Apr 1852), 6

Sandy Banks, 'Sandy Banks's Criticism of Hayfield's Bird's Eye View', *Glossop Record* (4 Nov 1865), 2

'Scotforth township meeting', *Lancaster Gazette* (30 Mar 1889), 7

'Serious accident to a coachman', *Lancaster Gazette* (6 Jun 1891), 5

Silkstone Valley Walks: Silkstone Common to Falthwaite (Barnsley: Barnsley Metropolitan Borough, undated)

Smith, A.H. *The Place-Names of the West Riding of Yorkshire* (Cambridge: CUP, 1961–1963), 8 vols

Speight, Harry *Chronicles and stories of old Bingley. A full account of the history, antiquities, natural productions, scenery, customs and folklore of the ancient town and parish of Bingley, in the West Riding of Yorkshire* (London: Elliot Stock, 1898)

'Stealing eggs', *Burnley Advertiser* (26 Jul 1862), 3

'Superstition in the Fylde: Whitegate-Lane Boggart', *The Preston Chronicle and Lancashire Advertiser* (2 May 1857), 5

Sutcliffe, T. 'A Tour in Midgley', *Halifax Antiquarian Society* 28 (1928), 113–57

Sweeney, P. 'The Dumber Boggert' (Merrin: D. Alexe, ND) [one-page bill]

Taylor, Henry *The Ancient Crosses and Holy Wells of Lancashire* (Manchester: Sherratt and Hughes, 1906)

'Ten Hours Factory Bill', *Poor Man's Guardian* (13 Jun 1835), 4

'The 'Freetown Pie' – Witchcraft Revived', *Bury Times* (6 Dec 1862), 2

'The Bradford Corporation Bill', *Yorkshire Evening Post* (14 May 1901), 6

'The Brutal Murder of a Housemaid Near Lancaster', *Manchester Courier* (18 Jan 1866), 4

'The Copp Boggart', *Preston Chronicle* (21 Dec 1872), 3

'The Ghost of John Parkinson's Farewell', *Preston Chronicle* (29 May 1880), 6

'The Miner and the Ghost', *Nottinghamshire Guardian* (31 Dec 1887), 8

'The Roman roads of Lancashire', *Manchester Courier* (19 Oct 1850), 5

'The Spaw "Boggart"', *Bolton Chronicle* (19 Jan 1839), 3
'The Spital Estate', *Derbyshire Times and Chesterfield Herald* (4 Jun 1932), 3
'The Starling Bridge Boggart', *Blackburn Standard* (2 Jun 1894), 3
Thornber, William *The History of Blackpool and its Neighbourhood* (Nelson: 1985, Galava [reprint of the 1837 original])
'To Be Lett', *Leeds Intelligencer* (25 Jan 1796), 1
'To Be Sold by Auction', *Chester Courant* (4 Apr 1797), 3
'To brick makers', *Leeds Intelligencer* (13 Feb 1787), 1
'To the Editor of the Bradford Observer', *Bradford Observer* (1 Jun 1837), 7
Turner, John Horsfall 'Fragments of Local History: No 10, Place Names', *Brighouse News* (Apr 1869) [undated clipping without page or number, recorded http://www.yorkshireindexers.info/wiki/index.php?title=Brighouse_Place_Names, accessed 8 Jan 2020]
'Ulleskelf (Near Tadcaster)', *Yorkshire Gazette* (19 Oct 1844), 1
Uttley, Alison *Ambush of Young Days* (London: Faber and Faber, 1951)
'Valuable Freehold Estates', *Bradford Observer* (21 Apr 1870), 2
'Valuable freehold farms', *Leeds Mercury* (4 Jun 1825), 1
Wainwright, F.T. 'Field names of Amounderness Hundred', *Transactions of the Historic Society of Lancashire and Cheshire* 97 (1946), 71–116
Waugh, Edwin *Sketches of Lancashire life and localities* (London: Whittaker, 1855)
Wesleyan Missionary Society', *North Devon Journal* (14 May 1863), 5
West, Thomas *A Guide to the Lakes* (Kendal: William Pennington, 1812 [1778])
Wigfull, Chas. S. 'Alton Addenda', *Derbyshire Advertiser* (6 May 1927), 31
'Woodman House Estate', *Leeds Mercury* (24 Feb), 4
'Wrightington Cycle Tragedy', *Lancashire Evening Post* (25 Feb 1941), 5
'Yorkshire freehold estates', *Leeds Intelligencer* (16 May 1805), 4
Young, Simon 'Boggart Hole Clough: Sources, Publics and Bogies', *Transactions of the Antiquarian Society for Lancashire and Cheshire* 109 (2013), 115–144
Young, Simon 'In Search of Holden Rag', *Retrospective* 35 (2017), 3–10

Corpus Three: Boggart Census

Preface

In March 2019, Dr Lynda Taylor interviewed, on my behalf, her father-in-law, Arthur, about his boggart memories. Arthur, born 1926, had some remarkable recollections. I found it extraordinary that these ideas were still alive in the twenty-first century, fifty or sixty years after I thought they had died out. I had at the same time been reading, with my students, *Chewing the Fat: An Oral History of Italian Foodways from Fascism to Dolce Vita* by Karima Moyer-Nocchi, which collects memories as a way of recording and writing food history. Inspired by Arthur and Moyer-Nocchi, I decided to gather boggart memories to help with my work on Victorian boggart folklore. Between July 2019, when I launched my survey in *Fortean Times*, and late October 2019, when I stopped the survey, I sought out boggart memories from boggartdom: the territories that the boggart once haunted. I managed to gather in about eleven hundred, which are listed here by area. These memories include around 400 negative memories. For me, at least, negatives are quite important in determining where and when boggart beliefs died out. I asked for memories for those born prior to about 1970; when offered I included later memories, too.

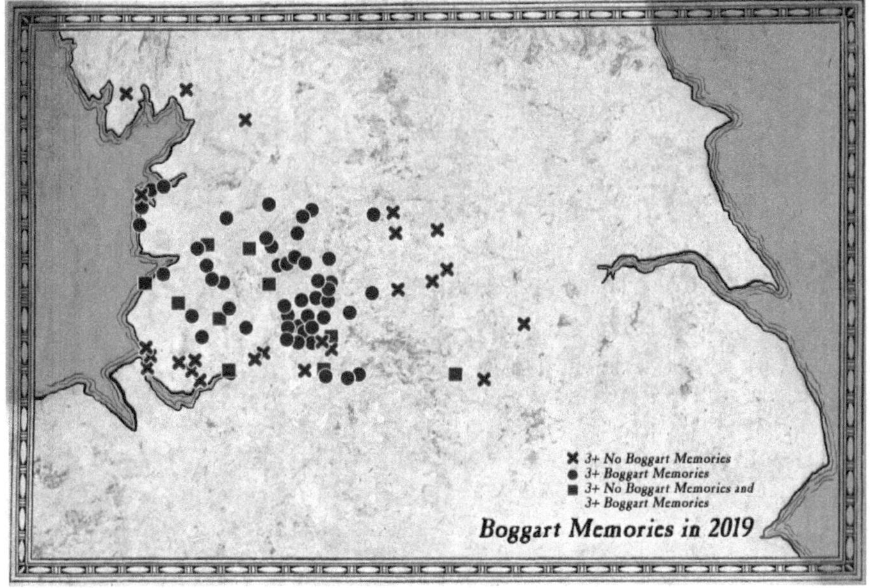

Each entry has the decade in which the person was born (when I was able to determine it), their sex and the source of information (C = 'chat' i.e. an interview; E = email; F = Facebook; FG = Facebook Group; FGH = Facebook Group via Holly Elsdon, a contact in the Calder Valley; FM = Facebook Messenger). I had very little knowledge of Facebook before the project began; I hope to write more on its potential in folklore collection at a later date. I have numbered entries by community, usually in the order in which I gathered in the information. I did this so that I could easily, over the next years, add further entries. If you have boggart memories please send them in even if you are reading this in 2050 (I'm, in every sense, an optimist): simonyoungfl AT gmail DOT com.

Editing conventions

I have corrected misspellings: e.g. 'acording' was changed to 'according'. I have respected, though, the individual spellings of supernatural creatures. I have altered punctuation for the sake of clarity, including brackets. I have not changed the language or grammar even when a sentence was clearly wrong, save for apostrophes. I use [square brackets] to insert information or to introduce words to make accounts clearer. I have written out all numbers save for dates (e.g. '6' became 'six'), and I expand abbreviations (e.g. 'approx.' becomes 'approximately'). I gave up on 'emoticons' because they were not easy to transfer into MS Word; I have mixed feelings about this as I discovered that they offer an impressive metalanguage of their own. I only very rarely cut respondents' text. Even when not writing about boggarts, folklore matters often come up and these may be of interest to readers. I have put house and personal names as 'XXX'.

I am in the debt of several editors, journalists and eleven hundred contributors. I would like to particularly thank by name eight people who went far beyond the call of duty. I'm incredibly grateful to: Holly Elsdon (Calder Valley), Lucy Evans (Leeds), Georgina Ormrod (Burnley), David Pattern (Kirklees), Ray Sutcliffe (Littleborough), Lynda Taylor (Greater Manchester), Stephen and Anne Young (Lancaster).

Lancashire

Accrington 1 (La). 1950s/M/E., 4-9-19. 'When I was a child, I thought a boggart (or bogey-man) was a small, ugly, scary goblin which lived in a hole in the ground and came out to kidnap naughty children at night as a punishment for not doing what they were told. My parents used the word "bogey-man" more than "boggart", as a threat, as in "The bogey-man knows what you're doing and will come and take you away if you don't behave yourself." I only remember one grandparent but can't remember her ever threatening me in any way. I've not heard my children or other younger members of the family use the word "boggart" or "bogey-man", even though I know I occasionally used the same threat with my children as my parents did with me. Forty-odd years ago when I was in my early twenties, I used to live very close to Boggart Hole Clough in Blackley (suburb of Manchester) and worked at the children's hospital opposite the clough. Local children seemed very aware of the malicious nature of the boggarts who, according to the folklore, lived there so they tended to stay away from the clough when it was dark, if they had any sense. I suppose that parents would warn children off going there in the dark not because of any belief in boggarts, but because of the risk to children of getting lost and/or hurt due to the waterways, steep slopes, dark woods and deep undergrowth. We moved away from the area before my eldest child was old enough to play outside on her own, but I too would probably have used the folklore to scare her away if she had been older! I don't recall any particular incidents in or around the Clough being attributed to boggarts during the time I lived/worked there. I grew up in Lancashire in the late 1950s/1960s.'

Accrington 2 (La). 1950s/M/F., 11-9-19. 'We had boggarts in Accy in Lancs. So my dad said if owt went wrong.'

Accrington 3 (La). 1970s/M/E., 14-10-19. 'I've just finished a book myself about the paranormal in Lancashire, and I included a short section on Boggarts. The term "Boggart" is something I grew up with and my granddad used to tell me tales of a Boggart who lived under the canal bridge at Church near Accrington. I suspect he was trying to keep me away from playing near the canal when I was an unruly child! This was in the 1970s. Funny you should ask that [was it Jenny Greenteeth], because that's exactly the name he gave it! [Jenny Greenteeth: extract from the book] The Leeds to Liverpool canal winds its way through the Lancashire countryside connecting the port of Liverpool in the west, to the urban conurbations of Manchester and Leeds in the east. Once a thriving thoroughfare of trade, the working canal boats have long gone to be replaced by pleasure craft and residential narrow boats. My maternal great grandfather worked the canal barges at the turn of the twentieth century, and my grandfather Bill told me that as a child he was deterred from playing near to the canal with warnings a Boggart called "Ginny Greenteeth" who lurked under the swing bridge at Church. Shaped like a horseshoe, the canal basin at Church was a loading and unloading point for coal and finished cotton for the local weaving mills. Deeper than the canal at either side, it was said that if you fell in the weeds along the bottom would reach up and entangle your legs, pulling you down and drowning you in a few minutes. Worse still, Ginny Greenteeth would wait under the swing bridge and pull children down to a watery grave. My grandfather said as children they were genuinely frightened of the tale. No local child went swimming in the canal, or skated on it during the coldest winters. If you did, Greenteeth would 'ave you! As a somewhat rebellious child, I often played near the canal and on the swing bridge, much to the annoyance of my grandparents, peering over the wooden railing to see if I could catch a glimpse of the evil Boggart, but I never did!'

Accrington 4 (La). 1940s/M/FG., 14-10-19. 'Growing up, I never heard the word "boggarts" until I started to read Lancashire folklore which has lots of mentions of it. In his famous poem "Come Hooam to thi Childer an' me". Edwin Waugh wrote in one verse "Hes t'boggarts ta'en owd o' mi dad?" who has a major drink problem. The word appears in several dialect dictionaries – see WRIGHT *English Dialect Dictionary*, which will give instances where it appears in several counties. I grew up in the 1940s and 50s.'

Accrington 5 (La). 1960s/M/FG., 14-10-19. 'I grew up in Accy born 1961 and was led to believe that boggarts lived near canal bridges, a bit like trolls... lol.'

Accrington 6 (La). ???/M/FG., 14-10-19. 'My dad said boggarts did it when string always got knotted, jerseys all inside out, also newspapers stuck together. Bet you've had that Boggarts!'

Accrington 7 (La). 1960s/M/FG., 15-10-19. 'I was a child in the 1960s, early 1970s, and grandma/mum used to say "the Bogeyman will get you," if you stayed out late. Don't know if that was a shortened version of the same thing, but they both came from Yorkshire?'

Accrington 8 (La). 1950s/F/FG., 15-10-19. 'Born in Accrington in the 1950s and lived there for fourteen years, then Oswaldtwistle. Never heard the word – any memories? [Other FB user responds: it may be a false memory but did mum once describe Jinny Greenteeth who lived down Antley back as a boggart? Certainly references to a boggart in the Lancashire Legends book]. I remember Jinny Greenteeth but not the boggart bit.'

Accrington 9 (La). ???/F/FG., 16-10-19. 'According to my mam, there were boggarts on the bottom rec that came out when it was getting dark (I'm sure it was true but never hung around to find out). I know and Jenny greenteeth in the canal who grabbed kids who got too near the water… It's a bloody wonder we left the doorstep!'

Accrington 10 (La). 1960s/F/FG., 16-10-19. 'Apparently my Grandma used this term on an Aunt, who she didn't like very much, and when she came up to visit, my Grandma would say "uh boggart's back". [Age estimated from FB page].

Accrington 11 (La). 1960s/M/FG., 15-10-19. 'I'm familiar with the word "boggart" and remembering hearing some older Accringtonians use it when I was growing up. But it was certainly a rare word. I was born in 1962. My mother, who grew up in Clitheroe in the 1930s and 1940s, used to recall a story of when she and her friends dressed as ghosts and a neighbour exclaimed: "Eeeeh boggarts!"'

Accrington 12 (La). 1950s/F/FG., 15-10-19. 'I was born in Accrington in the early 1950s, I know the term Jinny Greenteeth referring to the green pond weed on top of lodge water (the water that served mills) and was always told to keep away or she'd get you. Suppose it was sensible, kept you away from the water! Know the Bogeyman too. I have heard of the boggart but not sure where from as I now live near Wigan and think I've heard it over here. [Other adds: yup Jinny was a water resident. Antler back [?] where I was told she lived was right next to one of the lodges].'

Accrington 13 (La). 1940s/F/FG., 15-10-19. 'Born in the 1940s. Only heard of t' Bogiemen, mum said we had one in the cupboard under the attic stairs and I wasn't to go in there!'

Accrington 14 (La). ???/M/FG., 17-10-19. '"Johnny Dark" lived, in some families, understairs cupboards when I was a lad [no boggarts]. I don't know... I must have been a good lad so I never got the opportunity to spend time in the dark cupboard for a chat with him. The only Boggarts I have heard about are the original miners of the Sabden Treacle Mines. But that's another story...'
Adlington 1 (La). ???/F/F., 6/9. 'We never went near the canal lived in Adlington, but ginny green teeth would drag us in. It was grandma that used to tell us "Boggerts". Don't stay out in the dark or they would take us. Another one was Jonny Cobler. He used of come round Adlington selling firewood pushing a little truck. If we didn't do as we were told he would take us. [On Jenny] Slimey green on top of water.'
Anfield 1 (La). ???/F/FG., 15-10-19. 'Born in Kirkdale, grew up in Anfield, it was always the Bogeyman. Never took the same form but was always large and black.'
Ashton-in-Makerfield 1 (La). 1900s/F/FG., 18-10-19. 'My grandmother – born 1903 in Ashton in Makerfield used to threaten to turn into a boggart and go up through the hessoil (the gap under the fireplace) and come back to haunt us!... Left school at fourteen and her first job was as a sugar boiler in the Santus sweet factory where her father was the manager. He was a founder member of the NUM on the Lancashire coalfield and a very active local politician. She lost two younger brothers to diphtheria and used to tell me about living through the General Strike of 1926 when married to a miner they lived on 6d (2.5p) per day!'
Ashton-On-Mersey 1 (La). 1950s/M/FG., 26-9-19. 'I grew up in Ashton on Mersey and this poem has always been in the family [Dumber Boggart Poem from 19C]. Dumber Lane was an old track to the village at the time. We thought of them as bogeymen. Before any street lighting on a dark winter's night, travelling outdoors down a country lane must have been scary.'
Ashton-Under-Lyne 1 (La). 1960s/F/FG., 21-9-19. 'I grew up in Ashton-under-Lyne. Born in the 1960s. Remember threats of "if you don't behave the boggart'll get you." We lived in a terraced block and the kids played out in the back ginnel where we were convinced there were boggarts hiding in dark corners. A stronger memory is of a neighbour who was a millwright locally. Must have been born in the 1920s. Told stories of milk engines "going boggart" – running out of control and going faster until they broke or worse, caused accidents and major damage.'
Ashton-Under-Lyne 2 (La). 1950s/M/FG., 22-9-19. 'I was born 1952 and lived in Ashton until 1970. The only time I heard the word "boggart" was in reference to "Boggart Hole Clough".'

Ashton-Under-Lyne 3 (La). 1950s/F/FG., 22-9-19. 'I was born in Ashton and definitely heard the word "boggart" as I grew up in the 1950s. I was warned by my grandmother never to go down her cellar steps or the "boggart" would get me. There was also a "boggart" who lived in the Clough. If I was fidgety, my great aunt who lived with us would tell me to sit still "thou art like a boggart". Hope that helps.'

Ashton-Under-Lyne 4 (La). 1960s/F/FG., 22-9-19. 'My grandma was born in Ashton in the 1900s and she used to say to us "he/she is as faus as a boggart", faus meaning false, and the saying used to mean that someone was being nice to you but that they were up to no good. I was born in the late sixties and our family still use it.'

Ashton-Under-Lyne 5 (La). 1960s/M/FG., 22-9-19. 'Don't recall ever hearing the word "Boggart" as a child, but the Boogeyman was someone who all the kids were familiar with in the 1960s/1970s. The threat of the Boogeyman getting us was usually used in regard to places that we shouldn't go or play, but sometimes used as a threat to make us behave or stay put. are these two names for the same thing, I wonder. Yes, born and still living in Ashton.'

Ashton-Under-Lyne 6 (La). 1980s/F/FG., 23-9-19. 'Always thought my dad said "beggart" but maybe he meant "boggart". He said it when I was naughty as a kid, lol. Ashton 1980s.'

Ashton-Under-Lyne 7 (La). 1950s/M/FG., 23-9-19. 'Never heard of it [boggart], lived in Ashton from 1950s till 1970s.'

Ashton-Under-Lyne 8 (La). 1940s/M/FG., 23-9-19. 'Born in Ashton in 1940 and left in 1966 and I have never heard the word "Boggart".'

Aspull 1 (La). 1960s/F/FG., 21-9-19. 'I grew up in Aspull (b. 1964) two miles outside Wigan on the Bolton side, a very localised community rooted in mining and farming but with Irish community too (probably going back to construction of the mines and canal network, Leeds Liverpool canal). The top end of Aspull was known locally as Irishtown in the early twentieth century – the Irish mother of one of my dad's friends famed for smoking a clay pipe. One set of grandparents were from Aspull, the other set from Wigan town (granddad b. 1895 and Marsh Green, granny b. 1898). My Wigan grandparents (name XXX) mentioned boggarts when we were young: it would have been anything from 1964 to 1975 when they chastised us for cheekiness: "tha'r a boggart!" and even "tha'r a marsh boggart!" Once we'd stopped laughing we begged to know what a boggart was, or the difference between ordinary boggarts or marsh boggarts but I don't remember getting a description! But we called each other "boggarts" after then whenever occasion called.'

Aspull 2 (La). ???/F/FG., 15-10-19. 'My grandma used to say the cart horse 'took boggarts' and kicked cart over in her thickest Aspull accent.'

Aspull 3 (La). 1950s/M/FG., 17-10-19. 'Gorses Brook, on the way to Blackrod. I remember in the late 1950s people used to scare you with Gorses Boggert is after you. I lived in Ratcliffe Rd, not far off.'

Aspull 4 (La). ???/F/FG., 17-10-19. 'I was born in Aspull. My family had a farm. We had two shire horses to pull the plough etc. The horses were named Tommy and Dinah. One day Tommy had Boggarts. He was running round the yards my Uncle George Wilkinson trying to grab the reigns. George was shouting to me to get in the house. Finally, both my uncles TM and George got him under control. Whew. Thank Goodness. The farm was XXX Bolton Rd. Aspull. Next to the Running Horses pub.'

Astley 1 (La). 1970s/F/FG., 7-10-19. 'Astley Moss, when I was young we went potato picking. An old farmer told us that boggarts lived in the peat bog trenches that had been cut. From that moment on peat bogs after dark, no thank you.'

Atherton 1 (La). 1950s/M/F., 7-9-19. 'When I was a kid in the 1950s I grabbed hold at the back of a greengrocer's cart pulled by a horse. I was wearing roller skates and the noise of the skates on the cobbles made the horse run away fast or "tek boggarts" as my gran used to say. Meaning as though it had been startled by a boggart. I held on for dear life and nearly hit the factory wall. I describe it in my autobiography *The Thirty Bob Kid*. Sadly I have never heard the phrase used in recent times. I grew up in Atherton. My gran was born in 1881 and she used the term "took boggarts". That was probably the first time I had ever heard it. I don't think Boggarts were discussed as mischievous presences who caused havoc around the house unless you left them a saucer of milk or something. Perhaps we were just lucky in avoiding them!'

Atherton 2 (La). 1930s/M/FG., 5-10-19. 'Word "boggarts" used in our house up to at least the mid-1970s, at least by my dad, but he came from Atherton, in Leigh. The phrase it came in was "it's tekken t'boggarts" i.e. it has gone a bit crazy, and he said my nan used to use the word when the milk-man's horse ran wild and hurtled up the street with bottles flying everywhere. Absolutely not the same as "away with the fairies." Dad also remembered being frightened away from local canals by the story that a creature called Jinny Greenteeth would rise out of the slimy depths and drag you in. Born 1930, moved to Fleetwood from Leigh in the early 1950s, died 2012. My uncle Vincent (his younger brother by several years, who died a couple of years ago), used these dialect words and many more. He never moved from the old family house and his accent was so strong that my husband (a Londoner) found it a challenge to understand him.'

Atherton 3 (La). 1960s/M/FG., 7-10-19. 'I live in Atherton and boggarts was used as a threat to young children if they did not do as was told (was used in my family) and yes there is a place in Manchester called Boggarts Old Clough near Blackley.'

Atherton 4 (La). 1960s/M/FG., 7-10-19. 'Lived in Atherton fifty-five years. Familiar with "bogey man" but never heard of boggart.'

Atherton 5 (La). 1970s/F/FG., 9-10-19. 'My mother said if a horse ran away it had "taken boggerts". Yes, in the 1970s. Born and bred Atherton. I would have known [what a boggart was].'

Audenshaw 1 (La). 1950s/F/FG., 2-10-19. 'I did. My father used to tell us that Jinny Greenteeth, the Boggart of Fairfield Wells would come and get us if we didn't behave. (1950s). [FB user added: My gran used to scare me with someone called Velvet Ellen as well as Jinny Greenteeth.] Fairfield Wells (an apt toponym) is on the border between Audenshaw and Higher Openshaw, Manchester. I should imagine that at one time Fairfield like Audenshaw was a small hamlet. They have merged since and become very urbanised.'

Audenshaw 2 (La). 1960s/F/FG., 2-10-19: 'Born in Audenshaw in the 1960s, know about the bogey man but never heard the word "Boggat" used in our house.'

Audenshaw 3 (La). 1950s/M/FG., 2-10-19. 'Always the "bogey man" will come and get you…, I've never heard the word "boggart". I was born St Anne's Rd Audenshaw, 1950.'

Audenshaw 4 (La). 1950s/M/FG., 2-10-19. 'There was a bogart or ghost that appeared at certain times on the "forty steps" near the Snipe Estate. Yes, it was a widely used term in the 1960s. The story was something about the spirit of a railway workers wife or sweetheart that killed herself forty steps from the bottom of the staircase of "The Steps" that went up the side of the Railway bridge near of the line that ran alongside Aldwyn school next to the Snipe football field. Her ghostly shape was sighted drifting along the footpath over the bridge on the anniversary of her death or when someone was going to die! A more recent one was the bogey man who haunted the Gunpowder Shack on Ashton Moss near the pond next to the Snipe Estate. It was a brick bomb proofed shed used for storing ammunition for a nearby anti-aircraft battery in WW2. Again a ghostly light as a harbinger of doom!'

Audenshaw 5 (La). 1940s/M/FG., 2-10-19. 'Just spoken to my Dad who is in his 80s and was an Audenshaw resident until the 1980s. He says "boggart" is a no for him too.'

Audenshaw 6 (La). 1940s/F/FG., 3-10-19. 'Always bogey man around Lumb Lane, Audenshaw *circa* 1946.'
Audenshaw 7 (La). 1940s/M/FG., 2-10-19. 'I grew up in Audenshaw 1945–1960 and can't ever remember hearing that word.'
Aughton 1 (La). ???/F/FG., 5-10-19. 'I grew up in Aughton near Ormskirk and lived on a farm dating back to the 1600s. Rumour had it that the Aughton Boggart lived in one of our barns… I used to run past it when it was dark! Sadly not the time frame you are looking at. This was the 1980s.'
Aughton 2 (La). 1950s/M/E., 9-10-19. 'I grew up in Aughton during the 1950s. The word [boggart] was fairly well known in those days to us children. Bold Lane, Aughton which originally ran between Prescot Road and Holt Green was, I believe, previously known as Boggart Lane. Today Bold Lane runs between Town Green village to Holt Green. The section between Town Green Village and Prescot Road is now known as Town Green Lane. We were told of the Boggart down Bold Lane as children. In those days Aughton was a truly rural community with few houses and many farms. Walking down Bold Lane in those days especially on a winter's evening with mist everywhere, it was not hard to imagine the Boggart leaping out from behind a hedge. Certainly we were cautioned as children to beware of the Boggart. I think it was a means of making sure we came straight home from school in those days, especially during the winter evenings. Of course everyone walked the mile or so to and from school in those days as there were few cars.'
Bacup 1 (La). 1960s/F/F., 7-9-19. 'I grew up in Bacup, East Lancs which is where my dad was from, too. All I remember is walking in the hills with him and him telling me about boggarts that lived in holes and carried their heads under their arms to frighten folk and anyone who saw one was never seen again. But I always wondered how you could know they had seen one if nobody saw them again! My mum was brought up in a West Yorkshire mining village and one of her sayings was "Off at boggart" to indicate running away fast from something that spooked you.'
Bacup 2 (La). 1930s/M/E., 23-9-19. 'My father Fred was born in Bacup in 1937 (now deceased) and often told us of The Time He Saw The Boggart. It's possible he wrote it down in his memoirs but unfortunately I can't access this right now. He was larking about on the moor with some friends – I guess they were all somewhere between nine and thirteen. They were confronted by what he described as a small man about three or four feet high, dressed in old-fashioned clothes. They all immediately and simultaneously fled in terror, vaulting high hedges in their path, until they were too exhausted to run any further. Decades later he still believed this to have been a boggart and was

quite serious in his recollection of it, like he could still remember how scared they all were by the encounter. Naturally, the rest of us in the family think of it as an amusing tale of our ancestral homeland (our family moved to Penzance in 1984). He did have a few good ghost stories in his repertoire… [subsequent email] I will certainly check the memoirs when I can. One detail I neglected to mention about the Boggart's clothing was that it was tattered.'

Bacup 3 (La). 1980s/M/FG., 17-10-19. 'Yes me. My paternal grandfather used to say 'orrid or dirty Boggart when I was little. He always told me it was a troll who lived up on't moor. Well early 1980s for me. My granddad though was born in 1928. No he was born in Salford, near chimney pot park. He lived in Whitworth for forty years and had a shop in Stacksteads.'

Balladen 1 (La). 1950s/F/FG., 20-9-19. 'Jinny Green teeth lived under the bridge in Balladen village. We were terrified of her. I was born in 1956 and have known about Jinny for as long as I can remember. "Boggart" was a common word then. There was a boggart in every deep dark pool of water.'

Ballam 1 (La). 1950s/F/FG., 27-9-19. 'I lived in Ballam between Blackpool, Lytham and Wrea Green. Yes, I remember hearing boggarts mentioned in early 1950s.'

Bamber Bridge 1 (La). 1960s/F/FG., 28-9-19. 'Mum used to tell us to be careful boggarts don't get you. Never know what she meant though we lived in Bamber Bridge. [Aged guessed from Facebook page]'

Bamber Bridge 2 (La). 1950s/F/FG., 3-10-19. 'As a brownie in Bamber Bridge we sat in a circle to keep the "boggarts" out. Early 1960s. And I remember "granny" green teeth too.'

Banks 1 (La). 1950s/F/FG., 29-9-19. 'Born 1951, lived in Banks up to 1971. Heard the word "Boggart" as a deterrent for us children to not stray too far. Didn't work!'

Banks 2 (La). 1940s/F/FG., 29-9-19. 'My Mum still uses that word saying "the boggarts will get you" if you go out in the dark. She is eighty-three.'

Banks 3 (La). 1940s/M/FG., 29-9-19. 'I lived in Banks in the 1940/1950s and the word [boggart] was used by my gran to frighten us, to keep us from [the] wandering creature from the swamps or marshes.'

Banks 4 (La). 1960s/F/FG., 30-9-19. 'In Banks we heard the old folk talk in dialect about Sand Bowers, sand bears on the beach at Southport and Moss Boggarts, false apparitions or imaginative scary ghosts. There was a saying, "faus as a boggart", false as a boggart. I was born in 1965.'

Banks 5 (La). 1940s/F/FG., 2-10-19. 'Never really heard any of my family talk about Boggarts, just lived with ghosts. I lived at XXX Farm, Banks, from 1949. My Dad kept cows in the shipping adjoining the house and we always thought the banging were the cows, but when they went the banging carried on. Not on about this, but the banging got louder and louder and then an apparition of a lady in a crinkly, shiny black full skirted dress appeared with a black veil and carrying like a folder under her arm and remember lacy fingerless gloves. Always came in the front room by the fireplace. The banging would get quieter and she would fade away. Your Lady with the trunk brought it back to mind.'

Bardsley 1 (La). ???/F/FG., 22-9-19. 'My dad used the word if he saw someone dressed a bit too creatively. He would say: "flaming hell! She looks a right boggart on that"! I will sometimes use the phrase myself. Thank you. I didn't know the meaning of it. BTW my dad was born in Rochdale and grew up in Bardsley, Oldham.'

Barrow 1 (La). 1950s/F/FG., 17-10-19. 'I'm from Barrow, born late 1950s, then Blackpool from mid-1960s. Definitely heard the word "Boggart" associated with boggy areas.'

Barrow-in-Furness 1 (La). 1950s/M/F., 13-9-19. 'My town is covered in that Map. We were told never go near the water, i.e. fresh water like reservoirs because the water boggarts would get you! Funny you should mention Ginny Greenteeth, my older brother would make me put the bedroom lights out every night. He would shout quick Jimmy Greenteeth was under the bed and was going to grab me by the legs. Every night I would make a leap of faith diving on to the bed scared stiff. Years later, I learned of Ginny Greenteeth, who was live [*sic*] in the Canals and would grab children if they went too near the bank. It was just a legend to stop the kids wandering near the water. This was around the Manchester area. I come from Barrow in Furness that was Lancashire until the boundaries were changed, we still have Lancashire accents here, not Cumbrian. So I guess my brother and other local kids misheard the name of Ginny and said Jimmy, but I'm pretty sure the legend was about Boggarts in a roundabout way? Yes, late fifties. I think you could be right about Jimmy/Ginny thing. Still it frightened the crap out of me. Lol, I'm just wondering if the name Boggart could have anything to do with the moss. I think is called Bog Wart, I also think they maybe a medicinal value, and would naturally grow in Boggy ground. Just a Thought?'

Barrow-in-Furness 2 (La). 1950s/F/F., 13-9-19. 'My nan used to say if I went through the iron works tunnel in Barrow-in-Furness the boggarts would get us. Used to run through it screaming. The 1950s. Actually anywhere you weren't supposed to go they would get you and just for the record I saw the ghost of a monk at Furness Abbey in Barrow. [Other FB user: I live in Barrow and I've heard that one. We used to go down to Cocken Tunnel (under the slag bank) is that where you mean] No that was up the dingle (as we called it) on way to Ormsgill Pub… Ironworks tunnel was by Gradwells now the Hungry Horse. Hindpool Rd led you near channel and bottom of iron works.'

Barrowford 1 (La). 1970s/M/FG., 23-9-19. 'There was a Boggart Stile in Barrowford when I was a kid where a monster lived.'

Barton 1 (La). ???/M/FG., 29-9-19. 'Plenty of boggarts down Station Lane in Barton, Houses and Farms named after them. It was a regular meeting spot for boggarts in days gone by.'

Bentham 1 (La). 1930s/M/FG., 4-10-19. 'I have lived in Bentham all my life. I am eighty-two years old and I have never heard the word "Boggart".'

Bentham 2 (La). 1960s/M/FG., 5-10-19. 'I grew up in Mewith, just over a mile outside Bentham in the 1960s. "Boggart" was not a term I remember being used either at home or at school when I was growing up. Don't remember hearing the word used until I was in my thirties or forties. "Bogey Man", yes. "Boggart" definitely not.'

Bentham 3 (La). 1940s/M/FG., 5-10-19. 'Born and brought up in the 1940s, 1950s in High Bentham. I too have never heard the word "boggart" in any context.'

Bentham 4 (La). 1940s/M/E., 9-10-19. 'I was born in High Bentham 1947. Stories were told by young teenagers to my peer group (nine-ten year olds) about boggarts. One supposedly lived in a field drain in a local farmer's field. The field drain was made of slabs, rectangular two feet by two foot six open at both ends and thirty to thirty-five feet long. When the wind blew it made a resonating moaning noise. On 4 Nov (mischief night) the teenagers went Boggarting which involved rolling up a newspaper and pushing it up the roof drainage down pipe and setting fire to it which made a loud moaning noise. Fortunately down pipes were all cast iron and as far as I know no damage was caused to the houses. I noticed XXX made a comment and he lived in the same road.'

Billinge 1 (La). 1950s/F/FG., 18-9-19. 'I was born late 1940s, lived in Billinge. I remember the word "boggart". Similar meaning to bogey man. Jinny Greenteeth described the green algae on the surface of a pond in my early years. I still use the expression today.'

Billinge 2 (La). 1960s/M/FG., 14-10-19. 'In Billinge (near Wigan) we used to say 'he's t'en (taken) boggarts' meaning someone had gone mad or was possessed. A spooked horse was also said to have "t'en boggarts." Boggarts were supposed to live in Crank Caverns and would eat people who went into the caves. Then there was Bowser – a great black hellhound…Yes. 1960s. Then there was Jenny Greenteeth… She lived in ponds and had weeds or algae for hair. If you went into the pond she'd wrap her hair around you and drag you to the bottom. That's if the pond had a bottom, of course. Some were bottomless. Are you aware of the Crank Caverns legend? It was covered in the *Liverpool Echo* (I think) a very long time ago. More recently David Icke covered it too. He probably thinks it's true. Just google Crank Caverns. Man-eating goblin things! They sound like Tolkien's orcs. We used to go down them to scare ourselves but never saw anything. Some of my friends were stuck down there overnight once and emerged safe, sound and uneaten the next day.'

Billinge 3 (La). ???/M/FG., 17-10-19. 'I'm from Billinge near St. Helens. I've heard the term "boggart" but not sure where from. But did know they were mythical creatures like the bogeyman.'

Blackburn 1 (La). 1980s/F/F., 29-8-19. 'I was an 1980s child... But surprised my grandparents didn't share this with me... They grew up in 1940s/50s and were a very big influence in my early introduction to all things fae, goblins, witches and the like. My grandpa in particular always told us stories about magical places through the "magic eye" which was an eye shaped knot on a tree in their garden! He was also known to make paper fairies with tea lights behind and get us to watch them from the window which of course we believed were real... When the wind blew out the candles it was because the fairies had seen us watching! In the morning there would always be mushrooms for us to collect! Such memories! But I don't recall the boggarts!'

Blackburn 2 (La). 1930s/F/FG., 17-9-19. 'My mum used to say "stop making Bogarts" meaning stop making a fuss. She is in her eighties and from Blackburn. I've just asked her about it, she says boggarts meaning "trouble." However, she probably picked up the phrase from my dad's mum who came from Rotherham, Yorkshire originally.'

Blackburn 3 (La). 1940s/F/FG., 26-9-19. 'I was born in 1944 and lived on the outskirts of Blackburn (Brownhill). I have never heard of that word. [subsequent comment] Yes heard of the Bogeyman but not Boggart.'

Blackburn 4 (La). 1950s/M/FG., 26-9-19. 'Bogart Bridge between Downham and Barley. Supposedly a black dog haunting there. I saw it in a book about Lancashire haunts and other stories. Try looking up Pendle sculpture trail. Interesting at Barley. But as XXX said it was always the mysterious Bogey Man that scared us. Also I heard the phrase "ran at Bogart" meaning ran away fast.'

Blackburn 5 (La). 1940s/F/FG., 26-9-19. 'I was born also in 1944. Lived Mill Hill, Blackburn My parents were in their forties when I was born (mum died ten months after). My sister was born in 1927 and [I] never heard that word. Although not relevant to your book heard lots of old things from my grandma.'

Blackburn 6 (La). 1950s/F/FG., 26-9-19. 'Heard of it and put it in practice when our kids were little, especially on Sunday mornings when they jumped in bed with us. We had them hiding under the bedclothes saying Boggarts are coming, Daleks on their way. My son the eldest child loved it as my two girls thinking it was true! Typical lad but all in good fun and often remember those happy days. [Age estimated from Facebook page].'

Blackburn 7 (La). 1960s/F/FG., 26-9-19. 'I was born in 1962 and grew up at Shadsworth, Blackburn. We never used the word "boggart", it was bogeyman for us. I think I was a teenager before I heard of boggarts and thought of them as being in the rural areas.'

Blackburn 8 (La). 1950s/F/FG., 26-9-19. 'Born in 1956, Blackburn, heard of bogeyman, not boddards [corrects to "boggarts" in subsequent comment].'

Blackburn 9 (La). 1940s/F/FG., 26-9-19. 'Never heard the word "boggart" until I read a children's story to my grandson seven years ago. Born in Blackburn 1945.'

Blackburn 10 (La). 1950s/F/FG., 26-9-19. 'Born 1954 and remember well "the bogeyman will come and get you" from my older sister, I think. Sorry no boggarts only bogeyman. Yes, Blackburn.'

Blackburn 11 (La). 1940s/F/FG., 26-9-19. 'Good morning Jean. I've never heard of it [boggart] before and I was born in 1940. I've heard of bogey men.'

Blackburn 12 (La). 1960s/F/FG., 26-9-19. 'Hi born and raised with bogart lore. Jessica Lofthouse has an interesting story on a Clitheroe bogart in her book *Lancashire folklore*. Yes I did [grow up in Blackburn] and came back after thirty-four years in Wiltshire four years ago. I teach a short local history course for BwD Adult Learning. Jessica Lofthouse is wonderful. I remember watching her on TV as a child. My grandmother was from Banks near Southport and a country girl at heart. She told me many ghost and folklore stories which fascinated me. As a young girl I would go to the library (museum) every week and read all I could on witches, bogarts and the like. My Father would also tell me local folklore tales which I have passed to my children. When the bogart appeared in Harry Potter my girls knew that's not what they are really like! I think you can find JL on YouTube *Look Northwest*.'

Blackburn 13 (La). ???/M/FG., 27-9-19. 'There are a few farms on Whalley Old Road, which is the high road from Blackburn to Whalley. We knew one of them as the Boggatt House.'

Blackburn 14 (La). 1960s/M/FG., 28-9-19. 'My dad told me there was a boggart in Pleasington called the Pall Mall boggart. But that is all I know. I wonder if anyone else has heard this tale. He heard it from my grandma when he was a child.'

Blackburn 15 (La). 1980s/F/FG., 4-10-19. 'Hi, don't know if this is any good to you and your book but my nan used to tell me of a lady called Jenny Green Teeth that lived in the pond up Witton Park, Blackburn also there is a vape company based in Burnley that sells a liquid called boggart's breath. It's called the Lancashire Steam Company. No sorry I can't remember my nan mention boggarts, but she always told me about Jenny. It would have been late 1980s early 1990s. This was around Johnstone Street Blackburn. I lived in Accrington and visited every weekend. But has always stuck in my mind as it terrified me at the time! Lol, I'll ask my dad and see if she mentioned them to him.'

Blackburn 16 (La). 1950s/F/FG., 9-10-19. 'Born in Blackburn 1950s and never heard the word.'

Blackburn 17 (La). 1950s/M/FG., 9-10-19. 'Our scoutmaster (Holy Trinity, 3rd Blackburn – early 1960s) used to take us on night hikes. He would warn us to be beware of the boggarts that lived in the Trough of Bowland and on Darwen Moors.'

Blackburn 18 (La). 1940s/F/FG., 9-10-19. 'Born in 1942, heard it used many times, my husband also says it was used in his childhood.'

Blackburn 19 (La). 1940s/M/FG., 9-10-19. 'I was born in the late 1940s and never heard the term. It's a word I've heard more in the Manchester area (e.g. Boggart Hole Clough).'

Blackburn 20 (La). 1940s/F/FG., 9-10-19. 'Born in Blackburn 1941 heard it used by grandma.'

Blackburn 21 (La). 1950s/F/FG., 9-10-19. 'Born in Blackburn 1952 and I don't remember every hearing of a Boggart.'

Blackburn 22 (La). 1970s/F/FG., 9-10-19. 'As a young girl in the 1970s, my Grandmother used to tell us not to go in the cupboard under the stairs as the big hats would get us. I had no idea what they were, but they sounded scared [scary?] enough to stop me finding out, lol. We lived in Blackburn.'

Blackburn 23 (La). 1960s/M/FG., 9-10-19. 'I grew up in Blackburn (born 1966) to Scouse parents so whilst it wasn't a creature really known in our house my friend's grandparents had tales of boggarts. They also made an appearance around Halloween in "scary" stories at school.'

Blackburn 24 (La). 1960s/M/FG., 9-10-19. 'I grew up in Blackburn in the 1960s and 1970s, lived in a traditional area (Audley) and worked in the mill. I never heard this term ["boggart"] used. Maybe it just passed me by.'

Blackburn 25 (La). 1950s/M/FG., 9-10-19. 'A Boggart was recognised by the squelchy footfalls in the dark. Always at the other side of the hedge or treeline, and always just behind the one listening. We grew up knowing about them in the 1950s and it has always been part of our culture. The people who live in Belthorn were known as "Belthorn Boggarts", and I'm sure that I've heard the expression "Ossy Boggarts" for the people who live above the lamp in Oswaldtwistle. There was for many years, if not decades, only one street lamp in Oswaldtwistle, near the Library consequently some folks lived lower down the village, and some lived higher up.... above the lamp. No one ever "saw" a Boggart, that was their secret, but they were frightening to hear them "squelch" when wandering home late at night, and usually heard when staggering back from the local hostelry. I do believe that I myself was followed for almost a mile by one of them on the road from Darwen across to Tockholes, never seen, but always heard, and always too close for comfort. I am also convinced that is where the sport of jogging originated, getting away from the Boggarts as quick as possible, and that is also why one never sees a happy jogger. [Replying to a comment from another user.] Sorry XXX, thought it was Boggarts, now I come to think of it, Ossy Gobbins sounds much more likely.'

Blackburn 26 (La). 1940s/M/FG., 9-10-19. 'Moved to Blackburn from Chorley in 1948 as a three year old and I've never heard the word before.'

Blackburn 27 (La). 1940s/M/FG., 9-10-19. 'Blackburn in the 1940s/1950s, never heard the word.'

Blackburn 28 (La). 1980s/F/FG., 9-10-19. 'I was born in Blackburn in 1967 and grew up there. Parents (born in 1940s) and both sets of grandparents (born around 1915) were all from Accrington and Clayton-le-Moors but I have never heard the word "Boggart" used by any of them.'

Blackburn 29 (La). 1940s/F/FG., 9-10-19. 'I was born in Blackburn 1947 but never heard that word "Boggart".'

Blackburn 30 (La). 1970s/F/FG., 9-10-19. 'Boggarts. What an interesting subject. I was born in Blackburn 1967. My dad was from Great Harwood, mum from Blackburn, both born in the 1920s. If I stayed up late as a kid – so the mid-1970s onwards – dad would call me "The Midnight Boggart". Maybe because they were from an older generation they knew about them? I must have asked what one was, and they will have told me, but I can't remember any specific tales. Both my parents' grandparents were born in Ireland.'

Blackburn 31 (La). 1940s/F/FG., 10-10-19. 'I was born in 1944 and my granddad used to use the phrase "don't do that the boggart will get you" or "don't go in there the boggart [is] in there". My dad didn't really use the phrase after granddad died. The saying fizzled out in our family, but [I] can still hear him saying that.'

Blackburn 32 (La). 1960s/F/FG., 10-10-19. 'We knew the term "bogey man" as kids growing up in 1960s, Blackburn Lancashire.'

Blackburn 33 (La). 1950s/F/FG., 11-10-19. 'Boggarts live in holes in the ground, like trolls. When my son was small (1980s) his granddad told him a hole beside the path on the field behind our house on St James Road was a boggart hole. He [son] always ran past it. Boggarts are a bit like a scary, big, black dog, though that might be a description of the barghest. I've always known about boggarts (grew up in the 1950s).'

Blackburn 34 (La). 1960s/F/FG., 11-10-19. 'My parents were born and bred in Nelson, Lancashire in 1934. I grew up in Blackburn, Lancashire in the 1960s and never heard the word "boggart", but maybe bogey man came from that? I'll ask my parents if they remember and get back to you.'

Blackburn 35 (La). ???/M/FG., 11-10-19. 'As a now "senior" Lancashire Lad, I had never heard this word until I took some youngsters to the Youth Centre in Cumbria in the 1970s where the leader introduced them to the Boggart, who was known to roam the grounds at night devouring all and any who might be out there when they shouldn't be. It worked (with some). Keswick, but it was "Irish" man, who was youth leader, who lived a lot of his life in "Blackburn, Lancashire" very complicated.'

Blackburn 36 (La). 1940s/M/FG., 12-10-19. 'My husband still says it when he sees anything ugly: "Who'd frighten a boggart". LOL. Yes. His Mum always spoke in a broad Lancashire dialect. We were born in Blackburn in 1940s.'

Blackburn 37 (La). 1950s/F/FG., 13-10-19. 'I have heard people speak about a boggart in the Blackburn area. That was in the 1950s.'

Blackburn 38 (La). 1950s/M/FG., 15-10-19. 'Born-bred in Blackburn from 1965 – Boggarts were little trolls who lived in caves and on the Moors between Darwen and Bolton.'

Blackley 1 (La). 1940s/F/E., 6-9-19. 'I grew up in Blackley Manchester near a park called "Boggart Hole Clough". According to local legend, there was a farm in the valley and a spirit lived there. When he was annoyed he would turn the milk sour and do other objectionable things. I made sure I never went down into the valley where there was a cafe unless my dad was there. We now live in Hazel Grove and it's a word nobody knows here. My own children know the word because they've been to the park but the grandchildren don't know the word.'

Blackley 2 (La). 1960s/F/F., 9-9-19. 'Where I grew up in Manchester, the local park is called Boggart Hole Clough. Was told it was a witch.'

Blackley 3 (La). 1940s/M/FG., 15-9-19. 'Not in Littleborough but when I grew up in north Manchester, we used to play in Boggart Hole Clough in Moston/Blackley. There were two tales of the Boggart being trapped in his hole. One was that the large stone fountain in the valley was built to keep it in and the other that the large stone at the left hand side of the main path up to the lake was doing the same thing? Never thought about it until seeing your post. I was born 1947 so would be a regular in the park probably from 1953/1954 up to the early 1960s.'

Blackley 4 (La). 1950s/F/FG., 21-9-19. 'I went to Blackley Convent Prep School as a child – 1956 to 1964, the Rochdale Road entrance to Boggart Hole Clough adjoined our school, up a short little side road – Blackley Library across this little road. We used to go on school nature walks in there! [but no boggarts]'

Blackley 5 (La). 1960s/M/FG., 27-9-19. 'Our old English teacher used to regale us with ghost stories about Boggart Hole Clough (he seemed to prefer this to actually teaching English). This would have been around 1970. Nothing else to add really, but he did spin a good yarn.'

Blackley 6 (La). 1960s/F/FG., 27-9-19. 'Boggart Hole Clough in Blackley. Scared the life out of us as kids. My father-in-law used to tell my son that the boggart lived in the clough. That was the 1980s, but it went way back before then.'

Blackley 7 (La). 1950s/F/FG., 1-10-19. 'I was born and brought up in Blackley, Boggart Hole Clough was our local park. Moved to Rainhill over thirty-one years ago. We were always told that the boggarts were creatures that lived in the Clough and came out at night to waylay anyone passing by. We always came home before dark for sure.'

Blackley 8 (La). 1970s/F/FG., 4-10-19. 'I lived facing Baileys Woods on Dam Head Estate in 1973. We were told by our librarian that it was a farm before and the boggart from the clough would steal things and leave lights on in Dam Head Farm buildings. So we should take great care as we lived on the edge where the boggart left the clough and came through Baileys Woods to the houses facing the woods. I moved out in 1985 but we never experienced a boggart visit thankfully.'

Blackley 9 (La). ???/M/FG., 12-10-19. 'Nothing to add really except growing up in Blackley I spent a lot of my time in the oddly named Boggart Hole Clough. *Wikipedia* gives an explanation for the name, "It has been claimed that the clough is haunted by a boggart, a mischievous spirit found mainly in Lancashire and Yorkshire, perhaps in an attempt to explain the unusual name." No sorry, we never really thought about it, just thinking it had a weird name, unlike the traditionally named Queen's Park down the road. It was only as you got older you wondered how it had gained its name, thinking it must be from some mystical past.'

Blackley 10 (La). 1970s/F/FG., 12-10-19. '1970s growing up. Later years moved to Blackley Bogart Hole Clough. Only story I ever heard of was the white lady often seen on the hill at the main gates on the left. Bogart Hole Clough had walkways small river and park full off greenery. I visited this place months ago. Not changed. Reminds me more of a forest.'

Blackley 11 (La). 1960s/F/FG., 17-10-19. 'Born in Moston 1960. Then moved to Blackley, 1965. My mum always told me about the boggarts in the Clough lived under the bridges and anyone staying in there after dark would be taken away and eaten by the boggarts. [Added comment from other FB-user: 'yeah, under the bridges is where they lurked.]'

Blackley 12 (La). 1970s/F/FG., 18-10-19. 'I lived in the bungalow in Boggart Hole Clough park, my dad used to frighten us with stories of the boggart. I'm forty-eight years old so I don't know if that fits your time frame. My husband who is fifty-nine also used to be told stories of the boggart from his granddad. No, he's a Mossley lad born and bred.'

Blackley 13 (La). 1980s/F/FG., 7-11-19. 'I grew up in the 1980/1990s in Blackley and because of the name of our local park I'd heard of boggarts. The stories about them stealing things and turning the milk sour. We would do night walks in there to see how deep in we got before getting scared. I was always one of those who ran out screaming after about two hundred metres – for no apparent reason. Never saw a boggart or heard of anyone who did. But was still scared of them while in the Clough.'

Blackley 14 (La). 1950s/F/E., 22-11-19. 'Evil supernatural creature. Parents used [the word "boggart"].'

Blackpool 1 (La). 1920s/F/F., 12-9-19. 'Here is my mother's story, slightly edited from its inclusion in Nick Redfern's book, *Men in Black: Personal Stories and Eerie Adventures*. My mother tells me that when she was a young girl in Blackpool, living near the airport at Squires Gate, she had an experience which shook her to the core. Aged around fourteen years – so that would be just pre-war, 1936 or so – she was coming home from work as an apprentice dressmaker one winter evening around 6 pm. To reach her house she had to walk along Squires Gate Lane which is a long road that goes past the airport and had fencing all around the surrounding field at the time made of wooden panels. She was on the opposite side to the airport preparing to cross when a light caught her eye, seeming to shine out from behind the fence as a paling was moved to one side. It dazzled her a bit and she was puzzled but security was tight there and she assumed at first it was a night watchman. While she was thinking this she was astonished, and then terribly frightened, to see a "little man" emerge, followed by two others, each holding a bright lamp or electric torch and moving quietly as if cautious not to disturb anyone. Now, by "little" she says they were probably around her own height, making them maybe four feet ten to five foot tall as she was a tiny woman and hadn't finished growing at the time. They were slender but a bit stocky around the middle and had spindly arms and legs. Their attire consisted of an all-in-one kind of black or dark-coloured jumpsuit with a closely-fitted hood and their faces peeping out looked very pale, almost luminous. She remembers their eyes very vividly – huge and bright "shining like carriage lamps" with big black pupils. They reminded her of pixies from children's book illustrations but she "knew" they were "something else" and that she wasn't really meant to have seen them. There was absolute silence – as there so often seems to be in these sort of accounts – no traffic and she was freezing cold, from fright as much as the winter weather. Suddenly, one of them caught her eye and "looked almost as startled as I was" to see her seeing him. To her horror, he – she felt they were male – began to take steps to cross the road, indubitably to "make contact" with her. She was too terrified to scream so ran, silently, fearing they would make chase, taking a slightly longer route home and never stopping for breath until she reached the front door where her pounding alerted my grandfather. All she could say was that there were, "little men" at the airport field and was helped in, half fainting. Of course, Granddad assumed she'd been assaulted and dashed out to inspect the road where he saw nothing amiss. When at last she was able to speak coherently she described the beings to my grandparents who mused she may have seen the Boggarts – Lancashire imps – having an evening out. "Poor lass, they were t'Boggarts", Granddad mused – which probably wasn't much comfort! My mother says she "knew" that the little men "knew" she was "a child" and told each other this by a kind of whispering language which wasn't English but which she nevertheless understood, perhaps telepathically. Even in her eighties she could recall this experience with utter clarity as one of the strangest and most terrifying of her life, worse than any during the War. We often sat in that field together, me and Mum and I never felt it was an evil place – just "odd" somehow, even when the buttercups and daisies were in bloom and the fence had long since been demolished. I only knew the word from my Mum and Grandparents. I recall at junior school we read *Folk Tales of Lancashire* – not sure of the author – and I think a boggart was included there.'

Blackpool 2 (La). 1960s/M/FG., 27-9-19. 'I was born in Blackpool in 1961. Boggarts were definitely around in my childhood, especially when we were in the cubs and scouts. Camp fire stories always included a good scary boggart story.'

Blackpool 3 (La). 1950s/F/FG., 28-9-19. 'I've heard the name boggart used lots of times. I think it was a naughty being who hid in the shadows and put spells or curses on you and took great delight in scaring you. I have a friend called John Lamb who is an author and he mentions boggarts in some of his books. Steeleye Span sing of a boggart called Long Lankin, don't they? Seem to recall that I have always known the word, but it wasn't until I read some books in the last few years, that I heard the name again. I have friends who are of the Wiccan faith and they use the term a lot. I'm now unsure if Long Lankin/Lamkin was an actual physical boggart or imaginary fear, but I'm sure someone told me it was a boggart who lived in the moss and scared babies and children in nurseries – I could be wrong. Boggarts and fairy funerals I've read about. Wasn't Jenny greenteeth a boggart or was that a term used for green slime or both? Well they [Wicca] have mentioned her/it [Jenny Greenteeth]. They describe it as a being in ponds or bogs and it causes the green slime on top, ha ha. Having said that I did know that before they said. Some of them genuinely believe In Fairies and goddesses. Boggarts are mentioned too but not sure if they think of them as real. When I was in the RAF there was an imaginary being called a Gremlin. You blamed it for putting "a spanner in the works" – ha ha – which I suppose is a type of boggart!'

Blackpool 4 (La). 1950s/F/FG., 28-9-19. 'Is there a Boggart Hole Clough somewhere in the east Lancs area? Thank you for that. It's a phrase I often hear in my childhood! My mother was a Mancunian, and my father was born in Farnworth, the phrase was quite common in my childhood, though less so when we lived in the Fylde. My husband, who is from Uppermill in Saddleworth is also very familiar with the phrase. He tells me that there is a Boggart Hole Clough in Saddleworth.'

Blackpool 5 (La). 1940s/M/FG., 28-9-19. 'I grew up in Blackpool, born 1946, and read about boggarts as a young boy. They were not spoken of at home, but I heard occasional references at primary school and from friends when playing out.'

Blackpool 6 (La). 1970s/F/FG., 30-9-19. 'My dad, in the 1960s, used to say there were boggarts about, meaning ghosts. When my daughter was born in the 1980s, she had white hair and he used to call her a boggart jokingly! Yes, he was born and bred in Blackpool.'

Blackpool 7 (La). 1970s/F/FG., 6-10-19. 'I remember going to Pendle Hill with my parents when I was young and going into a little shop at the bottom of the hill and being bought a Treacle Eating Boggart (from the treacle mines under Pendle Hill). I still have my fluffy Boggart. Would have been late 1970s/ early 1980s. I'll try to find the Boggart later and put a picture on. I'm a Blackpool girl but have lived in Fleetwood for about the last eighteen years.'

Blackpool 8 (La). 1940s/F/FG., 6-10-19. 'I was born in 1948 in Blackpool and grew up in Bispham. I never heard the word "Boggart" but heard about Bogey Men.'

Blackpool 9 (La). 1960s/F/FG., 16-10-19. 'I was a child in the 1960s, grew up in Bispham, Blackpool. I never heard the word "boggart" when I was growing up. Probably not much help, sorry!'

Blackpool 10 (La). 1950s/F/E., 17-10-19. 'I grew up in Blackpool in the 1950s and 1960s. "Boggart" was a term used by my mother to signify a kind-of ghost, a bit like Ginny Greenteeth.'

Blackrod 1 (La). 1960s/M/FG., 14-10-19. 'I grew up on Blackrod in the late 1960s till the 1980s and have never heard that word until reading this post.'

Blackrod 2 (La). 1970s/M/FG., 14-10-19. 'Hi as kids in the 1970s used to talk about Gorses Boggart which lived between Aspull and Blackrod.'

Blackrod 3 (La). ???/F/FG., 14-10-19. 'My mother-in-law Doris called her sister Alice "the boggart".'

Blackrod 4 (La). 1950s/M/FG., 14-10-19. 'Grew up in Blackrod in the 50/60s but never heard "boggarts" as a phrase. We did refer to bogeymen to frighten kids. Amazing how the baddies were always male in days gone by.'

Blackrod 5 (La). 1950s/F/FG., 14-10-19. 'I grew up in Blackrod. I have heard of "boggart". Isn't it a little person? I might be totally wrong? I lived there and grew up there in the 1950/1960s.'

Bolton 1 (La). 1980s/M/E., 15-7-19. 'I read with interest your information request in the above issue and would like to relate a brief story I was told by my grandma in the early 1980s. We come from Bolton in Lancashire, and during WW2 my grandma (nanna) worked the farmland, I suppose as a land girl, around the town. The image of our town as a large industrial city is not without credence. However, it is surrounded by farms and moorland that give rise to several supernatural tales, including the phantom hitchhikers and screaming skulls from Turton Tower. I was told, along with my cousins, that on a farm now long gone in the Breightmet area of the town, near the long gone Breightmet Hall, some work was done for an elderly gentleman farmer type. He related that many years previously as a boy, there was indeed a boggart who lived on the farm. This entity was extremely well behaved and industrious, provided he was left alone. He wanted no help, or things done on his behalf. If his wishes were respected, unpleasant tasks were tackled with relish, mucking out, rat catching, and general heavy labour. It was stated he once shifted almost 1.5 tonnes of dressed stone from a waggon to where a building was to be erected overnight. The farmer's daughter, only a child at the time, made the Boggart some clothing and a pair of clogs, being shown how to by a seamstress who was told the clothing was for dolls. On seeing the gift, the boggart apparently made himself known to the farmer the following day, stating in thick Lancashire Dialect, "New clooas (clothes), new clogs, new wood? Boggarts a'gooin, and ah'll de nay Moore good!" He promptly disappeared and was never seen again. It is probably only a story, insomuch as it's difficult to believe that dressed stone in that quantity could be shifted by a tiny boggart, or a child with no experience could knock up a pair of serviceable clogs. What strikes me about it is this... The story related above would date to some time in the last two decades of the nineteenth century. At this time the town was more or less at its zenith, the most important cotton spinning and bleaching town in the world, and therefore already a centre of research and scientific endeavour. That such an old belief could persist two miles from its centre is fascinating and shows just how durable these beliefs are. When the old hall fell under the wrecking ball in the late 1940s, several country belief items were recovered, such as a mummified cat, charms and hexes carved not beams and walls, and pots of pins and other sundry items. An early council estate stands on the site now and all traces have been obliterated, although several pictures exist on the website of the museum. All this smacks of FOAF tales, I realise that, but it's also worth noting that Manchester's Boggart Hole Clough is perhaps eight miles away, suggesting the area had its resident share, imagined or not! Unfortunately I cannot furnish you with the farmer's names, as I don't know them, and my nanna died in 1998. Good luck with your quest and I look forward to reading your findings, sharing the hope that there are still folk about who can put flesh on the bones. The word [boggart] crops up in at least one placename, Boggart Hole Clough. Although the word is not in common use, I distinctly recall a lesson at primary school, I would've been around seven years old, when a dialect speaker came into school to help preserve old speaking terms and phrases. The thought being that such talk was dying out under the Mancunian influence on television and radio. Moving onto folklore, this man produced a somewhat terrifying, to my young mind at least, a picture of a boggart. He told us the name of the entity although most called it a troll, maybe because there was a bridge in the immediate background of the picture. I would imagine this is prevalent elsewhere, but there are many local history societies here, who do similar work in visiting schools and bringing history to young people. I would imagine the word is still in circulation although not widely used. However, my eleven year old son has just told me that a boggart is a fairy, he was told this at school, whilst my daughter who is six says it is a "not very nice monster"! She has seen a picture in a picture book and prefers the word "troll".'

Bolton 2 (La). 1950s/F/FG., 10-10-19. 'Born 1956. Lived in Bromley Cross, Bolton until 1971. Lived in Darwen ever since. Never heard of boggarts – only bogeymen. Very scary.'

Bolton 3 (La). ???/M/FG., 15-10-19. 'I grew up outside of Bolton in Lancashire and we used the word.'

Bolton 4 (La). 1970s/M/FG., 18-10-19. 'Never heard of the Boggart but was always fearful that if we got up in the middle of the night the Bogey man would come and get us.'

Bootle 1 (La). 1950s/F/FG., 18-9-19. 'Born in Bootle 1955. Never heard of boggart but was terrified of the bogeyman!'

Bootle 2 (La). 1950s/F/FG., 27-9-19. 'I was born in 1952 in Bootle, my dad was from Fazakerley, my mum from Essex and I never heard this expression. All I knew was "bogey man".'

Bootle 3 (La). 1950s/F/FG., 27-9-19. 'Called the bogey man in 1950s, Bootle.'

Bootle 4 (La). 1950s/F/FG., 27-9-19. 'I was born in Bootle in 1955 and have never heard this expression.'

Bootle 5 (La). 1940s/M/FG., 27-9-19. 'Sound like I'm the old geezer here. Grew up in ford, next to the cemetery, always the bogeyman, this was the forties.'

Bootle 6 (La). 1950s/F/FG., 27-9-19. 'Bootle, 1955–1966 never heard of it. However, the bogey man will get you was a common word.'

Bootle 7 (La). 1940s/M/FG., 28-9-19. 'I was born in 1947 and never heard of a boggart. The two tales told the most in Bootle, were the headless coachman of Bibbys Lane, and Spring Heeled Jack who appeared all over Liverpool.'

Bootle 8 (La). 1950s/F/FG., 28-9-19. 'Bootle. I'm the 1950s/60s. Never boggart always bogeyman!'

Bootle 9 (La). 1960s/F/FG., 28-9-19. 'Plus the green man of the Leeds Liverpool canal but never a word "Boggart". No idea but whenever I crossed over the canal bridge leading to Derby Road, where all the warehouses and the old Blackledges factory was, my older cousin always said the Green Man would get us.'

Bootle 10 (La). ???/F/FG., 17-10-19. 'Lived off Marsh Lane during that time and the talk was about "Bibbys Ghost". Never heard of Boggart. More info about it please.'

Bootle 11 (La). 1930s/F/FG., 17-10-19. 'I was born in Bootle 1931, never heard of that word at any time. I had heard of Ginny Greenteeth. Don't remember any others at this time. Sorry, good luck.'

Britannia 1 (La). 1960s/M/FG., 21-9-19. 'I was born in 1969 and definitely was told about boggarts. A boggart was meant to be attached to moors and quagmires. I always called the creature under my bed the boggart. Also when I was little and could hear the foxes scream at night I thought that they were boggarts and my parents did nothing to dissuade me of that notion. Brought up in Britannia. Boggarts were unkempt men with slimy hands, a ghost of sorts.'

Broughton 1 (La). 1970s/M/FG., 29-9-19. 'I heard the term [boggart] regular, brought up in the 1970s on a farm in Durton Lane called Jumps Farm. Ghostly figures.'

Burnley 1 (La). ???/M/E., 18-9-19. 'I read the piece on the local newspaper's *Lancashire Telegraph* website and I live in Burnley although I'm not native to Burnley, I consider myself as Burnley bred and I have read quite a few books about weird stuff in the Burnley area and I once read a book by Whittaker (first name unknown) who wrote of the boggart of Hollin Hill, Burnley. As the story goes children in the Hollin Hill area of Burnley (Burnley Wood at the top of Hollingrieve Road) started to disappear and an investigation turned up that a boggart was responsible. The local mayor gave the boggart a chance to return the children, which it agreed provided that there should always be a holly tree growing on Hollin Hill and if the trees should disappear the boggart will return to take more children. So the mayor ordered hundreds of holly trees to be planted in the area, but in subsequent years due to people spreading, building houses, encroaching on the area and stealing the holly trees for Christmas activities, the holly trees on Hollin Hill have reduced in number, the last time I was there there was only three... Does this mean there will be a return of the Hollin Hill boggart? Who knows! Apparently this must be "true" as it was written in the town's annals and recorded for prosperity. Then there is the story of Black Shuck (sometimes boggarts can come in the shape of giant red eyed dogs apparently) of Church Street again in Burnley. But that is another story I have had personal acquaintance with...'

Burnley 2 (La). 1950s/F/E., 12-9-19. 'My best friend's mum, born in Burnley and living in the same area as my mum. She was born in 1959. She only considers boggarts to live under bridges. She didn't seem to know much about what they might do. She knows of Boggart Bridge and said she learned about it in school. She is also unaware of any other local boggart stories. Her family did not tell tales of any other local creatures of mischief.'

Burnley 3 (La). 1940s/F/E., 12-9-19. 'My mother was born in Burnley in 1943. She considers boggarts to be spirits that typically live under bridges, but also in woods. She considers that they cause accidents and aren't friendly. The only boggart she is aware of locally is Boggart Bridge at Towneley, but she doesn't know the tale around this one. She says the only times her family used the word were jovial words against each other. Her parents did not tell her of any other local boggart stories and it seems her awareness of the Towneley Boggart is from living in that area.'

Burnley 4 (La). 1940s/F/F., 2-9-19. 'There's a Boggart Bridge above Towneley on the Burnley to Todmorden railway line. The word "boggard". The word was a familiar one. However, it was spoken with some humour. I was brought up in a household of faith with acknowledgement to the existence of evil in the world. I was also told fairy stories of different cultures and loved hearing them. My mother talked of herself being 'fey' meaning she perceived ideas of strange creatures. My mother talked of Ginny Greenteeth. This was in Burnley in the 1940s and 1950s. I'd be seven in 1950. I asked questions. I had parents who explained ideas to me. We talked. I was a good reader but I was also read to. My mother was fascinated by legends and fairy tales. My dad was a classical scholar and a teacher. I adored Greek myths and tales of belief as well as Bible stories. Still do!'

Burnley 5 (La). 1950s/F/F., 4-9-19. 'If I was naughty, in Lancashire I was told that the bogey man would get me. [So you never heard boggart?]. Yes, but the commonly used term was bogey man.'

Burnley 6 (La). 1980s/F/F., 4-9-19. 'I have always lived in Burnley (Rosehill area and now I live at the bottom end of Thursden Valley at Lane Bottom). I was born in the 1980s. I don't have a particular memory of becoming aware of boggarts. I guess I've always been aware of the concept due to spending lots of time at Towneley Park growing up and always having a natural interest in local folklore and a personal interest in all things magical and of that ilk. My mother and uncle use the word "boggart" as a jovial jibe for each other, meaning nuisance, I guess. They were both born in the 1940s. I imagine the fact my parents were older means I was exposed to the word more than someone with younger parents may have been. My son obviously knows what they are as we go walking in the local countryside a lot and we live close to the laid boggart of Extwistle. So he knows all about the mischief that one caused. Otherwise there aren't many people I come across in daily conversations who know what I mean when I talk about boggarts and I was actually very surprised in the last year or two that many people from my age through to those in their mid-fifties had no clue what I was talking about! Even those who live in Burnley with its many historical boggarts. Looking at your map I think you already know the boggart stories that I am familiar with, so I don't think I can add to that. Do you know of the Bee Hole Boggart? Apparently that resided near where Turf Moor football ground is and when human skin was found in shreds on some thorn bushes, it was supposedly this boggart that was the culprit for the murder. If it helps, in addition to the fairy well on your map, there is another not far from the Extwistle boggart that still exists today. Although it was used as a water supply well and now is encased with stone with a metal lid on it. And to answer your last question, what does boggart mean to me: I understand boggarts to be *genius loci* that are shape shifting, often malevolent spirits that cause trouble, sometimes of a fatal nature. To me they're always watching, even if they're not in a corporeal form. They can be tiny, or make themselves into large creatures and may even present as weather phenomenon such as mist or fog. But they always like to cause trouble, even if they've been laid to rest, unless some bargain has been made by someone of great wit and guile. As I have a toddler who enjoyed watching the 1966 cartoon of *The Grinch* last year. I am inclined to think that the Grinch may be a modern equivalent of a boggart with some variations.'

Burnley 7 (La). 1960s/F/F., 12-9-19. 'I was told about the Rowley boggart when I was a teenager. I'm sixty-one now. I'm in Burnley, Lancashire. I'd heard of it but not took much notice. It was only when a group of us got together and started telling stories. Like a little elf/imp like but evil spirit.'

Burnley 8 (La). 1960s/M/F., 12-9-19. 'In the grounds of Towneley Hall in Burnley there is a bridge called "Boggart's Bridge". [Boggarts] were ever present when I was a child. My Mother would scare us with tales of Jinny Greenteeth. Yes, when I was a small boy some seventy years ago, our mothers and dads used to excite our little minds with stories of hauntings, ghouls, and beasties.'

Burnley 9 (La). 1950s/M/FG., 21-9-19. 'Went to Burnley grammar school in the 1960s and remember some of my mates went to Towneley Hall and all said were chased by Towneley Bogart! Late one winter night. Sorry lost touch with all of them now sadly. My dad was a night watchman at Towneley Hall and they were all convinced grounds were haunted and hall. This was during World War 2, I believe. Sadly my dad passed away a few years ago.'

Burnley 10 (La). ???/M/FG., 28-9-19. 'My dad was a local historian in Burnley and told me that a boggart is similar to a dwarf possibly a ghost who would come through the house in the middle of the night and clean up, arrange things and the house would be better organised. Not sure if this helps?'

Burnley 11 (La). 1950s/F/FG., 3-10-19. 'I live in the Leyland area but am originally from Burnley. Born in the 1950s I regularly heard about the Boggarts living and working in the Treacle Mines in Sabden. I visited the Treacle mines quite a few times but sadly they shut down as a visitor attraction many years ago. Interestingly one of the phrases used in my childhood was "setting off at Boggart".'

Burnley 12 (La). 1950s/F/FG., 9-10-19. 'Yes, I heard this word off an old farmer when we saw a ghost back in the 1960s. [Age estimated from FB page.]'
Burscough 1 (La). 1960s/F/FG., 28-9-19. 'Ginny Greenteeth lives in the Leeds Liverpool canal… Usually hanging around the bridges. If a child went too near the canal she would drag them in by her long green fingers that you could see floating on top of the water(weeds). I think in Burscough it was used as a deterrent to stop kids going too near the water when they were little, but I think if you check XXX's group Images of Burscough there are posts that tell it is a myth that is circulated around Lancashire in different forms, usually concerning waterways and lakes. I will say this though. I'm now fifty-five and I still don't get too close to the canal. She's there waiting! I did get told of the treacle eating boggarts from Sabden. The ones that live in the Sabden treacle mines. Do they count?'
Burscough 2 (La). 1970s/F/FG., 3-10-19. 'My grandparents had a "boggart" room in their house on Liverpool Road Sth up by the Bull and Dog Garage! Petrified us as kids! Late 1970s early 1980s.'
Burscough 3 (La). ???/F/FG., 9-10-19. 'We had a boggart room in our house. It is a shower room now.'
Burscough 4 (La). 1960s/F/FG., 9-10-19. '1964–1973. Never heard the word "boggart". Good luck with your research.'
Burscough 5 (La). 1960s/M/FG., 9-10-19. 'My Mam always mentioned Boggerts being about especially under the Stairs when I was growing up in the 1960s. (1964? to 1970-ish). It was meant to scare me and my sister away from the understairs cupboard we had, which coincidentally hid her Xmas/Birthday Presents from prying eyes. It worked though until we needed to put a shilling in the Gas Meter in there.'
Burscough 6 (La). 1960s/F/FG., 10-10-19. 'We still use the word "boggarts" at home. Yes and my husband, my mum and dad used to say it too. My mum was Burscough born and bred but my dad was from Yorkshire, but he may have picked it up from my mum.'
Burscough 7 (La). 1950s/F/FG., 10-10-19. 'Remember Ginny Grinty and Bogyman but not Boggarts. I was born in 1953, and as a child Ginny Grinty in my upbringing was used as a deterrent as we lived so near the canal we were told Ginny Grinty lived in there and other dangerous places. Other people may have other examples.'
Burscough 8 (La). 1950s/M/FG., 10-10-19. 'My family came from Burscough and I was born in 1959. I like XXX remember stories of Ginny Grinty. Although I remember her being called Jenny Greenteeth. No Boggarts, although I am sure I came across a few during my army training days…'

Burscough 9 (La). ???/M/FG., 10-10-19. 'Like many, I don't remember "boggart" but I do remember Ginny Grinty who lived in the canal behind Vic Street to claim any foolish, unwary, young children who ventured onto the canal bank alone. Where did that myth come from, I wonder?'

Burscough 10 (La). 1950s/M/FG., 10-10-19. 'I was born in 1950 and brought up in Burscough but don't recall boggarts. Ginny Greenteeth was often a threat my parents used.'

Bury 1 (La). 1960s/F/E., 4-9-19. 'I always think of Boggart Hole Clough in Blackley. To me a Boggart is a mischievous, cheeky creature. Small, fat, stumpy legs and big eyes. I have no idea where that image comes from as I don't recall anyone, parents or grandparents talking about or telling stories about boggarts. It's not a word we use in my family at all. Born in Bury, Lancahire in 1961.'

Bury 2 (La). 1940s/F/E., 5-9-19. 'The first and only time I've heard was the word was "Boggart Hole Clough" (and even then I thought it was "Boggart Hall Clough") – a "park" outside of Middleton. Grew up in Bury in the 1940/1950s.'

Bury 3 (La). 1950s/M/E., 4-9-19. 'To me, a boggart is a small creature who comes to live in your house if you are unlucky. Responsible for things going wrong, and once you get one they are impossible to get rid of. They make milk turn sour, just when it's too late to get some more, hide your keys when you need to go out etc etc. My mother used to talk about them when I was little. Locally-ish there is of course Boggart Hole Clough near Blackley (Google). Other snippets there! There is the story of the Lancashire farmer who was unable to grow anything in a certain field, no matter what he did or what he planted. He was scratching his head, puzzling over it when he heard a little voice "I want 'alf". He looked round and there, seated on a small stone, was a boggart. "I want 'alf" he repeated. "If tha dussn't give me 'alf, nowt'll grow in this field". The farmer thought a bit then said "right dust tha want the 'alf that grows above the ground or below the ground?" "Above the ground". So the farmer planted potatoes! When the boggart realised this he flew into a terrible rage and said "Tha's cheatin'! I'll have another do. This time I'll have th' alf that grows below the ground." So the farmer planted wheat! The boggart flew into such a rage he blew himself up! Lived in Bury all my life (seventy-three). Another story concerns the couple who had a boggart they couldn't get rid of no matter what they did. Finally, they decide to wait till it was asleep, and packed up a cart in dead silence so as not to wake it. They tiptoed out, just in time to hear another boggart say "Are you going somewhere?" Their boggart replied "Aye, we're flittin."'

Bury 4 (La). 1970s/M/FG., 27-9-19. 'My dad used to talk of boggarts, I grew up in Bury he was Moston. Of course, there is Boggart Hole Clough in that area as well. I still use the word "boggarts" and jokingly threaten their existence to my children.'

Bury 5 (La). 1960s/F/FG., 4-10-19. 'I grew up in Bury, Lancashire but moved to high Bentham in 1996. I've never heard a word about boggarts here. My granddad told us about them when we were children, so late 1960s. He described them as little goblin-like creatures that you could spot hanging upside down in trees. He said they lived in holes in trees and lived off sheep muck. Also, and I never heard this from anyone else, he told us about wierwacker birds, he said they looked like small storks but flew backwards so they could see where they had been, also so they didn't get dust in their eyes. He also claimed if they wanted to they could disappear up their own backside! Have you ever heard that tale? I loved those stories as a child and looked hard but saw neither.'

Bury 6 (La). 1950s/F/FG., 17-10-19. 'We had boggarts in Walshaw, Bury. 1950s.'

Cadishead 1 (La). 1950s/F/FG., 26-9-19. 'Grew up in Cadishead, born 1955. Never heard "boggart" but 'the bogey man' was a frequent threat. My gran was "proper Lancysheer" and spoke with strong dialect, eg used "thee, thou and tha" and words like "clempt" and "skrieking".'

Cadishead 2 (La). 1960s/F/FG., 26-9-19. 'I grew up in Cadishead and also was threatened with the bogey man.'

Cadishead 3 (La). 1930s/F/FG., 26-9-19. 'Born Cadishead 1937. Often heard of bogies or the bogyman but never boggart.'

Cadishead 4 (La). 1950s/F/FG., 26-9-19. 'I too grew up in Cadishead. Born 1959. Never heard of "boggart" either!'

Cadishead 5 (La). 1950s/F/FG., 26-9-19. 'I was born in 1959. Lived in Cadishead/Irlam. I have never heard the word ever, but was told watch out for the bogey man.'

Cadishead 6 (La). 1950s/F/FG., 26-9-19. 'I was born 1959. My Nan referred to the "Bogeyman" but never "boggart". We lived in Cadishead.'

Cadishead 7 (La). 1930s/M/FG., 27-9-19. 'My Grandmother and my Dad, both living in Cadishead and Irlam 1930s–1960s. (Dad born 1935, don't know about Gran). Always came out with this word when I was growing up and they didn't like the way I looked: "Tha favvers a Boggart!"'

Cadishead 8 (La). 1960s/M/FG., 27-9-19. 'Born and Bred in Cadishead from 1965. The first time I heard the term "Boggart" was looking at the map of Blakeley near Middleton, Boggart Hole Clough.'

Cadishead 9 (La). 1950s/F/FG., 27-9-19. 'Born here 1955. Never heard of the boggart, only the bogeyman! Parents were from Yorkshire though so I grew up using two "languages"!'
Carleton 1 (La). 1960s/M/FG., 26-9-19. 'I recall a boggart hanging round Robins Lane, Carleton. I was a young boy from Liverpool never heard of them, moved to Carleton in 1968/1969 aged six. Sure I heard of them now and then through 1970s. That and Green Ghost of Carleton, too, at crem.'
Carnforth 1 (La). 1980s/M/FG., 16-10-19. 'So I was born in 1985, and have always been told about boggarts by my grandpa, who was born in 1934. No, I grew up in Carnforth and Whittington, and my grandpa was brought up in Carnforth and Nether Kellet.'
Chipping 1 (La). 1940s/F/FG., 26-9-19. 'I'm born and brought up in Chipping, still use the word "boggart". I was born in the mid-1940s and a boggart was the one that made doors slam, or loud noises.'
Cheadle 1 (La). 1940s/F/FG., 29-9-19. 'I was born in and grew up in Cheadle during the 1940s and 1950s (at that time Cheadle was not part of Stockport but had its own identity as Cheadle and Gatley UDC). However, I don't remember the word "boggart" being used but rather the derivative bogey man. He was a threat lightly used by many mums and dads with little effect.'
Cheadle 2 (La). 1950s/F/FG., 29-9-19. 'I grew up in Cheadle, Hulme, near Councillor Lane. Born in 1946. Never heard of the word "boggart".'
Cheadle 3 (La). 1950s/F/FG., 29-9-19. 'I grew up in Cheadle in the 1950s but never heard the word "boggart".'
Chorley 1 (La). 1950s/F/F., 31-8-19. 'Yes, my mum used to talk about them. I thought she had made them up. Chorley, Lancashire 1954.'
Chorley 2 (La). 1940s/F/F., 11-9-19. '"Boggerts" was used a lot in my childhood, early 1940s. I've been known to say it to this day!'
Chorley 3 (La). 1960s/M/FG., 24-9-19. 'I live in Hest Bank just north of Lancaster. My link to "Boggarts" comes from my late father who was born in Withnell Fold near Chorley in 1924. He grew up that part of Lancashire backing onto the Pennines, Brincall Moor, Houghton Tower. I was born in 1966 and used to visit relatives in this area until the 1980s. [On] childhood walks along the disused railway line from Chorley to Blackburn there were derelict level cross and house near Brincall. "Oh the boggarts live there" and the same was said about the derelict farms on the Moore. To me, if you didn't want people to go to a place or children to be good tell them "Boggarts" are there. I cannot recall the term "Boggart" being used in this part of Lancashire.'
Chorley 4 (La). 1960s/M/FG., 29-9-19. 'I never came across Bogarts growing up in Lancashire in the 1960s and 1970s. Ginny Greenteeth was the

one to look out for! No I only read about Boggarts when I was much older. Ginny Greenteeth lived in the weeds in ponds and streams and would pull you in if you didn't watch out!'

Chorley 5 (La). 1940s/M/FG., 9-10-19. 'I am eighty and I have always known of Boggarts. I was told as a little lad that Boggarts were bad spirits who cause mischief to happen and they would also scare people by making noises. I was born in Chorley and have lived in Euxton fifty years. I have heard of the Euxton Boggart but know nothing else about it.'

Chorley 6 (La). 1990s/M/FG., 17-10-19. 'I may be a lot younger than the time you have been talking about but have loved reading all these comments. But one common thing that caught my attention as [I] have heard about it myself is people saying it may be the same as the bogeyman. As a young child I was told that the bogeyman would come for me if I misbehaved and it was my parents and grandparents that both told me the same but I was born in Preston and lived in Chorley until I was about nine. But I know my grandparents was told the same when they were children and they came from Stoke and Manchester and even though I grew up and stopped believing the stories I still find some enjoyment when I come across things like this when others have heard similar stories.'

Chorley 7 (La). 1950s/F/FG., 18-10-19. 'Only thing I can remember as kids was told to be careful near the old hall down Bagganly Lane. Beware of the Bagganly Boggart. No late 1950s and early 1960s.'

Chorley 8 (La). 1940s/M/FG., 18-10-19. 'My Dad was always saying Boggarts and old men will get me if don't behave myself. I think I was more scared off with the thought of the old men as I could picture them, but was always confused what a Boggart would look like, and still to this day I have no clue. Maybe you can end my seventy-six years of wondering. I grew up in Chorley, in the 1940s. First down Moore Road then in the 1950s Eaves Lane. Was always scared the Boggarts would get me while walking back home in twilight from ort Nab or back from Empire cinema and the flickering gas lamps, that caused long shaky shadows down the steps of Peterwink.'

Chorlton 1 (La). 1950s/M/E., 4-9-19. 'What does the word "boggart" mean to you? I have only heard of the word "Boggart" in relation to "Boggart Hole Clough Park" in North Manchester. Did your parents and grandparents use the word? No. Do your children, nephews and nieces use it? No. Do you know any stories about boggarts – or places especially associated with them? No. Where did you grow up, and in what decade? Chorlton in South Manchester. Born 1955 and lived there until 1977.'

Chorlton-on-Medlock 1 (La). 1940s/M/F., 4-9-19. 'I remember going to Boggart Hole Clough with my brother when I was little. Firstly I was about ten years old. In 1955. We went to a local pond to fish. I was born in Chorlton on Medlock, 1945. All the kids at my school knew about the boggarts. Not sure about what they were. Hope this is some help. I now live in New Zealand. So the time delay is a key factor.'
Chowbent 1 (La). 1950s/M/FG., 7-10-19. 'I grew up in Chowbent in the 1950s but never heard the word "bogarts"!'
Clapham 1 (La). 1910s/F/FG., 9-10-19. 'My Mother used the word, she was born and lived her early life on a farm at Keasdon near Clapham. You can also find this word used in the Tom Pig books by Alison Utley. Born 1912.'
Clayton 1 (La). 1930s/M/FG., 28-9-19. 'Whenever we heard noises in the bushes as kids my dad used to say it was "the Bogarts"! He was from Clayton and his dad would scare him with it! He was born in the 1930s. His dad was very cynical and told him lots of scary stuff like this. He also gave my dad a book called *Runaway Rufus and the Goldbag Gnome*. Scared me too when I was young. I think my dad said the Bogarts were from New Mills! Sorry to be so vague.'
Clayton-Le-Moores 1 (La). 1950s/M/F., 31-8-19. 'There is a local legend where I live that the Boggarts live in the canal in Clayton Le Moores and they would attack the unwary. It's an old Lancashire folk tale that near the canal lurked Boggarts who would get you. Personally, it was over sixty years ago when my grandmother told me that one and she died in the mid-1960s. Yes, I was born in 1955 and I have forgot the amount of folk lore she used to tell me. [Asked about Jenny Greenteeth.] My Grandmother used to talk about Nana Greenteeth which was the nickname for an old Lodge in Oswaldtwistle which is not the nature reserve at Foxhill Bank in Oswaldtwistle. I haven't heard the name Greenteeth for decades. [On Lucette local boggart] It must be fifty years since I heard that one, but my memory is not as good as it used to be.'
Clayton-Le-Moores 2 (La). 1980s/M/FG., 9-10-19. 'A famous boggart lives at Clayton Hall, Clayton le Moors. I heard the word "boggart" a lot growing up. Aye Google Clayton Hall boggart there's even a stone nearby that has the word "boggart" written on it. It will just give you some info on Lancashire boggarts that may be helpful.'
Clayton-Le-Moores 3 (La). 1970s/F/FG., 16-10-19. 'Never heard of big bogart but I do remember the green teeth to stay away from canal all these years I thought nana was saying Johnny not Jinny ha. Yep, I'm fifty now but every day I used to walk down canal bankung with my eye rolling telephone pull along [?] and I would want to look at the ducks and nana would say: "ooo don't go too close or Jonny green teeth will come and get you". Ha.'

Clitheroe 1 (La). 1940s/F/F., 29-8-19. 'I was born in 1945 in Blackburn, Lancs. Grew up and still [live] in Clitheroe, Ribble Valley. My parents explained boggarts as mischievous creatures. If we were being very silly they would say we were acting like a boggart. We were never quite sure where they were supposed to live... I will have a think about it, see what I can remember. They were described more as mischievous, definitely not evil or menacing in any way.'

Clitheroe 2 (La). 1980s/F/FG., 17-9-19. 'I was told of stories as a child of the Sabden treacle mines and the treacle eating bogarts!'

Clitheroe 3 (La). ???/F/FG., 19-9-19. 'My mum said that she grew up hearing about boggarts. She says it was a mischievous little creature that lived in the woods, nothing to be scared of but if anything went wrong/got lost etc it was down to the boggart!'

Clitheroe 4 (La). 1940s/M/F., 8-9-19. 'I was born in 1944 at XXX Whalley Road in Clitheroe and am an old boy of Clitheroe Royal Grammar School. We were often told about Boggarts when we were children and told that they lived at the top of the stairs in the roof space or even in any dark space like cellars etc. We had lots of simple fables in those days like the Sabden Treacle mines and Pegganells Well down near the river. We called the opening into the roof space at the top of the stairs, the Boggart Hole. Boggarts were portrayed as evil monsters to us as kids. We were genuinely scared of boggarts. Never saw one I must admit but we were always wary of dark spaces as we made to believe these were boggart holes.'

Clitheroe 5 (La). ???/F/FG., 17-9-19. 'I use the word [boggart] to scare my child. I've no idea to what foul creature it relates but it sounds good when mixed in with ghouls, goblins, ghosts, banshees and all other manner of things that go bump in the night!'

Clitheroe 6 (La). 1970s/F/FG., 17-9-19. 'Not boggart, but have you heard of Ginny Green Teeth? My dad told me about her, and his mum told him when he was a boy.... My dad said she lived in the canal and would drag you in and under if you strayed too close....'

Clitheroe 7 (La). ???/M/FG., 17-9-19. 'We were told of the bogart as kids and that the loft hatch was the bogart ole (hole) and he would come down it and get us take us away if we didn't behave. When upstairs if we heard a noise creak the wind up in the attic there would be a stampede down the stairs to take refuge behind the settee where our mum and dad sat. It was described as big and dark an you couldn't ever see its face. [I] will speak with my brothers and sisters and see if they can say more!'

Clitheroe 8 (La). 1950s/M/F., 8-9-19. 'Boggart stories abounded in our house in the 1950s and 1960s. And I mentioned "boggarts" to my kids in the 1980s. I was raised in Clitheroe, Lancashire. Boggarts, my mother told us, lived exclusively in dark places; caves, cellars, attics and even in the outside lavatories. The fear of boggarts were used by my mother as an effective control tool over me and my six siblings. She never described fully as to what a boggart actually looked like. "Ginny Green Teeth" also featured in her horror stories. When I talked of boggarts to my children it was in a light-hearted way and in the context of "what my mum used to tell us". I don't think they have passed the "boggart" folklore onto their children. My wife was keen not to scare the children and so I was discouraged from telling boggart (or bogie man as my wife called them) stories. Ginny Greenteeth (Jenny Greenteeth) was a wizened old woman who used to live near Brungerly Bridge on Waddington Road (over the River Ribble). She died by falling into a well whilst drawing water and her spirit haunts the banks of the Ribble and that people have mysteriously died whilst walking along the bank, their deaths being attributed to "Ginny Greenteeth"'.

Clitheroe 9 (La). 1960s/F/FG., 4-10-19. 'Can't say I ever heard of a boggart. Clitheroe 1967–1978. Great Harwood 1978–present.'

Clowbridge 1 (La). 1940s/M/FG., 9-10-19. 'I was born in 1944 and lived in the tiny village of Clowbridge (between Rawtenstall and Burnley) until I was eleven. I remember well my Granddad talking about the Boggart, as in "the Bogart will come and get you if you're not good." Or "don't go there, that's where the Boggart lives". It was obviously a term used to frighten children.'

Collyhurst 1 (La). 1950s/M/F., 12-9-19. 'Until the age of eight, I was raised in Collyhurst, North Manchester. There was a park near Moston called Boggart Hole Clough. There have always been stories of Boggarts, dark forces and Fairies! We were raised with them, we never doubted their existence. When we were naughty, we were always told that we'd be taken by the Boggarts, and that the Fairies would report us to Father Christmas, who would put our names in the naughty children's book and we wouldn't receive any Christmas presents! But we always did! 1950s into early 1960s. A hairy malevolent troll like beast, as found in the *Lord of the Rings*, something akin to a bogeyman! Yep and a Boggart, with Fairies thrown into the mix, this was found to be more so around wakes week, when the Nook was always flooded and boggy; and they worked in comparative unity, which is something you don't normally hear of where Boggarts are concerned! Yep! I heard of Ginny too! There was also said to be one at Daisy Nook!'

Collyhurst 2 (La). 1940s/F/FG., 28-9-19. 'Children had a lot of freedom to roam when I was growing up (late 1940s onward) and it was common for mum to use the terms "Boggart" to warn you about the dangers of falling down in holes or steep places, and "Ginny Greenteeth" to keep you away from the canal. She tried to scare you into being good and safe. Sorry, should have said we lived in Collyhurst and Miles Platting. [Boggart =] A bogeyman who lived in dark places, and was wet and muddy.'

Collyhurst 3 (La). 1950s/M/FG., 9-10-19. '[I] was born in 1950. I spent most of my childhood in Collyhurst, Manchester. My Dad was born in Moston area of Manchester, adjacent to Boggart Hole Clough, so from my early childhood I was aware of the term Boggart, because of my Dad and also the fact that his parents lived all their lives in that area. We knew the "legend/folklore" of what and who the Boggarts were and where they supposedly lived. We were told that they lived in a hole in certain trees, but I've also been told that there were other holes that they lived/hid in. Obviously as kids it was more of a spooky folklore tale and as kids was constantly exaggerated and added to in typical kids fashion. I've lost count of how many of us kids had given an account of how each one of us had actually seen or had an encounter with one of these creatures. Amazingly once one kid had described this little black devil like pixie creature lurking around the base of a dark hole in an ancient tree in the "Clough", it was soon agreed by us all that these were indeed Boggarts because we all definitely had seen the same things. I ended up in adult life living literally opposite to Boggart Hole Clough and I don't mind admitting that my kids grew up knowing my childhood account of these "creatures". Further perpetuating the myth and I can honestly say without any form of real fear of them, as indeed myself and my brother grew up. No fear other than our typical childhood fantastic imagination and it really was just part of our childhood. Incidentally, the name Boggart Hole Clough was and is the source of many an amusing misnomer. Probably the most common one I've heard both past and present is "Bucket Ho Clough". Great memories indeed. I know I've not provided much on the actual folklore, but it is a personal and priceless memory of mine.'

Collyhurst 4 (La). 1960s/F/FG., 9-10-19. 'I was taught the boggarts lived in Bogart o Clough and were like the wombles. Kingsley Crescent, Collyhurst 1967.'

Collyhurst 5 (La). 1960s/F/FG., 9-10-19. 'I went to school just round the corner from Osborne Street. My gran and mother used the wash house there but my gran had to walk along Osborne street back to Miles Platting on the corner was and think still is a old mill on top was a iron like fixture that looked like a chair. We were told that. "Ginny green teeth" lived there. She sat up there to see who was being naughty. This was between 1950 and 1958. No. [For boggarts.]'

Collyhurst 6 (La). 1940s/F/FG., 9-10-19. 'I was born in 1941, lived in Slater Street. Used to go to the clough at weekends. For some reason I thought it was called Bucket o Clough, till I wrote an essay after having been there the teacher asked me where it was. I hadn't [heard of boggarts] till that day. Teacher told the class about them. I still got 6d (old money) for my essay, lol.'

Collyhurst 7 (La). 1950s/F/FG., 12-10-19. 'My decades were 1950s and 1960s. I lived in Higher Blackley, but my Gran lived on Grangepark Road which is opposite the gates to the Clough on Charlestown Road. We spent a lot of time in the Clough, with our Mum, Aunt and Gran, and cousin. We knew the Boggart was a baddie, like the Bogeyman! There is a pathway near to where an old tearooms used to be, also a bridge and ninety-nine steps leading off it. We always said the Boggart was under the bridge and got over the bridge quickly. Lol.'

Collyhurst 8 (La). 1940s/M/FG., 12-10-19. 'Hello. In the 1950s, when I was a very young policeman, Boggart Hole Clough in Blackley was part of the section I first patrolled. It was of a hilly terrain and thickly wooded for the most part and was a beat which was patrolled on a bicycle. The trees which lined both sides of the many cindered pathways were of great age and therefore tall and heavily branched so that the slightest breeze, at night would cause them to moan and groan. It also seemed at night, that somebody was walking behind you. The Clough was only a section of the beat covering the district, and there being a boating lake and buildings which housed the rowing boats, together with two cafes within its cartilage. The beat constable was required to examine those buildings at least twice during a tour of duty. Similarly, so as to avoid a prolonged cycle ride to reach the other side of the patrol we were obliged to cut through the clough. A young officer on his first night shift had been allocated the Boggart Hole Clough beat, having been shown round it on a day shift some weeks previously, and at the station whilst waiting for the instructions of the sergeant, the older bobbies began to discuss the boggart. "There's a full moon I see": said one. The others went on to remark that the spectre will be about the clough. They then left for their various duties. One of the officers had sped from the station and quickly cycled to an old rain shelter some yards into the clough and when the nervous probationer rode along the nearby path, the hidden copper let out a terrifying drawn out screech. The timid bobby left his bike and ran back to the main road. He worked the rest of the shift on foot, returning at dawn to collect the beat bike. A few weeks later he resigned from the police service having discovered that it really wasn't for him.'

Colne 1 (La). 1970s/M/FG., 27-9-19. 'I've heard of it [boggart] from my youth but not heard it since or remember where I'd actually heard it from. XXX or XXX are good on all things Colne. I was born in 1975, maybe it was something that was mentioned at infants/junior school.'
Colne 2 (La). 1970s/F/FG., 30-9-19. 'There used to be a Sabden Treacle mine visitor attraction and was full of little Treacle miners. Imaginary characters including the Treacle boggart. My mum bought me a little furry grey Treacle boggart, but I doubt I have it now.'
Colne 3 (La). 1950s/M/FG., 9-10-19. '"Off at boggart" meant running off, like a horse startled by a boggart. Also as a verb, as in "Wheer ar ta boggartin' off to?" I only knew the word in the sense of running when I was a kid in the 1950s. Didn't find out that boggarts were troll-like creatures until much later. Boggart Hole Clough is a grand northern placename.'
Croft 1 (La). 1940s/F/FG., 16-9-19. 'Yes my dad used the word "boggart". He was born in Croft in 1909 and I grew up in the 1940s in same place.'
Crompton 1 (La). 1960s/F/FG., 25-10-11. 'My mum used to tell me a story about graggly bones coming up the stairs one at a time getting closer and closer to my bedroom door then she would grab me and scare me to death and this was at bedtime in a creepy old farmhouse. She was born near high Crompton but had relatives in Milnrow and Newhay. Yes, a boggart I'm sure. I think the story came from her mother, passed down. I haven't scared my kids with the tale though.'
Cronton 1 (La). 1970s/F/FG., 28-9-19. 'We still use the word "Boggot" to the kids, lol: i.e. "the boggots will get you". Lol. Halton View and Cronton areas. As I said we still use this word "Boggart". Referring it to an evil spirit or monster lurking in the shadows lol. Now, I've just spoken with hubby who is much older than me and he mentioned the name of a road or area called Boggart Old Clough. Maybe top end of Cronton/ Rainhill. I will go and do a google search lol. Actually think it was more towards Tarbock area. Hubby 1950s and me 1970s/1980s. Lol. Oh my word we used to call it "Jimmy Green Teeth". Lol. We used to put the washing line prop across the grass/ lawn in the back garden. And we had to walk along the prop from one side of the lawn off the path towards the other side onto the boarder/soil. I suppose it was a variation of a bridge and water and keeping you away from deep water and the water's edge as you described in your comments, lol.'
Cronton 2 (La). 1950s/F/FG., 29-9-19. 'Born Cronton in 1956 moved Rainhill late 1960s. Only heard of the boggy man that came at night if you were naughty.'
Cronton 3 (La). 1950s/F/FG., 14-10-19. 'I was born in 1951 and grew up

just on the outside of Cronton from 1956 at the time (Lancashire). It's [boggart] not a term I have heard in the area, but I have read it in books though.'
Cronton 4 (La). 1950s/F/FG., 14-10-19. 'I lived in Cronton until I was twelve (1956-68) and don't recall hearing "boggart" at all.'
Crumpsall 1 (La). 1950s/F/FG., 26-9-19. 'I grew up in Crumpsall in the fifties and regularly played in Boggart Hole Clough. I have vague memories of my dad telling us that Boggarts were bad, but can't remember why!'
Crumpsall 2 (La). 1950s/M/FG., 26-9-19. 'I was born in Crumpsall in 1958 and lived there for the first forty-three years of my life, we went to Boggart Hole Clough regularly as children then played football there as adults. We were told Boggarts were little imps. Like mischievous beings who would play pranks on you, we were told to watch out for them when we went to the fair at the Clough at night-time or the evening. What do you mean as kids? As a sixty-one year old man I still believe in them. Yes of course we believed in them, my older brothers would try to scare me with them when we went to the fair as children. My mum used to always say behave or the Boggarts will come for you as we were leaving to go to the fair without her. It kept us on our toes. We would play up to each other that we didn't believe in them. But I think deep down we did because our parents spoke about them. I know I personally did.'
Crumpsall 3 (La). 1960s/M/FG., 26-9-19. 'Spent many happy hours in Boggart Hole Clough in the 1960s when it was a beautiful day out with a packed lunch of meat paste butties and bottle of water the story my mum told was the "Boggart" was a naughty imp who, if it found children being naughty, would encourage them to be even naughtier so as to get them in more trouble and on occasions would tempt them into the depths of the Clough to take them to their lair never to be seen again, and I am assuming that is where the "hole" comes from. No never heard that [story of boggart being buried under stone] from my mum but I'm of the opinion all mums had their own version of the story just to frighten the children to come home before dark.'
Crumpsall 4 (La). 1960s/F/FG., 26-9-19. 'Born 1965 Crumpsall and grew up there. Used to go to Boggart Hole Clough park when growing up. There was a rectangular boulder rising from the ground and my dad once told my brother and me (probably in the early 1970s) that it was where they had buried the Boggart when he died and accidentally left one of his feet sticking out of the ground. The Boggart, to me, was a giant.'
Crumpsall 5 (La). 1960s/M/FG., 27-9-19. 'I think anyone growing up in Crumpsall would know the word "Boggart" from the Clough all the others

have mentioned. I was born in 1960, and I probably took it as just a name until adults, usually my parents, explained what it meant. Somehow, I always associated the big dip in the ground at the corner of Rochdale and Charlestown Roads as being the boggart's hole. But [I] think that was just my imagination! Should've made clear, born and grew up in Crumpsall.'

Crumpsall 6 (La). 1950s/F/FG., 27-9-19. 'Born in Crumpsall 1957. I was told they lived in the bushes in the park. Scared the life out of me.'

Crumpsall 7 (La). 1960s/F/FG., 27-9-19. 'Born Crumpsall, 1961. Always told [about] the Boggart. "He" lived under a big rock that used to be I think near Boothhall hospital entrance.'

Crumpsall 8 (La). 1950s/F/FG., 4-10-19. 'Born in 1950 in Crumpsall and all the populous knew of Boggart Hole Clough and thought of it as being a bit spooky.'

Dalton-in-Furness 1 (La). 1950s/F/FG., 28-9-19. 'I grew up in Martin and Dalton in 1950s, 1960s. Never heard [of] them [boggarts].'

Darwen 1 (La). ???/F/FG., 28-9-19. 'My husband uses the word [boggart] lots. He comes from Darwin Lancashire. Not a word I was familiar with myself.'

Denton 1 (La). 1940s/F/FG., 4-10-19. 'I didn't move to Euxton till I was twenty-four so would seem to miss out on your target. However, I was born in Denton, Manchester (now Tameside) in 1948 and also lived in Dukinfield and Ashton-under-Lyne in the 1960s where Boggarts were well known. A popular picnic area was Boggart Hole Clough and we were often told as kids "behave, or the boggart will get you". I never heard any specific tales about Boggarts though it just seemed to be a general notion of the Boggart or Bogeyman being a danger.'

Denton 2 (La). 1930s/F/FG., 2-10-19. 'I always remember bogey man 1930s and 1940s. Grew up in Denton 1935 to 1955. Married an Audenshaw boy. Moved to Australia in 1964.'

Droylsden 1 (La). 1950s/F/FG., 22-9-19 'My father came from Blackley and lived near Boggart Hole Clough. He used to tell us that he played there as a child. We lived in Droylsden. I was born 1953. To be honest I can only recall that he lived near it and it was a scary place to play. Sorry I can't be of more help.'

Droylsden 2 (La). 1940s/F/FG., 13-10-19. 'I was born at home in Droylsden in 1948. Never heard of boggarts but the bogey man, oh yes. Scared the life out of me.'

Droylsden 3 (La). 1950s/M/FG., 13-10-19. 'Lived in Droylsden since I was born in 1951. Never heard of a Boggart.'

Droylsden 4 (La). 1940s/F/FG., 13-10-19. 'I grew up in Droylsden in 1940s/1950s. If I was trying a fast one on my Mother she would say "you're as farce as a boggart". Still don't know what she meant.'
Droylsden 5 (La). 1940s/F/FG., 13-10-19. 'Born in Droylsden in 1949. Lived there for fifty-eight years and still visit family. I don't recall ever hearing "boggart" mentioned. My husband used to live in Blackley and played in Boggart Hole Clough!'
Droylsden 6 (La). 1950s/F/FG., 13-10-19. 'Born in Droylsden 1951. Lived here all my life and never heard boggart mentioned except for Boggart Hole Clough.'
Droylsden 7 (La). 1950s/F/FG., 13-10-19. Droylsden 1950s, 1960s. Never heard of Boggart but lived in Blackley in 1970s and obviously Boggart Hole Clough.'
Droylsden 8 (La). 1950s/F/FG., 13-10-19. 'I'm from Droylsden born 1956, never heard or used the word "Boggert". Very interesting though?'
Droylsden 9 (La). 1950s/M/FG., 14-10-19. 'I was brought up on Hawthorn Road on the edge of the moss and was told as a youngster: "If you don't go to sleep the Moss Bogarts are coming." That was mid to late 1950s.'
Droylsden 10 (La). 1950s/M/FG., 14-10-19. 'Born mid-1950s, Manchester Road Droylsden. Heard of the bogeyman but don't remember boggarts. However, I was working in Hyde in the 1970s and when I reported a broken roller towel in the gents a local woman said "it's tekken boggarts" which she said meant it was broken.'
Droylsden 11 (La). 1950s/M/FG., 16-10-19. 'Born in 1956 in Droylsden and definitely knew about boggarts. I was given an explanation that term (and bogey men) arose from the oppression of the Catholic religion when priests would [hide] in panels or other nooks and crannies in houses to avoid capture. Any noises they made would be put down to boggart or bogey man. I think Boggart Hole Clough still exists in Manchester.'
Droylsden 12 (La). 1940s/F/FG., 18-10-19. 'My mother was born in Droylsden, 1947, and brought up same area. My grandfather (her father) used to mention boggarts to her but he was from Wales.'
Droylsden 13 (La). 1970s/F/FG., 21-10-19. 'Pretty sure one of my sisters used to terrify me as a kid telling me boggarts lived in the clough and would get me if I was there in the dark. Early 1970s. Yes, born and bred [in Droylsden]. It was the local clough, between Clough Road and Littlemoss area. There was a path that ran along the back of XXX's yard and across the wooden railway bridge (monkey bridge?). Used to be terrified of going along there on my own, particularly if it was getting dark. Never really strayed much onto the clough because of it.'

Eccleston 1 (La). 1960s/F/FG., 3-10-19. 'I was born 1969 and my dad often referred to anything that was a mess as it "fathered a boggert's nest". We were from Eccleston and my dad caught a lot of expressions from his mother who was from Standish. I thought a boggert was a stuffy man.'
Edenfield 1 (La). 1940s/M/FG., 17-10-19. 'I was born in 1945 and remember lots of references [to] "the boggart". My dad worked at XXX's farm in Edenfield a village not far from Rossendale and after the harvest and the hay bales were stacked to the roof in the hay barn, us kids used to play hiding away amongst the hay bales. But when my dad got fed up with looking for us all he had to do was just say: "if you don't come out now I'll send the Bogart in to get you". That was enough we used to run out with fear in our eyes. Still don't know why.'
Edgworth 1 (La). 1930s/F/FG., 18-10-19. 'Boggarts were a familiar lot to me growing up in Edgworth in the 1930s and 1940s. Scary things like unaccountable sounds or happenings. Grownups would put it down to boggarts.'
Edgworth 2 (La). 1970s/F/FG., 18-10-19. 'Hi. I grew up in Edgworth in the 1970s/1980s. I was told by my dad that Hob Lane, off Blackburn road in Edgworth, was called that because of the Hob Goblins that lived down the lane. My dad's friend lived in the cottage at the very top of the lane and had told my dad the story. He had lived in Edgworth all his life, as had his parents. Also heard of the word "Boggart" not sure whether it's linked. Just googled it and the head of the Boggarts was called Hobs. [FB user adds: You are probably aware that a "hob" was a form of boggart. Hob Lane is at north end of Edgworth village, leading down to Wayoh reservoir. Maybe some mileage in looking into that placename?]'
Edgworth 3 (La). 1950s/F/E., 20-10-19. 'I grew up in Edgworth late 1950s/1960s never heard of bogarts! Until my Cumbrian mother-in-law used to refer to her tiny corgi cross Jack Russell dog (? no one is quite sure what she was but looked like a tiny fox) as a bogart when she was having what we all called a "silly session", chasing around, snapping and barking at nothing in particular, just for the fun of it. Have you looked at the TWA DOGS INN, Keswick. They have a REAL Specimen of a bogart there! I did, however, scare myself silly watching *Quatermass and the Pit* in the late 1950s. The capsule was found in HOBBS Lane. Where I lived in Edgworth. Perhaps some research is needed into Hob Goblins too! Good Luck and if you do find a bogart please send me a piccie. My mum-in-law's family hailed from Siloth/Wigton area. She was born and raised at Wheyrigg farm, outskirts of Wigton.'
Edgworth 4 (La). ???/M/FG., 23-10-19. 'With a dad from Blackley, Manchester who grew up playing in Boggart Hole Clough and a Mum from

Middleton both born in the 1930s I heard various stories of Boggarts and even a couple of poems as a kid. So, whilst we talked about them in the family. I don't remember hearing any from the other kids.'

Edgworth 5 (La). 1960s/M/FG., 24-10-19. 'I never heard that word. I lived in Edgworth from birth in 1966 till 2010. My mum never used it. She was born and died in Edgworth.'

Edgworth 6 (La). ???/F/FG., 7-11-19. 'My granny had a well in the bottom of her garden Sharples Meadow Edgworth. She told us granny green teeth lived at the bottom of the well and would get us if we went near it.... [Other user: I caught frogs in Gran's well. It looked Soooooo deep. Maybe thats why I now have a fear of "dark water".] Could be. Frightened the life out of me.'

Edgworth 7 (La). 1930s/F/FG., 7-11-19. 'Me and my family Edgworth/ chapel town /Broadhead since 1936 we all use the word "boggart". Mum's now eighty-three and she mentioned them the other day.'

Euxton 1 (La). 1980s/F/FG., 4-10-19. 'I was born in the 1980s and still heard about boggarts from my grandparents [confirmed Euxton]. Yeah, usually when my nan couldn't find something she claimed it must have been the boggarts.'

Euxton 2 (La). 1950s/F/FG., 4-10-19. 'Hi, I grew up in Euxton in the 1950s but never heard of the word "Boggarts"'.

Euxton 3 (La). 1950s/F/FG., 4-10-19. 'XXX, and I grew up together and went to Euxton C. of E. school together in the 1950s. Sorry but I have never heard anyone talk about Boggarts.'

Euxton 4 (La). 1960s/F/FG., 4-10-19. 'I was born in 1965. I'm 53. My dad always used to say there were boggarts in the woods in Croston as you come into the village.'

Euxton 5 (La). 1970s/F/FG., 4-10-19. 'Brought up in Euxton (1970s) went to St Mary's School. Heard stories of boggarts both at school and, I'm pretty sure, at Brownies!'

Euxton 6 (La). 1970s/F/FG., 4-10-19. 'I grew up in Euxton in the 1970s and my dad always told me to mind out for the boggarts. Used to scare the life out of me. He's eighty-seven now and teases his grandchildren about the boggarts.'

Euxton 7 (La). 1970s/F/FG., 4-10-19. 'I was born and bred in Euxton, 71. I had heard about "boggarts" and used the word when out riding and my horse spooked at something, lol. I also remember the Sabden treacle mines, they have treacle eating boggarts that live there.'

Euxton 8 (La). 1960s/F/FG., 4-10-19. 'I was born in 1964 and lived in Euxton all my life, until four years ago when I moved to Chorley. "Owd Shap

Boggart" was always being mentioned in our house. My Dad, now 90 and my Granddad were always trying to frighten us children with "Owd Shap Boggart". [Didn't know who Old Shap was].'

Euxton 9 (La). 1960s/F/FG., 4-10-19. 'Grew up in Euxton, 1960s and 1970s, my mum used to say the word "boggarts", as a scared character or troll. She would say be careful or the boggarts will get you!'

Euxton 10 (La). 1960s/F/FG., 4-10-19. 'Born in Euxton lived there all my life – when something spooks or runs off "its taken Boggarts"! Or "teken boggarts". My mum is from Adlington though and she used to talk about some men that used to hang around in the park area that her mother used to tell her and her sisters to stay away from and she used to call them "Crow Boggarts". I assumed they maybe worked in the pits or coal mines so that's why they were black as crows. But I can ask her for more info if you need me to. She was born in 1940.'

Euxton 11 (La). 1970s/F/FG., 4-10-19. 'I grew up in Euxton. My uncle used to tell a story about the Boggart of Euxton Parish, which apparently lived in the field at the back of our house. My cousins then used to go home to Leyland, while my brother and I would lie awake, scared half to death that the Boggart would emerge and eat us! I lived in the row of houses on the Leyland side of Packsaddle bridge. Little bit earlier, probably late 1970s.'

Failsworth 1 (La). 1950s/M/F., 29-8-19. 'First off I grew up in the North West, a village called Failsworth which is now part of greater Manchester, but in the 1950s we weren't. Our own council, police force and countryside mostly all around. So grandparents and great uncles and aunts told stories which I'm afraid I don't remember much of but [boggarts were] big and hairy and very black, then another was small and angry and very hairy. Hairy was the main thing. Moved away in the late 1970s and didn't have children until the 1990s and never passed on the stories to my daughter as they were forgotten. Sorry. The boggarts were used as a type of bogey man thing to get us kids to behave I think. Sorry I don't know anyone who has these stories. My gran always told us if we stayed out after dark the Bogarts would get us little ones.'

Failsworth 2 (La). 1960s/F/FG., 23-9-19. 'I grew up in Failsworth in the 1960s and 1970s. I knew the word "boggart". I used to love cycling to Boggart Hole Clough in Blackley to play. Searching the woodland trying to find the mischievous goblin that was supposed to haunt the area. As the light faded I was sure I could feel him watching me and cycled home top speed, terrified he might chase and eat me. Guess today's children probably think a boggart is just a shapeshifter from the Harry Potter novels.'

Fallowfield 1 (La). 1950s/F/E., 30-9-19. 'And I did hear about boggarts from my mum in the 1950s. I was aware of Boggart Hole Clough and something that lived amongst the rocks there? Plus one of my mum's favourite book (and still mine) is *Waste Castle* by W. M. Letts. It's set in Manchester and the little girl who tells the story is scared of a particular lane. My mum said it would be a boggart! "But one of the girls at school had told me a horrid story about this lane, that it was haunted by a lame old woman who came hobbling after you at dusk and caught your dress. In the rainy dusk the lane looked long and dreary. I felt that I simply could not go. I set off running, and I ran as hard as I could; I felt sure that I did hear someone following me, but perhaps it was the noise my heart was making." So really it was from Didsbury/Fallowfield where I grew up not Gorton (where I went to school because my dad was headmaster at Thoams Street) that I heard about boggarts. The main terror in Gorton was the brook – we had a rhyme about it that I'll send you if I can remember it. But not boggarts. My dad grew up in a haunted house in the grounds of Manchester Grammar School – must have told you about that and revisiting it a couple of years ago? But he just said it was something that took doors off the hinges, rang bells etc and was there as a presence. I don't think my dad used the word "boggart".'

Fleetwood 1 (La). 1960s/F/FG., 28-9-19. 'Hi, I was born in Fleetwood in 1968, and my mum (who's now seventy) would often say "you little boggart" to me, with the same tone as I would have called my own children "little monkey". It wasn't used in a negative way, and was often accompanied by laughter. She used it if I was maybe a bit cheeky etc. I heard her use it quite a lot, but it was long forgotten until I read your post! I never asked her what a boggart was. However, I will ask her next time I see her. She's a retired head teacher and her degree was in English, so I'm certain she will be interested. [Mum was not in brownies, though respondent was].'

Fleetwood 2 (La). 1940s/F/FG., 5-10-19. 'I was born in Fleetwood in 1949 and have never heard the name "boggarts" mentioned. It may be common in other parts of Lancashire, but I don't think it is local to Fleetwood.'

Fleetwood 3 (La). 1950s/F/FG., 5-10-19. 'Born in the 1950s in Fleetwood, never heard of the word "Boggart". But like the lady in earlier comment parents used to scare children with Ginny Green Teeth, if they didn't behave.'

Fleetwood 4 (La). 1950s/F/FG., 4-10-19. 'I was born in Fleetwood in 1957 and lived there til 1986. I heard of them and was often warned not to go near ponds and dykes as Jenny Green teeth lived in them and pulled kids under water. My grandmother on Mum's side was a Scot and I can remember her telling this to my sister and myself. Yes I was told so. [Jenny a boggart]. Didn't stop me going to ponds though.'

Fleetwood 5 (La). 1950s/F/FG., 11-10-19. 'In this care home I asked and most born in 1920/1930s remember those as just ghosts not a threat. I was born in 1950s and had never heard the word. Do not know if relevant but one of Irish family know other words.'

Fleetwood 6 (La). 1960s/F/FG., 18-10-19. 'I grew up in Fleetwood during the 1960s and 1970s and we used to play a chasing game on the street called Brownies, Boggarts and Bluebirds. The Brownies were like elves/pixies and the Boggarts were mean goblin-type creatures and the Bluebirds were the goodies. I was quite used to hearing the term "Boggarts" during my childhood. Hi, I wasn't in the Brownies myself but others may have been so maybe it did come from there.'

Fleetwood 7 (La). 1950s/F/E., 2-11-19. 'Grew up in 1950/1960s, first in Fleetwood, then in Cleveleys. Left the area in 1972. My mother always used to say "the Boggarts" were around if there was an unexplained problem in the home! E.g. we had a big solid chair with bun feet and one fell off unexpectedly so Mother blamed the Boggart! Mother originally came from Accrington, so maybe it's a Lancashire thing. My father came from Preston and he also knew all about them! I have lived in different places in the UK and Canada, have ended up near Lincoln but only ever heard of Boggarts in Lancashire!'

Formby 1 (La). 1940s/F/FG., 21-9-19. 'I was born in 1946 and grew up in Formby/Freshfield until 1953. We moved to Southport until 1955. My parents then moved to Birkdale and then Hillside and I left the area in 1968. I do not think the term "Boggart" was ever used at home or school, but the term "Bogieman" was used.'

Freckleton 1 (La). 1950s/F/FG., 4-10-19. 'My Grandma used to call hedgehog poo boggart muck. 1950s Freckleton. Boggart = Something scary.'

Furness 1 (La). 1970s/F/FG., 21-9-19. 'I grew up in the 1970s in South Cumbria, and a Boggart was classed as a cheeky, mischievous little creature that lives in nature.'

Fylde 1 (La). 1960s/M/FG., 17-10-19. 'I grew up in the Fylde in the 1960s and 1970s and remember my Dad talking about a Boggart. I could be wrong but I seem to remember R.G. Shepherd, who had a weekly column on a Saturday in the *Evening Gazette*, writing about Boggarts. His column was in the paper throughout the 1970s and it was called "In The Country", and he wrote about country life, folklore, wildlife, local characters etc from the Over Wyre area of the Fylde.'

Fylde 2 (La). 1970s/F/FG., 17-10-19. 'I grew up in the Fylde in the 1970s and definitely knew the term [boggart].'

Fylde 3 (La). 1990s/F/FG., 17-10-19. 'We went on residential school trips to Patterdale in the 1990s and were told stories about boggarts on the walks. Each instructor had a slightly different description though and definitely not a term we heard outside of the Lake District.'

Grange-Over-Sands 1 (La). ???/F/F.,12-9-19. 'When we moved up from the South East to south Cumbria in 1971 we inherited a small holly tree near our front door. When I told an elderly friend that we intended to cut it down she said: "beware as it will let the boggart into the house". From memory I think we still got rid of it? Never heard of boggarts in Kent although I do recall being scared of the boggy man. Grange-over-Sands, South Cumbria overlooking Morecambe Bay.'

Grange-Over-Sands 2 (La). ???/F/F., 13-9-19. 'Grange over Sands used to be in Lancashire. The boundaries were changed in 1974, and it became Cumbria, perhaps the boggarts moved too. My grandmother often warned us that they were watching us. Born and bred in Grange over Sands, I am fourth generation of our family to be in Grange. Yes, if we misbehaved we would be chased by the boggart and if he caught us we would be put in the glory hole which in Gran's house was the under stairs space filled with all unused junk. But it was pitch black and as a child a terrifying place. But if we wanted to please the boggart we had to polish his boots until they shone and leave them by the door to the glory hole. Being cheeky and badly behaved was not allowed but I'm very good at polishing boots!'

Great Harwood 1 (La). 1930s/M/FG., 19-09-19. 'My dad (eighty-four next week) talks about Boggarts. He's Great Harwood. Is that close enough? I'll ask mum to ask him'.

Great Harwood 2 (La). 1960s/F/F., 29-8-19. 'I was brought up by grandparents in a town called Great Harwood in Lancashire. My grandparents and my dad used the word in the 1960s. He used the word to scare us saying "the boggarts are coming to get you". He never actually said what boggarts were, but I built up an image in my little girl mind of a sort of dark swamp goblin. Grandparents teach us so much, if only we listened more often before it's too late.'

Great Harwood 3 (La). 1970s/M/E., 29-8-19. 'I have been asked [by] my mother-in-law to contact yourself regarding the origins of the word "boggart", so I'll try to answer in order of requests. I was born very late 1970s and am from Great Harwood near Blackburn. We used to get told when we were kids that strange happenings or sightings of ghosts were boggarts. It was my late father who told me it meant ghost or poltergeist.'

Great Harwood 4 (La). 1960s/F/E., 4-10-19. 'Hi, I grew up in Park Road Great Harwood in the 1960s. Boggarts were never mentioned in my home, but the bogey man was. You were threatened with him if you did anything naughty or if we were out playing in the dark. In my mind I associate boggarts with more of a rural area, of a person or being who lives in or around marshland. Hope this helps. History and memories are very important.'

Great Harwood 5 (La). 1990s/F/FG., 4-10-19. 'My Granddad used to tell us stories about boggarts when we were little. That was in the early 1990s though – Great Harwood.'

Great Harwood 6 (La). 1950s/F/FG., 4-10-19. 'I never heard "bogart", my mum was a "southerner". But she did warn us about the pooka, a huge rabbit (aka Harvey in the James Stewart film of the same name). Never sure what the pooka would do. Great Harwood, 1950s.'

Great Harwood 7 (La). 1950s/F/FG., 5-10-19. 'My Granddad used "Yon Boggart in't coal house" to scare me. Great Harwood 1960s to 1980s.'

Great Harwood 8 (La). 1920s/F/FG., 5-10-19. 'I was born in Great Harwood in 1929 and still live here. Uncle Alec used to tell me: "Tha'd better be off afore t'boggarts catch thee." I thought boggarts were huge black bats who could carry me away. I was frightened of them and used to avoid walking past the back streets where they might be waiting for me.'

Great Harwood 9 (La). 1970s/F/FG., 10-10-19. 'Yep the word "bogart" was used in our house when I was a little girl. Not in specific stories. I assumed it was just another name for the bogeyman. I was born, 1971.'

Great Harwood 10 (La). 1960s/M/FG., 16-10-19. 'I grew up in Great Harwood in the 1960s and I was told that there were boggarts in the fields by the top road to Blackburn, near to what is now the Spice Lounge (previously the Shepherd's Rest and the new inns).'

Great Harwood 11 (La). 1960s/M/FG., 21-10-19. 'Camped as a Christ Church scout in the 1960s at Bowley Great Harwood and we were told that the Bowley boggart would prowl at nite! Maybe coming from where XXX said, never saw one but heard sounds… Bloody scared us'

Halsall 1 (La). 1960s/M/FG., 4-10-19. 'I grew up in Halsall. We were told not to go too near the canal as Ginny Greenweed – a green monster with long fingers – would pull us under. [Boggarts] No I don't think so.'

Halsall 2 (La). 1970s/F/FG., 17-10-19. 'We grew up in the 1970s in Halsall and my brother was and still well known as "Boggert". I have tagged him above. He may be working today, so might be a while till answers. He got it from a very young age, prob when five. He was very, very naughty. [Brother adds: 'I got the nick-name when I was very young. My auntie lived in Yorkshire where they used to use that term all the time. Anyway I had a few friends over and my mum told them all a bit of a made up ghost story really, including the term 'bogarts' in it hence how I got my nick-name, since then its stuck, lol.'] [Mother adds: 'my son XXX nick-named boggart, got the name because of being naughty. An auntie told him if he didn't behave the boggart would come. He would run around shouting "boggart". All his friends called him boggart at school. He's now in his late 40s and some still call him "boggart". If you ask anyone in Halsall and about "do you know boggart" they'll probably say "yea, it's XXX". The auntie was from Yorkshire and boggarts are well known there'].'

Halsall 3 (La). 1960s/M/FG., 17-10-19. 'I lived on Watson House farm from 1964 to 1974. With my twin brother XXX, mum XXX, Grandmother, XXX and Grandfather XXX. They used to tell us about the bogarts down the moors. The "moors" being the cart track down to the fields which led eventually to Clock House Farm. They also used to tell us about "Jenny" or "Jinny" Greenteeth, a water witch who would drag us into the water if we played around the canal, pits or ditches. (I'm a bit of a musician in my spare time, I've actually written a song about Jinny Greenteeth and an instrumental called Clock House. I've also written about the man in a boat on the side of the church). I have many powerful, inspiring and happy memories of growing up in Halsall. Good luck with your project.'

Hambleton 1 (La). 1970s/F/FG., 17-9-19. 'Where the Grange (house/old farm) is in Hambleton used to be called Boggart Yate/gate (in the long distant past). My Dad's family used to own it and he was born in the 1950s, but doesn't really know why it had that name.'

Hambleton 2 (La). 1970s/M/FG., 13-10-19. 'In the 1970s and 1980s I lived in Hambleton and there was for a while a restaurant called "Ye Old Boggery Gate". I vaguely remember older people in the area mentioning that a boggart was occasionally seen and that the gate was where he was hung. Unfortunately, I cannot substantiate this but maybe one of the group has more info?'

Hareholme 1 (La). 1940s/M/FG., 20-9-19. 'Born in Hareholme and spent my pre-nursery days in Sandybank with my grandma. If I was playing up she'd say "Boggarts'll get thee if tha doesn't buck up". I was at times threatened by "Mad Ab". I believe he was a real local character but have no idea who. I was born in 1948 so it would be early 1950s.'

Harpurhey 1 (La). ???/M/FG., 17-10-19. 'Lived in Harpurhey and moved to Blackley. Used to go to Boggart Hole Clough as a kid rowing on the lake with my dad. As we got older. We used to walk to my gran's in Moston through the clough. We knew about the boggarts (the little people) who live in the clough, in the dip near the cafe. The boggarts were naughty fairies.'

Harpurhey 2 (La). 1930s/M/FG., 17-10-19. 'I was born in Harpurhey in 1939 and it was always referred to as Boggart Hole Clough so I have heard the name all my life. Just thought it was a mischievous being, was not really scared.'

Haslingden 1 (La). 1960s/F/FG., 20-9-19. 'My husband and I are keen walkers so when walking over Holcombe Moor and seeing walkers in the distance we refer to them as "boggarts" and I thought I just made it up, but reading this made me think maybe it came from my childhood. Brought up in Haslingden in the 1960s. We live in Spain now and always refer to people we see in the distance as "boggarts".'
Haslingden 2 (La). 1950s/M/FG., 21/9/19. 'Haslingden mid-1950s to late 1960s. "Off at boggart" used a lot also "bogey man" which I assumed was a derivative of boggart. No [boggart] was just a general saying used by all. The only meaning I knew was off at a rush, in a hurry.'
Haslingden 3 (La). 1950s/M/FG., 21-9-19. 'I was in a play put on by Haslingden arts' club which had a boggart as one of the characters. This would have been in the late 1960s. I'm afraid I can't remember the name of the play, it was a long time ago. That was the first time I heard the word, as far as I know. I grew up in Haslingden. Sorry, don't remember that. I would have been around thirteen-fourteen.'
Haslingden 4 (La). ???/F/FG., 17-10-19. 'My Grandmother used to talk of being chased by a Boggart back in the early 1900s on the moors above Prinny Hill, Haslingden. Always took this with a pinch of salt (which was wise as Boggarts can't cross salt).'
Helmshore 1 (La). 1930s/M/E., 4-9-19. 'Boggart is a poltergeist. I was born in 1933 and lived as a child within three hundred yards of the Boggart House described in my publication. Everyone in the village used the word, though few residents took the idea seriously. I have no children, and I doubt if the word is used or even understood by the younger generation. The Boggart House was demolished long ago and is remembered only by the elderly.'
Helmshore 2 (La). 1970s/F/FG., 20-9-19. 'Grew up in Helmshore in the 1970s and 1980s and remember my brother buying a treacle-eating boggart from Sabden.'
Helmshore 3 (La). ???/M/FG., 17-10-19. 'There was a fun run in Helmshore called the boggatts jaunt in the 1990s.'
Helmshore 4 (La). ???/F/FG., 17-10-19. 'Probably too late timewise but only heard of "boggarts" when I drove to work at Queens Park Conservation Studios in the early 2000s. Thought this was very quaint and didn't think much of it until there was I think a murder there. Locked my car doors to and from work after that! Then at St Veronica's my daughters were in the choir and Mrs XXX taught them a song about "Boggarts" and they sang it at Preston Guild Hall where the lovely Diane Oxberry was the presenter for the evening. The girls were very taken by it and used to sing it at the

tops of their voices in the car for years after! So the word has some mixed memories for me.'

Heywood 1 (La). 1940s/F/ E., 8-9-19. 'Sorry for the delay – been delving into a couple of Lancashire dialect books I have to see if there was any mention of boggarts – there isn't. To me a boggart is an evil old tramp-like person who kidnaps children! Grandma Gordon (Auntie Tags) often mentioned the boggarts will come and get you if you are naughty! Parents didn't mention boggarts but did mention the bogey man – it's a wonder we didn't all grow up with nervous dispositions. Children, nephews and nieces do not use the word as far as I know Do not know of any stories about boggarts, but I did work at ICI in Blackley and spent many a lunch hour in Boggart Hole Clough! Grew up in Heywood, Lancashire in the 1940s and 1950s.'

Heywood 2 (La). 1930s/F/E., 8-9-19. 'In response to your earlier email, I imagine a boggart, as a female creature of evil intent, living beneath water, especially deep, murky ponds in isolated places. When I was young, I remember passing Boggart Hole Clough on the bus route into Manchester and my Mother saying it was a place best avoided, as nasty things had occurred there. I don't think my parents talked about boggarts as I was growing up. The only other creature I heard of, which could be classed as a boggart, was Jinney Greenteeth. My childhood friend lived in Hopwood, on a farm, through which the canal flowed. Her mother used to warn us to keep away from the bank, or Jinney Greenteeth would spring up from under the reeds, grab us and take us under the water. I was born in 1937 and grew up in Heywood, Lancashire.'

Heywood 3 (La). 1920s/M/E., 12-3-19. Lynda Taylor interviewed Arthur Taylor (born April 1926). 'He told me that: "Nothing will ever grow except grass in any boggart field". I asked if he was talking specifically about the boggart field at Gristlehurst. No – any boggart field, he said. But he didn't know of any other, but knew this was a fact. Gristlehurst in the Census is deemed a hamlet. There are two or three dwellings there... Arthur grew up with the expression "The bogey-man will come for you" and he was clear that a boggart was "a little elf – a bad one. Not just mischievous, but bad, evil". Specific, not generic. Now, in his childhood and teens he didn't live at this end of Heywood; he lived on the Manchester side, two to three miles away. I'd be surprised if his understanding came from any knowledge of the Grizlehurst boggart (too rural). He did know, of course, about Boggart Old Clough. He said he'd visited the Clough as a child – he thought probably on a Sunday School trip. He didn't see the irony.'

Heywood 4 (La). ???/F/FG., 19-9-19. 'I didn't move to Littleborough until 1973. However, I grew up in Heywood where people talked about the

Gristlehurst Boggart, if that's any interest to you. Yes, it would have been in the sixties that I heard of it. It was said to throw people about of bed and move things around in the house. Grizlehurst Farm is still there but the old hall was gone before I was born. Legend has it that it was buried with a cockerel with a stake through its heart, yet continued to cause mischief. I would refer you to Edwin Waugh, as one of his books of *Lancashire Sketches* opens with a chapter on the subject, although you may find the dialect heavy going!'

Heywood 5 (La). 1950s/M/E., 4-9-19. 'Well, I used to pass Boggart Hole Clough every day going to work (at ICI Blackley) and my Father was born round the corner from it. I never gave the word "Boggart" much thought, but when asked, my Father did tell me that the clough was the home to a nasty evil little being that could cause all sorts of trouble, and the "hole" was where it lived. But he never used the word in any context, not to me anyway. I had the feeling from him that parents took advantage of this story as a scare tactic, to try to keep their children out of the woods and out of danger! As you know I grew up in Heywood and in the 1950s.'

Heywood 6 (La). 1950s/F/E., 4-9-19. 'Some strange goblin-like creature who lives in forests or woods. Yes, in relation to Boggart Hole Clough. No children etc. Boggart Hole Clough. They lived in the trees. Heywood in the 1950s.'

Heywood 7 (La). 1940s/M/E., 4-9-19. 'Never encountered this word before today. Heywood, Lancashire. 1940s/1950s. My wife claims the word is linked to "Boggart Hole Clough".'

Heywood 8 (La). 1950s/F/E., 30-9-19. 'Boggart: a malevolent supernatural creature – worse than mischievous – found in both country and town. I think of a boggart as male. He has his own defined space and woe betide anyone who crosses the liminal boundary. This space could be a field or hole, but equally in town, a house or public building. Some of the stories told to you are very reminiscent of Scandinavian tales of elves, so I'm wary of getting the two confused. But where elves could often be helpful and were always physically attractive, I don't perceive either characteristic in the boggart. The very choice of word "boggart" suggests an unattractive, earthy figure. My children don't use the word. It was quite a common admonition in the late 1950s that the bogey-man would come to take you away if you were being naughty, but I don't recall my parents referring to the boggart itself, except in Boggart Hole Clough – about six miles from where I lived. The connection with the boggart didn't stop anyone going for an afternoon out, including (ironically) Sunday School trips. Not for me; for XXX. Later – in my twenties – I came across the tale of the Grislehurst Boggart, as I lived across the road from it.

I then traced the tale in Waugh's account (and, of course, went to look for it). Born in Heywood in the 1950s.'

Hindley 1 (La). 1950s/M/E., 10-10-19. 'I've seen your post as regards Boggarts and I'm sending you my memory. I'm sixty-six now and was born in Hindley but have lived in Atherton since 1979. As a kid in the late 1950s my granddad was telling my dad about our local rag and bone man doing his rounds. When he came into our street his mild gentle horse reared up neighed loudly then set off galloping towards the next street. The rag and bone man, with neighbours, chased after his horse and cart and finally calmed his horse down saying it had never done that before. My granddad told him "Thee 'orse went Boggart!" When I asked him what a Boggart was he said it's a small elf-like spirit that plays bad tricks or pranks on people. Every time the rag and bone man came into our street his horse would shy from that spot and had to be coaxed forward. My granddad often told me never to go into a local lodge alone, called the Deep Pit, as a Boggart has already pulled two young lads under and drowned them. I do ghost walks around Atherton and collect ghost stories from locals and one elderly gentleman told me that his dad told him to keep away from the area in Atherton called the Valley as a local Boggart there has a habit of pushing people into the brook or making the stepping stones wobble when anyone walked across the brook. Whilst metal detecting in the Valley one morning I found a rusted tin close to the Valley brook's bank and when forced open it contained a small piece of parchment with a spell to a water sprite or Boggart, dated to the 1870s, asking them to take away a wart. The tin also contained a horsehair ring for the sprite and a feather writing quill. I hope this information is useful.'

Hindley Green 1 (La). 1890s/M/FG., 17-10-19. 'My Granddad was born in 1898, in Hindley Green Wigan. He used to tell us a story about the local Boggart house. He said that early one morning a friend and himself were out picking coal. 1930s depression. Apparently there was a bridge just ahead, underneath the bridge was the Boggart houses. He said they both saw a man sat on the bridge, and the man was only wearing a nightshirt! Odd... Anyway, as they got closer the man just disappeared in thin air, scared my granddad's friend half to death. When they got home, they told the story to family and friends. They were told that a man who lived in the houses had jumped off the bridge, and unfortunately died, the description they gave, was apparently very accurate, and they didn't walk past that area again. [Did you grow up with boggarts?] No, just the story!'

Hoghton 1 (La). 1950s/M/FG., 28-9-19. 'Hoghton near Preston. Heard and used the term "boggart", 1957.'

Hollingworth 1 (La). 1960s/M/FG., 26-9-19. 'Clegg Hall boggert when we was kids. Hollingworth lake, 1960s 1970s.'
Hollingwood 1 (La). 1940s/F/FG., 26-9-19. 'Haven't heard of boggarts. I lived in Hollingwood, from 1947 to 1967.'
Hooley Hill 1 (La). 1950s/F/FG., 7-10-19. 'This isn't Hyde, but my grandmother lived in Guide Bridge, an area called Hooley Hill. My granddad had an allotment there. She would say, "the hens won't lay if there's boggarts about." This was 1950s and I had no clue what she meant. She would literally just state it! My mum would not explain so I presumed it would scare me.'
Horwich 1 (La). 1940s/F/F., 8-9-19. 'Grew up in Horwich near Bolton and my father and his family came to live there in 1926 from Rawcliffe in Yorkshire. I grew up with my grandparents and I never heard that word [boggart] mentioned. I was born in 1947.'
Horwich 2 (La). 1960s/F/FG., 14-10-19. 'My dad used to tell us the boggarts lived under the stairs. I'm from Horwich, Bolton Lancashire. 1960s.'
Hothersall 1 (La). ???/F/FG., 13-10-19. 'I was told to beware of the Hothersall Bogart. I lived in Hothersall at the time. 1985. The person who warned me was Longridge born and bred. He's late seventies now. I've never heard anyone else use the word!'
Hurlston 1 (La). 1980s/M/F., 21-9-19. 'There is a house just by Hurlston Hall that I know as "The Boggart House". I will find out its proper name and let you know. You might want to interview the owners. I was born in 1984 and lived in Parbold all my life so this house must be quite notorious that I know of it and by that name.'
Hurlston 2 (La). 1930s/M/FG., 4-10-19. 'My Dad used to say there was a Bogart at Hurlston Hall which on dark mornings with only a storm lamp in the stable, the horseman would yoke the horse on one side and the Bogart would yoke the other side. [Age from FB page]'
Huyton 1 (La). 1950s/F/FG., 27-9-19. 'I'm nearly sixty-five, born in Huyton and never heard of a Boggart until I lived up in Lancs after I got married. But before 1975 (I think) Huyton was in Lancashire so most prob the older generation had said it. We had Johnny Blocker.'
Huyton 2 (La). 1940s/M/FG., 27-9-19. 'I've lived in Huyton for seventy-nine years. Never heard the word used but I do know there was a lot of marsh and bog land around the area way back. Perhaps the word related to legendary stories about these areas i.e. Bog arts or stories.'
Huyton 3 (La). 1960s/M/FG., 27-9-19. 'Lived in Huyton all my life, fifty-four years. Never heard anyone use the word "boggart".'

Huyton 4 (La). 1960s/M/FG., 27-9-19. 'Huyton, 1960s, never heard of boggarts.'
Huyton 5 (La). 1940s/M/FG., 30-9-19. 'Lived in Huyton 1948 until 1971. Never heard the term "boggart". 'Bogeyman' rings a bell perhaps there is a connection.'
Ince Blundell 1 (La). ???/M/F., 31-8-19. 'When I was a child if I denied doing something (breaking a glass or spilling a drink etc), my great grandmother who was a from Lancashire would say must have been a bogart! My great grandmother was from Lathom in Lancashire. She grew up in that area then moved to Ainsdale. My grandmother and mother talked about boggarts as well. If anything went missing it must have been a bogart. We also knew about water boggarts who lived in water. I have a field with ponies, chickens and ducks. I still talk about boggarts with the children who come! I have a fairy garden but leave out larger things that we say belong to our boggarts. I'm in Ince Blundell in Sefton. Our boggarts are very badly behaved!'
Irlam 1 (La). 1950s/F/F., 9-9-19. 'I grew up in the Lancashire area and my older cousin talked of Boggarts when we were little to scare us. My cousin lived on a farm on Chat Moss, Irlam. It's Greater Manchester now but I think it was Lancashire when I was a child. This was the 1950s and I don't remember what he said other than the Bogarts are coming and I recall that wasn't a good thing! I grew up in Irlam, Eccles and Cadishead. I would not have heard about Boggarts any other way until a few years ago when I was looking at Fairies in a Jar and there was one. It was a company based in Birmingham that made and sold them.'
Irlam 2 (La). 1950s/F/FG., 26-9-19. 'I grew up in Irlam, b. 1959, and like XXX the bogey man was always "lurking" in our childhood; especially linked to the farming areas of "The Moss". My Great Uncle used to talk about a Boggart, but he grew up in Chorlton, South Manchester and I believe had family near Boggart Hole Clough, North Manchester.'
Irlam 3 (La). 1960s/F/FG., 26-9-19. 'I've never heard this before but threatened with the bogeyman if we were naughty. Born 1964. Grew up in Irlam.'
Irlam 4 (La). 1960s/F/FG., 26-9-19. 'Grew up in Irlam in 1960s. If anything mysteriously disappeared in the house my mum used to say that the boggart had taken it. She lived in Irlam all her life and died two years ago aged ninety.'
Irlam 5 (La). 1960s/F/FG., 26-9-19. 'Yes definitely threatened with the bogey man, and the cupboard under the stairs was always called the bogey hole. Earlier [than 1970s] it's always been used in the family going back two generations that I know of. [Age guessed from FB page.]'

Irlam 6 (La). 1960s/F/FG., 26-9-19. 'I was born and grew up in Irlam. Born 1966. Don't remember the word "boggart" but bogey man yes!'
Irlam 7 (La). 1960s/F/FG., 26-9-19. 'As I was led to believe the bogey man resided on the field/rough grassed area at the back of my Granddad's house on Alexandra Grove in Irlam.'
Irlam 8 (La). 1950s/M/FG., 27-9-19. 'Born 1951 in Irlam. Never heard "boggart" used.'
Irlam 9 (La). 1960s/F/FG., 27-9-19. 'The Bogey Man was always a threat! Born 1964 and grew up in Irlam.'
Irlam 10 (La). 1940s/M/FG., 28-9-19. 'My mam told me that if I was naughty the man with the barrow would get me. No boggart was never mentioned. Bogeyman was but it was the man with the barrow that scared me the most. I was born in Irlam in 1947 and have lived here all my life. [FB user added: I wonder if that is an expression passed down which relates to how they used to collect bodies during the plague? It would be enough to put the fear of God into any child, I imagine!]'
Irlam 11 (La). 1950s/F/FG., 29-9-19. 'Attended the Brownies in Irlam around late 1950s, early 1960s. Part of a verse we used to sing about the fairy ring was "to keep the bad boggarts out and the good fairies in".'
Kirkdale 1 (La). 1960s/M/FG., 18-9-19. 'Born in Kirkdale in 1958, bogeyman yes, boggart no'.
Kirkdale 2 (La). 1960s/F/FG., 13-10-19. 'Bogey man as well. Kirkdale 1960. Still in Kirkdale.'
Kirkdale 3 (La). 1940s/F/FG., 12-10-19. 'Born 1941... Grew up with the term Bogey man never knew the origin... Born Kirkdale.'
Kirkdale 4 (La). 1960s/F/FG., 13-10-19. 'Born in the fifties in Kirkdale and knew of the bogey man. Never met him, thankfully.'
Kirkdale 5 (La). 1950s/F/FG., 16-10-19. '1950s, the bogey man or old nick.'
Kirkdale 6 (La). 1940s/F/FG., 7-11-19. 'Born Kirkdale 1947, bogey man.'
Knowlsley 1 (La). 1980s/M/FG., 28-9-19. 'Would spring-heeled jack class as a boggart? We heard about that as kids. A demon who attacked people and could vault away from the Victorian police who tried to capture him. I'd heard the term once or twice this was in the 1980s in Knowsley. Though we mainly just called them "monsters" which I guess is an Americanism.'
Lancashire 1. 1970s/F/FG., 20-9-19. 'I'm forty-four and I remember the word "Boggart" as some sort of naughty little creature. I always remember a cartoon in the 1990s called the Treacle people from Sabden Treacle Mines in Lancashire and the writers referenced the Boggarts regularly. Yes, definitely

my parents used to say to us when I was little to watch out for the Boggarts, they'll get you. It was usually when we were out near rivers, I was born in 1975. Funnily enough we are moving from Barnoldswick to over Manchester way and there's quite a few places that are named boggart. There's Swan Lane in Hindley Green that the locals call Boggart Lane.'

Lancaster 1 (La). 1950s/F/E., 31-8-19. 'For me a Boggart is a slightly malevolent rural dwarf. My father and paternal grandmother would refer to them occasionally. My grandmother lived on the Cumbrian coast, Cockermouth on the extreme west coast. The family were Rievers. Boggarts were associated with Ireland. I was born in Lancaster and grew up in the 1950s.'

Lancaster 2 (La). 1970s/F/F., 31-8-19. 'Born in 1971. I'm forty-eight. Born and bred in Lancaster, Lancashire. Never heard of them either.'

Lancaster 3 (La). 1950s/F/FG., 14-10-19. 'We definitely had boggarts in Lancaster when I was growing up in the 1950s and 1960s.'

Lancaster 4 (La). 1980s/F/FG., 14-10-19. 'We used to say things were "bogging", I guess it's derived from "boggart". That was in the 1980s in Lancaster, scruffy, smelly horrible. Like something that's crawled out of a bog [Another FB user: 'Bogging meant disgusting, something that isn't very nice.'] Hence why I think it's derived from "boggart" as that does too.'

Lathom 1 (La). 1950s/F/FG., 9-10-19. 'I remember being told not to go somewhere because the boggart would get you and not to go near the water because Ginny Grinty would get you. This was in the 1950s in Lathom.'

Leece 1 (La). 1960s/M/F., 13-9-19. 'Boggarts Bridge was a place we were scared about crossing in the 1960s. It was between Leece and Gleaston on the Furness Peninsula in South Cumbria. I think adults built up the story to scare children. Not sure if it's named on a map. Think it was a story passed down by mouth.'

Leigh 1 (La). 1950s/F/F., 12-9-19. I remember the word "boggarts" from when I was growing up and always related it to the bogeyman! Arrrrrghhhhhhh! I was born in St Helens but lived in Leigh from the age of ten months. I was growing up in the 1950s. I'm now in my seventies and I can't really remember who said it I just know I heard it. Don't think I was ever really frightened though.'

Leyland 1 (La). 1950s/M/F., 29-8-19. 'Bogerts were always after us into mid late 1950s in Leyland. We were usually doing what we shouldn't'.

Leyland 2 (La). 1950s/M/FG., 3-10-19. '"Don't go into Stannings Wood, the Boggarts will get you!" Lol. Boggarts were more believable than the "Fan-Tailed Water Rabbits" meant to keep kids away from the water in Stannings Wood in the late 1950s early 1960s (unsuccessfully I might add). Lol, not joking (as such) when I was in the cubs/scouts (circa 1960–70) "bogarts" were frequently referred to and various other things were thrown in one being "Fan-tailed Water Rabbits" which were (apparently) the things which you almost think you see out of the corner of your eye when travelling through a wood which you're not supposed to be in. They [the rabbits] are (supposedly) fairly harmless but don't go near them and appear to scare you away from where the "Boggarts" are as they live deep in woods and farmers' fields (especially those you're not supposed to be in, if I remember the tale correctly).'

Leyland 3 (La). 1910s/F/FG., 3-10-19. 'My mum often mentioned "boggarts". She reckoned there was one in Nixon Lane, Leyland, and there was supposed to be a boggart just where Yewlands Drive in Leyland joins School Lane. "There used to be a narrow lane there and it was called Boggart Lane. It was supposed to be haunted by a headless woman. Most people who had to use School Lane on dark winter evenings usually kept to the opposite side of the road until they had passed Boggart Lane" from *Memories of old Leyland* by B. Morris. Note: Nixon Lane is Moss Side, Leyland and School Lane goes from Asda to Golden Hill Lane, Leyland. No, its not rude: she was born in 1912.'

Leyland 4 (La). 1960s/M/FG., 3-10-19. 'Grew up in Leyland in the late 1960s/70s but used to visit my grandparents in Eccleston every week. My Granddad regularly told us of the tale of the "two boggarts sat in a cave". A tale I tell my kids now. [on Facebook Messenger] Hi, in reply to your message (on Leyland memories) my Granddad would say "Two Boggarts were sat in a cave. One said 't' tother, 'nah Jem, tell us a tale' and so the tale began… two boggarts sat in a cave. One said 't' tother, 'nah Jed, tell us a tale' and so the tale began… 'Two Boggarts were sat in a cave…" Repeat indefinitely! He proper enjoyed telling this and I like seeing how long it takes before someone clicks.'

Leyland 5 (La). 1950s/M/FG., 3-10-19. 'My husband grew up in Leyland in the 1950s and he's never heard the word "boggarts"'.

Leyland 6 (La). 1940s/M/FG., 3-10-19. 'Growing up in 1940s, 1950s. If your parents didn't want you to go somewhere they told you the biggest [presumably an auto correct mistake] will get you.'

Leyland 7 (La). 1960s/F/FG., 3-10-19. 'Stories of boggarts used to give me the collywobbles. "The boggarts will get you" a term I heard. I was born in the sixties and spent most of childhood in Leyland.'

Leyland 8 (La). 1950s/F/FG., 3-10-19. 'I was born in late fifties. My Dad used to use the term frequently. I thought there were boggarts under my bed at night! Yes, I was born in Leyland, as were my Mum and Dad. We moved to other parts of Lancashire for a short spell then back to Clayton le Woods just outside Leyland.'

Leyland 9 (La). 1960s/F/FG., 3-10-19. '1960s in Lostock Hall not far from Leyland. "Boggarts" were prowling about after dark in the fields... Worst of all were the "Crow Boggarts" the supreme of all scary things.'

Leyland 10 (La). 1950s/F/FG., 3-10-19. 'I grew up in Leyland from 1956. I was told the boggarts lived in the woods and came out at night.'

Leyland 11 (La). 1930s/F/FG., 4-10-19. 'I was born in Leyland in 1936 and have lived here all my life. When I was young my dad would tell us the boggarts would get us if we didn't behave. I always thought they lived on Farington Moss.'

Leyland 12 (La). 1950s/F/FG., 3-10-19. 'In the 1950s I was told the legend of how the "Boggart Cat" was responsible for the parish church being built where it is. There was supposedly a plan to build it in Dawson Lane (perhaps so it could serve Whittle-le-Woods as well as Leyland). Stones for the foundations were take there and left overnight, but in the morning they had been moved to the site of the present St Andrew's. They were taken back, but it happened again. So two men were posted as night watchmen. The following morning, one of them was found in Dawson Lane a gibbering wreck, driven out of his mind. The other was with the stones in what's now Church Road and told of giant cat which picked up the stones in its claws and took them to its "preferred" site. The superstitious locals decided it was some sort of a sign, decided to build the church where it is now, and the "Boggart Cat" was never seen again! I seem to remember seeing a drawing of the event in a book, perhaps one by *Leyland Guardian* founding editor George Birtill.'

Leyland 13 (La). 1950s/F/FG., 3-10-19. 'My dad was a Mancunian and told us tales of a boggert, used to scare us daft. He [the boggart] lived on the moors [of] Saddleworth but used to come down to watch naughty children and if you didn't behave and be good he took you back and you had to live in the cave on the moors. You could see people but they couldn't see you. Used to frighten us half to death. I would have been about six years of age. My brother eight. Born in 1957.'

Leyland 14 (La). 1950s/M/FG., 3-10-19. 'My husband says, as a child, he was told that a figure carved in stone on the side of the parish church in Leyland was a boggart watching out for naughty children! Yes, born 1952'.

Leyland 15 (La). 1950s/M/FG., 12-10-19. 'I grew up in Leyland, Lancashire and always remember knowing the word "boggart". My Mum came from Blackburn and moved to Leyland about 1935. I don't know if I got the word from her. I always thought it was just a country name. Something along the lines of a troll, or something that appeared out [of] a bog/marsh to cause mischief or terror!'

Leyland 16 (La). ???/M/FG., 17-10-19. 'Wow. My dad has used the word "boggart" for as long as I can remember when hearing or seeing something he couldn't identify. I just thought it was a word he'd made up.'

Leyland 17 (La). 1960s/F/FG., 17-10-19. 'As children we were told stories of the Mayfield Boggart. Our parents said if we didn't come home by dusk the boggart would snatch us. Once a girl went missing... Everyone said it was the boggart [born 1967].'

Leyland 18 (La). 1950s/F/FG., 17-10-19. 'I was born in Leyland. 1954. My dad was also born in Leyland and spoke very broad Lanky. He used to talk of Boggarts under the bed at night! Very scary.'

Litherland 1 (La). ???/F/FG., 28-9-19. 'Bogey man yes and Ginny greenteeth in the water. Lived in Litherland.'

Litherland 2 (La). 1950s/M/E., 1-10-19. 'We didn't use the term "boggart" unfortunately. I was wondering if you had "The White Lady of Croston" on your list. As school kids we visited The Royal Umpire Museum and were regaled by folk tales of the White Lady and they scared us s***less! I grew up in Litherland. Born 1958.'

Little Harwood 1 (La). 1970s/M/FG., 26-9-19. 'I presume the threat from parents to do as you were told or the Bogeyman will come and get you is a derivation. Oft quoted fifty years ago around Little Harwood.'

Little Harwood 2 (La). 1940s/F/FG., 30-9-19. 'I grew up in Little Harwood. My mother would tell us to be careful when going near the backs because the bogeymen would get you. Never knew where it came from but always ran past the backs to be safe.'

Little Lever 1 (La). 1950s/M/E., 5-9-19. 'What does the word "boggart" mean to you? I vaguely knew of the term "boggart" when I was a child as my family of origin were traditional Lancastrians who remembered all the old superstitions including Ginny Greenteeth and the Bogey Man. The terms were used primarily to ensure that we remained safe. For example: "Don't go into the woods alone or the Bogey Man will get you". In more recent times Terry Pratchett has used Boggarts frequently in his Tiffany Aching series of books for younger children. In these books Boggarts will take the form of your worst nightmares. Did your parents and grandparents use the word? Do your children, nephews and nieces use it? Not my mother as she was Canadian but my father and my various Aunts and Grandmother. It was a term that was mostly used by the women in the family. Do you know any stories about boggarts – or places especially associated with them? As mentioned above. Places that had some form of inherent danger; the woods, the canal, old and dilapidated buildings… Where did you grow up, and in what decade? I grew up in a small village called Little Lever in Lancashire in the 1950s. The idea of using these old tactics to scare children into: a) doing as they are told; or b) keeping them away from places you don't want them to go has become very un-PC! Besides which, children are far more sophisticated these days and would check it out on YouTube!'

Little Lever 2 (La). 1980s/F/FG., 18-10-19. 'It's not Edgworth but Little Lever has Miner Miner 49er don't know the ins and outs of the story (mining disasters happened) but it was as if you don't get in miner miner 49er will get you. This is an old mining community if that helps. Not sure about "boggart" (had to Google) it, but he used to haunt areas not built on because there is a mine underneath so I thought it could count. Just reread messages it apparently was on Ladyshore field by the canal [that there] was a boggart named Miner 49er to scare the kids you could see the miner's lamp and scraping of mining tool.'

Littleborough 1 (La). 1950s/M/FG., 15-9-19. 'We always called it Clegg Hall Bogart. Friend coming back from haymaking at dusk saw something peering over the high wall we were passing. He legged it and we only caught up with him at the Blue Ball. He was on his third pint by then. Late 1960s, maybe 1968. We were coming down the lane in an old Land Rover with the top off. He was sat in the back then just jumped out as we were going slow and all I saw was him dash past like old nick was after him. I was twenty-two. Born 1946. The guy who ran was older, about twenty-eight or thirty. I worked as a millwright during the day fir a ebor [?] engineering who built woodworking conveyors and also did mill work like boilers and general engineering. We converted a water wheel back from electricity to water at Allison's flour milling in Castleford. [Other FB user writes: 'For him to jump out the back of the Land Rover he was sat in and run for his life the boggart must've given him a fright! If you go up that way this story originates from the long wall up Branch Road not necessarily the hall itself.'] There are many tales of scary stuff when you speak to the elderly who had stories handed down about the local area, some is fact and other fiction just to scare kids from going somewhere or going out at night.'

Littleborough 2 (La). 1960s/M/FG., 15-9-19. 'I grew up in the 1960s when most local people in Littleborough knew the story of the Clegg Hall Bogart mainly due to Rev. Oakley's book *In Olden Days*. The topic is still talked about on this page and "Remembering Littleborough" page. Possibly, mostly older generation on there as it was the original Littleborough page for people to talk about days gone by. Yes I have a copy of *In Olden Days* a great book but not too accurate in its history content.'

Littleborough 3 (La). 1950s/F/FG., 15-9-19. 'My Mum used to say, when she was annoyed with my Dad "that bugger will live to be a Boggart!" meaning a great age. She was right. He lived to be ninety-four. She also always said don't flit on a Friday as the Boggart would come with you! I seem to have in the back of my mind that farmers used to put "supper" out for the Boggart and were always wary that if they forgot they would find Boggart mischief in the morning!'

Littleborough 4 (La). 1950s/F/E., and FG., 4-9-19. 'My wife, aged seventy-one, born and bred in Littleborough. There was a hillside quarry in Shore Littleborough called the Boggart Hole. (1950s). [User on Facebook, when we were growing up as kids up Shore we called it the Balder Hole. It was used for many years to dump rubbish from the cotton mill. Other user: I commented to Simon on the supposed existence of the Boggart Hole at the top end of Shore Road. Up to now, I have only seen one confirmation that it was known as "The Boggart Hole." Can anyone on here please confirm if they also heard it called this? It is the small quarry on the unbuilt section of Shore Road, where it narrows down, and where I guess that it was unlit many years ago. Other user: seem to remember it was used as a refuse dump by LUDC. Lots of people used to dig it for bottles. Other user: 'There was the bogey hole on the left-hand side about fifty yards up from Lakeland House. When I was young it was frequented often by a man of the road. He might have been a bit scruffy but he was well mannered and did odd jobs. That would be in the 1950s.' [confirmed photograph of hole] 'Probably looks very much overgrown nowadays. Some knew it as the Bogey Hole others referred to it as the Boulder Hole. Not very big. Maybe the source of enough stone for one large dwelling or the wall opposite.'

Littleborough 5 (La). 1990s/F/FG., 15-9-19. 'My dad used to call me a little boggart when I was naughty. Yes definitely in the 1990s.'

Littleborough 6 (La). 1960s/M/FG., 15-9-19. 'My mother would mention the Birch Hill Bogart and the headless nun, both hung around on't Peddlers. This is a colloquialism for the pathway between Wardle and the King Bill (William IV) pub at the top of Shore. She told me the story about Ned the clogger who had a footwear business on Ramsden Road. It seems he was returning from the King Bill and he saw what appeared to be a woman stuck in mud at a point where the brook (stream) crosses the dirt path. The story goes that Ned shouted to the woman, "Art stuck lass?" The figure turned to him and he noted her absence of a head. The figure then disappeared in a puff of smoke. The story went on to say that Ned was never the same again and died shortly afterwards. Now I know this story is open to many hypotheses. Three possibilities are. A rumour put about by wives of drunken husbands to keep them out of the alehouse. A rumour put about by the landlord of the Hare and Hounds to stop his customers straying. Or finally was it just that Ned had supped too much in't King Bill. Whatever the reason. It's a brave mon us goes oer't Peddlers in't dark I'll tell thy. [age estimated from Facebook]. [One FB user added the comment: 'Bloody 'ell! I go over Peddlers on a regular basis on my way home from work. Last winter went over a couple of times in the dark mornings, once when it was covered in snow. Must of been the first person over Peddlers that day, it was pitch black and very eerie. Sharn't be doin' it again!']

Littleborough 7 (La). 1960s/F/FM., 20-9-19. [Question asked: 'Hi XXX, I was intrigued by your answer about boggarts. Did your family use the term in Littleborough in the 1960s? What did it mean to them. Thanks!'] 'Yes they did and it meant a ghost/ghoul type apparition which was mean and horrible.'

Littleborough 8 (La). 1970s/M/F., 12-9-19. 'We used to "set off at boggart" meaning we would run off at speed as if we were being chased by a boggart. (Rochdale/Littleborough area). Not entirely sure [what a boggart was] just meant shifting fast!'

Littleborough 9 (La). 1950s/F/E., 25-9-19. 'Born in Littleborough, brought up in the 1950s. Has heard of Boggarts, but doesn't know what they are.'

Littleborough 10 (La). 1960s/M/E., 25-9-19. 'XXX (is a farmer) born in Littleborough brought up in the 1960s, has heard of Boggarts. It appeared that his grandmother born in the 1890s invented the "Boggart of Elees", to frighten him into keeping away precisely from Elees, where a man with a bad reputation for his behaviour towards children lived. XXX isn't quite sure what a Boggart is, but thinks it is something to do with a Bogey Man.'

Littleborough 11 (La). 1930s/M/E., 28-9-19. 'I was born in Littleborough in 1939 and was aware of the story of the Clegg Hall Boggart and in later years of Boggart Hole Clough. I was probably in my early teens when I first heard of the Clegg Hall one as that was when I started to wander far and wide. There was around that time a short comical story about a man who spent a night in Clegg Hall and was awakened by the boggart crying "There's only thee and me" to which the man replied "Aye, and there'll only be thee when I get my clogs on". Edwin Waugh tells a similar story about the resident ghost of Boggart Hole Clough who's about to follow the family to their new home. I assume that you've read his story of the Grizlehurst Boggart. If this is a record of an actual conversation, rather than a product of his imagination then it's a fascinating glimpse of the world they lived in. The saying "Going off at t' boggart" was in common use in Rochdale in the 1950s which I took to mean running away, but occasionally it would mean someone going off the subject. Lancashire can be a difficult language. I doubt that I'd have heard of such a thing at that time. This is because my mother and sister were both educated at the convent school and "talked posh". My father rarely spoke and was not from Lancashire and grandparents were either dead or not on speaking terms. Our bogeymen at the time were Herr Hitler and his friends. I suppose that I became bilingual; speaking Lancashire at school and "the Queens' English" at home. This is a vast amount of information on the subject and most interesting. The frequency of the word 'hole' makes me wonder if it could be a corruption of "hollow". The area isn't known for natural holes in the ground but there's an abundance of dells and cloughs. I can only think of one hollow locally – Grotton Hollow in Oldham, but no doubt there are more. The description of the resident spirit at Boggart Hole Clough sounds like a typical poltergeist story with the presence of young children. It's intriguing that boggarts inhabit the general area which saw the sudden growth of population in the early years of the industrial revolution. How many families who made the change from agricultural workers to mill hands had children who were traumatised by it. I don't know what research has been done into the poltergeist subject, but I recall a family who were affected by it and in former times it would be easier to refer to it as a "boggart" than a poltergeist. It's easy to forget what a different, superstitious world we lived in before television, so many things were considered to be unlucky, such as walking on the cracks in the paving. My father who was an engineer with his own business, always opened the door during a thunderstorm to let the thunderbolt out which could come down the chimney. Then there was the mad bull which lived in a barn. The building was used as a joiners' workshop. Nobody ever saw or heard the bull but we all believed that it was real. Perhaps several boggarts were invented like the bull to keep nosy kids away.'

Littleborough 12 (La). 1950s/F/FG., 28-9-19. 'Yes – maybe something Irish, or to do with a demon. Littleborough.'

Littleborough 13 (La). 1970s/M/FG., 14-10-19. 'I grew up in the 1970s knowing about the boggart of Clegg Hall, not far from the border of West Yorkshire (Littleborough, Lancashire), but its use was definitely dying out.'

Littleborough 14 (La). 1970s/F/FG., 17-10-19. 'We were told stories of the Clegg Hall Bogart at home and school in the 1970s. At school we did a local history project on the large halls around Littleborough (Stubley, Clegg, Stansfield etc).'

Littleborough 15 (La). 1940s/F/FG., 17-10-19. 'Brought up in Littleborough from 1948 till I married in 1970. Never heard the word "boggart" but we had bogey men! This just made me remember I used to get a book out of Littleborough library that was all about Littleborough ghost stories. Frightened me to death, lol.'

Littleborough 16 (La). 1940s/F/FG., 17-10-19. 'I lived in Little borough from 1941 till 1970. My Grandmother had a saying "faus as a boggart" which I took to mean sly or crafty as a boggart.'

Littleborough 17 (La). 1910s/M/FG., 17-10-19. 'My father who was born in 1918 used to say when we were watching the TV during the 1960s about singers with excessive eye makeup: "She looks a boggart".'

Littleborough 18 (La). 1920s/F/FG., 17-10-19. 'I remember singing moonlight starlight. I hope there are no bogarts tonight.' [Daughter writes: 'my mom is ninety-two but she's pretty good on Facebook. I was born in 1961 and "boggart" was a term frequently employed in our house re ghouls and ghosts'].'

Littleborough 19 (La). 1970s/M/FG., 17-10-19. 'I did but it was from reading about Clegg Hall, so the use of the word was obviously of historical context from the reading rather than from "live" conversation (although I did get the meaning of the word from my dad when I asked him). I have noticed it being used a bit more frequently in films. In fact yesterday I watched *Seventh Son* (crap film) which used the term to describe a monster (rather than something more akin to a ghost as I understood the term growing up) and of course it's used in the "Harry Potter" franchise. Yes, so I probably would have been reading and talking about this around 1976.'

Littleborough 20 (La). 1900s/F/FG., 17-10-19. 'My Mum used to tell me about the Handle Hall Boggart, says she was delivering eggs one dark evening when she was a young girl, as she went up the lane something jumped on her back. She ran home minus the eggs and her Father said that would have been the boggart. Yes, born in Littleborough 1902 and me 1940.'

Littleborough 21 (La). 1950s/F/FG., 17-10-19. 'I was born in Littleborough 1954 and my mum (1926) often used the phrase "he's a right boggart" meaning unpleasant, bad tempered.'

Littleborough 22 (La). 1950s/M/FG., 23-10-19. 'Born and bred in Littleborough; 1950s. My parents and Grandparents often used to refer to the Clegg Hall Boggart; especially as one lot lived at Smithybridge, and not too far from Clegg Hall. Scary when you're a kid and the place looked really spooky.'

Littleborough 23 (La). 1970s/F/E., 1-11-19. 'I came across your name via a folklore Facebook post that said you were interested in boggarts, particularly from those in the Calder Valley region? I was born in Littleborough in 1973, which is right on the West Yorkshire border near Todmorden. We have an old hall near our house called Clegg Hall which I grew up hearing stories about its resident boggart, who was an evil uncle who apparently threw two orphans (heirs of the estate) over a balcony and was henceforth doomed to haunt the place (some say that it is the children than haunt the place). Hope that was useful. You may well have come across the story already but just thought I would share.'

Liverpool 1 (La). 1950s/M/C., mid-August 19. Didn't know the word or Ginny Greenteeth.

Liverpool 2 (La). 1950s/M/FG., 18-9-19. 'Born in 1949, I'd never heard of a boggart until I moved to Manchester in the 1970s.'

Liverpool 3 (La). 1960s/F/FG., 18-9-19. 'Born 1956 never heard the word [boggart].'

Liverpool 4 (La). 1960s/F/FG., 18-9-19. 'Born 1957 never heard of the word [boggart].'

Liverpool 5 (La). 1960s/F/FG., 18-9-19. 'Born late 1950s. The word "boggart" was never used. However, the bogeyman was used.'

Liverpool 6 (La). 1950s/F/FG., 15-9-19. 'I'm from Liverpool and the word "bogart" meant I was a scruff and I was, lol [age from FB page]'.

Liverpool 7 (La). 1950s/F/FG., 18-9-19. 'Growing up in suburb of Liverpool in 1950s. The Bogey Man was our biggest fear of ever [every?] meeting.'

Liverpool 8 (La). 1940s/M/FG., 18-9-19. 'Born and brought up in late 1940s and 1950s in South Liverpool: no memories of the word then. You must know that Liverpool is really not part of "old Lancashire", but more Irish, Welsh and Scots etc mixture.'

Liverpool 9 (La). 1970s/F/FG., 20-9-19. 'Hi Simon, just read your Facebook on Liverpool boggarts. Thing is it's quite a Lancashire word, so I assume mainly top end of Liverpool may have more use of it? I have no family memories other than the word "bogey men". There was a boggart supposed to roam Childwall Woods. Also some areas have buggins in Merseyside and Wirral. Maybe a derivative. (I saw someone commented on a boggart in Walton, but think they may have misread in a book for Walton in Preston, not the pool). Kirby had leprechauns! Hi, was from reading Childwall Valley Road area. Hope it helps. Yes from Liverpool, 1970 era. But I didn't live in south Liverpool (where Boggart was mentioned). I'm from north Liverpool.'

Liverpool 10 (La). 1950s/M/F., 29-8-19. '"Boggart" was used to describe a malevolent spirit, something that might be called a poltergeist in recent years I think. I also think it is the origin of the word "Bogeyman". My gran reckoned the crypt and graveyard of the Anglican Cathedral in Liverpool was teeming with them.'

Liverpool 11 (La). ???/F/F., 4-9-19. 'Remember that word [boggart]. It's an old Lancashire saying, not heard for long, long time.'

Liverpool 12 (La). ???/F/FG., 17-10-19. 'Heard of the term [boggart] when I lived in Cheshire. Always thought it related to creatures of marshy places. I'm a Scouser, never heard it in Liverpool. Think it was Risley Moss near Warrington. Remember where I heard the name. A boggart used to inhabit Whitley Reedbed near Antrobus in Cheshire. All drained now but it was once the biggest Reedbed in Cheshire. Suggestion that the boggart was the booming of a Bittern?'

Longridge 1 (La). ???/M/FG., 17-9-19. 'Both "boggart" and "Ginny Green Teeth" were used in our house. Boggarts lived in the woods.'

Longridge 2 (La). 1970s/F/FG., 26-9-19. 'I'm Longridge born and bred and still use the word "Boggart". Grew up through the 1970s and 1980s. Mind you some would say I've never grown up! I use it if I hear a strange noise in the house or if my van or motorbike isn't running properly. The Boggarts have got to it!'

Longridge 3 (La). 1970s/M/FG., 26-9-19. 'They used to say one lived in Bluebell Wood, Cow Hill, Grimsargh. Have a look it might agree to an interview. Yes, early 1970s. There's a stagnant pond in the wood, and this is where said Bogart hangs out. Possibly a way to stop children being near the pond. [I asked if Jenny Greenteeth] Yeah, [I] read the replies, it rekindled a memory! It's just come to me now, my mum used to say that was the name of the boggart in Bluebell wood at Grimsargh, too!'

Longridge 4 (La). 1960s/F/FG., 26-9-19. 'I'm Longridge born and still here. We still talk about boggarts. There is one at the bottom of Hothersall Lane. It's a stone face in a tree, have the story in a book somewhere.'

Longridge 5 (La). 1960s/F/FG., 26-9-19. 'We use the word "boggart" all the time! I think XXX might have also used it on the odd occasion [FB friend responded: 'I used it yesterday at work in fact!'] [Age guessed from FB page].'

Longridge 6 (La). 1960s/F/FG., 26-9-19. 'Definitely a knowledge of the word "Boggart". Hennal Lane, Walton le Dale has quite a famous one... Never heard of one in Longridge though. [Asked if she would have recognised the word] Oh yes... but it was other places that had Boggarts. Not Longridge. We just had ghosts. Too posh for Boggarts. Lol. [Age based on Facebook page].'

Longridge 7 (La). 1990s/F/FG., 26-9-19. 'Might be a bit outside the area you are looking at but there is place up near Haslingden moor with a folklore story about a boggart called Jenny Greenteeth? I can put you in contact with the person who can tell you the background to it. I'd never heard of [boggart] it till my friend told me the story of Jenny about a year ago! I will pm you now.'

Longridge 8 (La). 1940s/M/FG., 27-9-19. 'Grew up in Longridge born 11/10/1947. The use of the word "Boggert" was common in our family. At the ripe old of eight I think the imagination would have conjured something wild and wonderful and being one of thirteen kids would have helped. Have you heard this prayer "From goalies and gousties and long leggetty beasties and things that go bump in the night, Lord protect us"?'

Longridge 9 (La). 1970s/F/FG., 27-9-19. 'Scruffy boggart. Used growing in the 1970s. My most recent use (for her person) who's been fly tipping up Chapel Hill. Scruffy boggert.'

Longridge 10 (La). 1950s/M/FG., 27-9-19. 'I was born in Longridge in 1953 and lived there until 2003. My granddad who hails from Hesketh Lane near Chipping used to tell me scary stories about boggarts when I was little. There's a place called Boggart Hole Clough near Manchester. A boggart was a spook or ghost. He used to say places were haunted by them. Sometimes my mum and I would visit him in Hesketh Lane and we would go by bus so when we left we'd have to walk down the lane to the junction of the Chipping to Longridge road to catch the bus. If it was dark when we left he'd whisper to me "Mind the boggarts don't get you" just as we were leaving. I would be looking into every dark corner on the walk down the lane (which wasn't lit in those days). The only lights would be those at the Dog and Partridge.'

Longridge 11 (La). ???/M/FG., 10-10-19. 'My Dad and Granddad used to talk about Boggart Corner around the back lanes of Longridge. I think it was a small bridge over a brook.'

Longton Marsh 1 (La). 1950s/F/F., 29-8-19. 'Little village off the A6 south of Garstang, north of Preston called Barton, has a Boggart House on Station Lane. I was raised on Longton Marsh on the Ribble estuary and we were told about boggarts being nasty. I was born in 1954. My Dad was from Wigan, my Mum from Suffolk. The farmers round the Marsh must have told their kids about Boggarts. My Dad certainly passed on threats about Boggarts.'

Lower Ince 1 (La). 1950s/M/FG., 19-9-19. 'Grow up in Lower Ince born 1951 and never heard the word. Hubby born in Wallgate and he never heard it'.

Lumb 1 (La). 1950s/F/FG., 21/9/19. 'Bogart was referred to in our house as setting off at boggart, like starting to run fast and Mad Abb was just that, somebody going crazy. I lived then in Lumb in the 1950s and I've been told there's a place called Boggart Clough in the Dean area of Lumb. Mad Abb was a real person lived in Bacup, real name Abraham Dewhurst. I'm not sure [location of Clough] but have messaged someone who lives in Dean and they should know. Will let you know if I find out.' [FG user added: 'There are two farms up Dean Clough head and Clough bottom that was Bogart Clough on the foot path to Bacup'.]

Lumb 2 (La). 1960s/F/FG., 23-9-19. 'I agree with XXX and my cousin XXX. My parents, grandparents and other relatives talked about "going off at t'boggart" meaning setting off at a run. I still use this expression myself! Kids were also warned that if they misbehaved, the boggarts would get them. I was also born and bred in Lumb, Rossendale and grew up there in the 1960s and 1970s. Thanks XXX for the info on "Mad Ab". I use this expression too but didn't know the history.'

Lumb 3 (La). 1970s/F/FG., 25-9-19. 'I didn't know that they were monsters but as a child growing up in Lumb and Water, the old folk used to say "set of'at boggart". This used to mean that someone had suddenly set off going somewhere very fast as if running away from something. This would have been 1970s.'

Lydgate 1 (La). 1930s/M/FG., 13-10-19. 'I remember my mother talking about boggarts, as in, "the boggarts must have taken it", if she had lost something and couldn't find it. I grew up in the 1930s up Knotts Road, Lydgate.'

Lytham 1 (La). 1970s/F/FG., 3-10-19. 'XXX, never forgotten your crow boggart story. It's actually my sister's story, so can't remember much detail. Happened in the late 1970s, I think, and involved an old farmer discovering what he thought was a dead body, but was luckily "nowt but a crow boggart" that being a scarecrow! My sister tells it better.'

Lytham 2 (La). ???/F/FG., 17-10-19. 'Don't know why, but my late father always referred to the Christmas turkey as the boggart. Yes, father grew up at 1 Victoria Street. We grew up in Mornington Road.'

Manchester 1 (La). 1940s/M/E., 4-9-19. 'Boggarts are mischievous imps/sprites who are capable of causing mayhem. They live in dark places, under bridges etc. We and our children know the folklore about Boggarts. Boggart Hole Clough, Blackley, Manchester is a large wooded park belonging to Manchester City Council. A "hole" is the Boggart's home. "Clough" is a dark, steep sided, wooded area. We grew up in North Manchester near Boggart Hole Clough and spent much of our childhood playing there in the 1940s/50s and 1960s. Many years ago, when our children were young, a play titled "The Boggarts of Boggart Hole Clough" was performed at Manchester University theatre. My children were taken to see it by their school. Can't remember ever being frightened of Boggarts etc by our parents. The main stories our children remember are those referring to the "ugly trolls" who lived under bridges.'

Manchester 2 (La). 1960s/F/FG., 20-9-19. 'I'm originally from Manchester, in one of the suburbs of Manchester there is a large park called Boggart Hole Clough, where, it is rumoured, a Boggart has haunted the area for many years and still does to this day. We spent many a happy hour as children searching for it. Nope, we never found the boggart sadly. I'm going back to the 1960s.'

Manchester 3 (La). 1950s/F/E., 5-9-19. 'What does the word "boggart" mean to you? Nothing. We do have Boggart Hole Clough in Blackley, Manchester where I used to go as a child. Manchester, 1950s.'

Manchester 4 (La). 1940s/F/FG., 21-9-19. '"From Boggarts and blisters and fell-walking sisters, dear Lord deliver us." Fell-walker's prayer. This was on a postcard in a shop in the Lake District in the 1950s. I used to go youth-hostelling in those days. I also used to play tennis in Boggart Hole Clough. I can remember older people saying that Boggarts turned milk sour, and stole babies. I have no experience of this! The caption for the poem was a fell walker's prayer.'

Manchester 5 (La). 1960s/F/FG., 27-9-19. 'We lived in Manchester and visited Boggart Hole Clough many times – it was a special day out. If we moaned at home time mum used to say the boggarts lived in the clough and we had to leave before dark or they would get us. Early 1960s.'

Manchester 6 (La). 1940s/M/FG., 27-9-19. 'My dad talked about Boggart Hole Clough but I didn't know where it was, I just remember him talking about it. He always said, when talking about it, that he wouldn't like to spend the night there.'

Manchester 7 (La). 1970s/M/FG., 29-9-19. 'I grew up in north Manchester. My childhood was spent playing in Boggart Hole Clough and full of stories of boggarts and fairies and sleeping giants. Boggarts are creatures to be appeased, an angered boggart will follow you home and cause mayhem. Once in your house, you can never get them out. Never invite them in! They creep about in the night between dusk and dawn. They are as big as a horse, as fast as the wind and mean as the devil. Boggart stories were used as warnings from adults and to scare the life out of us by older siblings and cousins. They steal small children and eat dogs. I spent hours looking for the boggart hole – quietly hoping not to find the entrance to their lair. Yes, 1970s. I have to admit telling my own children stories of the boggarts, fairies and sleeping giants too.'

Manchester 8 (La). 1960s/M/FG., 29-9-19. 'I grew up knowing of the "Bogey Man". I was born in Manchester in 1968 and moved to Stockport in 1973 (my parents are Manchester families for a couple of generations). In the 1970s my parents would use the terms about the bogey Man as would my friend's parents. Looking back I've just assumed it was a way of making sure we didn't stray too far and were home when expected for fear that there was a bogey man out there who would get you.'

Manchester 9 (La). 1950s/F/FG., 10-10-19. 'Grew up in Manchester in the 1950s, when it was still Lancashire. There was a woodland area around there somewhere called Boggart Hole Clough (although we always called it boggatall clough). My mum said that's where boggarts lived. She never said what boggarts were but we didn't like the sound of it just the same.'

Manchester 10 (La). 1940s/M/FG., 16-10-19. 'Legged it from the Clough when one of us kids thought we saw it. 1940s.'

Manchester 11 (La). 1950s/F/FG., 17-10-19. 'I grew up in Manchester in the 1950s and one place I hated visiting with my grandparents was Boggart Hole Clough, a place where boggarts used to dwell according to my mother. It was in fact a park set in ancient woodland with steep ravines and is now a nature reserve. If we misbehaved we were threatened with the boggart and as a child I used to have nightmares of a monster coming to eat me! I heard recently that there is a brewery called Boggart Hole Clough and on Googling today I found the tale of the green boggart here.'

Manchester 12 (La). 1950s/M/FG., 17-10-19. 'Fantastic that you are doing this research. Growing up in east Manchester in the 1950s, I well remember the term "boggart", and the place, Boggart Hole Clough too. I have a book which may be of interest with regards to the use of northern dialect words, such as "boggart", which you probably are privy to. I'll give details should you wish.'

Manchester 13 (La). 1970s/F/FG., 17-10-19. 'We always played in Boggart Hole Clough as kids. There was a lot of different stories about the boggart. We sat in there at night telling stories. It was great fun. I lived on Ashley Lane growing up in the 1970s. Don't think we was ever scared of it.'

Manchester 14 (La). 1950s/M/FG., 17-10-19. 'Bogart Hole Clough is still there and is very popular. The Bogart must be there causing mischievous happenings. "The Clough" as it was known had a very large wooded part with streams and sells [?]. Just what the bogarts like. Don't get caught in the Clough after dark. The Bogart will have you. Got the kids home in daylight anyway.'

Manchester 15 (La). 1990s/F/FG., 17-10-19. 'I'm twenty-five and I used the boggart to scare my children (five and three) into being good whilst we're in the Clough. We spend a lot of afternoons/weekends there. They both think the boggart come out when it starts to get dark, but hides out in the Clough watching for naughty people during the day, so that he can eat them when it's dark. Been told his favourite meal is naughty children. It works. They play nicely and behave when we're there.'

Manchester 16 (La). 1960s/F/FG., 17-10-19. 'I grew up in north Manchester near Boggart Hole Clough and when I moved up to Lees no-one I spoke to knew anything about boggarts or had ever heard of them. Was born in 1966. Local legend – the family in the end cottage next to Bogart Hole Clough were so fed up of the milk turning sour and all the other things the boggart did to them that they decided to move away. After they had loaded everything they owned into the horse and cart and the old man got up ready to get the horse moving a bounce came from the milk churn "nah then, where we goin". They didn't bother and put everything back in the house'.

Manchester 17 (La). 1960s/M/FG., 21-10-19. 'Not a term I recall, from either HG [?] (second half of 1950s and 1960s) or my earlier time in Trafford Park (1948 to 54). But my parents were from South Wales and Tyneside, so if a regional word I wouldn't have heard it from them! Bogey Man, yes, a much more widespread contraction, I imagine.'

Manchester 18 (La). 1950s/M/E., 22-11-19. 'Evil creature. Father and friends used the word. Only [knew] the association with Boggart Hole Clough.'

Marton 1 (La). 1950s/F/FG., 27-9-19. 'I grew up in Marton, my mum was from Cumberland (Cumbria) she believed in the bogey man. That was in the fifties.'

Middleton 1 (La). 1950s/F/F., 1-9-19. 'I grew up in Middleton, Manchester. There was a [park] not far from my grandma's house called Bogat Hole Clough. It's still there near Crumpsall. My Gran used to say if we didn't stay away the boggats would take us down into the Clough to a secret hole, and we would never be seen again. Being of an impresionate age, it worked on me, and have never been there since, even though the council (I think) have cleaned it up and put walks through about 1959/1960.'

Middleton 2 (La). 1950s/F/F., 1-9-19. 'When I was a child we were told that a boggart or green man lived in or near the canal. This I think was used by adults to frighten us to keep us away from dangerous places. Middleton near Manchester. I now live in Lytham St Annes still in Lancashire, but have not heard of any boggarts round here. Think it is more of an east Lancashire thing with the hills and valleys. I was born in 1946 so was used in my childhood. Moved to Lytham St Annes in 1965. [Asked whether the green man was Jenny Greenteeth]. Yes, but it was Jinny Green Teeth, in my day.'

Middleton 3 (La). 1950s/M/FG., 21-9-19. 'I was brought up in Middleton. Born in the 1950s and we used to go looking for them in Boggart Hole Clough Park in Blackley. To be honest, I think we were looking [for a] wizened old man with maybe an animal's head, on the lines of Puck from *Midsummer's Night*.'

Middleton 4 (La).1950s/M/E., 4-9-19. 'I was born in 1952 in North Manchester (specifically, I grew up in Middleton) and so whenever we went into Manchester we would pass Boggart Hole Clough. So I have known the word for as long as I can remember. Indeed, it was only when I moved south in 1979 that I realised it was a local word not a national one. For me a boggart was always mischievous bordering on the evil, though I don't recall the idea of a boggart ever being used as a threat (not in the sense that my grandmother might say, do that and the devil will get you). Physically, I picture boggarts as rather like dwarves: small, humanoid, gnarled. But I don't know where this image came from, I have no memory of ever seeing a picture of a boggart. Because of Boggart Hole Clough (which I think I have only ever entered perhaps once or twice in my life) I used to think that boggarts only lived there. Away from the Clough you would never see them. I should mention that my father's favourite mild expletive was "well I'll be buggared." But because of his accent, this always came out as "well I'll be buggart." So I think that for a long time I was probably confused between "boggart" and "buggared". I'm not sure what that says, either about me or about boggarts. My parents and my maternal grandmother (who lived with us and was originally from Oldham) all knew and used the word "boggart". My maternal grandfather was from Wales; he died when I was very young so I have no idea whether he knew the word or not. My paternal grandparents lived just outside Blackpool, but were both originally from Scotland, and I don't recall either of them ever using the word. I have no children, nephews or nieces so I have no idea about whether the word has survived into the next generation. My wife is from Oxford, but did know the word before she met me because she has always been a keen reader of writers like Alan Garner.'

Middleton 5 (La). ???/F/FG., 15-9-19. 'There is a Boggart Hole Clough in Blackley on the way to Manchester. My mum who is from Middleton says that when she was young if you were scared they would say you were "boggart fiert"'.

Middleton 6 (La). 1950s/M/F., 29-8-19. 'Next to where I lived in Manchester was a piece of parkland known as "Boggart Hole Clough", in Alkrington, Middleton. Born in 1951 the only reference to a boggart I ever heard from my family was the name of this little 'park', Boggart Hole Clough.

It stood next to the main Manchester-Rochdale road. In later life I recall hearing the word "boggart" on a TV programme which served to remind me of this little Park in Alkrington. I only ever walked the place once with my mother and sister who had contrived to create a magical atmosphere by hiding small value silver coins along the short route we took. I still don't know how or when they carried out the hiding of the coinage.'

Middleton 7 (La). 1940s/M/FG., 14-10-19. 'As a youngster in Middleton, there was an old lady, forgotten her name, used to look like a witch and we kids used to call her "Nan Boggart". Do not understand where the name came from?'

Middleton 8 (La). ???/M/FG., 7-11-19. 'I am Lancastrian born, but have lived in Cowling, North Yorkshire for forty nine years. Growing up in the fifties in Middleton near Rochdale I recall visiting Boggart Hole Clough. When out in the village on dark autumn nights, older women would frighten us young lads with tales of "The Black Boggart". In recent years I wrote a magazine article about exploding/ bursting steam engine flywheels: "Chasing the Boggart"'.

Miles Platting 1 (La). 1950s/F/FG., 10-10-19. 'Bogart hole clough but didn't realise what a bogart was. Grew up in Miles Platting and Ancoats. We had legends of Ginny green teeth in the canal though! [age guessed from FB]'

Milnrow 1 (La). 1970s/F/FG., 15-09-19. 'My mum was born on a street next to Boggart Hole Clough in Moston, Manchester. Growing up in Milnrow I also heard of the Clegg Hall boggart. [What about Clough?] Not really. Most of the stories I was told by my Grandma were about the war and how a bomb drifted from over their street and landed in the Clough, with a crater there to this day. Many stories were told about the Clough but not why it was called what it is. Sorry if this is no help to you. Was born in 1971 and I remember at about the age of seven being given a book called *Lancashire Ghosts* and there was a section on boggarts. The accompanying picture was of a small, stocky bald-headed, bearded man throwing plates in front of a horrified woman. I always think of this whenever I heard the term. The book also mentioned the Clegg Hall boggart but I can't remember exactly what was said though. I have a feeling I may still have the book somewhere. I'll look for it.'

Milnrow 2 (La). 1950s/M/FG., 12-10-19. 'Stanny Brook Park in Milnrow supposed to have had a boggart. I was born in 1959.'

Milnrow 3 (La). 1960s/F/FG., 12-10-19. 'I know the word and know it refers to say a bogey man. Banded about in the 1960s. Milnrow.'

Milnrow 4 (La). ???/F/FG., 12-10-19. 'One of my relatives used to dress up as a Boggart and jump out from side of Clegg Hall at our kids when they walked past. No early 1970s.'

Milnrow 5 (La). 1960s/F/FG., 12-10-19. 'From Milnrow born 1960 and my brother always said the boggart would get me if I didn't behave. He told me there was supposed to be a boggart at Stubley Old Hall in Littleborough and had something to do with a passage from there to Clegg Hall which is also suppose to have a boggart.'

Milnrow 6 (La). 1970s/M/FG., 13-10-19. 'Still hear [boggart]. My ma and older Milnrow relatives use the word "boggart" today. And my Grandma Nellie (born 1907 and who was brilliant on local folk tales and dialect) used to frighten me as a young lad with tales of local boggarts. She also used to tell me a strange tale of three boggarts that were like large dogs, with 'een (eyes) as big as tupenny pies and were called "Knock 'em down", "Creysh (crash) 'em down" and "Knock 'em flat to t' floor"! I was born in 1972 and grew up in Milnrow so they have certainly persisted locally. If you want to learn more about local boggarts, including their names, I strongly suggest you read Ammon Wrigley's *Saddleworth Superstitions and Folk Customs*. It's a scarce book but local studies libraries should help. Another bit of my grandma's boggart story has come back to me the following lines: "Owd Georgie Jammy came leathering down t' street, his face as white as a puddin' clout (cloth for rag puddings)," shoutin' "do let me in, I've sin a boggart!". Sorry I can't piece together the whole story. I was very young! Also, could you let me know when your book comes out? I've just remembered another local boggart reference! Milnrow had a local character called Hubert (he died in his late 70s about 2005 I think). He was always round at my Granddad Harold's and he used to tell me about a strange local chap from when he was a lad who had the nickname "Randall Boggart". I'm sure he told me he was basically a tramp who often slept rough near Butterworth Hall (an old part of Milnrow). Perhaps he was a bit scary to the local children hence him being given the name "boggart". I've never heard bogie for a boggart in Milnrow, only boggart. We did use the term bogie, but that was a homemade car/chariot thing made with a plank of wood and old pram wheels.'

Milnrow 7 (La). 1940s/M/FG., 18-10-19. 'Growing up in Milnrow in the late 1940s and 1950s I heard the word "boggart" from time to time used by older people. Always referring to ghosts I think.'

Milnrow 8 (La). 1950s/F/FG., 18-10-19. 'We definitely used "bogeyman" but heard "boggarts" used as well. Born in 1950 in Milnrow. Bogeyman would come and get you if you were bad. Boggarts I always thought lived in the bogs or marshy land or dark woods.'

Morecambe 1 (La). 1950s/M/F., 31-8-19, 'Knew the word growing up in

North Lancs. Came on Bogart Hole when I moved to Rossendale. 1950s, 1960s, Morecambe, Lancaster area, East Lancs.'

Moston 1 (La). 1960s/M/FG., 26-9-19. 'In the 1960s my brother was very ill and had to spend a long time in Booth Hall hospital. My mum had no choice when visiting him but to leave us play in Bogert Hole Clough park. There we heard stories of the bogert that once resided there and the mischief he would get up to. Playing tricks and harassing the local population.'

Moston 2 (La). 1960s/M/E., 25-9-19. 'I'm just responding to an article I've just read regarding Boggarts so I'll tell you the little information I have on the subject. I used to live in Moston, a suburb of Manchester. As a child I used to visit a park in Moston, not new Moston which sprouted up in the 1960s but "Old" Moston with its huge three-storey Victorian property. There behind the Ben Brierley pub is one of the entrances to Boggart Hole Clough, a medium size park. At the bottom of one of the hills by a footpath is a stone about ten inches high and about ten inches diameter. Local folklore says the local boggart is buried under that stone, and if you don't say "hello" when you pass he will jump up from below and grab you… with dire consequences. So if you ever make it there, be sure to say hello! No 1960s, but I'll forgive you… The fact is my parents lived in the park grounds in prefabs just after the war. I have elder brothers and sisters who lived in the park and were playing in the "Hollows" a particularly spooky part of the park in the 1950s. I went to school near there and visited the park thousands of times, so it's always been part of the folklore as I grew up. I'll pass your info onto them and see what they say. Good luck.'

Moston 3 (La). 1960s/F/FG., 27-9-19. 'My wife lived in Moston on the other side of Bogert Hole Clough from Booth Hall and as a child she was told that the bogart lived under the bridge at the bottom end of the Clough. I take my dog in there every night and I still haven't seen him [the boggart]. 1960s/70s I think her parents and most parents in the area used the tale to stop them straying into the park.'

Moston 4 (La). ???/M/FG., 27-9-19. 'Oh it's such a long time ago but if I recall it right it was a local in the park who told me. I am sure that there was a mention of the Boggert in a book on the history of the park. He was a little old man with a stick and a floppy hat. He was good at hiding and could move fast, disappear in a blink of the eye. When it was farmland around there and he was upset with a farmer, he would turn his cow's milk sour or let the pigs out any kind of mischief. He was a bit like a hob goblin. The person who had offended him would have to leave a gift out. I think food was the going rate, to appease him [the boggart]. Parents when scolding their children, would threaten them. "If you don't behave the Boggert will get you and take you away". I hope my memory serves me well. I love folklore and local history. Let me know how you get on with your research.'

Moston 5 (La). 1950s/F/FG., 28-9-19. 'Born 1951 lived in Moston six years moved to Blackley Village. Practically grew up in Boggart Hole Clough in school holidays. Thought boggart was a boggie man. Aw no really sorry [no stories]. Don't think was ever really frightened of him. But you always felt a presence.'

Moston 6 (La). 1950s/F/FG., 9-10-19. 'I've heard this word all my life, I was born near Boggart Hole Clough park in Monsall, Manchester. We used to be scared to death if we was still in the park when it was going dark in case the Boggart "got us" lol.'

Moston 7 (La). 1940s/M/FG., 13-10-19. 'I can't confirm the veracity of this story, but here it is as told to me by my grandmother in the early 1950s. I was born in 1947. Someone has already mentioned Boggart Hole Clough. Apparently it got its name following a series of incidents when a ghost or Bogart, used to jump out of the bushes and frighten young women walking through this isolated area. It would have been sometime in the late 1800s when her father (or grandfather, I can't remember) was walking through the area when he saw the Boggart up to its usual tricks, frightening a young woman. He was on his way home from work and was carrying a tin plate which he took with him to eat his meals from at the mill. When he saw the Boggart he threw the plate at him (bear in mind this was before the invention off the frisbee) and it struck him [the boggart] on the head knocking him to the ground. On getting closer he saw that he actually knew the man well, who with his dying breath said "Aye Tom, tha's killed me". They used to talk like that in them days. So there we have it, my Great Grandfather killed the Ghost of Boggart Hole Clough. Either that or my grandmother was a good storyteller.'

Nateby 1 (La). 1970s/M/FG., 20-9-19. 'Hubby grew up with Crow boggart. (Snot Monster). It's what came out of your nose... Crow Boggart. Basically Snot. Ha, ha! He was born in Nateby 1976, but he has been bought up with Lancashire twang. He still talks like that. Sorry born 1974. Oops not gonna live that down.'

Nelson 1 (La). 1950s/F/F., 29-8-19. 'I haven't heard of them and I was born and bred in the middle of this area! I was born in 1946 in Lancaster, my parents moved back to Nelson in 1947 so I was raised in Pendle Witch country, I remember most of my childhood very well and no one ever mentioned boggarts.'

Nelson 2 (La). 1950s/F/F., 29-8-19. 'We were always warned about the "Bogeyman" when we were kids in Nelson. No I don't think [I heard of boggarts] but I'm presuming that they are the same thing [as bogeymen]?'
Nelson 3 (La). 1950s/F/FG., 27-9-19. 'The word "boggart" was used in our house, all through my childhood, in the same way as "bogeyman". In fact, I always thought that the bogey part was a shortening of "boggart". I was born in 1957 but by the time my three sons were born, in the late 1970s and early 1980s, I never heard the term "boggart" used, only "bogeyman".'
Nelson 4 (La). 1960s/F/FG., 7-10-19. 'I grew up in Nelson. Lived there 1960s to present day. I've heard the word "Boggart" but never knew what it referred to other than some scary small creature. Never heard any stories.'
Nelson 5 (La). 1950s/F/FG., 7-10-19. 'I grew up in Nelson 1950s/60s and never came across the word "Boggart" until I started working in Manchester and heard of Boggart Hole Clough.'
Nelson 6 (La). 1960s/M/FG., 7-10-19. 'I'll have heard the word "Boggart" used in the context of "She were off at Boggart to the shop before it closed". So I took that to mean running fast. This was in the 1940s.'
Nelson 7 (La). ???/M/FG., 7-10-19. 'I took school parties to Ingleborough Hall in Clapham in the 1970s and every time we went on a Boggart Hunt one of the evenings.'
Nelson 8 (La). 1940s/F/FG., 7-10-19. 'I grew up in Nelson in the 1940/1950s. If anyone was running as fast as they could, they were said to be off at Boggart. [But what is a boggart?] Just someone going fast. We had so many sayings in those days, you just seemed to copy off your mum and dad and grandma and granddad.'
Nelson 9 (La). 1950s/F/FG., 7-10-19. 'Lived in Nelson from 1957 to 1986. Bogart meant speeding off with the wind behind you, possibly fear. Running it. Moving very fast. No, not exactly, but as a child you understood that it was not normal as in normal human behaviour. There was a mystery attached to it as you only said "I ran like Boggart" if you were scared.'
Nelson 10 (La). ???/F/FG., 17-10-19. 'I grew up in Nelson Lancashire. My dad used to say he or she is off at Bogart when someone was running fast.'
Nelson 11 (La). 1950s/M/FG., 18-10-19. 'There's a Lancashire expression that was very common; "He's off at t'boggart!", meaning setting off running. I never understood it but feel sure that I used it. I vaguely remember a "Boggart Hole" as well, but can't recall the location. No doubt there would be many places that were dangerous for kids to play in and hence the name used to scare them away. Sadly I doubt that around my childhood area of Nelson there would be any one location with the name. Maybe just, as I said, a name used

for various places to frighten off kids. I'll ask on the relevant 'Then and Now' groups. I think that there was a Burnley coal mine called "Boggart Bridge". 1950s for me. As kids we really did get everywhere. "Be home before it gets dark or else or the Boggart will get you?" Maybe? Did "Bogeyman" evolve from "Boggart"?'

Newchurch in Pendle 1 (La). 1960s/F/FG., 7-10-19. 'I grew up in Newchurch in Pendle in the 1960s through to the 1980s and remember hearing the word "Boggart".'

Newhey 1 (La). 1950s/F/FG., 18-10-19. 'Was born in a terraced house on Bentgate Street, Newhey 1957. I used to say "Raggle Boggart". Think it may mean a ghostly shape?'

Newhey 2 (La). 1950s/F/FG., 12-10-19. 'Born in 1974 and we still say the word "boggart". There's an old myth that Ogden in New Hey has a boggart – The Ogden Boggart.'

Newhey 3 (La). 1970s/F/FG., 13-10-19. 'My big brother used to threaten me with the bogart, from me being about five, 1970, to me being [in my] early teens. Newhey born and bred.'

Newhey 4 (La). ???/F/FG., 16-10-19. 'You have reminded me of "Jimmy Boggart" a tramp who was a traveller fierce red hair. He was still about in the 1960s and when he visited Newhey he came and slept in Coldgreave. An itinerant farm worker. Travelled with an old bike which he never rode, just pushed. The "owd georgie jammy" tale was also told to us, but can't recall much of it. Your words simply reminded me of it.'

Newton 1 (La). 1960s/F/FG., 7-10-19. 'I was born in Newton in 1962 and was often frightened by my Dad and older siblings with stories of the Bogart. Especially around Halloween.'

Newton 2 (La). 1950s/F/FG., 7-10-19. 'I was born in Newton Hyde. Never heard of Boggart but my Granddad used to say there was a Bogey Man in the cellar to scare us. [Age guessed from Facebook page.]'

Oldham 1 (La). 1940s/M/F., 4-9-19. 'The word hasn't completely died out in the Oldham area of Lancashire. "It's tecken boggart" for instance. And Boggart Hole Clough is not so far away. When I was young tecken (taken) boggart referred to when a carthorse or a cotton mill steam engine would, for no explainable reason, become violently out of control. In the case of a mill engine, this could be a very dangerous situation and would need all the intuitive skill of the mill engineer to bring it back under control. I remember many years ago reading a list of Oldham district boggarts given in the local newspaper. I grew up in the 1940s. Up to recently we had a marvellous local evening newspaper, the *Oldham Evening Chronicle*, which had a weekend edition

sometimes containing features on local history and folklore. I'm sure the list of local boggarts was in that edition. The paper is no more, but I believe the archive might be held at the council's Local Interest Centre.'
Oldham 2 (La). 1950s/M/E., 4-9-19. 'What does the word "boggart" mean to you? A malevolent spirit. Did your parents and grandparents use the word? Yes. Do your children, nephews and nieces use it? No. Do you know any stories about boggarts – or places especially associated with them? Yes, my father told this local legend about a boggart which lived in Boggart Old Clough which I took to be near Blackley, Manchester where my father came from, but I might have been wrong. The Boggart lived in a cottage with a family and they got so fed up with it mischievously interfering with their daily lives that they decided to leave. They loaded up a cart with their belongings and were just about to leave when the Boggart jumped on too and said "I'm coming with you."! Where did you grow up, and in what decade? Oldham, 1950s.'
Oldham 3 (La). 1920s/F/FG., 21-9-19. 'My wife always used the word and is seventy-six years old. It was used by her mother who is aged one hundred and one and is a native of Oldham.' [See Southport 9.]
Oldham 4 (La). ???/F/FG., 21-9-19. 'I don't know if this any interest to you but in the late 1970s I worked on a nursing home where one of the residents [Oldham]... spoke of the boggarts when she became stressed. She would have been in her 1980s then and in her confused state she said that they were tormenting her. Good luck in your research.'
Oldham 5 (La). 1980s/F/FG., 22-9-19. 'I grew up in Oldham and heard about boggarts in the 1970s. I'd have said it was some sort of creature from folklore who was responsible for causing havoc in the area – I remember reading stories about them.'
Oldham 6 (La). 1960s/M/FG., 22-9-19. 'Simon, hi. I have read some of your work on line. I remember "The Boggart" myths from early childhood in Oldham and onward in Springhead from 1960s and 1970s. My feeling is it is more Lancastrian than Yorkshire. However, there is some missives here: https://huddersfield.exposed/wiki/Boggart that may debunk that myth. There is of course The Boggart Stones, a local sandstone outcrop on the peak between the Holmfirth road and Uppermill, though this may be a local name than an actual official OS name.'
Oldham 7 (La). 1950s/M/FG., 23-9-19. 'I worked in cotton mills for a good many years and I remember several older ladies saying "my frames took bogart". Meaning something has gone wrong with the machine. 1965 onwards. It was usually when all the ends were broken or the machine wouldn't stop for some reason.'

Oldham 8 (La). 1960s/M/FG., 14-10-19. 'I was born in Oldham, Lancashire in 1964 and fairies, boggarts etc. were familiar beings being recounted to me in tales by my grandma. I'm sure you will have heard of the Chamber Hall Boggart in Oldham. If not, please reply for further details. To this day, whenever I walk down by Chamber Hall Close (where the sadly demolished medieval hall once stood) I say 'Hi' to the sleeping boggart! People think I am crazy but I retain a belief in supernatural spirits etc. They are still out there but cannot be heard or seen amongst the crass clutter we have created in our "modern society". One day, things will be as they once were. OLD NEWSPAPER REPORT. Chamber Hall is doomed! Unless public opinion can express itself forcibly and clearly, there seems to be no possibility of the ancient home with its interesting out-buildings being preserved. Ignominious demolition threatens the Hall that was the seat for over three centuries of the Tetlows, the residence of Sheriff Wrigley, most prominent Cromwellian magnate, mansion of the stately Georgian Gregges of Chester, abode of the still more famous "Chamber Ha' boggart". The residence itself has been rebuilt more than once. The farmhouse behind it is part of an earlier Chamber Hall, but that too is only a comparatively modern representative of the first Hall. Chamber appears on the stage of history in the thirteenth century as the marriage portion of one of the heiresses of the Oldham of Oldham. Tetlows and Their Successors. When the first Tetlow of Chamber built the Hall and brought his bride to be mistress of it, it would be one of the very few houses that possessed a separate reception room, that is to say, a large upper storey, and not merely attic rooms in the gables. This proud distinction gave it the name it has ever since borne. There was no town of Oldham in those days. What is now the great and populous County borough of Oldham was then just "Kaskenmore" a territory open and mostly barren "forest" land with but few clearings. Another generation was to pass away before St Mary's Church would provide a nucleus around which the settlements would congregate and begin slowly to evolve the Oldham of to-day. The community was a purely pastoral one. Quite possibly some of the coal on the surface was worked here and there by the settlers. They did their own spinning and weaving of course for their home-made garments. But they wrested a very precarious living from the soil, of which a few plots only would be of any value for growing their scanty grain crops. Oatmeal and ewes' milk must have been their staple food for the most part. Handing down the Hall from father to son, the Tetlow family remained at Chamber for over three changeful centuries. Some of the family in the sixteenth century began to work the coalpits on a fairly large scale for those days. From Chamber Hall came the gentle mother of Lawrence Chadderton, for whom Emmanuel College,

Cambridge, was built in 1584, one of the most eminent Elizabethan divines, and one of the 47 translators of the English Authorised Bible of 1611. As a boy Lawrence must often have played and worked in the old barn still to be seen. This mediaeval barn just to the south of the house is the most ancient building now remaining in Oldham and is so finely proportioned that from the architectural as well as from the historic point of view it would be a thousand pities if it should be destroyed. It has of course been often repaired and perhaps partly rebuilt. The date which appears on it with initials, "G.W. 1640 I.W." no doubt commemorates one of these restorations. The initials are those of George Wood and his wife Jane, daughter and sole heiress of Robert, the last male representative of the Tetlows of Chamber Hall. An Influential Wrigley. In 1646 the Woods cut off the entail and sold the property to Henry Wrigley. Probably he built the present cottage to the north, a small two-storey block with an external stone stair. It has a date-stone "H.W. 1648" over the doorway; and he seems to have used the upper room as a receiving house and warehouse for fustian brought in by the weavers from their cottages far and near. Henry Wrigley was the chief antagonist of the incumbent of Oldham Church, the Rev. John Lake, a stout "Church and King" man. Their controversies were acute. It is pleasant to remember, however, that forty years later Wrigley would have been delighted to have heartily supported his old opponent when as Bishop of Chichester, Lake stood out as one of the "Seven Bishops" for English liberties in 1688. Wrigley became High Sheriff of Lancashire in 1651, and was one of the largest employers of labour – agricultural, textile and colliery – for many miles around. He was for many years the most influential man in Oldham. He was one of the executors of the will of Humphrey Chetham, and so concerned in the foundation of the very earliest public library in England – that of Chetham's Hospital, still so full of interest and beauty. His granddaughter, Martha, married Joseph Gregge, Esq., of Chester, in 1680, and until quite recently the Hall remained in that line. The name "Gregge Street" – now renamed Grange Avenue – commemorated those owners. Captain Benjamin Gregge became High Sheriff in 1722, and of Mrs Gregge it is recorded that she was 'beautifully fair' as well as distinguished by "ornaments of mind". The front of the Hall was rebuilt, probably in Captain Gregge's time, and is a good example of early Georgian domestic architecture. The old oak from the interior has largely disappeared. The Boggart. Mr James Dronsfield has told us in "Ouselwood" the story of the famous boggart, the tradition having been a live one in his infancy, a hundred years ago. The boggart used to play all sorts of noisy pranks on the inmates of the Hall. Food had to be placed for it each night to keep it from being too troublesome. One night a new maid to whom the task was allotted, tempted by the daintiness of the titbits left over from a dinner-party, ate them herself, then, saying "Churn milk and barley bread is good enough for boggarts" left only the latter in their place, in a bowl. Then she finished her ironing and went to bed. A few minutes later terrified shrieks came from her room. The boggart had appeared and repeating the scornful words "Churn milk and barley bread" had indelibly branded her with the hot smoothing iron. The story of the "flitting" abandoned when the boggart promised to accompany his hosts, is told of this as well as of other boggarts. After all, why should they not act in the same way under similar conditions? At last it became necessary to exorcise the intruder. After prayer and fasting the boggart consented to be removed, stipulating only that a live game-cock should be buried with him beneath the doorstone. This granted after the final "Amen" the doorstone suddenly cracked right through the middle, and a sepulchral voice declared. So long as hollins and ivvens are green Chamber Ha' Boggart will ne'er more be seen. It is only fair to the boggart, however, to add that only three years ago I was told by the lady of the house that mysterious noises, sometimes like the sound of a loud insistent knock, were still heard in the dead of night in its old abode! The boggart was also said to sit sometimes upon a rail under a large thornbush on the opposite side of the lane, and old inhabitants tell how in their childhood very few Oldham people would have dared to go along Chamber Lane after nightfall. A suggested practical use for the historic buildings is that the Hall should become a Branch Library and Reading Rooms: the Barn a "Regional Museum" for larger historic objects such as looms, e.g.: and the smaller range a Museum which could easily be put into shape in order to relieve the congestion in the present Municipal Museum. MORE RECENT QUOTE ON TETLOW FAMILY WEBSITE. "When working in Oldham recently and being very near to the site of "Chamber Hall" I spoke to an elderly local lady. She said when she was a little girl it was still standing, say around 1925. She said it looked a very dark and forbidding building. She and the other children used to run past it. They named it "Mother Black Jacks".'

Oldham 9 (La). 1950s/F/FG., 14-10-19. 'I remember being warned about the Boggart as a child in Oldham along with Ginny Greenteeth 1950.'

Oldham 10 (La). 1950s/M/FG., 14-10-19. 'I'm sixty-seven, born in Oldham, so I grew up in 1950s and 1960s. Boggarts were definitely mentioned by people who spoke the dialect, like my Uncle Jim. He was born at the beginning of the twentieth century. He spoke the dialect all the time. He mentioned boggarts. He lived on Oldham Edge (so called because it edges onto the moor). I learned that there were some boggarts around Delph and up into Saddleworth. So, people were still talking about them into the 1960s.

After that we became sophisticated and modern and our folk heritage became a "folksy" embarrassment. I would probably have said it was some kind of malevolent spirit up on the moors... and laughed at the idea. There was some relationship with Jack o' Lantern. I remember a teacher saying never to follow Jack o' Lantern and they were in league with boggarts. (Maybe it was just to warn us about straying too far off the path.) Now we have internet trolls. Far more dangerous.'

Oldham 11 (La). ???/M/FG., 18-10-19. 'I was born in Oldham and we used to go to boggart hole clough. It was near Avro Factory. We never saw any but if you went today they may still be there they supposed to be a cat like creature. My dad said that he saw them as he worked at the Avro Factory. He used to work nights, so maybe that is when it came out.'

Openshaw 1 (La). 1960s/M/FG., 27-9-19. 'Lived in lower Openshaw and at the bottom of Clayton there was a bit of wasted land behind Gorton monestry with a little brook running through it and mothers used to tell their kids it was haunted at night by the Blackey Brook Boggart in the early 1960s.'

Openshaw 2 (La). ???/M/FG., 28-9-19. 'I still live in Openshaw as a kid my dad told [me] "be careful the boggart will get you".'

Openshaw 3 (La). 1940s/M/FG., 28-9-19. 'I lived in Openshaw from 1945-1965 never heard or warned of the boggart.'

Openshaw 4 (La). 1940s/M/FG., 28-9-19. 'I lived in Higher Openshaw from 1947-1968. We had a cellar with very steep steps and to keep us away from them Dad said the Boggart lived down there.'

Openshaw 5 (La). 1960s/M/FG., 2-10-19. 'Born in Openshaw but never heard of boggart until I moved to Harpurhey then was Boggart Hole Clough. I was born Openshaw 1962 and left 1968. I think a lot still goes on in the clough in the way of witchcraft and seances. My sister lived by the side of there and spoke about stuff going on.'

Ormskirk 1 (La). 1960s/M/FG., 28-9-19. 'I grew up in Ormskirk in the 1960s and have never heard of this. But my parents were from up north so maybe that's why.'

Ormskirk 2 (La). 1960s/M/FG., 28-9-19. '"Bogarts" was a term used when I was a lad in the 1960s. What about Ginny Greenteeth?'

Oswaldtwistle 1 (La). 1940s/M/FG., 17-10-19. 'There was a Boggart in Oswaldtwistle "Jinny Greenteeth" my Aunty called it... This was in the 1940s when I was young. But I bet done [?] people these days have heard of her. My aunty told me she [Jinny] lived in a pond up Foxhill. The saying was "be good or Jinny Greenteeth will get you". Still look behind me when I go up Ozzy.'

Out Rawcliffe 1 (La). ???/F/FG., 20-9-19. 'My family lived in Out Rawcliffe and their farm was known as Boggart House and boggarts are still spoken about in my household.'

Out Rawcliffe 2 (La). 1960s/F/FG., 24-9-19. 'I grew up in Out Rawcliffe in the 1960s/1970s and yes the word "bogart" was often used in and around our very old farmhouse, usually to try and keep us kids out of mischief. "Don't go in there, Boggarts will get thee!" etc etc. Anything that was a bit scary was always down to boggarts, chuckle. I'm from a very big Over Wyre family and I think everyone young and old will still know what a Boggart was. I would say boggarts are still going strong all over Lancashire. To us they were another word for ghosts.'

Over Wyre 1 (La). ???/M/FG., 20-9-19. 'Over Wyre boggarts were always known as "cat boggarts" that lived in the shadows of dark country lanes. They were knocking about in Hambleton in the 1980s and in Preesall in the 1970s.'

Over Wyre 2 (La). ???/F/FG., 18-10-19. 'I spent my teen years Over Wyre... Ghosts and similar were referred to as "boggarts".'

Padiham 1 (La). 1950s/M/FG., 9-19-19. I grew up in Padiham at that time I remember a boggart bridge. Hope this helps.'

Padiham 2 (La). 1970s/F/FG., 12-10-19. I read of a boggart that lived under a bridge in read [?]. It's a long time ago. I can't remember where I read it. I can't. But I always assumed it was the one at Devil's Elbow as I can really imagine a boggart living there. I'll try and see if I can think what I would have been reading forty years or so ago that mentions it.'

Pendle 1 (La). 1970s/F/FG., 20-9-19. 'My gran used to talk about treacle eating boggarts that lived in Pendle Hill. 1970s and 1980s. She lived in Sabden for years and we all knew of them. There was a museum in Sabden as well but that for me was when I was a teen.'

Pendle 2 (La). 1950s/F/F., 4-9-19. 'There were tales of boggarts when I was young in the 1950s up i'th'ills i' Pendle country, and black dogs. There was even one under the bridge at Boggart Bridge on Todmorden Road, near Towneley, and you had to greet him as you passed over. One also resides at the Devil's Elbow as you come up the brew from Whalley to Read, you have to say "hello Mr Boggart", as you travel the tight bend or you're in for trouble. In 1950s Burnley boggarts were part of the folklore, as far as I remember they were a malevolent spirit, and harm would befall you at Boggart Bridge or the sharp steep bend at Devil's Elbow but would they not harm you as long as you respected them, hence the greeting as you went over the bridge. They were a spirit of the water or woods (like the Scandinavian trolls). "T'boggart'll get you", was a threat to misbehaving children though – a bit like a bogeyman. They weren't all bad because there is a legend of a boggart who lived at Barcroft Hall, which is a bit further along the road from Townley and also near Boggart Bridge, this was an industrious spirit who did the housework at night when everyone was in bed, leaving the hall spick and span for the morning. One night the housewife stayed up to watch and saw this little creature was very raggedly dressed so she made a new set of clothes and left them out, he danced around in them then vanished. She never saw him again. The black dog was a ferocious creature that would chase you across the moor, one was supposed to inhabit Turf Moor where Burnley Football club now is. That's all I can remember but the area of Pendle was filled with stories of spirits. The tale of the Lancashire witches is pure fabrication but based on the imaginings of a group of silly women fictionalised by Harrison Ainsworth. When we go home to Burnley up Whalley Brew we still say "hello Mr Boggart" as we go round the tight bend to placate the spirit that lives in the steep wooded area. The Greeting Mr Boggart was a Burnley thing everyone did it at some time though probably it had died out by the 1950s. Our Girl Guide leader lived at Boggart Bridge and she obviously perpetuated it with us guides. But it definitely was a tradition at Whalley Brew too, that was a particularly dangerous stretch of road famous for accidents. Incidentally I think there was a belief that the boggarts were the "guardians of the gate", i.e.the entrance to the underworld in the mysterious places they inhabited.'

Penwortham 1 (La). 1940s/F/FG., 21-9-19. 'My other halls [?half's] Nan who lives in Penwortham is in her eighties and uses the word. If a horse pulls up and starts a commotion she would say "oh look its takin Boggarts!" Interestingly I found this online just now where the same turn of phrase has been used.'

Penwortham 2 (La). 1960s/F/FG., 3-10-19. 'Yes! I was born in Penwortham in 1966 and my Granddad used to tell tales about "boggarts" in the early 1970s. Can't remember the tales so much as the name, I used to love the word. I'm sure I have a book somewhere, which was his, with Lancashire ghost tales including boggarts.'

Penwortham 3 (La). 1920s/M/FG., 4-10-19. 'My father used to talk about boggarts all the time, especially in winter nights when it was dark and windy. He used to tell us to be careful or the boggarts will get us. It frightened us to death! He was XXX's and XXX's grandfather. Yes, he was born in Preston but lived in Penwortham since 1922 and died in 1984. I must say when mentioned "boggarts" he always giggled so we wouldn't really be frightened.'

Penwortham 4 (La). 1960s/F/FG., 18-10-19. 'I asked my dad who was born in Preston 1942. He lived Ashton/Ribbleton didn't tell me a lot, but said a common term in Preston while he was growing up and has Irish origins and his family definitely didn't have any! I was born 1970 grew up in Penwortham and never heard of them. I grew up in Penwortham in the 1960s [dates muddled here] and never heard it used at home but had seen the word in stories I think. Has Irish connotations.'

Pilling 1 (La). 1940s/F/FG., 21-9-19. 'Definitely Ginney Greenteeth too. If you went too close to the dyke she would grab you and gobble you up. I was born 1948. But the dykes were all around Pilling and they had like a green algae type plant that grows over the surface and I think the Jinny Greenteeth story was to stop us going too close and drowning because in those days we would just go out and roam freely around the countryside with no adult supervision. [If someone had asked about boggarts in 1950.] I'd have said a scary ghostlike headless creature that hid in Staffords wood and would steal children. Ha! ha! I did believe that then but also I was told that it was also a headless horseman who galloped down the lane at midnight.'

Pilling 2 (La). 1950s/F/FG., 20-9-19. 'My grandparent's farmed at XXX Farm, Pilling and the road down to it (off Garstang Road) is called Boggarts Lane. As a child in the 1950s my older cousins would terrify me with stories of Boggarts as we walked past the wood. Nothing to do with ghosts but during WW2 American GIs were stationed each side of the lane. Whites on one side and coloured on the other which is terrible.'

Pilling 3 (La). 1970s/M/F., 2-9-19 'Many moons ago I used to live in Pilling, there was a road we called Boggert Lane. I lived in Pilling about fifty years ago, I can't remember anything about the lane in question, as I don't believe in ghosts and ghoulies.'

Pilling 4 (La). 1970s/F/FG., 24-9-19. 'Born in 1978. Grew up hearing about boggarts lived in Pilling. I'd have said it was small ugly troll/goblin creature that came out in the dark and it was something to be scared of.'

Pilling 5 (La). 1950s/F/FG., 28-9-19. 'I used to live in Pilling and lived down a road called Boggat Road. It was named that because of something bad that had happened years ago. [Age guessed from FB page].'

Pilling 6 (La). 1930s/M/FG., 11-10-19. 'I spoke to mum and dad this week. My dad is from Pilling and my mum from Stalmine and both heard of boggarts when kids from parents. My dad's mum was born in 1905 and dad in 1935 and he said there was said to be a Boggart down Smallwood Hey (main road) that jumped out on people at night. He said he thought it was a story to get kids home before dark. Hope that helps.'

Pilling 7 (La). 1950s/F/FG., 15-10-19. 'I remember "back in the day" a second cousin of mine used to tell the best boggart tales, we would go into his Granddad's barn, climb the ladder and sit in the hay loft on Eagland Hill (always referred to as "on" Eagland Hill not at) and he told us the best scary stories. This would be early to mid-1960s when we were all young teens. He called the boggart "Ichabod". Fifty years on I can't remember his stories in detail … but they were very happy (if slightly scary) times. By the way Eagland Hill is a hamlet near Pilling in Lancashire.'

Pinnock 1 (La). 1920s/M/FG., 5-10-19. 'Lads used to make "Bogeys", old pram wheels with a piece of wood on top for a seat and rope attached to steer and they were said to be what boggarts rode on according to my uncle who was born down Pincock in 1925.'

Poulton 1 (La). 1950s/M/FG., 26-9-19. 'I grew up in Poulton in the 1950s/1960s and I can't remember hearing the word. I think I first came across it in literature, as an adult.'

Poulton 2 (La). 1950s/F/FG., 26-9-19. 'I was born in 1952 and lived in Poulton-le-Fylde until my twenties. My mother was District Commissioner for Girl Guides and ran the 2nd Poulton Brownie pack. Growing up, I was well aware of the term Boggart and, searching my memory just now, decided it was through Brownies that I must have heard it. Please look here https://en.wikipedia.org/wiki/Brownies_(Scouting) second paragraph! It never occurred to me that boggarts were just a Lancashire phenomenon – I presumed everyone knew about them. Boggarts were naughty goblin-like creatures but I honestly can't remember much more detail about them. Our Lancashire pronunciation was of course boggert and not bog-art. Then, of course, boggarts turned up again in Harry Potter which is probably the first time my husband (from Sussex) heard the word. Since then, whenever we hear our wardrobe creak in this old Suffolk house we say "uh-oh, boggart!").'

Poulton 3 (La). 1950s/F/FG., 26-9-19. 'I heard the word often when growing up in Poulton from the late 1950s. If we misbehaved, Mum would tell us "You'd better be good or the boggarts will get you" – I think a boggart was the Lancashire version of the bogeyman. Dad used to tell us about Boggart's Wood, but that could have been a nickname for Brockholes Wood (known as Tee Wood) because he used to walk through there as a child and said it was scary at night.'

Poulton 4 (La). 1960s/F/FG., 26-9-19. 'My Granddad used to talk to me about boggarts. He described them as mischievous woodland creatures. Never frightening. He was born in 1912 and from the Clitheroe area, but lived most of his adult life in Cleveleys. The era he was telling me the stories was when I was four or five, so early 1970s. Also later on, in early 1980s, a teacher at Cardinal Allen High School Fleetwood used to warn us about boggarts roaming around in the dark at Castlerigg in Keswick in the Lake District. I'm sure he only did this to stop us unruly teenagers from venturing out at night whilst staying there during our final year of high school!'

Poulton 5 (La). 1970s/F/FG., 27-9-19. 'I grew up with Ginny Greenteeth [in the 1970s]. We used to go for walks in the countryside to see where she lived. I lived in Poulton-le-Fylde. Have always loved folklore and legends. Yes, I used to read about them [boggarts] and my dad would tell me stories about Ginny Greenteeth living in the woods. Only that she was a skinny ugly old hag that lived in a den in the woods and ate naughty children!'

Poulton 6 (La). 1950s/F/FG., 27-9-19. 'Just to confirm, my older sister remembers boggarts from Brownies, not from any other source. Her husband (also a Poultonian) has never heard of them.'

Poulton 7 (La). 1940s/F/FG., 27-9-19. 'Bogy man we called it. Years later I heard of boggarts. Yes [Poulton] from a few weeks old. My Mum was from Bacup and said "Bogie Man". Boggart was heard from other people or books. Don't remember schoolfriends from Poulton ever saying it. My Dad didn't use any of those words. He was from Yorkshire family but born in Cumberland (Cumbria). I would think that Bogie man is referring to Boggarts. Just a slang name. My Mum mentioned it a lot.'

Poulton 8 (La). 1960s/F/FG., 17-10-19. 'All I remember is being told that if I didn't behave myself the boggarts would come and get me. Not my parents who said that to me so not sure who it was.'

Preesall 1 (La). 1950s/M/FG., 20-9-19. 'Born in Preesall in 1951 and lived there until 1967. Cannot remember any reference to Boggarts in ghost stories etc. Was scared of the headless horseman of Hackensall Hall though!'

Preesall 2 (La). 1960s/F/FG., 20-9-19. 'I was born in 1966 and loved to hear my mum and dad tell tales of boggarts on England Hill Moss! A great one about when The Old Ship in Pilling was an ale house and a man walking home encountered a boggart who relieved him of all his money in a card game!'

Preesall 3 (La). 1950s/F/FG., 20-9-19. 'I was born in the 1950s and as a child always was told stories about mischievous boggarts by my father who was born in Nateby in 1926. Sorry not in any detail but I remember how they scared me and my sister, it made us a little afraid of the dark, and what might be hiding in dark corners.'

Preesall 4 (La). 1970s/F/FG., 20-9-19. 'Hasn't died out in my family.... I was born in 1973 and boggart is still a word I hear when family is about. I was born and bred Over Wyre in Preesall and lived on a farm till I was twelve. Youngest of three daughters, others are sixty-three and fifty-six. Boggarts were under your bed or at the back of the barn and messed with things in mischief...

And my parents (still alive at eighty-three and eighty) used it all the time. There's also the saying "there's no bigger boggart than yourself" that I still say now to my kids. Even my southern husband knows what a boggart is after being married for sixteen years! Yeah no worries! If I remember I will talk to my mum and dad this weekend and see if they can remember where they got it from.'

Preesall 5 (La). 1960s/M/FG., 21-9-19. 'Had an interesting chat only last week to do with this subject and that with reference to the Hackensall boggart maybe brought about by the smuggling on the river Wyre to ward off people at night as smugglers went about their business. [Did you grow up with boggarts?]. Yes, grew up with the likes of ginny green teeth, and the headless horseman.'

Preesall 6 (La). 1960s/F/FG., 25-9-19. 'My dad and granddad used to tell me there was boggarts at the end of the pea row to stop me pinching them… It didn't work! I was born and bred in Preesall.'

Preston 1 (La). 1970s/M/F., 29-8-19. 'Preston born and bred and never heard of them.'

Preston 2 (La). 1950s/F/F., 4-9-19. 'The stone is in Written Stone Lane near Longridge and the story is that if the stone is ever moved the person moving it would be in trouble with the local boggart who lived under it. The lane was a favourite spot for blackberrying in autumn for my family. I grew up in the Preston area and still live here. It is a story I seem to have known about forever, as the story of the Pendle witch trials. Passed it on to my children who are now grown up and hopefully they will pass it on to the grandchildren. I suppose I would have said [a boggart] was a kind of mischief making ghost. Though neither child asked! I was a child in the 1950s and 1960s in the Preston area, but of a Scottish family. The Scots are pretty good at tales of mysterious beings too!'

Preston 3 (La). 1950s/F/F., 8-9-19. 'I was born in 1952 in Preston and lived here all my life. Yes I heard boggart and bogey man as a child and even now the bogey man is used by some older people to frighten children. Needless to say I wouldn't say that to a child. But I had it said to me by my parents not to frighten me but to speed me up. Comments like "be home before it's dark or the bogey man will get you". I grew up in a town but it was more country people used "boggart". What I understood was that boggarts lived on poor land that was uncultivated and yes they supposedly frightened people and livestock. Sheep, cows etc would run away, birds would fly off and horses would rear on their hind legs. I've never given it any thought before. But I think it was a bit like Father Christmas. Once you got to a certain age you stopped believing. However I'm not saying they don't exist... just that I never saw one. Yes both of those. Bannister doll was well known in Preston and a true story. In fact, I'm sure there was a book written about her by someone in Preston. I'm not sure who the author was. But maybe Amazon have it or Waterstones in Preston where I think there was a book signing by the author. Now Ginny Greenteeth was mentioned a lot in our house growing up. Usually at teeth brushing time. From what I was told she did exist and was a lady who was quite frightening in appearance. And as a child you don't want that. In those days Preston was an industrial town and dark and dismal. You can see photos on Flickr and videos on YouTube. So all these things you believed as life wasn't very bright in the northern towns. But we never saw fairies but was once shown a fairy ring in someone's garden.'

Preston 4 (La). 1950s/M/FG., 28-9-19. 'Born in Preston 1952 and left in 1967, but I cannot recall hearing this at home or anywhere else. Hope this helps.'

Preston 5 (La). 1950s/F/FG., 28-9-19. 'Preston born and bred 1956 heard the expression but can't put it into context – never heard it at home.'

Preston 6 (La). 1950s/M/FG., 28-9-19. '1950s Preston. Never heard Boggarts.'

Preston 7 (La). 1950s/F/FG., 28-9-19. 'This was in late 1950s onwards. I remember my nana (born 1909) telling me about "Boggart's Pit Wood" in Treales, near Preston. A pit was a pond. Don't know anymore about the Boggart who was supposed to be there though.'

Preston 8 (La). 1950s/F/FG., 28-9-19. 'Born in Preston Royal Infirmary in 1951, left in 1964. I never heard the word at home or anywhere, sorry.'

Preston 9 (La). 1950s/M/FG., 29-9-19. 'Born in 52 in Preston, grandparents and parents both talked about Boggarts in a sort of scary way especially on country walks and finding boggy, marshy areas where the Boggarts might grab your leg and pull you into the bog so crossing boggy marshy ground was made quite exciting. I carried on the tradition in and around our Devon village with our grandchildren!'

Preston 10 (La). 1950s/F/FG., 29-9-19. '50s born and bred, never heard the word before.'

Preston 11 (La). 1960s/F/FG., 4-10-19. 'I was born in 1966 in Deepdale, Preston and although I cannot remember the word "Boggart" (although I have heard it subsequently), I was terrified of Jenny Green Teeth. Was she a kind of Boggart I wonder? My mum said she lived in the Ribble and would pull you under the water.'

Preston 12 (La). 1950s/F/FG., 4-10-19. 'I was brought up in the 1950s/60s and I was frightened to death of the witch that lived in the outside toilet. My brothers said she came when you pulled the chain. Needless to say I pulled the chain and I ran like hell.'

Preston 13 (La). 1960s/F/FG., 4-10-19. 'About the boggarts I grew up in Preston town in 1960s and people seemed to know about one in Gregson Lane. Also the older folk called them bargeists? The original story made it into a reading scheme in 1980s!'

Preston 14 (La). 1940s/M/FG., 5-10-19. 'Born in early 1940s in Preston. My mother used the term as an affectionate term to us for being a nuisance ("You little Boggart!") when appropriate in the 1940s and early 1950s.'

Preston 15 (La). 1970s/F/FG., 12-10-19. 'First time I ever heard "bogart" was a few years ago from someone from Preston who now lives in Hoghton as far as I know. He will be in 1970s. Just used to tell the kids they [boggarts] lived in his garden as had a large uncultured one great for kids.'

Preston 16 (La). 1950s/F/FG., 17-10-19. 'Preston 1954. Would be told if you don't get to sleep the bogey man would get you.'

Preston 17 (La). 1950s/F/FG., 17-10-19. 'Preston 1951, also told about the bogey man, never heard boggarts mentioned.'

Preston 18 (La). 1950s/F/E., 31-10-19. 'Was just doing a bit of online research about Mischief Night traditions in Lancashire and happened upon your survey. I was born in Preston in 1957 and grew up in Fulwood. I certainly grew up knowing that boggarts would get you if you weren't careful. I can't remember ever being told quite what they were like but, in my mind – as a Brownie – they were like extremely naughty imps or goblins. I may have misremembered this, but I'm pretty sure that my friend XXX, lived on a farm in Barton, near Preston, which was called Boggart Farm. I will look it up but you can probably check yourself. It was the XXX family farm for many years I believe. Hope this is helpful! I've just checked and the farm I mentioned is actually Boggart House Farm. It's still in the XXX family and still producing milk. They may be able to help you with the origins of the name of the farm.'

Prestwich 1 (La). 1950s/F/FG., 17-10-19. 'I grew up in Prestwich in the 1950s and there was a Boggart Hole Clough we used to talk about. I'm not sure now, but I think it was on the other side of Heaton Park from us around Blakeley way. I would have said it was a Bogeyman ... to be feared. It was never linked with the park. Just a place somewhere on the other side of the park from where I lived as a child.'

Prestwich 2 (La). 1970s/F/FG., 17-10-19. 'Never heard of the term, only in relation to Boggart Hole Clough. However, so grew up in the 1970s and lived on Deyne Avenue, where there was originally a Deanery, and believe me, there were plenty of "boggarts" or poltergeists as we called them in many of the houses on the even side.'

Prestwich 3 (La). 1970s/F/FG., 17-10-19. 'I grew up in Prestwich in the 1970s and used to visit Boggart Hole Clough (it's in the Lower Broughton Area) but I only knew what a boggart was from reading old stories. I was never aware of any stories linked to the park though.'

Prestwich 4 (La). 1960s/F/FG., 17-10-19. 'I grew up in Prestwich in the 1960s and have heard of Boggarthole Clough which is in Blackley but never knew what a boggart was but assume some sort of folk monster as you say… Presumably one resides in the Clough!?'

Prestwich 5 (La). 1940s/F/FG., 18-10-19. 'My friend and her brother used to go in Boggart hole clough, she said they had such strange experiences in there that they stopped going. Other people have said the same. I've lived in Prestwich all my life. Since 1948.'

Prestwich 6 (La). 1960s/M/FG., 18-10-19. 'Born in 1960 and only really ever heard of Boggart Hole Clough, but no associated stories. However, I do have an old book, *Lancashire Stories* by Frank Hird (1912) that has two stories on boggarts. One is The Clegg Hall Boggart (Rochdale) and the other is The Boggarts Clough. I will scan these as jpeg's and send in two emails.'

Prestwich 7 (La). 1960s/F/FG., 18-10-19. 'Born in the early 1960s. In the 1970s I'd want to play in Prestwich Clough and would be warned that the bogart would be looking for me. Not sure who warned me but feel it was older teens and adults. They'd be teasing me by saying that I was Jinny (I'm Jenny) Greenteeth. The memory is very vague. There didn't seem to be any threatening overtones. It was as though it was just a fact that a Boggart lived in the clough.'

Prestwich 8 (La). 1960s/F/FG., 18-10-19. 'Grew up in Prestwich in the 1960s and always knew what Boggarts were, possibly because of Boggart's Hole Clough.'

Prestwich 9 (La). 1960s/M/FG., 18-10-19. 'Born in 1962 and grew up in Carr Clough I am aware of the mythical creature called a Bogart. It's in the same category as goblins and trolls. My recollection is they came out into the clough to prey on young children at dusk. I got this story from older kids trying to scare us whilst walking through the clough after cubs. We were in the twenty second Prestwich and would walk down from St. Mary's church and up again to the crossing of St Ann's Road and Lowther Rd. There would of been half a dozen of us most weeks but you were always a bit wary going through the clough after dark.'

Prestwich 10 (La). 1940s/M/FG., 23-10-19. 'I was born in 1944 and remember my father explaining what Boggarts were. This was in response to my questions about Boggart Hole Clough. [How did he describe them?] Only that they were mythical creatures bent on mischief.'

Prestwich 11 (La). 1960s/F/FG., 24-10-19. 'As children we used to walk to our Grandma's (she lived on Venwood Road) sometimes down St Ann's road and sometimes down past St Mary's church and through the Clough. We were also told to beware of the boggart! I didn't hear about Boggart Hole Clough until years later when I and one of my sisters worked for Thorn Consumer Electronics and one of the other workers, George, who lived nearby mentioned it. I assumed from then on that all Boggarts lived in cloughs. Walking to Grandma's. 1960s.'

Prestwich 12 (La). 1950s/M/FG., 24-10-19. 'Born 1955 and can't recall ever hearing the word, Prestwich.'

Rainhill 1 (La). 1950s/M/FG., 28-7-19. 'When I was growing up in the 1950s I knew a boggart was a monster that us kids use to talk about. Not a clue [as to gender], rightly or wrongly us kids just thought that a boggart was a monster of some sort, lol. [Later added.] A boggart is a shapeshifter that usually lurks in dark spaces. It has no definite form, taking the shape of that which is most feared by the person who encounters it. When not in the sight of a person, it is believed to look like a dark blob.'

Rainhill 2 (La). 1960s/F/FG., 28-7-19. 'I've never heard the word and grew up in the 1960s 1970s, 1980s in Rainhill. New one on me.'

Rainhill 3 (La). 1940s/M/FG., 28-7-19. 'Born in 1942 Rainhill. Never heard of a boggart, but plenty of bogey men.'

Rainhill 4 (La). 1980s/M/FG., 28-7-19. 'Also aged forty-two and lived almost all my life in Rainhill but never heard the word "boggart".'

Rainhill 5 (La). 1950s/F/FG., 29-7-19. 'I grew up in Rainhill in the 1950s. Can't say "boggart" is a word I'm familiar with. Boggy men, yes! Maybe derived from boggart!'

Rainhill 6 (La). 1950s/F/FG., 28-7-19. We have the Clough in Rainhill but I haven't heard it referred to as Boggart Clough though I'm familiar with the word "Boggart". Ginny Greenteeth lives in the ponds round the Clough! No I don't think so [Jinny a boggart] cos I think boggarts are male. She is female. it was a bit confused with Bogeyman I think too. I'm not being very helpful am I!? Rainhill born and bred growing up in the 1950s. Ginny lived in the ponds underneath the green algae bloom which our family still call, Ginny Green teeth. My Mother is ninety-eight and sharp as a pin. She grew up in St Helens. I think the Ginny Greenteeth came from her. She certainly uses it as a name. Just asked my husband about bogarts. He has never come across it but always knew about Ginny Greenteeth when growing up in very rural North Wales in the 1950s. I suppose it kept us safely away from water of unknown depth!'

Rainhill 7 (La). 1970s/F/FG., 17-10-19. 'A bit out of your date range. I was born in 1972. I'd never heard of a boggart until I moved to Staffordshire. The kids make them here in forest school. They're some sort of creature that lives in the woods.'

Rawtenstall 1 (La). 1920s/F/F., 8-9-19. 'Well the word "boggart" is still in use in Lancashire. When I met my future mother-in-law I was confused when she said someone was "off like the boggart!" Never heard it before. My MIL was born in 1923 in the Rawtenstall area. I met her in Baxenden in 1997. She was using that phrase then and had all her life. According to my husband, she used it when referring to someone rushing off somewhere suddenly: "ee, he were off like a boggart". I lived in Fleetwood at the time and had never heard the phrase before so it struck me as odd. My MIL died in 2014, still using the phrase. I lived in Liverpool until I was eight, then Fleetwood. I never heard it anywhere before I came to East Lancashire. I was born 1949.

Rawtenstall 2 (La). 1940s/F/FG., 21-9-19. 'I grew up in Rawtenstall in the late forties and early fifties, I never heard of the Boggarts though.'

Rawtenstall 3 (La). 1960s/F/FG., 20-9-19. '[Boggarts were] The little people, the night spirits. Rawtenstall, 1960. Believe it or not Mummy [told me] but she was Scottish. We lived in Rawtenstall for twenty years so she must of been told a story. Just asked one of my brothers. He remembered after I told him (watch out for the boggarts). He's much younger than I and again Rawtenstall born. We've all left for thirty years now.'

Rawtenstall 4 (La). 1950s/M/FG., 23-9-19. 'Grew up in 1950s and early 1960s. We were always told to be in before it goes dark when playing out after school or the boggarts will get you. Rawtenstall, and Goodshaw chapel, the old village on the hill.'

Rawtenstall 5 (La). 1960s/F/FG., and E., 13-10-19. 'Rossendale in Lancashire where I was brought up had boggarts as scary beings everywhere – anywhere dark or dangerous. Under bridges, in tunnels, lurking near lodges (large ponds). Those ponds had boggarts that would pull you in and drown you. I remember my friend's dog that refused to cross bridges and that was put down to animals knowing where boggarts were hiding. I lived in Rawtenstall at the time which was from the early 1960s through the 1970s up to 1980. I went to high school in Waterfoot where these beliefs still held sway with people from there and Bacup. Small holes in the ground not lived in by animals were called boggart holes and we would poke sticks down hoping they would bite! I did write on Facebook I believe for you but wondered if you need the same here? If I can remember any more stories I will email. I've asked my mother and she only knew the same sort of thing as myself – she lived in Bacup in Rossendale and grew up as a war baby. I didn't really get many stories about boggarts from home, but school was a real place for very old-fashioned things even for that area. St Marys in Rawtenstall was my infant/junior school and Bacup and Rawtenstall was my high school. Compared to my friends through the valley the stories and activities we did at St Marys were much more detailed, antiquated and interesting. I remember with so much fondness, especially Easter! I've had a word with friends and a gentleman my age didn't know the word "boggart". He used bogeyman for the same set of fears. Oh and some boy at my infant school would say he had a boggart on his throat not a frog in his throat. Just remembered.'

Ribbleton 1 (La). 1940s/M/FG., 18-10-19. 'I asked my dad who was born in Preston 1942. He lived Ashton/Ribbleton didn't tell me a lot. But said a common term in Preston while he was growing up and has Irish origins and his family definitely didn't have any!'

Rishton 1 (La). 1960s/F/FG., 5-10-19. 'A bogart was like a bogeyman something to scare young kids from doing something dangerous the one I remember being told about was granny green teeth who lived under canal bridge who would pull you under water if you went near. Rishton, 1960s.'

Rishton 2 (La). 1950s/F/FG., 9-10-19. 'I remember mum talking about the 'Dunkenhalgh boggart' just thought it was a ghost or something? I also remember Ginny Greenteeth from the canal! Born and lived in Rishton 1950s to 1970s.'

Rixton 1 (La). 1950s/M/FG., 26-9-19. 'I was born in 1957 and grew up in Rixton and Irlam. I had never heard of Boggarts until 1979 when I saw a little production at the Library Theatre in Manchester called The Boggarts Of Boggart Hole Clough.'

Rochdale 1 (La). 1940s/M/E., 4-9-19. 'What does the word "boggart" mean to you? An evil spirit. Did your parents and grandparents use the word? Yes. Do your children, nephews and nieces use it? No. Do you know any stories about boggarts – or places especially associated with them? Only Boggart Old Clough in Rochdale. The family who had lived there had been so afraid of the Boggart that they had left hurriedly, never to return and the house was left to go to ruin. As a child I went there once on Halloween with some other kids and frightened ourselves to death waiting for the Boggarts to appear – which, of course, they didn't! Where did you grow up, and in what decade? In Rochdale in the 1940s and 1950s.'

Rochdale 2 (La). 1970s/M/E., 28-9-19. '1970s, yes heard of them from period dramas. Rochdale.'

Rochdale 3 (La). 1920s/M/FG., 10-10-19. 'My father, who was born and raised in Rochdale, would often use the expression "run like a boggart!" when encouraging someone to sprint or move fast when playing sport. When questioned on what a boggart was he informed me that it was a troubled spirit who haunted the nearby moors, appearing and vanishing quickly. He often referenced boggarts when describing someone who looked pale and sickly. He was born in 1923, died 1990 and was always proud of his "Lanky" heritage. Even though he lived and worked in Southport he often resorted to speaking in dialect. All "thee" and "thou"!'

Rochdale 4 (La). 1950s/F/FG., 14-10-19. 'I grew up originally in Rochdale in the 1950/1960s but the word "Boggart" was a familiar word particularly in a place called Boggart Hole Clough in Blakeley Manchester. My parents always mentioned it as well so that goes back to the 1930s. As a child it was a common expression. So always in our vocabulary as my parents used to meet in Boggart Hole Clough in their "courting days" just after the war. Where it originated from I have no idea. Boggarts I thought were like mythical creatures.'

Rochdale 5 (La). ???/M/FG., 14-10-19. 'Small world. I was born in Rochdale (Witworth area). My dad was known as the badger man. The brocks came down off "Owd Betts" hills around Whitworth and dug under buildings. Dad captured them and released them back on the hills. He would talk about spooky areas up there freaked him out sometimes. Boy had to dig deep there into the memory bank… Why do I know about Boggarts? Cos I do. Where from? Hmmm got it! My dad was a fan of Mike Harding (the Rochdale cowboy). Think he did sketches involving boggats. Going to lie down in a dark room now.'

Rochdale 6 (La). 1950s/F/E., 23-10-19. 'Hi I was born in 1955 and my mum used to say that we were watching the Boggarts if we stared into the coal fire when it was lit. She said Boggarts lived in amongst the orange and yellow flames of the coals. She still says it now. No problem we were both born in Rochdale, Lancashire. My Mum was born in the 1930s and was a weaver. As a child we had a coal fire in the family home until the 1970s.'

Rochdale 7 (La). 1960s/M/E., 23-10-19. 'We knew all about Boggarts from a song passed down by my granddad called "Come Whoam To Thi' Childer An' Me". The Oldham Tinkers do it, but we knew it as little children in the 1960s. My mum, XXX used to sing it to us. We lived in Castleton Rochdale but the Granddad in question lived in Bamber Bridge Preston. He had been a teacher all his life and knew a great many such songs or stories.'

Rossendale 1 (La). 1960s/M/E., 8-9-19. 'What does the word "boggart" mean to you? Some sort of animal creature/possibly half-man and half-animal. Associated with darkness. 2 Did your parents and grandparents use the word? Maternal grandmother from Burnley used boggart; paternal grandparents from London did not use it, nor did my parents. Parents in law (from Colne, Lancashire), still use boggart to describe furious running, such as when two dogs are chasing each other; they are said to be "boggarting around". Do your children, nephews and nieces use it? Not to my knowledge. 3 Do you know any stories about boggarts – or places especially associated with them? No. 4 Where did you grow up, and in what decade? Rossendale, Lancashire. 1960s/1970s.'

Rossendale 2 (La). 1960s/M/F/FG., 21-9-19. 'Boggarts were big black dogs, red or yellow eyes over the tops at night if you saw it someone was going to die but my parents got us excited about seeing them we used to look out for them. XXX, XXX remember we saw them at Arnside Knott and Liskard amongst other places? We thought we did [saw them], kid's imaginations... Late 1960s early 1970s.'

Rossendale 3 (La). 1970s/F/FG., 21-9-19. 'Growing up in Rossendale in the 1970s the term "boggart" would be used by my mum as a way of saying setting off fast/rushing without thinking – "off at boggart." I don't recall anything else.'

Rossendale 4 (La). 1980s/F/FG., 25-9-19. 'I'm in the Rossendale Valley, Whitworth and people used to say they live in Healey Dell. They are little troll creatures.'

Rossendale 5 (La). 1960s/M/FG., 25-9-19. 'We definitely had a Boggart in the loft from the late 1960s until the loft conversion circa 1977. It explained any creaks and groans that came from upstairs.'

Rossendale 6 (La). 1950s/M/E., 1-11-19. 'I just came upon the piece in FLS news and immediately realised I had to contact you! My mother used to tell me I looked as though a boggart had been after me whenever I looked particularly dishevelled, a frequent event. We lived in the Rossendale Valley between 1958 and 1964, then we moved to West Lancs. Mother (born 1923) had a very traditional East Lancashire (Crawshawbooth) upbringing, in great poverty, during the Depression, and spoke Lancashire dialect when she wasn't trying to be posh. A great many words in that dialect derive from Old Norse. My father (born 1916) was also from East Lancashire (Waterfoot) but rarely mentioned any local legends. My grandparents were no longer around when I was growing up and we didn't have close ties with other kin. Possibly because the Moors Murders were going on in the early 1960s, I was no longer allowed to run wild on the hills, and I picked up the idea that there was something terrifying and monstrous out there... perhaps I made up my own "boggart" as I don't think my mother ever explained exactly what she meant. I imagined a drowned creature had crawled up the stairs to hide under my bed, necessitating a flying leap into bed from the bedroom door. Years later, reading of bog burials, I wondered about archetypes and collective memory, or perhaps my mother had told stories that I no longer remember. About ten years ago, while researching for an article on Beowulf, I remembered the boggart and did a little reading... Beowulf and his mother were said to live among wolves and there are stories of boggarts as black dogs (e.g. the Kinder Boggart in Derbyshire). I came across a reference to one Yorkshire name for a creature like a boggart – Grindylow – which sounds awfully like Grendel, the monster in Beowulf, but can't remember where I found that – sorry! I found *Beowulf and Grendel: The Truth Behind England's Oldest Legend*, by John Grigsby (2005) useful in reading about Grendel and boggarts. There's also the legendary Black Annis or Anna, who lived in a cave in Leicestershire, with some similarities to Grendel's mother and could well be described as a kind of boggart, as she was said to pounce upon unsuspecting children. There do seem to be connections between ideas from the Boggart Lands (love the name!) and Scandinavia. I have a daughter and granddaughter both of whom now live in Stockport, but I don't believe I ever mentioned boggarts to either of them.'

Rufford 1 (La). ???/F/FG., 3-10-19. 'My neighbour in Rufford used to refer to the house up the road as the Boggart House. He died in the 1990s.' Another user added: 'this was Field House. My dad was born there.'

Rufford 2 (La). 1950s/F/FG., 3-10-19. 'I was born in Rufford in 1956 and lived there until 1974 – I now live in Rufford again. I remember being told "the boggarts will get you" if I was being naughty!'

Rufford 3 (La). 1930s/F/FG., 3-10-19. 'I was born in 1935 and my dad was born and grew up at The Hermitage, Flash Lane, Rufford. There was a small room above the front door there which was known as the boggart room all his life and when we visited the current owners twenty years ago they confirmed several spooky happenings which they had experienced themselves. They were sensible, elderly people not inclined to make anything up!'

Rufford 4 (La). 1940s/F/FG., 11-10-19. 'I'm XXX's older sister and remember the word in the 1940s and 1950s. I always thought that because of Martin Mere the surrounding area was like a bog and that's where the word came from.'

Rufford 5 (La). 1930s/F/FG., 11-10-19. 'I grew up with boggarts late 1930s onwards round Mere Brow and Holmeswood. They skulked around in the dark and lived in old buildings and along wooded lanes. And we were also wary of slimy Jinny Greenteeth in pits and ditches.'

Rufford 6 (La). 1970s/M/FG., 11-10-19. 'I was camping in the New Forest circa 1970 and at dusk we went on an organised hunt for the Boggart in the woods. We occasionally saw a shadowy figure in the distance. Great fun.'

Sabden 1 (La). 1950s/M/FG., 7-10-19. 'I remember hearing of a Boggart at Sabden fold and a Boggart of the clough on Pendle in the 1950s, early 1960s. Both referred to mischievous spirits in the area. Out of interest, Harrison Ainsworth uses the term Boggart in his book *The Lancashire Witches* in the 19th century.'

Salesbury 1 (La). 1940s/M/FG., 13-10-19. 'I grew up in the mid-1940s to mid-1950s and I was warned when walking homegrown [*sic*] Bolton Hall up lovely hall to my home in Wiltshire after dark to be aware of the boggarts in the Ditch. So I sang all the way up, lol.'

Salesbury 2 (La). 1970s/F/FG., 13-10-19. 'Growing up in Salesbury in the 1970s and 1980s, boggarts were bad/evil spirits that lived at the bottom of the garden. I don't know where or when I learnt the word.'

Salford 1 (La). 1950s/F/E., 2-9-19. 'What does the word "boggart" mean to you? An outside spirit, large, hairy, earthy smelling and a vague humanoid shape – something to be afraid of. Similar to the bogeyman under a bed but not found in bedrooms, and not tied to bridges like trolls. Found outside in the dark. Sometimes it just liked to scare children away but not harm them specifically. Did your parents and grandparents use the word? Do your children or nephews and nieces? Much older siblings used it to scare me. I didn't see much of grandparents and don't remember them using it. I'm thinking I read about boggarts too. I never used it with my own children. Do you know any stories about boggarts or places especially associated with boggarts? Not sure, I read a lot of fantasy stories as a child but do not remember any particular reference. Where did you grow up and in what decade? I was born in part of what is now Salford in 1950, and grew up between there, Venezuela and Barbados, then we moved to the south of England from age seven. My mother lived in Lancashire until her mid-1930s [*sic*].'

Salford 2 (La). 1930s/F/E., 11-9-19. 'To me, a boggart is a goblin/sprite which is an awful nuisance, but not vicious. It makes the cows kick over the milk cans, or stops the butter coming, but doesn't hurt human or animal. As far as I know, a boggart is male. My mother (my father was from London and my grandparents dead before I was born) did not refer to boggarts. She didn't approve of "silly nonsense". She did, though, jokingly refer to Jinny Greenteeth. My children do refer to boggarts. They like to keep regional expressions alive.

I know only the well-recorded tale of the boggart of Boggart Hole Clough. I was born in 1934 in Salford, but heard of boggarts only when I started work, in Blackley.'

Salford 3 (La). 1950s/F/FG., 28-9-19. 'I became aware of the word, growing up in Salford, when I was sent for regular treatments at Booth Hall children's hospital, which was at a place called Boggart Hole Clough. As a child of ten or so I looked up the toponymy and came across the haunted farmhouse story. So I understood a boggart to be some kind of poltergeist. Coming to live in Blackburn in 1979, I found the word not used or understood much despite other archaic words used daily, such as "a-gait" (going on about). Born late 1950s, attended Booth Hall 1966 onwards. I was always a history nerd, word collector and fascinated with the occult. Our house held many old books that I browsed freely. So words like boggart, yutick, and such just may have come my way in any case. My mother used to mention Jenny Greenteeth and Spring-heeled Jack, but never seriously. I think they were current stories when her mother was a child, in the late 19th century. Eerily accurate. Her mother came from Woolston, and was very superstitious crossed with fanatical Catholicism. Covered all mirrors and hid shiny objects during thunderstorms and sat under the stairs singing hymns. Saw signs of death, gentleman visitors, unlucky colour combos, etc. After green comes black. Eeh, she was a cheerful soul.'

Salford 4 (La). ???/F/FG., 17-9-19. 'I grew up on the Salford/Prestwich border and there was a place locally called Boggart Hole Clough where the "bogeyman" was supposed to live.'

Salford 5 (La). 1940s/F/E., 22-11-19. 'Spirit or elf full of mischief or malevolence. Parents and grandma used "bogeyman" to be scary particularly at night. I vaguely remember a story about a cobbler who used a boggart to work through the night and who evidently came to a sticky end. I've visited Boggart Hole Clough.'

Scarisbrick 1 (La). 1960s/M/FG., 15-9-19. 'Brought up in Scarisbrick and heard it [boggart] regularly from my Grandparents. Plenty. They were used as a threat to make you behave as 'The Boggart will get you' also there were places where the Boggart lived. Old Lancashire language isn't it, neither on my father's side were very travelled my father was the first to go anywhere distant [date from Facebook page].'

Scarisbrick 2 (La). 1970s/F/E., 28-10-19. 'My friend shared a social media post that you're interested in boggart stories from Lancashire. I'm from Scarisbrick, and boggart stories were a big part of growing up in the 1970s, passed on from parents and grandparents. Just checking you are indeed "the boggart man" before I send tales to someone completely random! [Later email.] OK, so I grew up in Scarisbrick, born 1970. My granddad and my nan were both born there in the early 1900s; the family goes back generations in Scarisbrick, Halsall, Rufford. In the 1970s we lived in Hurlston Green in a row of cottages that family had lived in since the mid-1800s. My grandparents had moved to live on Wyke Cop near the moss. My Nan's mother and grand-mother had both worked as out servants at the half timbered Hurlston Hall, long since demolished. My nan told me that there was a well there where you could leave the buckets out overnight and the boggart would fill them up. But you mustn't wait up to try and see him or he'd throw the buckets down the well. There was also apparently a bloodstain on the steps which would always return after being scrubbed away. There's a line of wells through Scarisbrick, and another was in the back yard, long since capped over. My nan told me this was how the boggart got around the village. In my Great Auntie Alice's cottage next door the stairs were said to be panelled with panels from Hurlston Hall, and she wouldn't change them or "the boggart wouldn't like it". Not surprising, they were very nice wood panels! Down the footpath at the side of the cottages was Sandy Brook which runs through Ormskirk and on to the moss. There was a plank bridge over it which my nan said to be careful of when crossing, and thank the boggart. Children around Hurlston Green were always told tales about what the boggart might do if there was anything dangerous they had to be careful around, or to keep them in their beds at night. The spookiest story though was about how the boggart didn't like being trapped, and would tell you if there was a death. We had a door in our house we didn't close if we were eating a meal as it would shake, and I saw it happen a couple of times until my mum got a doorstop! She wasn't from the village and hadn't grown up with the tale! The story about the boggart informing you of a death haunts me even today. When my granddad passed away, there was a loud knocking on the front window, nobody was in sight. Ten minutes later we were called by our dad to say he had passed away. He told us next day that the old story went that the boggart always did this when someone died away from home. Hope those stories are useful to you! We don't live in Scarisbrick now, but I've told my son the stories, and he loves them!

Shaw 1 (La). ???/F/FG., 15-9-19. 'I live in Shaw. As a teenager my friend and I used to attend Royton Youth Club. One weekend trip was a midnight outing "Boggart Hunting". We and a coach full of youth club pals went on Saddleworth Moors to hunt. Needless to say we found nothing but had a great laugh trying.'

Shaw 2 (La). 1960s/M/FG., 12-10-19. 'My Mum would warn me that "Billy Boggart" would get you if you stayed out too late as a kid in the 1960s! Now

I tell our grandchildren the same threat! Born and bred in Shaw then moved to Newhey in 1970.'

Silverdale 1 (La). 1950s/F/F., 13-9-19. 'My Nana came from Silverdale and boggarts were plentiful in Lancashire and if you didn't behave they would come for you. Well, she used to say that the boggarts lived in holes in the ground and caves and although I can't remember her describing them, I thought they were like goblins but that could be my imagination. This would be in the 1950s and 1960s.'

Silverdale 2 (La). 1960s/F/FG., 17-10-19. 'I heard of both bogeymen and boggarts but thought of them as quite different beings. Bogeymen came to get you if you misbehaved but boggarts would get you if you strayed into their territory.'

Skelmersdale 1 (La): 1950s/F/F., 2-9-19. 'Not [note?] where I live there was a place near the local coal mine called "The Boggart House" supposed to be haunted. I was born in 1950 then our little town was mostly rural. It was chiefly a mining area in the 1800s. The last mine still working in the 1950s. I think "boggart" was thought of a ghostly sort of thing. As our town expanded in the early 1960s taking in the over spill population from the Liverpool area new housing was built. There are a couple of websites which keep good records of the history of our area "Memories of Skelm" and "Skelmersdale Heritage Society" photographs and stories keep popping up all the time. It is really good to see the old town scenes I remember from my childhood. The Boggart house has been mentioned a couple of times on "Memories of Skelm". I cannot remember the exact location of where it was myself though. I think I've heard it [i.e. boggart] mentioned by parents and other members of my family. The men were mostly coal miners… My Dad worked on the coal face for a lot of his life and worked at Sutton Manor colliery during the Second World War. My Maternal Granddad/Great Uncle both fought in the Great War 1914–1918. I never heard them speak of the war at all. But I think they understood that word "boggart" to be a ghost or spirit of some kind. Sorry cannot be of more help. I myself have not heard the word mentioned in a long time only on the website "Memories of Skelm" and only in reference to the "Boggart house".'

Skelmersdale 2 (La): 1950s/F/FG., 15-9-19. 'My Granddad called scarecrows "crow boggarts". "Boggart" refers to a ghost too. The "boggart house" is a haunted house.'

Skelmersdale 3 (La): 1950s/F/FG., 20-9-19. 'Hi. I was brought up in Skem all my life. I was born in 1965 and my Grandparents referred to "Boggarts" frequently. It would be around the time the Skem Dev Co were building the housing estates on farm-land between the old town and Ashurst beacon. The area was always described to me as Boggart land and it was not recommended to venture there after dark. As a young child, I questioned this, as I hadn't a clue what a boggart actually was. I was reliably informed that a boggart was a ghost or spirit, and not a friendly one!'

Skelmersdale 4 (La): 1980s/F/FG., 15-9-19. 'I grew up in Skem in the 1980s. My Granny and Uncles told us about boggarts – mischievous creatures who hid things etc. I think they were suppose to "haunt" houses.'

Skelmersdale 5 (La): 1950s/F/FG., 15-9-19. 'My mother used to say if you don't behave yourself yon boggart will take you away. That was the later 1950s. My granddad would say the same if we youngsters were going into the outbuildings. It was a way of keeping us from going messing with his things. If our floorboards were creaking at night I thought the boggart had got in. This would be in 1960s. Granddad was born in 1898.'

Skelmersdale 6 (La). 1950s/M/FG., 15-9-19. 'Growing up in Skem when I was a kid if my mum or dad called me a "boggart" it meant I was a scruffy sod after being on the moss all day. They were right. Born 1953.'

Skelmersdale 7 (La). 1960s/M/FG., 9-10-19. 'When I lived in owd Skem, there was an old derelict house next to St Pauls church which all the kids christened the boggart house, there's no way you would walk past it on your own. Spooky.'

Skipool 1 (La). ???/M/F., 29-8-19. 'Wow that's really interesting because my great grandparents were from Skipool. She said that when she was courting, they were chased by a boggert. Which was some sort of cross between a human and a fly I think!'

Smallbridge 1 (La). 1950s/M/E., 4-9-19. 'Me I am 68 born in Smallbridge. My father used to threaten us that the Bogey Man would come and get us as a way of frightening us. 1950s.'

Smallbridge 2 (La). 1950s/F/E., 26-9-19. 'I have just seen your post on the Wardle and Smallbridge History Group Facebook page. As I understood it when growing up (born 1953 in Smallbridge, not living in Nottingham), a boggart was simply a malevolent spirit. Living only a few miles from the wonderfully named Boggart Hole Clough, few people locally can have failed to hear the word! You might like to have a look at this article about Clegg Hall, written by Brian Clegg (not from the Hall!). Born 1955 in Smith Bridge.'

Smallbridge 3 (La). 1940s/F/FG., 4-9-19. 'I can't remember this being [Clegg Hall Boggart] referred to when I was growing up in Smallbridge (born 1945). For us it was the Bogey Man! A dark and mysterious thing with no definite description. To us it was a ghost in Clegg Hall.'

Smallbridge 4 (La). 1940s/F/FG., 26-9-19. 'Smallbridge nineteen forties and fifties. We heard of the Clegg Hall Bogart, but as XXX said it was always the mysterious Bogey Man that scared us. Also I heard the phrase "ran at Bogart" meaning ran away fast.'
Smallbridge 5 (La). 1950s/F/FG., 18-10-19. 'My Dad used to tell us about the Clegg Hall Bogart at Halloween. Born Birch Hill 1950s. Lived Greengate then Smithy bridge until the 1990s.'
Smithy Bridge 1 (La). ???/F/FG., 15-9-19. 'Born and bred in Smithy Bridge and definitely grew up knowing about the Clegg Hall Boggart was always scared of going up the bonk when it was dark.'
Smithy Bridge 2 (La). 1940s/F/FG., 17-10-19. 'I'm sure like other myths it was a scare technique to keep people safe from real predators. We had the Clegg Hall Bogart no idea why, and Nanny Green Teeth who waited in the canal weeds to pull children into the water if they got too close to the edge. From 1945 in Smithy Bridge.'
Smithy Bridge 3 (La). 1950s/F/FG., 17-10-19. 'I lived in Smithy Bridge for three years 1956 to 1959 there was talk of a boggart at Clegg Hall. Occasionally heard weird sounds in the evening when walking along the canal across from the Hall. My house in Littleborough was haunted. Apparently a man was found dead at the bottom of the cellar steps and people said his son pushed him down. On several occasions while in the back room of the house I could smell pipe tobacco and a man would be standing at the window. When I went to the door there was nobody there. The man that died smoked a pipe. I am a believer in Spirits. Yes. [to an inquirer] When we were over in the UK in 1968 XXX met you and your sister on the rec and she told you she used to live in your house and it was haunted. XXX will be sixty this year so not sure if it was you or your sister, that she spoke to. We were back in the borough from May 1968 to September 1968 intending to stay, but my son had very bad eczema while we were there and in Canada he didn't have it, so we came home in time for the school year September.'
Southport 1 (La). 1940s/M/FG., 20-9-19. 'I remember the term "boggarts" from 1950s. Used to describe unfortunate events. Southport 1943–1970. Lately I think the word "gremlins" replaced it.'
Southport 2 (La). 1950s/F/FG., 20-9-19. 'I was born in 1953 in Southport and never heard of that word [boggart].'
Southport 3 (La). 1960s/M/FG., 20-9-19. '1960s, never knew "boggarts"'.
Southport 4 (La). 1960s/F/FG., 21-9-19. 'If I remember rightly boggarts were mischief makers in the Brownies. Perhaps rephrase that to Brownie lore, they weren't members of the pack. Yes, here in Southport early 1960s.

We used to dance round a circular rug with and owl on a mushroom in the middle and sing about how good it was to be a brownie. If you stood on the rug the boggart would get you (and this in a Methodist establishment too!).'

Southport 5 (La). 1950s/F/FG., 21-9-19. 'I was born in 1953 in Southport and never heard of that word.'

Southport 6 (La). 1950s/F/FG., 21-9-19. 'Remember [boggart] being mentioned as I grew up in Southport. 1943 to present day'.

Southport 7 (La). 1960s/M/FG., 21-9-19. 'At primary school in Southport in the late sixties I remember being taught a song with the lines: "Dwarves live underground, Dryads in Trees, There are Trolls and Goblins and Imps and Ogres, Bogey-men, Kelpies, but rarer than these, And very much nicer is such a rogue, As the Railway Boggart, he doesn't clank chains, But has lots of fun in railway trains." I'm pretty sure I didn't dream this... If I remember right, it was part of a songbook.'

Southport 8 (La). 1960s/F/FG., 21-9-19. 'My friend and I used to use the reference section at the town centre library in the late 1960s. There was a book in the architecture section which had photos of old Lancashire houses which had been destroyed either by neglect or fire. One such house was reported to have been haunted by Noman the Boggart. We read it as Norman and thought it was hilarious. We had to look up the word "Boggart". Neither of us had heard of the word. When the library was revamped I was told that those books had been moved to Bootle... Don't know why.'

Southport 9 (La). 1950s/M/FG., E., 21-9-19. 'I was always told that a Boggart was somebody who couldn't stay still.' [in later email]. 'As I have stated on Facebook the term BOGGATS was used to describe anybody or animal etc who could not keep still. My wife always used the word and is seventy-six years old. It was used by her mother who is aged one hundred and one and is a native of Oldham. I hope this info is of use to you.'

Southport 10 (La). 1950s/F/FG., 21-9-19. 'Southport 1940s. No mention of boggarts.'

Southport 11 (La). 1940s/F/FG., 21-9-19. 'Born 1946 and grew up in Southport. Never heard the word "Boggard" until today.'

Southport 12 (La). 1950s/F/FG., 21-9-19. 'Born in Southport in the era you mention but can't say I ever came across the word "boggard".'

Southport 13 (La). 1950s/F/E., 26-9-19. 'I got your email address from XXX (we both dance with XXX). I'm a storyteller, mainly working in Lancashire, and a member of the SFS so have posted XXX's post on their FB page too – hopefully this will get you some more responses. For my own part, my earliest memory of hearing the word "boggart" was as a small child (late 1950s or early 1960s) from both my grandma and a great aunt, who would raise their eyebrows if I misbehaved/spoke out of turn/etc. and say, "You're no better than Newhall Boggart." However there was never any explanation of who or what this was. Both ladies were born and bred in the Crossens/Southport area, in the 1890s. Another great aunt (originally from Preston I think), used to tell me a boggart story about one who was originally helpful on a farm, but turned bad and was eventually caught and buried under a big stone. Hundreds of years later, a farmer decided to use the same stone in a barn building, but his family were plagued with bad luck ever after and had to leave the farm. The details would change a bit every time she told me the story. My only other childhood memory of boggarts was a playground (long rope) skipping rhyme, "The stars are shining, the moon's so bright, the boggart can't come out tonight." Chanted with a strong rhythm, emphasis on shi, bright, can't and night. Whoever was skipping in the rope had to jump out and the next skipper jump in exactly on the beat of "night" – if either failed they were "out" and had to turn the rope instead of skipping. Hope these are of interest. Nowadays I often introduce traditional storytelling to school groups by talking about J.K. Rowling's Dobbie, and the similarities between his story (freed by the gift of a sock) and some of the Lancashire boggart tales (where the helpful boggart disappears after receiving a gift or thanks), with the idea of showing children how traditional tales are full of good ideas to borrow and reuse in their own stories. I grew up in Churchtown (Southport) and went to Churchtown infant and junior schools.'

Southport 14 (La). 1950s/M/FG., 29-9-19. 'My Grandma used to say "The Bogey Man" don't know if it was short for Boggart. Yes 1950s, 1960s. No born in Southport but moved to Ormskirk in the 1950s. She was also of Irish descent.'

Southport 15 (La). 1960s/M/FG., 4-10-19. 'I just read your piece on the Burscough Community Forum. I was born in 1967 and grew up in Marshside (north end of Southport) and grew up familiar with the word in the 1970s and understanding it was some kind of mythical marsh creature. Three of four grandparents born in the area and family traced back to area since 1670s. Where I grew up is next to Ribble Estuary saltmarsh – just inland (nearer to where I now live) is the drained lake – Martin Mere. As a young kid I'd go off onto the marsh birdwatching (I'm still a keen birder) on my own and my Dad and my Uncle XXX would often say "mind them boggarts". At age sixteen (1983) I started work at WWT Martin Mere and I do remember boggarts being referred to in a home context. I've attached pics from a book I just checked and pic of title. I've heard a mate of mine from up the road in Tarleton who is the same age as me mention boggarts – I'll ask him. Cheers. Have a look at the Lancashire dialect Facebook page and perhaps the Lancashire Wildlife Trust.'

Southport 16 (La). 1950s/M/FG., 14-10-19. 'I come from Marshside in Southport and was born in 1950. I heard tales of a boggart of Martin Mere all my early life. A big black dog with red eyes. Can't remember why or what it did tho!'

Southport 17 (La). 1970s/F/FG., 14-10-19. 'I grew up in Southport and heard of boggarts as a kid (1970s). Isn't there a Boggart Hole Clough over Bury way?'

Southport 18 (La). 1950s/M/FG., 17-10-19. 'Grew up in Southport early 1950s to 1970s. Yes, I heard about Boggarts and spent a night in a number of haunted houses in South West Lancs when I was a student. A group of us did this for fun and we all knew about Boggarts. One place we visited was known locally as "Boggarts Hall".'

Southport 19 (La). 1940s/F/FG., 17-10-19. 'Born 1945 my Nan used to say "Boggarts" if anything was out of place? However, she never elaborated as to who or what they were? Nan was born in Liverpool in 1889 but placed in an orphanage with her sister in Formby. It is described as an Industrial school on the census. I traced the family on Genes Reunited! Industrial schools were set up to train orphans in domestic service! My Nan was sent to be in service within a titled household! So I'm presuming as earlier relations were of Irish descendants. It's a name for troublesome gremlins? Like we say nowadays if something has been moved mysteriously?'

Southport 20 (La). 1950s/M/FG., 17-10-19. 'I was born in Marshside in 1954. Never heard of Boggarts until much later in life but never in connection with Southport.'

Southport 21 (La). 1950s/F/FG., 17-10-19. 'I was born 1956 in Southport raised in Crossens. Never heard that word [boggart].'

St. Helens 1 (La). 1940s/F/FG., 28-9-19. 'My grandparents lived in The Sutton area of St Helens and they talked of Boggarts on t'moss I was led to believe that they were witches. I grew up in the 1940s. When it was stormy and windy we were told by my grandfather that the boggarts were out on the moss. I don't know why but I always thought of them as being Irish. But memories can be confused when you are thinking of almost eighty years ago.'

St. Helens 2 (La). 1920s/F/FG., 1-10-19. 'My mother is ninety-eight and sharp as a pin. She grew up in St Helens. I think the Ginny Greenteeth came from her. She certainly uses it as a name. My Mother never heard of boggarts growing up in St. Helens in the 1920s.' [Duplicates Rainhill 6]

Stacksteads 1 (La). 1960s/M/E., 15-2-21: 'I was brought up in Stacksteads near Bacup. The boggart was used to scare us to stop us from wandering up onto the moors to play. And don't go near the old pits because the Boggarts will drag you in and you will never be seen again. That was for me, late 1960s'.
Stalmine 1 (La). 1930s/F/FG., 20-9-19. 'Carr Lane Boggart in Stalmine, also Jinny Green Teeth. 1937 to this day.'
Standish 1 (La). ???/M/FG., 17-10-19. 'I've lived in Standish all my life and my grandparents still use the word "boggarts" to describe the dog when he's having a mad session of running around! For example, "ey up dogs taken boggarts!"'
Storth 1 (La). 1950s/F/FG., 17-10-19. 'I grew up in Storth in the 1950s and lived there until 1982. I never heard the word "Boggart", in all that time.'
Storth 2 (La). 1950s/F/FG., 18-10-19. 'Lived in Storth at XX Shaw Green and as I was growing up playing out till it got dark our mum and dad used to get us into the house saying the bogeyman would be out soon and would get us... Don't know if this is same. [Age guessed from FB.]'
Storth 3 (La). ???/F/FG., 18-10-19. 'Bogey men was used in our house as children. My ancestors belonged to Storth. Whether or not that was derived from boggart. My husband's mate was known as "Boggart"!'
Stretford 1 (La).1950s/M/F., 11-9-19. 'As a kid, we used to call an old lady neighbour, 'The old boggart'. [Boggart] was an expression which my Mother and her friends used from time to time. Stretford, Manchester in the 1950/1960s.'
Tarleton 1 (La). 1980s/F/FG., 29-9-19. 'My grandparents in Tarleton definitely used the word "boggart" in the 1980s when I was a child – e.g. If the door blew open slightly when no one was there – they would blame the boggart. Send a join request for the Banks and surrounding areas history group as I bet lots of the older members on there have heard this word.'
Thornham 1 (La). 1950s/M/FG., 17-10-19. '"off at boggart" still used in our house for anything that sets off unexpectedly quickly. No, born in Balderstone and lived Thornham mid-1950s to mid-1960s then Bamford. Got expression from my Dad who was a Rochdalian.'
Thornton-Cleveley 1 (La). 1930s/M/FG., 12-10-19. 'My dad, who is in his eighties, has often talked about boggarts. He said there was a Bourne Hall Boggart, a headless horseman that rode on particular nights. Bourne Hall was an old building on top of a hill in Thornton, that was around in the 1300s, and had priest hide holes from the time of Henry VIII. We lived just down the road from the Hall. Suggest you ask what people know about this in the Thornton-Cleveleys Past site.'

Thornton-Cleveley 2 (La). 1970s/F/FG., 17-10-19. 'My mum remembers Boggart Hall Clough in Manchester which was known in the 1970s as a lonely wild bit of land. I also had a friend who told me of boggarts living on Underbank Road in Thornton, though he was possibly just being mischievous. He's now sadly died and I'm very sorry that I can't talk to him anymore about these things.'

Thornton-Cleveley 3 (La). 1950s/F/FG., 17-10-19. 'I grew up in Thornton in the 1950s and 1960s. I heard the word "boggart" from my uncles mother and as I was led to believe it was a headless horseman! [Another FB user writes: "The Bourne Hall boggart?"; another user: "I have heard about The Bourne Hall boggart also".]'

Thornton-Cleveley 4 (La). ???/M/FG., 17-10-19. 'In Thornton library when I was a kid there was a terrific selection of local history books. One that sticks in my mind brought together a lot of the mythology of North Fylde, for example the story of when Preesall Moss suddenly rose twenty feet and shifted whilst farmhands watched. One story that sticks in my mind was the Hambleton Boggart, which was a large, cat-like creature which lived in the hedgerows of the lanes over Wyre. It would occasionally jump out and grab a lone passer-by, dragging them into the hedge where they would fight it and the thorns to escape, returning home scratched and dishevelled. This almost always happened to people who were coming home from the public house after a long session...'

Thornton-Cleveley 5 (La). 1960s/F/FG., 20-10-19. 'I was born and bred in Thornton and I'd never heard of bogart until diving a cave around Ingleton called Hurtle Pot where supposedly a bogart lived! Born in May 1960.'

Thornton-Cleveley 6 (La). 1970s/M/FG., 20-10-19. 'I was brought up in Burn Naze in the 1970s. Boggarts always seemed to dwell in places we were told to keep away from! As a kid I always imagined it like some horned devil like creature but that could [be] down to a Catholic upbringing.'

Thornton-Cleveley 7 (La). ???/F/FG., 7-11-19. 'I was born in Thornton. Mum used to tell us if we went near the Brooks, Granny Green Teeth would come out of the water and grab us. I used to tell my kids and grandkids, too. Scared us and my family to bits.'

Thornton-Cleveley 8 (La). 1950s/F/FG., 7-11-19. 'Yes, I was born and brought up in Thornton from 1951. I know of the saying "mind the Boggarts don't get you" too. We were told the saying "mind the Boggarts don't get you".'

Thornton-Cleveley 9 (La). ???/M/FG., 7-11-19. 'My father-in-law once told my kids about Boggarts living in the banks of the river Wyre. I will ask my kids if they remember the story and if they do I will post it.'

Thornton-Cleveley 10 (La). 1940s/M/FG., 7-11-19. 'My uncle used to live down Underbank in the 1940s and 1950s and when it was dark he used to cycle down the middle of Raikes Rd and Underbank whistling to himself to prevent the bogarts getting him!'

Tonge Moor 1 (La). 1970s/M/FG., 14-10-19. 'Do you know we have a cross on the outskirts of the village [Accrington], known colloquially as the "Headless Boggart"? There's a strange headless figure carved on it, this is the boggart. There's two legends associated with it. One is during the reformation a priest hid in a tunnel there to escape the Roundheads, but he never came out again, and his ghost is meant to haunt the place. The other is that when they dug land up to make a reservoir they found this strange headless creature and that is what is depicted on the cross. Well, I'm not originally from Blackrod, actually, I grew up the other side of Bolton (Tonge Moor) and I remember the kids going on about Boggarts on what colloquially was known as the Jolly Brows. I've lived in Blackrod for twenty years now. I like wandering around taking pictures of local stuff so I've got to know any interesting points of interest such as the headless cross. 1970s, 1980s lived just above Firwood Fold if you know it. A really old place. Spent a lot of time there as my parents ran the stables. I can tell you quite a few actually. Sure it's at the top of Grimeford Lane (but you have to cross the main road and keep its just on the triangluar junction. [Subsequent message.] Hi there. What would you like to know about Tonge Moor? I've got a few ghost stories about Firwood Fold. My friends and I used to go and walk on the Jolly Brows at night and I remember one guy talking about Boggarts. He was quite scared of them. If you mentioned it he thought it would likely summon one so he'd get anxious and tell you to stop it! Can't give you much more about boggarts apart from the rumours that they used to around on the Jolly Brows and you shouldn't talk about them or they might appear. I never saw one though! As for Firwood Fold, Our house backed on to Firwood Lane. It's a very old lane been a thoroughfare since Saxon times. Anyway my brother and sister's bedroom backed on to it and they always claimed that they could hear horses' hooves going down it in the middle of the night. You could have had a horse going down at about midnight but it would be strange! There was also legend about an old lady who used to visit sick children on the estate (its was a new housing estate replacing demolished Firwood Hall). A few local children said a nice old lady had paid a visit to them but no adults saw her and no one had any idea who she was! My mum said she saw a ghost in the grounds of Firwood Stables and that was an old lady.'

Treales 1 (La). 1940s/M/FG., 4-10-19. 'Brought up in the 1940s and 1950s.

My Mum used to talk about the Boggart Pits behind Treales C. of E. school.'

Ulverston 1 (La). 1950s/F/FG., 28-9-19. 'I grew up in Ulverston in the 1950s and 1960s. I know the word, not heard it for a long time, but may have read it. I doubt the knowledge came from my parents who were not local to the area.'

Ulverston 2 (La). 1950s/F/FG., 28-9-19. 'I grew up in the 1950s in Ulverston and never heard of them at all.'

Ulverston 3 (La). 1960s/F/FG., 29-9-19. 'I lived and brought up in Ulverston through the 1960s/1970s but never heard of the word

Ulverston 4 (La). 1950s/F/FG., 29-9-19. 'I think I heard of them through Brownies but that would be the 1950s.'

Ulverston 5 (La). 1960s/F/FG., 29-9-19. 'I grew up in Ulverston 1960s/1970s. Never heard of them.'

Upholland 1 (La). 1960s/M/FG., 13-10-19. 'I'm not from the Calder Valley, from Up Holland near Wigan Lancashire. Grew up in the 1960s and as kids we were told boggarts were said to be spirits that rose up out of the ground often to the sound of jangling chains.'

Walton-Le-Dale 1 (La). 1950s/F/FG., 4-9-19. 'We had Hennel Boggart in Hennel Lane. Walton le Dale in 1947.'

Walton-Le-Dale 2 (La). 1960s/M/FG., 4-10-19. 'In 1969–70 there was a radio for schools musical production called "The Railway Boggart". Can't remember much about it, apart from part of the lyric Something every stationmaster know is, how to grow lobelias and roses". I guess it was a BBC production. Thinking a bit more about it, my Dad (born in Walton-le-Dale in the early 1920s) would sometimes use "boggart" in place of "bugger", as in "it's a bit of a boggart". That could be a bit like Americans saying "darn" instead of "damn".'

Walton 1 (La). 1940s/M/FG., 18-9-19. 'I was born in Walton in 1942. I had never heard of a boggart until I worked in Skelmersdale. People in Skelmersdale used to call the scarecrow a "crow boggart".'

Walton 2 (La). 1940s/M/FG., 18-9-19. 'Born Walton 1939 the boggart of Cherry Lane was spoken about at home in Wellbrow road. Maybe because our name is similar. Thanks nice to hear it again. [XXX replied to this "The tale of the Boggart of Cherry Lane/Walton Hall goes back to the twelfth Century when King Henry II bequeathed the land and estate to Gilbert de Walton. Richard, Gilbert's son was a friend of Prince John, King Henry's son. Henry in 1185 sent John and his friend Richard to Ireland to quell the unruly Irish. They returned eighteen months later bringing with them two Irish colleens which they had captured. On a hired horse he set off to his father's estate in Walton and tied the girl by her hands to the stirrups. This meant she had to run alongside the horse over rough ground. On reaching the bridle path to Walton, now Cherry Lane, she fell and the horse threw its rider. Richard was enraged and he struck and hacked the unconscious girl at the neck with his sword then threw her body with the head hanging on by a thread into the nearby stream. From henceforth began the legend of the Boggart, i.e. the young Irish girl who was murdered, which was said to have appeared many time on the estate of Walton Hall."]

Wardle 1 (La). 1960s/F/F., 29-8-19. 'We had Ginny Greenteeth too. She would pull you into the water if you got too close. There were also lots of boggarts around as well... Basically they were anywhere adults didn't want you to go. I didn't like my hair being brushed when I was young, and people used to say that there were imps that would come in the night and steal children with "lugs" in their hair, take them to the nearest stream and drown them. It was all folklore going back generations. I think that it was adult trying to keep their children safe. I grew up in the late 1950s and 1960s. We had the freedom to roam around the village and surrounding countryside (usually as a gang of friends) at will. The only way that our parents could keep us safe was to tell tales of boggarts, bogeymen and faerie folk. The stories came back through the generations and were obviously well known amongst the villagers as we were all told the same stories even though our families weren't related. It certainly worked for me... I kept well away from the water (and there were lots of millponds in the village, all full of fish) because of Ginny Greenteeth! It was in Wardle, a village just above Littleborough, on the edge of the moors. I lived there from 1956 when I was born until 1968/9 when we moved over the hill to West Yorkshire (Hebden Bridge). It's great that you're keeping records of the folklore. Boggarts to me were small, gnome like creatures that lived in farm buildings and in quarries, caves and under rocks. The house ones lived with the family (unseen) and could be good or bad. If the family moved the boggart moved with them. The imps were small, not quite human creatures (think a mini Gollum) that would grab you by the hair and drag you down to the nearest river or stream and drown you... but only if you had "lugs" (knots) in your hair. Ginny Greenteeth lived in ponds and lakes and if you got too close to the edge would snatch you and you'd never be seen again. These are from my childhood. But all my childhood friends from around the village knew the stories, too.'

Wardle 2 (La). 1950s/F/FG., 15-9-19. 'I was born in Wardle 1950, our dad was the postman for the village and farms around Wardle, a farm on his route was always called Boggart House, a Mrs Kay lived there alone. The farm from what I can remember is situated in a valley. Passed Biggins Lodge over Clough House through the meadows going towards the old road to the Fisheries.' See Wardle 6 (La).

Wardle 3 (La). 1950s/F/FG., 26-9-19. 'My dad used to tell me and my pal that derelict Clegg Hall in the fifties had a boggert within. It was a ghost. The place was haunted we were glad to get past the hall fast no hanging around there for sure.'

Wardle 4 (La). 1950s/F/FG., 26-9-19. 'My Mum used it in an interesting way. Once we were in a wooded area and a horse came crashing through. The rider, though still in the saddle, had clearly lost control. My Mum shouted to me "Oh it's took boggart!" Presumably she meant that something had spooked the horse.'

Wardle 5 (La). 1940s/F/FG., 17-10-19. 'Men and women who were a nuisance or a bit shifty were also referred to as "boggarts" 1940–1950 up to now, specially by the older people.'

Wardle 6 (La). 1970s/F/FG., 17-10-19. 'I only ever heard it mentioned as in Boggart House in Wardle during my upbringing. [someone added: Me too, XXX. I recall visiting the old lady who lived there with my dad XXX (postman). I thought she was a witch and was scared that she was trying to poison me when she gave me sweets. I dropped them on the road out. I also remember an outdoor loo with a double wooden seat.] [Age estimated from FB page.]' See Wardle 2 (La).

Warrington 1 (La). 1940s/F/FG., 16-9-19. 'I grew up in the late 1940s and all through the 1950s in central Warrington but never heard the term used. I heard mum say if you don't go to bed, the Bogie man will get you. But "Baggart" and "Ghost" were never mentioned.'

Warrington 2 (La).1940s/F/FG., 17-9-19. 'I was born 1942 Warrington, [no?] boggarts, but there was the bogey man, which I would think derived from Boggart?'

Warrington 3 (La). 1950s/F/FG., 16-9-19. 'I grew up in the 1950s and knew of the Bogie man, but never heard of a boggart.'

Warrington 4 (La). 1960s/F/FG., 17-9-19. 'Boogie man the man under the stairs and if the wind was howling it was "Billie Wind" come to get you. Born in Warrington in the 1960s. My nana who was born in Glasgow but raised in Warrington from the age of eight always talked about Billie Wind.'

Warrington 5 (La). 1950s/F/FG., 16-9-19. 'Yes, Bogie man in the 1950s and 1960s but not boggart.'

Warrington 6 (La). 1940s/F/FG., 16-9-19. 'I've not heard the word "Boggart" just "the Bogey Man" and I was born in 1940s.'

Warrington 7 (La). 1950s/F/FG., 16-9-19. 'I was a child of 1950s and 1960s obviously heard of bogey man but never heard of the boggart. Never heard of the glosher man either until someone wrote a story about him. was it Wally Barnes (story teller, not glosser man)?'
Warrington 8 (La). 1950s/F/FG., 16-9-19. 'I grew up in Warrington in the 1950s and 1960s but never heard the term boggart just bogey man.'
Warrington 9 (La). 1960s/F/FG., 16-9-19. 'Born and bred in Warrington 1958-present day and only heard it [boggart] in Harry Potter films.'
Warrington 10 (La). 1950s/F/FG., 16-9-19. 'I too was born in Warrington in 1950 and left in 1982 but never heard of boggart. Heard of the bogey man though, who frightened us as kids!'
Warrington 11 (La). 1950s/F/FG., 16-9-19. 'I grew up in Warrington 1951 till 1973 only heard bogey man. Not boggart.'
Warrington 12 (La). 1940s/M/FG., 16-9-19. 'I was born 1937 and still live in Warrington and the only time I heard the word "Boggart" was a race horse owned and trained by a Mr. Barns from Warrington called the Boggart. I think [it] ran fourth in the Derby.'
Warrington 13 (La). 1950s/F/FG., 16-9-19. 'I grew up in the 1950s. Never heard of a boggart, bogey man yes. My husband was brought up in Bewsey in the 1950s and he heard of it. My husband had heard of a boggart. Says it's a mythical creature. Don't go into the woods in the dark the boggart will get you. It was frightening enough saying the bogey man will get you I would be hiding under the bed covers if someone said the boggart is coming to get you.'
Warrington 14 (La). 1950s/M/FG., 16-9-19. 'I was born in 1963 and I remember my grandmother (b. 1912) using the word "boggart". She was originally from the Moore area but lived most of her life in Fearnhead.'
Warrington 15 (La). ???/F/FG., 16-9-19. 'The Galosher man was a story told in Warrington from around the 1930s 1940s? Apparently he wore Galoshers (or Pumps as they are known in other regions), so that he could creep up silently behind his victims (usually female). There was also the Patent Leather Man during wartime, who had a fetish for ladies in patent leather shoes. I've also heard of Boggarts, but they were more known as Goblins who were mischievously wicked. If anything went missing around our house, or anything unexplained happened, my Mum would say "There's been Boggarts in here". My husband from Bewsey remembers being told of Boggarts down the "Gulley" between Bewsey Bridge along the railway lines from Bewsey to Whitecross. Maybe you should look up Wally Barnes' book?'
Warrington 16 (La). 1960s/F/FG., 19-9-19. 'We used to call each other crow boggarts and just looked it up and it's a scarecrow to scare the crows

as much as the boggarts scare humans. We said it growing up so late 1960s and the 1970s in Warrington.'

Warrington 17 (La). 1980s/F/FG., 10-10-19. 'I'm not sure if this is what you are after. I live in Gee Cross now, but I grew up in Warrington. My parents had some Story Teller cassettes and on long road trips, would play them to us in the car. One of them was called "The Great Big, Hairy Boggart". Myself and my sisters found the word "Boggart", very funny. We had never heard the word before. I'm a 1985 child so it's not the era you're after. I vaguely remember the Boggart being ugly, mean and selfish. The story was he wanted the farmer's land so the farmer outwitted him and eventually he left them alone. We loved the story it was our favourite and the only one I remember listening to. Ha!'

Warrington 18 (La). 1950s/F/E., 12-1-20: 'I was born in Warrington in 1953. The creature we were told to beware of was the bogey man. I only learned the word boggart as an adult when researching dialectology and folklore. Jinny Green teeth was the name given to the slimy weeds on the pond in the local park. No associated malevolent creature, just the weeds, but you were still warned to beware of them. There was often thick fog in winter (before the Clean Air Act) and we were warned that a "black man" would get us in the smog. Unfortunately, this led to white children being afraid of the very few people of colour around at the time. Since the boggart/bogey man is portrayed as black, I guess it wasn't deliberately racist in origin.'

For Warrington see also Shropshire 1 (Oth)

Waterfoot 1 (La). 1970s/F/F., 20-9-19. 'I grew up in Waterfoot in Rossendale in the 1970s. My Dad used to walk quite fast and was always ahead of us. Mum used to say that Dad was "Off at Boggart", which meant he was walking so fast because a boggart was after him. Boggart being a ghost.

Waterfoot 2 (La). 1960s/F/FG., 5-10-19. 'As I've read other people have written, we set off at "Boggart", speeding off. Also, our parents told us about a big scary black dog, with red eyes, roaming the hills at dusk and night time. This was something we were really terrified of seeing. This would be in the late 1960s and early 1970s, Waterfoot. [Was the dog a boggart?] Yep, it was, a very big scary beast.'

Waterfoot 3 (La). 1950s/F/FG., 9-10-19. 'I was born in 1952 in Waterfoot. I remember adults saying the Boogeyman would get you if you misbehave but I have never heard of the word "Boggart".'

Waterfoot 4 (La). 1950s/F/FG., 17-10-19. 'I was born in 1955 and brought up in Waterfoot. I'd never heard of the word "Boggart" until I drove past Boggart Hole Clough in Manchester.'

Waterloo 1 (La). 1950s/F/FG., 28-9-19. 'Born 1950 and grew up in Waterloo, never heard that word until now! Bogey men yes!'
Weeton 1 (La). 1960s/F/FG., 28-9-19. 'My Grandma and Great Aunt used to mention the "Staining Boggart". I remember reading about the "Weeton Boggart" too! 1960s and 1970s brought up near Weeton.'
Whalley 1 (La). 1950s/M/FG., 7-11-19. 'I was born in Whalley in the 1950s, but brought up in Accrington. My Grandfather would often talk about t' boggart.'
Wheelton 1 (La). 1950s/F/F., 29-8-19. 'My Gran used to warn me not to play by the canal or Ginny Green Teeth would get me! I think she was a Boggart. This was Wheelton – a village between Chorley and Blackburn in the 1950s. Although my Gran came from Fleetwood I also heard other children warn about it who lived near me. I was so terrified I used to walk on the opposite side of the road! Yes, I always thought the green weed was her hair! Whenever I asked where my Mum was my Dad would say "Run off with a bogeyman"!'
Westhoughton 1 (La). 1960s/F/FG., 15-10-19. 'My friend's Mum used to say "If you go any further than you are allowed, boggarts will have you!" Westhoughton Lancs. 1960–1970s. Forgotten about that word till I read your post.'
Whitefield 1 (La). 1950s/F/F., 29-8-19. 'I was born in Whitefield and a Sunday walk was through the clough a beautiful walk grass and trees. Was always called Bogart Hole Clough. Was told to behave or the Bogart may appear. I was five in 1953 and clearly remember the walks and hoping I would not see a Bogart. Never did hear a disruption [?] of one. Was enough to hear the name was always said quietly. Had a life full of fairy stories telling and writing them. But never about Bogart, would not dare to! My parents told us about them. I do not live in Whitefield now, but the area still has the name.'
Whitefield 2 (La). 1950s/F/ F., 31-8-19. 'Boggart Hole Clough, Whitefield and Prestwich, near Manchester. Used to walk down from Whitefield to the church where my dad worked. In Prestwich, I think the church was St. Marys. Disadvantaged [frightened?] on those walks. Lol. Just knew you had to behave. In the clough when walking because of the boggarts. I think it was passed down from my older sisters. We then went on to live in a graveyard because of my dad's job at the church. No wonder I have a good imagination. I could not say that the stories I have in my head are because of boggarts. Or because of where I lived. Early to mid-1950s.'
Whitefield 3 (La). 1950s/M/FG., 17-10-19. 'If [I were] fidgeting grandmother would say "Sit still! You're like a bouncing boggart".'

Whittingham 1 (La). ???/F/FG., 27-9-19. '[Niece asked: 'didn't great nana tell you and auntie Amanda a bogart story when you were kids?' The reply:] It was Grandma and she said there was a boggart at Chingle Hall. All she ever told me was that Chingle Hall had a boggart. My grandparents were born at the time of WW1 and they used a lot of Lancashire dialect.'

Whitworth 1 (La). 1970s/F/FG., 26-9-19. 'It's a well-used name in Bacup instead of ghost. There is a place called Tong Lane and its known for the Tong Boggart. It's also used in the mills and factories to describe something going wrong. (Running the boggart).'

Whitworth 2 (La). 1940s/F/E., 4-9-19. 'To me, boggarts were ghostly creatures that lived in marshlands (marshlands themselves being known as bogs). I don't remember parents using the word, but siblings did. I have not heard my own children using the word. I don't recall any stories. I was brought up in the Whitworth Valley, a stone quarrying area full of legends. I was born in 1938. Perhaps the ensuing war affected imaginations?'

Widnes 1 (La). 1950s/F/FG., 28-9-19. 'I remember being told the banshee will get you, and don't go near the pond as Ginny Green Teeth will pull you in this was the 1950s. No, no boggarts. Yes, I grew up in Widnes.'

Widnes 2 (La). 1940s/F/FG., 28-9-19. 'My grandmother used to refer to someone as a "boggart", if they were very cagey, mischievous or maybe dishonest. She would have nothing bad said about the gypsy and traveller communities, but said they were being confused with boggarts, and were NOT. Yes, I was born and raised in Widnes. 1941. My granddad was a somewhat kindly bent dock policeman. My grandmother was the local matriarch, who fed the poor kids in the neighbourhood and taught me by standing by her side with a basket of dripping sandwiches wrapped in newspaper for any child that was hungry after school... We also fed a local gentleman of the road called Matty Walsh. She used to give him sandwiches and a shilling every time he was around and called at our gate. My granddad was also a bookies runner, illegal but I told you he was a bent copper, but highly respected. He was Long XXX, 6'4'' talk and built like a ***** ***********: can't say that here! My grandmother also provided lodgings for the theatrical players at our local theatre, so I grew up around the seven dwarfs, the dame and countless others. I have lots of memories of those times, but now it is bedtime because tomorrow is my eighty-seventh birthday, and I need to be well awake for the festivities. Please come back if I can help any further.'

Widnes 3 (La). 1950s/F/FG., 28-9-19. 'My father-in-law said he knew them to be classed as mischievous figures who could looking at you whilst picking your pocket, if they'd robbed you, you'd been bogged. There is a place called

Bogart Hole Clough in Blakely Manchester. It was my Father-in-Law who was born in 1923 so I would imagine it was in the late 1920s and early 1930s in Widnes.'

Widnes 4 (La). 1950s/F/FG., 28-9-19. 'All I remember is being terrified of the boggarts when I was a kid in 1950s/1960s. My nan told us they were evil sprites that lived in the woods. I'm sixty-four now, never forgot about them. Yes, born February 1955, lived here all my life and would never live anywhere else.'

Widnes 5 (La). 1980s/M/FG., FM., 28-9-19. '[Boggarts] things on the golf course when a kid. And scared to death one night on there. It happened in 1977 when I was fifteen. I never went on there again in the dark. The night in question would have been late summer 1977. My parents' house and my mates five houses up from us backed onto the golf course, the other mate lived on another road. Prior to that a neighbour was talking to my parents and he claimed he had seen something on there before but hadn't a clue what it was. We had gone on there for a knock around, [with] a few golf clubs when it was getting a bit too late for golfers. Towards the fifth fairway we heard like a whispering, a gentle breeze then quiet. This happened again and again, we hid in a ditch and tried to look for a silhouette of someone against the lights. Nothing. We run around 100m away then the same noises. Fear set into us then, we ran to another ditch and hid, looking again for something, but nothing. The noise and breeze were right upon us this time we ran for home, three of us jumped the last ditch and into my mate's garden. XXX's dad said the three of us looked frightened to death when we burst through the kitchen door. Not one of us went on there again in the dark. In fact, we never talked about it. I couldn't tell you. I always knew it as a golf course grew up there since I was born. As kids we were always told it was haunted, even rumours of evil doings. But the word "boggart" was never used.' [Respondent volunteered all this as proof of boggarts, then said no use of word. I suppose the association with boggarts was made in his mind while reading my post.]

Widnes 6 (La). 1960s/F/FG., 28-9-19. 'Isn't there a house near Widnes called Brunt Bogart? I seem to remember it being for sale when I was very young and Dad wanted to view it but Mum wouldn't go because bogarts are evil. Yes, it would [have been 1960s]. No, we didn't talk about them otherwise. But I used to get books on folklore out of the library and boggarts cropped up in them quite a bit. [Mum chipped in on FB and added: there was a cottage called Brunt Bogart for sale many years ago we were considering buying it but when we looked the meaning of the name we decided against it!] My granddad used to scare me with Ginny Greenteeth as a child at Cronton, she lived in ponds and would drag you in. He called the green weed on top Ginny Greenteeth.'

Widnes 7 (La). 1930s/M/FG., 28-9-19. 'I remember as a youngster hearing scarecrows referred to as crow bogarts. Not often in Widnes but quite common around Ormskirk area. I heard it first from a friend who moved to Widnes from Ormskirk.'

Widnes 8 (La). 1960s/F/FG., 28-9-19. 'Never heard the term Boggarts. Bogeyman and Ginny Greenteeth yes. Widnes early 1960s. I'll see if my father-in-law knows anything, he's ninety-six so may know something.'

Widnes 9 (La). 1950s/M/FG., 28-9-19. 'I grew up in the Simms Cross area in the 1950s, and never heard of Boggarts. Look for info on "Spring heel Jack". You may find it interesting.'

Widnes 10 (La). 1940s/M/FG., 3-10-19. 'Well, I am seventy-seven, lived all my life in Widnes but never ever heard the word boggart'.

Widnes 11 (La). 1950s/F/FG., 29-9-19. 'And Jinny green teeth. She haunted the Bongs (waste land at Halton view Widnes). Maybe parents said it to keep us away. As a toxic stream ran through it. Water would change colours due to whatever a factory at top end let out into it. That was in the 1950s–1960s. No [for boggarts].'

Widnes 12 (La). 1950s/F/FG., 29-9-19. 'Grew up in Widnes in 1950s never heard of "Bogart". But bogeyman lived under the stairs and would get you.'

Wigan 1 (La). 1960s/F/FG., 17-9-19. 'I was born 1957 in Pemberton, Wigan. Never heard "Boggart" just "Bogey man" maybe it had changed the way we said it.'

Wigan 2 (La). 1960s/F/FG., 15-9-19. 'I originally come from Wigan, Winstanley area to be precise. Both my parents were from Wigan, and used the word "boggart" if my brother and I were dirty. I now live in Burscough and still call my husband a boggart if he hasn't had a shave for a couple of days. I am nearly sixty now, so my parents used the word in 1960s/1970s and probably beyond. Personally I love the word "boggart" and always thought it was a Wigan word, but maybe it's a Lancashire word.'

Wigan 3 (La). 1960s/F/FG., 17-9-19. 'I never heard the word "boggart", bogey man. Yes, boggart no. [Then later perhaps inspired by other posts] Just remembered that my dad used to say, "That horse has taken boggarts." Meaning the horse has run off. It was the 1960s. My dad came from Newtown, he taught me a lot of sayings. His favourite, on the last day of the school term was, "Did peawr dooer?" Meaning did you give the door a kick! My aunty came from Bamber Bridge. She has a broad Preston accent too!'

Wigan 4 (La). 1950s/F/FG., 17-9-19. 'Grandma used to use this word, if she wanted you to get out of her way, "tek thi boggerts!" She would say! This was a Lancashire saying. I grew up in Goose Green in Wigan, then Lancashire, until we had to be Greater Manchester, I always say "Lancashire" when anyone asks me where I'm from. Another saying was, "lay holes for medlars!" If you asked her what she was doing. Or what she had. In other words, mind your own business. Yes, I was born in 1955, so I was brought up at Goose Green, before they started building new houses. I and my sister who's a few years younger. I've lots of memories from about age of four. My mother worked and we lived next door to my grandmother, who lived with father, we never call him granddad lol and mum's sister auntie XXX and her husband uncle XXX! Who we also always gave his first name. They lived with grandmother, because my Auntie XXX was always poorly, she never had children and died at the age of forty-two, but she was lovely. And I'll always remember her blue slippers that she wore. And her funny way with money which she never spent, lol. Always had to have notes in her purse, and she could have twenty pounds in change, but she thought she had no money, lol, and in those days twenty pounds was a lot of money. Bless them! I loved them all, but the lady who brought me up was Auntie XXX! Mum's cousin who was like my second mum. She brought me up from one until I started school. Taught me most walking, going to toilet, numbers and letters. My mother work at the local mill. I was surrounded by love and sister too back in the day. In fact, it was a real community. I had more aunties back then, most of them not my blood. I really could write a book. Especially with my grandmother who was a very spiritual lady and who was a spiritualist. And saw spirit! She was a Methodist too and I believe her relatives built churches in days gone by! All these people who made do and mend had a great input in my life and in my childhood too! We called it Nanny Green Teeth, lol. Yes, you're right, before I said Jinny but didn't sound right. It bugged me then it came to me it was Nanny Green Teeth. The green slimy grass that grew in the brooks and streams around the fields at Goose Green! I thought our mam frightened us saying Nanny Green Teeth would get us lol. If you messed near the water! One way of keeping us away from water lol. Another story they told us, was about the Red Cloggs! We played out and it was getting dark mam would say, come in when it's getting dark or Red Cloggs would come and get you! When we asked what was red cloggs she said it was the feet with cloggs on covered in blood the miners wore, when they died in the mines lol. It's funny we ever survived to tell these tall stories lol. The mine she talked about was Blundell's tip and coal fields, in fact when just young girls my grandmother and her sister and some cousins were pit brow lasses. Grandma sat for hours telling us tales of what they had to do, sorting through the coal on coal belts. She said the work was hard and their hands where sometimes ripped by the sharp bits of coal shale etc, they wore thick stockings long skirts and sacking pinnies over the skirts and cloggs. If you couldn't afford stockings and you had just to wear the skirt and sacking your legs got chaffing. Thick shawls where worn scarfs covered their heads and then shawls covered them. Sacking over the shaws too. In winter she said it was terrible, rain made the woollen shawls heavy. I could imagine how they had to work. She said they were hard task masters! But she also said sometimes it was good the women would sing. Their hands were sore and had callouses in them. Bless them what a hard time it was for them.'

Wigan 5 (La): 1960s/M/FG., 18-9-19. 'My parents said a horse out of control had "Got boggarts" and run off. I just remembered, boggarts was also a name for fleas or lice on a pet animal. (Eg: "It's full o' boggarts" [perhaps fidgeting animals?]). Mum was from Poolstock and dad from Wallgate. Yes, I was brought up in Wigan. Still here.'

Wigan 6 (La). 1950s/M/FG., 18-9-19. 'My dad always used that word when calling someone. I still do sometimes. As in "Look at that Mon, the filthy bogurt."'

Wigan 7 (La). 1960s/M/FG., 18-9-19. 'Well, I originate from Wigan and the word "boggat" was used when you said "I've got a Bogart up my nose" not sure that helps your research or maybe it does.'

Wigan 8 (La). ???/F/FG., 13-10-19. 'I'm from Wigan but heard the word "boggarts" in the context of to run/get away from something fast? In the equine context probably, i.e. a horse giving it "full boggarts" from something it's spooked by.'

Wigan 9 (La). 1960s/M/FG., 13-10-19. 'I was born in Liverpool and my family moved to Wigan in the late 1960s. We used to visit Rivington Pike at weekends. I loved those visits and that probably explains why I now live in Blackrod. As a kid I was fascinated by the playground stories of Witches and Boggarts and all kinds of scary things "out on't Moors". I knew I was Lancastrian then, but this was "old Lancashire" and my teachers used to make a distinction in both religion and traditions between those of us with Irish descent and "proper Lancastrians". As far as we kids were concerned *circa* 1970 the Moors did contain Witches, and Boggarts, and other strange nocturnal creatures and they were real. Didn't know about Harry Potter … I just wondered where the Boggarts lived during the day when I was walking the Moors with my dad. Can't remember stories now, but there was a Jack O'Lantern too. And they all ate kids I think.'

Wigan 10 (La). 1960s/M/FG., 14-10-19. 'When I was growing up in Wigan in the 1960s I heard the term Bogeyman but not Boggart.'

Wigan 11 (La). 1970s/F/FG., 14-10-19. 'Boggy man we were also scared of as a child. My mum used to say if you're not good the boggy man will get you. Not at all never heard of "Boggart".'

Wigan 12 (La). 1930s/F/FG., 17-10-19. 'Hi, my mother lived in Scholes, Wigan and often told us as children of her fear as a child when the horses pulling carts and wagons would get the "boggarts" on the cobbled streets. Mum described the horse's fear and agitation. This would have been between 1930–1940.'

Wigan 13 (La). 1950s/F/E., 17-10-19. 'Just seen your post on FB. I grew up in the 1950s in Lancashire. My mother used to use the term "boggarts" to describe anything that moved jerkily or bolted quickly. For example, if horses were starting a race and became fractious, she would say they were taking boggarts.'

Wilpshire 1 (La). 1940s/F/FG., 26-9-19. 'Born 1948, lived in Wilpshire, was always aware of the word as a child. Boggarts lived in dark narrow clefts, especially around the Pendle Hill surrounds and preyed on unwary travellers and stray children! Left the area in 1963 for Westmorland, never heard the word there. Hope this helps.'

Winmarleigh 1 (La). 1960s/M/FG., 20-9-19. 'Folk of my parents age always said that Boggarts disappeared with the arrival of electric lights! We've still got them around Eagland Hill though. My son and family named their house Boggart Lodge, a combination of a name and Boggart. Age 57, Winmarleigh/Pilling.'

Wrightington 1 (La). ???/F/FM., 17-10-19. 'I lived near Boggart House, Wrightington and know a couple of stories about it. Morning, there was a Mr and Mrs XXX who lived in Boggart House about thirty years ago. Mrs XXX told me that she was at the sink in the kitchen one Sunday daytime looking out of the window and her daughter was sat at the kitchen table. She saw a little green man sat in the tree and called her daughter over to look. Her daughter saw him, screamed and walked away because it frightened her. My friends bought the house from the XXXs but they moved a few years ago.'

West Riding

Almondbury 1 (WRY). 1950s/F/E., 30-8-19. 'AB passed your enquiry on to me, as I grew up in Almondbury and Magdale 1950s/1960s, but I can recall no mentions of boggarts, or even Boggart's Eve, which features in Easther's *Glossary of the Dialect of Almondbury* etc. The worst childhood threat was "The bogey man will get you", and here in the Scottish Borders where I have lived for forty years eldritch creatures are "bogles" – surely no coincidence that they begin with the same three letters?'

Almondbury 2 (WRY). 1950s/F/FG., 16-10-19. 'I grew up in Almondbury in the 1950s and 1960s. Never heard any reference to them although my grandmother had lived in Almondbury since about 1912, I think it was...'

Almondbury 3 (WRY). 1950s/F/FG., 16-10-19. 'I was wondering the same thing as I lived in Almondbury in the 1950s and 1960s and have never heard of the word "boggarts".'

Almondbury 4 (WRY). 1950s/M/FG., 16-10-19. 'Grew up in Almondbury 1940s–1950s never heard the word at all.'

Almondbury 5 (WRY). 1950s/M/FG., 17-10-19. 'Born 51. Never heard boggard.'

Almondbury 6 (WRY). 1950s/F/FG., 17-10-19. 'I grew up in Almondbury from 1970 but never heard the word. However, my reason for posting is to ask if you've looked at Ogden water near Illingworth Halifax. I live near there now and there's loads about them [boggarts] there and the tea room which has now closed down (gutted it was lovely) was the Boggard Tea Room.'

Almondbury 7 (WRY). 1950s/F/FG., 17-10-19. 'I was born in the 1960s and grew up in the area. I am aware of the word, but it is not a word I have come across in common use locally. There is a place called Boggart Hole Clough in Blackley Lancashire.'

Aughton 1 (WRY). 1960s/M/FG., 13-10-19. 'Grew up in the 1960s in Aughton. Boggarts were ghosts.'

Baildon 1 (WRY). 1950s/F/F., 13-9-19. 'Always used the word "boggart", and still do. Friend also knew the word, something nasty that will get you! Baildon, 1950s, friend Shipley 1970s.

Baildon 2 (WRY). 1950s/F/FG., 14-10-19. 'I grew up in Baildon in the 1950s and cannot recall ever hearing the word.'

Baildon 3 (WRY). ???/F/FG., 17-10-19. 'Definitely no use of the word "boggart" and I had relatives who I knew and chatted with who were born in the 1880s.'

Baildon 4 (WRY). ???/F/FG., 17-10-19. 'According to John La Pages book, *The Story of Baildon*, there were several village superstitions, a dog known as the "guytrash", Padfooit whose chief haunt was Westgate, and several others. These all date from the nineteenth century. Holden Lane was known as Boggart Lane at that time and was supposed to have a spectre of its own. However, the weird and terrible cries said to emanate from the boggart turned out to be a screech owl! [other comment: The Guytrash was also known as "Bloodybones".] That's right. Padifooit was also a variation of the guytrash, and Bloodiboahns was said to haunt the area of Tentercroft known at the time as "Loin Spaht". Who knew Baildon had so many spectres?! [Other FB user: Chatterchains on Baildon Bank was another] [Still another: Haha. Remember "Chatterchains" and a massive almost hysterical gathering of kids around the paddling pool hoping to get a glimpse, probably around 1963. Some of us ventured up the Bank but were chased off. Sadly not by ghosts, just some bigger kids from the village.]'
Baildon 5 (WRY). 1950s/F/FG., 17-10-19. 'I was born in Baildon and grew up in the 1950s but never heard tell of Boggarts.'
Baildon 6 (WRY). 1960s/F/FG., 17-10-19. 'When I Lived in Baildon in the 1960s and used the word "boggart" to describe monsters on the moors.'
Bailiffe Bridge 1 (WRY). 1950s/M/FG., 14-10-19. 'Bailiffe Bridge then Rastrick 1950s and 1960s. Can't say I ever did [hear of boggarts growing up].'
Barnoldswick 1 (WRY). 1940s/F/F., 2-9-19. 'Now you've said "bogeyman". That's what I was told. I didn't recognize "boggart". I live in Barnoldswick which is now in Lancashire but was in Yorkshire when I was growing up. My parents and grandparents would say "If you don't..." that could be anything from going to sleep, finishing my tea, or whatever, "the bogeyman will get you". My husband comes from Burnley and he says it was the same there. We were both born in the 1940s so the time frame would be into the late 1950s.'
Barnoldswick 2 (WRY). 1950s/F/FG., 21-9-19. 'I grew up in Barlick in the late 1950s/early 1960s and although I'm pretty sure I was aware of the word [boggart] it wasn't a big deal in our house, as the family wasn't superstitious and didn't believe in stuff like that. Santa and the Tooth Fairy were as far as it went.'

Barnoldswick 3 (WRY). 1960s/F/FG., 23-9-19. 'I used to hear of the boggart, I always thought of him as a little traveling man who was very mischievous and would lure you into trouble? Born and bred in Barnoldswick in 1964'.

Barnoldswick 4 (WRY). 1960s/F/FG., 30-9-19. I was born in 1967. I'm from Barnoldswick. My parents used the word "Boggart" when I was growing up. To make me behave otherwise the boggart would come after me. It worked till I was at high school. But now it's not used like it was. There was a mill in Barnoldswick. Barnsey Mill. My dad was the transport manager and I use to go into his work. And he used to say the Barnsey Boggart is watching you. The mill was spooky especially when it was empty and it was night time, so we behaved so the boggart wouldn't get us!'

Barnsley 1 (WRY). 1950s/F/FG., 27-9-19. 'Boggarts were definitely spoken of in villages near Barnsley in 1950s. Twenty miles north of Sheffield. I was a Brownie however and we knew they were folklore not real.'

Berry Brow 1 (WRY). 1940s/F/E., 2-9-19. 'Thank you for forwarding Simon's enquiry about boggarts. Fascinating reply from XXX. Reminds me that Magdale itself was a bit magic, to us children, walking in Mag Wood, the Giant's footprint and snuffbox were magic but I seem to remember something more scholarly about "Mag" years later, and my mind is now fragmenting so I can't retrieve it. XXX you also lived close to Mag Wood and the spring that never gave out, my Mum said that in days of drought she remembered that there would be a line-up of people with water vessels at that spring in a queue waiting to fill up with drinking water (early twentieth century). I never saw it – don't know its location. I'm not surprised that XXX in Magdale was familiar with the frisson of anxiety about boggarts – Magdale was a little community in itself, a little outside the main routes of communication, a bit further from urban influence? More susceptible to fey ideas? As a child in Berry Brow, nearer to Huddersfield, in the 1940s and 1950s, the only Boggart I knew of was the farm called Boggard Ing (Ing=field), which was about a quarter mile up steep Park Lane from Berry Brow. The farmer was XXX, and his wife was somehow related to my Grandma XXX (born in 1870s.) Son XXX continued on at the farm when his parents died, we visited him too. We never felt anything spooky about the farm or its fields, and as children we never questioned the name; to us it just sounded boggy. This implies that the word "boggard" was meaningless to us youngsters. I have asked my brother (born 1935) who lives near Golcar, Huddersfield, about boggards in the Colne Valley – he has yet to ask a retired farmer who lives above Slaithwaite. My brother used to talk to all the old farmers in the 1950s and 1960s. My brother-in-law whose two grandmothers lived at hilltop farms in our region hadn't heard them mention boggards (perhaps old folk didn't want to smittle youngsters with their anxiety or fey ideas?) Did Methodism affect whether people were superstitious or not?'

Bradford 1 (WRY). 1940s/M/FG., 7-11-19. 'We used "bogie", presumably derived from the same word, 1940s/50s. But I would like to add that there was a "Boggart Lane" off Westfield Lane, Idle/Wrose (there is now a "Boggart Lane Close"; and there was a "Boggard Lane" in central Bradford. Its name was changed, early in the nineteenth century, to "Eastbrook Lane".'

Bradford 2 (WRY). 1940s/F/FG., 7-11-19. 'I was born in 1948 grew up in Bradford. I've never heard the word "boggart" at all.'

Bradford 3 (WRY). 1940s/F/FG., 7-11-19. 'Bradford – Bogie/Bogeyman were commonly used. "Bogart" rings a bell in relation to my grandma, who was born in Birmingham in 1885, moved to Bradford about 1910. 1940s, 1950s.'

Bradford 4 (WRY). 1930s/F/FG., 7-11-19. 'I was born 1939 in Bradford and never heard "Boggart". The word used here would be Bogeyman.'

Bradford 5 (WRY). 1950s/F/FG., 7-11-19. 'Grew up in the 1950s/1960s in Bradford and heard Bogey man never heard of Boggarts.'

Bradford 6 (WRY). 1930s/F/FG., 7-11-19. 'I was born in Bradford in 1934 and was brought up in the Wakefield Rd area at the very end of Bowling Back Lane. I was five when WW2 broke out. I have a very vivid memory of that time, but I never heard of that creature. The most scary thing we heard was Johnny Green Eyes, perhaps it was a more rural thing.'

Bradford 7 (WRY). 1950s/M/FG., 7-11-19. 'My dad referred to the white dot that appeared in the middle of the telly when it was turned off as "a Boggart" in the 1950s. Yes, he was Bradford born and bred but his mam came from Barnard Castle and her mam came from Cumbria so he may have heard the term from her. I've just Googled "Boggart" and it mentions Giggleswick, and my dad lived there a while as a child so he may have picked the term up there.'

Bradford 8 (WRY). 1930s/M/FG., 7-11-19. 'I was born 1933 in Great Horton Bradford and never heard the name.'

Bradford 9 (WRY). 1950s/M/FG., 7-11-19. 'I was born in Low Moor in Bradford in 1952. I know the name but think only generally not used from my area. Sorry can't help.'

Bradford 10 (WRY). 1940s/F/FG., 7-11-19. 'Born in 1942 both my husband and I have never heard the word "boggart". I lived in Eccleshill and he lived in Bradford Moor.'

Bradford 11 (WRY). 1940s/M/FG., 7-11-19. 'I grew up in Frizinghall in the 1940s-1950s and can't recall hearing that term [boggart].'

Bradford 12 (WRY). 1950s/F/FG., 7-11-19. 'Pasture Lane from 1950 to 1962. Brownie Guides. The Brownie Sixes are types of Boggarts. (I've been a Brownie Guider for thirty-six years, so often still come across Boggarts in stories.)'

Bradford 13 (WRY). 1950s/M/FG., 7-11-19. 'Was born 1950s, poet's corner BD3. Never heard then. But remember reading about Bradford boggart in library books Bradford library, 1970s.'
Bradford 14 (WRY). ???/M/FG., 7-11-19. 'Camping in Kettlewell many years ago a farmer once said "look out for the Boggart Phantom" when I was out walking late at night.'
Bradford 15 (WRY). 1950s/M/FG., 7-11-19. 'I grew up on Moore Avenue/ Wibsey area BD7 in the mid 1950s and 1960s – don't have any recollection of boggarts, but of bogey men and bogeys.'
Bradford 16 (WRY). 1950s/F/FG., 7-11-19. 'Born in West Bowling 1956, never heard the word "boggart".'
Bradford 17 (WRY). 1940s/M/FG., 7-11-19. 'Born in East Bowling, Bradford 1945, never heard that word.'
Bradford 18 (WRY). 1940s/M/FG., 7-11-19. 'Brought up in Girlington 1950s/1960s and never heard it said then.'
Bradford 19 (WRY). 1960s/F/FG., 7-11-19. 'Must have died out in Manningham before the 1960s and 1970s. As with other comments the bogeyman was used.'
Brighouse 1 (WRY). 1930s/F/FG., 18-10-19. 'I grew up in Brighouse from 1934 but I never heard of a Boggart!'
Brighouse 2 (WRY). 1930s/F/FG., 18-10-19. 'I remember Mr Blackburn at St Andrew's Junior School teaching us a song called The Railway Boggart, when I was in the first year, in 1970.'
Buttershaw 1 (WRY). 1930s/F/FG., 7-11-19. 'I was born in Buttershaw, between Halifax and Bradford 1935, my mum was born 1900 and she said "boggarts", I say "bogeyman".'
Conisbrough 1 (WRY). 1950s/M/FG., 7-11-19. 'Bogeyman is singular and very commonly used term. Never heard the word "Boggart" but assume it's must be a Southern version, certainly not common in the villages of Conisbrough and Denaby in the 1950s and 1960s. Also not heard of the "Bogeyman" for some time.'
Conisbrough 2 (WRY). 1940s/M/FG., 7-11-19. 'Yes, I was born in 1949 and remember my grandmother (born in Conisbrough) using the term "bogart" as a bogeyman. I'm sure you also know the park in Manchester known as "Boggart Hole Clough".'
Cowling 1 (WRY). 1910s/F/FG., 21-9-19. 'My Grandmother believed her house was visited by what she always referred to as Boggarts. On a number of occasions items would move around the house for no apparent reason. Items left in one room would appear in another room (mostly overnight).

Both my aunts readily backed up these stories. The house itself had formally been two houses and when the conversion was done one staircase was removed. On several occasions Gran and my aunties would clearly hear loud footsteps on the old (missing) staircase. No amount of reasoning would ever convince them otherwise. My Grandmother always referred to these visitations as "Boggarts". In fact, I can't recall her ever using any other term. She was from the Bolton Abbey in the Yorkshire Dales. It wasn't unusual to hear her use words I never came across elsewhere. 1910. Sorry I got a little carried away and didn't actually answer your questions. These stories came to me in the early 1970s. My Grandmother lived in Cowling, North Yorkshire.'

Cowling 2 (WRY). ???/F/FG., 7-11-19. 'Live in Cowling near Skipton/ Keighley also Colne. We have a Boggart Lane near Westfield Farm, Cowling Hill area.'

Delph 1 (WRY). 1950s/F/FG., 9-10-19. 'As a Delpher born and bred, I grew up with "boggarts" so to speak. I have always been a keen horse rider and when a horse spooked we said he has "taken boggart", or "seen a boggart", invisible to our human eyes but obviously visible to the horse! Likewise, if a person suddenly got frightened of something and ran off we would say "oh he's taken boggart". We thought boggarts were gnome- or troll-like creatures that lurked around the area intent on scaring people and animals. They were blamed for turning milk sour etc etc. The "black dog" was supposedly an apparition that roamed the hills around Friarmere and Castleshaw and if seen it meant that someone was about to die. I used to be frightened that I might see it when I was out riding. I never have done, but still am wary of the tale. My horse sees boggarts regularly! That is, he spooks at "nothing". Who knows, they may exist... Yes, grew up in the 1950s and 1960s. Good luck with the project. I find it all fascinating.'

Dewsbury 1 (WRY). 1960s/F/FG., 14-10-19. 'From Dewsbury born in the 1960s. Never heard of a boggart. It was the bogey man or George that lived in various places around my gran's house.'

Diggle 1 (WRY). 1960s/F/FG., 22-9-19. 'Born in 1961. Lived in Diggle then moved to Uppermill. No Boggarts here but plenty of fear of the bogeymen.'

Doncaster 1 (WRY). 1950s/M/FG., 7-11-19. 'Born end of 1950s (1957) and through 1960s in New Street, South Yorkshire. Typical high density, two up two down with a cellar come scullery, terraced housing near Balby Bridge, Doncaster with both grandparents and family living close by (Arbitration Street and Kelham Street, Green Dyke Lane). And yet, [boggart] not a term I'm familiar with or heard. Given that I grew up looking at a cemetery wall which made up the other side of the street) and behind which sometimes people hid and frightened folk by popping their heads up and making noises, I'm surprised it wasn't ever used. There was also a game where you had to run through the cemetery at night. Surely both times merited the use of the word [boggart] but no, never heard it.'

Doncaster 2 (WRY). 1950s/F/FG., 7-11-19. 'I was born in the late 1950s, and didn't encounter the word until I saw it in a child's storybook when I was teaching in 1980s. I think the word formed part of the title.'

Doncaster 3 (WRY). 1950s/F/FG., 7-11-19. 'Born in 1959 boggeymen yes I remember well. No, boggart is a myth. But have seen a blue orb and that's true.'

Doncaster 4 (WRY). 1950s/F/FG., 7-11-19. 'I am Doncaster born and bred and I was born in 1954 my husband 1952 and my husband has seen it referred to in books and we are pretty sure it's old English and the bogeyman derives from this word "boggarts". Hope this helps. Hence in my childhood and that of my husband they said the bogeyman is coming to take you away a term used to make us behave said as in bogey like in the nose.'

Doncaster 5 (WRY). 1950s/F/FG., 7-11-19. 'I'm Doncaster born and bred too. In the 1950s. Never heard of Boggarts (till Harry Potter) but like others was threatened with the Bogeyman coming to get me.'

Doncaster 6 (WRY). 1960s/F/FG., 7-11-19. 'I was born in Doncaster in the 1960s. Heard of bogeyman not boggart.'

Doncaster 7 (WRY). 1950s/F/FG., 7-11-19. 'Doncaster my auntie Jess told us the Bogey man would get us if we misbehaved. Was born in 1957 in Doncaster.'

Doncaster 8 (WRY). 1950s/F/FG., 7-11-19. 'Born in 1957. Raised in Cantley area. Never heard the word "boggart". Was always the Bogeyman.'

Doncaster 9 (WRY). 1950s/M/FG., 7-11-19. 'I grew up in Doncaster in the fifties: born 1947. I never heard the word "boggart".'

Doncaster 10 (WRY). 1940s/M/FG., 7-11-19. 'I heard it [boggart] lots of times growing up in Wheatley in the 1960s.'

Dunscroft 1 (WRY). 1960s/M/FG., 7-11-19. 'I was born in 1962 and lived my first twenty or so years in Dunscroft. I'd never really heard of a Boggart until about 2002. And that was only because of the Sheffield based morris team Boggarts Breakfast, which I'm now a member of.'

Earby 1 (WRY). 1940s/F/FG., 19/9/19. 'I lived in Earby from 1946 until 1961 and don't remember ever hearing the word "boggart". And though officially Earby was in Yorkshire at that time, both my parents were from Lancashire. When people ask me whereabouts I come from I'm never quite sure what to answer. It was Yorkshire when I left and then became Lancashire when I visited. I've lived in Tipperary for over forty years. That's much easier!'

Edenthorpe 1 (WRY). 1960s/M/FG., 7-11-19. 'Born in 1967, grew up in Edenthorpe and Stainforth, never heard the term "boggarts" but heard "bogeyman". Also my Grandparents used to tell me the 8 O'Clock Man was coming when they wanted to get me to go to bed! They said if I was quick he wouldn't catch me as he had a wooden leg! Scared me to death!'

Edlington 1 (WRY). ???/M/FG., 7-11-19. 'My old dad called me a "boggart". I was always having a good time playing in the wardrobe. He was from Durham, my mother was from Edlington. When I asked her what a boggart was she told me that I was.'

Elland 1 (WRY). 1980s/M/FG., 14/10/19. 'I was born in the 1980s. But I remember my Grandma tellling me about myths and folklore. She mentioned a boggart that lived by Elland Bridge. It would sit on a rock and follow you along the footpath.'

Elland 2 (WRY). 1970s/M/FG., 20/10/19. 'I was told of the Boggart stone in Elland, caused by impish boggarts sliding down it. Heard the tale in about 1980.'

Esholt 1 (WRY). 1960s/F/FG., 20/10/19. 'Not sure if it's of any relevance to your research but my eighty-one year-old parents have a few tales of spooky goings on in various houses they've lived in and around Esholt (and in the old Esholt Hall grounds). Esholt is a village steeped in history (up until recently it was also used as the setting for the Emmerdale tv series) and still has many ancient buildings and ruins of an old nunnery. They moved into Boggart House in about 1965 and finally moved out about five years ago to live closer to myself and my husband, so around fifty years in total. It was a fantastic place to grow up although a few strange things occurred. I remember mum's electric sewing machine started working on its own despite being turned off at the switch and my friend's car once moved around in the driveway despite the handbrake being engaged and doors locked. Not terrifying but definitely weird. At some point myself and two older sisters were told that a Boggart was a mischievous Yorkshire ghost who, amongst other things, liked to place a cold clammy hand on the face [of] people while they were sleeping. (I never felt anything but it's a wonder we ever slept soundly!). Older tales included ghostly noises and marble playing but that was before mum and dad moved in however I've attached an extract from a book that we found in Bradford Library a while ago. It may be of interest. My parents have experienced ghostly goings on within the grounds of Esholt Hall (more the "sense" of a presence and the dog behaving weirdly) and also at Esholt Lodge House (the sounds of marching soldiers despite no physical presence. Apparently the marching appeared to be moving in the direction of an old route taken by the Roundheads in the English Civil War). As a young child in another house in the village centre my sister complained of music being played in the night that prevented her sleeping. Mum was told that a lady who had since died was an avid musician and frequently played an instrument in the house. Hope that helps but if you want any further info my parents are very sprightly and happy to chat about Esholt and Boggart House if you're in the area or I can ask them any questions you may have.' [In a subsequent email, born 1963]: 'Mr and Mrs XXX [previous occupiers] had changed the name of the house on a gate sign to "The Firs" before my parents moved in but it was never changed on any legal document so my mum and dad just let it lapse back to Boggart House.'

Farsley 1 (WRY). ???/F/FG., 26-9-19. 'The bogeyman would get you if you walked on the cracks in paving. Grew up in Farsley.'

Fence 1 (WRY). 1940s/F/FG., 13-10-19. 'Brought up 1940s/50s in Fence, never heard the word "boggart". Well I was born early 1940s at Fence. My dad was born in Fence 1903. Don't remember him using it.'

Grasscroft 1 (WRY). 1960s/F/FG., 22-9-19. 'I grew up in Grasscroft and my parental threat was Ginny Green Teeth's pond. (To keep us away). When I was twelve (1975) I would visit my friends in Dobcross and the Boggarts were in dark places away from adults. I hadn't heard of them so I wasn't afraid as my friends were. And they really were!'

Greenfield 1 (WRY). 1950s/F/FG., 22-9-19. 'My grandparents used to use boggarts as a threat to make us come in from playing before it went dark. I was born mid-1950s and grew up in Greenfield. Also, don't know if this is outside your area but there is Boggart Hole Clough park in North Manchester. At first, probably a nameless horror, but as I read fairy stories and saw illustrations in them, I think my idea of a boggart developed into a goblin or troll type of creature.'

Halifax 1 (WRY). 1940s/F/E., 10-8-19 '"Boggart" means dirty, trouble-making, evil spirit that hides away. It's something – someone?! – to avoid, and is thus used by grownups to frighten children away from something/somewhere, as in "Don't go into the woods. There are boggarts there". No memory of parents/grandparents/relatives using the word. She first heard about them in the late 1980s – as in the story below. She grew up in Halifax in the 1940s and 1950s. It was before we got married which was in 1992. She told you about the garden at the Elland Health Centre where there was a stone slab, said to be a boggart grave which was haunted in some way. Apparently, each time XXX got a new cleaning lady in at this building, they were ok downstairs.

But when they went upstairs they got freaked out and kept resigning. Elland is not strictly Calder valley.'

Halifax 2 (WRY). 1950s/M/C., mid-August 19. Didn't know the word.

Halifax 3 (WRY). 1960s/M/F., 12-9-19 'Never heard of them? the word must have stopped being used before I was born? The only similar one I remember is a kid being told about the "Bogey Man".'

Halifax 4 (WRY). 1950s/F/E., 9-8-19. 'Hi. I have always thought of boggarts being like little imps that live under bridges or in corners of woods. I don't have a lot of recollections of the word being used but it must have [been] for me to know it. When I worked in Leeds there is a Boggart Hill area in Seacroft. There is a Boggart Lane in Norland/ Sowerby Bridge. My god-daughter asked me about the name a few weeks ago. Sorry no stories spring to mind. I was born and bred in Halifax from 1949.' [Respondent subsequently wrote that her sister had reminded her that they had, as children read a story about boggarts flitting.]

Haworth 1 (WRY). 1950s/M/E., 25-10-19. 'Morning, My name is XXX, and I grew up in the Worth Valley in Oldfield, close to Haworth in the 1960s. My grandparents lived in Oldfield from the mid-1930s to the early 1950s and again from 1964 to 1974. Though both were born in Keighley in the early 1900s and their ancestry remains within a ten mile radius of Keighley back to the beginning of the 1600s. But, as children, if we were running in and out of the house a lot, my grandmother would say "ee!, you're in and out like Butterfield Boggart!" And despite asking around I've never been able to find out who "Butterfield Boggart" was! Incidentally, we had a local historian who died earlier this year called Ian Dewhirst, who, in the 1960s, wrote a booklet called *The Haworth Water Wolf and other tales*. I can't remember much about the tale, except that you would swallow the Water Wolf whilst drinking water. I'm sure they will have a copy of this book in the Keighley Library, or, if you ask around on the local history sites "I Love Haworth and the Brontes", "Keighley and District Local History Society" etc. you may be able to find one. Certainly, the word "Boggart" is one I grew up with (born in the early 1950s), and one I still use in my poetry on occasion, but defining just WHAT a "Boggart" is or was is difficult! For myself, I am very interested in local history, especially in the area of the Upper Worth Valley, Haworth and beyond, and in the origin of our language and various words, for instance, as kids, we never "Played" out, we always "Laked out" and the Norwegian word for play is "Lek" so we appear to have a direct link back to the Viking era.'

Hebden Bridge 1 (WRY). 1970s/M/E., 21-7-19. 'If you mean reference to an evil spirit, then I certainly didn't know or use the word [boggart] when

I was growing up, and I don't know of anybody I knew in or around Hebden Bridge (or family close by) who did. Even having lived and worked in Scotland (with research on wetlands), I can't say that I ever heard anyone use the term.'

Hebden Bridge 2 (WRY). 1970s/M/E., 5-8-19. 'To your question, I can't think that we used that word [boggart] unless it came from a fantasy book.'

Hebden Bridge 3 (WRY). ???/F/FG., 16-10-19. 'We used to go bogart hunting up Hardcastle Crags. I used to stick googly eyes on a celeriac, and that was a boggart. One day I could only get a turnip, so did the same. We found the boggart and I was told not to be stupid Mummy, that's a turnip.'

Heptonstall 1 (WRY). 1950s/M/FG., 18-10-19. 'I'm sat with my father who grew up in Heptonstall in the Calder Valley in the 1950s and 1960s. He'd never heard the word [boggart] until Harry Potter.'

Hexthorpe (WRY). F/1950s/M/FG., 7-11-19. 'Born in the late 1950s in Hexthorpe. Never heard of boggarts.'

Hipperholme 1 (WRY). 1980s/M/FG., 16-10-19. 'Grew up in the 1980s. Born in 1981. I was aware of the term as we lived next to Boggart Lane in Hipperholme. This was a Bridleway between Northedge Lane and Bramley Lane. Probably back then, a grumpy spirit, or troll like charactor who might jump out on you. I was aware of the term from parents (Halifax and Keighley). But also told it was an old nonsense folk tale, and that they couldn't hurt me!'

Hipperholme 2 (WRY). 1950s/M/FG., 17-10-19. 'In Hipperholme there is, I believe, a lower boggart running between the grove and Bramley Lane, bridle path/footpath. It ran through a copse and I could see a boggart living there! The area I ran from in old times was a bog! [Age based on FB page guess]'

Hipperholme 3 (WRY). 1950s/M/FG., 18-10-19. 'Boggart Lane in Hipperholme. 1950s to present. I always knew a biggest [*sic*] as a ghost.'

Hipperholme 4 (WRY). 1950s/M/FG., 18-10-19. 'Boggart Lane, 1910.... We went down this lane to play in an old quarry in the 1950s. Just a name, nothing more back then.'

Honley 1 (WRY). 1950s/M/E., 29-8-19. 'I grew up in the 1950s and lived and still live at Magdale, Honley, in the Holme Valley, between Holmfirth and Huddersfield. I grew up with Boggarts as a presence in the local landscape, rather than household ones. They were only malign if you bothered them. There is a Boggart Lane about not far from Magdale in the vicinity of which I have since found there was a field name in the early nineteenth century of Boggart Ing. My father recollected relatives believing in Boggarts and having a fear of them and Will O the Wisps. The latter is my assumption from his description of them – I can't remember what term he used. As children we envisaged them as spindly, hairy, monkey/goblin like creatures with big eyes. I don't know where this image came from as I don't recollect them ever being described to me. Anyway, the belief was so ingrained that, even as an adult (though not in the least superstitious usually), whilst walking in the dark past numinous places – quarries, wells etc – I have felt a frisson of anxiety about their presence. I don't believe in their existence – except as a projection of anxieties about unseen forces which was probably more pronounced in the era before intense industrialisation.'

Huddersfield 1 (WRY). 1960s/M/FG., 21-10-19. 'I don't recall the word "Boggart" being used when I was growing up, though my family were quite superstitious. I was aware of the concept of house Brownies, elemental beings who help keep your home clean and tidy. I have also heard of a Barghest, if that's how it's spelled, a type of supernatural "demon dog", and there is supposed to be one on Ilkley moor though I've never encountered it. I think the Barghest is supposedly some sort of Astral entity, possibly conjured up by a Magician, rather than an elemental. I was born in Huddersfield in 1962, my parents were of the older generation born in 1920 and 1923. They both had practiced Scrying at one point, and attended séances. I had a grandmother who could read cards and tea leaves.'

Huddersfield 2 (WRY). ???/F/FG., 25-10-19. 'The word [boggart] was familiar to me as a child in the late 1950s early 1960s but not at home – in writing with stories written for members of Girlguiding – specifically Brownies. Probably in the Brownie annual which was sold and read nationally. The "beret boggart" has stuck in my mind as the "mr nobody" who had moved your hat! It therefore has never occurred to me that boggart was a northern word. My Brownie Annuals are sadly long gone but it would be interesting to know who the author was of the story/article. It would probably just be in one of them – somewhere between 1958 and 1962. I can enquire in Guide Leaders Facebook groups if you like. As a species we tend to hoard and value old materials like that and someone may know. Lots of early Brownie materials were based on such matters. Sixes were named after mythical creatures – Fairy, Pixie, Sprite, Ghilli Dhu etc. The Story of the Brownies was selected by Robert Baden Powell I believe as the basis for the helpfulness small children should display. And that is why the adult leader is traditionally called Brown Owl. Message me if you like.'

Idle 1 (WRY). ???/F/FG., 7-11-19. 'Was born and grew up near Idle in Bradford. My mum used the word "boggart" as you might say, "you little bugger", a non-swear word in Yorkshire. I knew it as meaning mischievously naughty.'

Idle 2 (WRY). 1940s/F/FG., 7-11-19. 'I grew up in Idle. we knew the word "Boggart" as a bad or mischievous mythical being who lived in the woods. we were told, if you go into those woods after dark the Boggart will get you. We never believed it of course. Sorry I did not say, it was in the 1940s.'
Ilkley 1 (WRY). 1950s/F/C., mid-August 19. Didn't know the word.
Ilkley 2 (WRY). 1940s/F/E., 12 Jan 2020. 'My son XXX who is an actor specialising in M.R. James Ghost stories showed me an article about your interest in Boggarts. I was born in 1942 in Ilkley in the West Riding of Yorkshire and was aware of the existence of the Boggart as an undefined but frightening presence. My mother had a helper with housework and childcare, an unmarried lady of indeterminate age who came from a village called Connonly near Silsden. She was called Miss Jackson and would stay for part of the week in our house. It was from her that I learned the threat "The Boggart will get You". I was never sure what the Boggart was but the name itself I found frightening and I had a dread of incurring its wrath. My grandmother who was born in 1880 in Leeds also spoke of Boggarts. I have always thought that Boggle Hole near Ravenscar North Yorkshire must be connected with Boggart. Your map was interesting as it seemed to include a pocket of Boggart references around the area of Boggle Hole.'
Leeds 1 (WRY). 1940s/M/FG., 26-9-19. 'I'd heard of the word in the family. I was born 1949. But Boggy Man was what we used. A creature of the night that could change its form. I guess many didn't get told the true meaning as it's so scary. My grandmother and mother would put on a Scottish accent. If you don't eat your porridge you won't grow up strong and the boggy man will get you. My mother's side originally came from Newton under Roseberry and Skelton in Cleveland.'
Leeds 2 (WRY). 1950s/F/FG., 26-9-19. 'Grew up in Leeds in the 1950s. Never heard the word "boggart" but was brought up with the bogeyman threat and the banshee. She stands under a lamp moaning and combing her hair. If you see her you're going to die! (My Gran was Irish). She told tales of the devil, leprechauns, banshees. No wonder I grew up scared of my own shadow.'
Leeds 3 (WRY). 1950s/F/F., 10-9-19. '[Boggart means] nothing apart from Boggart Clough. The bogey man was used when we were children as a fictitious scary man. Parents used "bogey man".'
Leeds 4 (WRY). 1950s/F/FG., 26-9-19. 'Grew up in the 1950s in Leeds never heard the word "boggart" other than an address, it was the bogeyman for us.'
Leeds 5 (WRY). 1950s/F/FG., 26-9-19. 'As a girl guide in the 1960s, when on camp, if you stood on the matting around the campfire, you would get the

"boggart" until someone else did it! I seem to remember it was a thing made out of potatoes and sticks... Hopefully others on here might remember better. It was, Crossgates Leeds 15. It sure wasn't a good thing to get the boggart, you looked to pass it on super quick.'

Leeds 6 (WRY). 1970s/M/FG., 26-9-19. 'I moved to Leeds in 1993 (Born in Cambridge in 1973). I have so long as I remember used the word (I know it as a fey who steals or hides things). I am not sure where I learned it. I know I have said it to friend of a similar age who grew up in Lancashire and she knew exactly what I meant.'

Leeds 7 (WRY). 1960s/F/E., 11-10-19. 'I grew up in the 1960s and early 1970s. I lived in Leeds and Wakefield. Boggarts were scary little buggers that might lurk on abandoned land or in the gardens of derelict houses. In my mind, they were related to the bogeys of the bogey hole – which could be the cupboard under the stairs, the cellar head steps or a boxroom/dark cupboard. They (boggarts) would try to trick you into deep potholes, dangerous sumps, old dams and such like. They liked bogs, delphs (quarries) and ruined factories too. Anywhere unsafe, shady and wildly appealing to us bairns (kids). I think they were frightened by light. They gained strength at dusk. There was Boggart Hill in Seacroft, and Boggle Hole at Robin Hood's Bay (where I went on my holidays) – so I knew they were real.'

Luddenden Foot 1 (WRY). ???/M/FG., 18-10-19. 'Noone remember the bogey hole at Higgin Dam, Boulder Clough? Used to spook me when I walked past on my own?'

Midgley 1 (WRY). 1970s/F/FG., 13-10-19. 'There was (is) a Boggart Farm in Old Town (I grew up in Midgely and Luddendenfoot). The current owners changed the name to Allswell. I never heard any specific stories about that farm but I knew/know what a Boggart was growing up. I also vaguely remember something about Heptonstall up way and Boggarts – I'll ask my Mum and Dad. Also maybe try XXX she runs the Hebden Bridge Ghost Walk (part of the Arts Festival). I was born early 1970s.'

Mirfield 1 (WRY). 1950s/F/FG., 16-10-19. 'When I was a little girl in the 1980s I used to play go and hunt boggarts in the woods with my granddad who was from Lincolnshire. He used to tell us we had to tuck our trousers in our socks so they couldn't run up our trouser legs! We have photos of us boggart hunting. Haven't heard it "boggarts" then until Harry Potter! Granddad would have been born in 1920s. Not sure if that's any help to you. I grew up in Mirfield. So just a few miles away. Granddad is from Mablethorpe.'

Moorside 1 (WRY). 1950s/M/FG., 22-9-19. 'Being a churchwarden back in the late 1970s and 1980s in Moorside, I recall our local vicar regularly had to visit and counsel younger members of the Sholver community who were reporting seeing will o' the wisps and the presence of boggarts in the valley below the estate. Generally they were suffering hardships like absent partners, failed marriages and real poverty, along with abusive behaviour all around. The name [i.e. boggart] came from the affected individuals, not the vicar, and the occupants of the estate were very widespread, including emergency housing cases from all over Greater Manchester... My wife's just told me that in Saddleworth, the terms Dobs and Bogs were synonymous when she moved here in the 1970s as meaning evil spirits. [On Boggart Hole Clough] I think about the place and it's mainly a deep gully with a pond at the bottom. I know that the place is a park and probably takes its name from the main feature. [in a response to someone else] Must have been pretty local as I remember Jenny Green Teeth! My mum came from Oldham and dad from Birkenhead, so all the colloquial stuff came from mum, and I think Jenny would be invoked if you didn't get off to sleep and behave. Of course you were quiet because of abject terror and sleep just ceased to be an option. if memory serves me right, she [i.e. Jenny] was resurrected by Mike Harding and the Oldham Tinkers folk songs in the 1970s! Reminiscing about childhood. I think one record may have been called Lancashire Hotch Potch.'

Mytholmroyd 1 (WRY). 1950s/F/C., mid-August 19. Interviewee didn't know the word as a kid, but later in life looked it up in a dictionary.

Mytholmroyd 2 (WRY). 1950s/M/FG., 16-10-19. 'Apart from when local news TV was doing patronising lightweight items, I never once heard the word "boggart" spoken in Mytholmroyd from 1953 when I arrived there as a young kid, to 1972, when I left. There was a tradition of "mumming" which involved groups of soot-faced men or youths entering houses on (I think) New Year's Eve, unannounced and uninvited, and making humming noises, before leaving, but that had probably stopped by the 1960s. I don't think it had anything to do with boggarts.'

Mytholmroyd 3 (WRY). ???/F/FG., 21-10-19. 'I lived in Calderdale for a great many years Mytholmroyd, Hebden and Todmorden. In my later years there I lived on the edge of a path that went past a place called Boggart Hall. I'd follow a particularly incredible pathway often with a raven overhead through a path of arching very old hawthorn and holly which had a terrible stench. Much, much magic and mystery came to me the further up that path I went. A golf course sits up to the right of the path UFO sightings have been up there for me though the walks to the left where there is a red and white spring and a gathering of many trees and shrubs walking onwards and upwards following the water course up to where it flows over a pathway. I often have walks where my mind is taken away from the now from the mundane to a different level that is very strong here the further up you go and again following the water courses. I could talk for many hours on this. But it is not really relevant to your question as I lived in the area from 1992-2018. I lived on Wellington Road walking up to the very top of it is a rusty railway bridge that leads to a field called Denis's field cross over the road in front of you and ahead is a steep stepped footpath of many, many steps take it right up to the top… Boggart is there at the top of those steps on the Right just above the Old Stansfield Hall (which has been made into flats). I cannot explain these things well for I have only walked there so I describe it as I would walk it.'

Netherton 1 (WRY). 1960s/M/FG., 14-10-19. 'Netherton 1960s, never heard of Boggarts.'

Netherton 2 (WRY). 1960s/F/FG., 14-10-19. '1960s never heard of them. Been talking to my brother about this. Were they also called Bogeymen? If so, yes. They were things to be feared.'

Netherton 3 (WRY). 1950s/F/FG., 14-10-19. 'Born 1958 – Netherton, Wakefield, never heard Boggart used in conversation.'

Netherton 4 (WRY). 1950s/F/FG., 14-10-19. 'Born in 1953 lived in Netherton until 1971. Never heard the term "Boggart".'

Netherton 5 (WRY). 1950s/F/FG., 23-10-19. 'Asked my mother who was born in Netherton in 1952. She has never heard of a boggart.'

Netherton 6 (WRY). ???/F/FG., 23-10-19. 'Never heard anything about boggart live there until getting married in 1971.'

Netherton 7 (WRY). 1960s/F/FG., 24-10-19. 'Born in Netherton 1961, grew up Sefton estate, "Bogeyman" for us too.'

Norland 1 (WRY). ???/M/FG., 17-10-19. 'Where I was born in Norland there is a Boggart Lane runs up from Sowerby Bridge to Norland. Not really. [Did family talk of boggart?] It's one of them where you wished you'd asked more questions when you were younger. It was really, yes [just a strange name].'

Oakenshaw 1 (WRY). 1950s/F/FG., 7-11-19. 'Never heard the word "boggart". It was the bogie man in the fifties I was born in Oakenshaw.'

Ogden 1 (WRY). ???/M/FG., 13-10-19. 'Bogart Lane at Ogden. Just off from the visitor centre at Ogden Water Nature Reserve. The story is bogarts come out at night to cause mischief in the woodlands.'

Ogden 2 (WRY). ???/M/FG., 14-10-19. 'There is a Boggart at Ogden, adjacent to the reservoir. The biggest bridge is by the remains of an old mill race. Until recently there was a cafe/tea room called The Boggart.'

Ogden 3 (WRY). 1960s/F/FG., 16-10-19. 'Born in early 1960s in Ogden.

Yes, Boggart a common word, used in rhymes and tales of folklore such as the Clegg Hall boggart, or which many ballads were written. The well known folk tune for Bonfire night "we come a cob coalin" the local words for this (as it changes throughout the country) used the word "Boggart" in a verse: "Down in yon cellar it is fair full of boggarts, they have eaten your stockin' and part of your shoe". It was used to scare you against going somewhere you shouldn't by your parents. The tale of the Ogden boggart seemed to come about to muster up trade for local businesses and was ridiculed by those who were born and bred many generations prior to this "new" tale gaining legs, I suppose a modern urban legend. [Other FB user added: 'The rag hole boggart, probably originating from Rag Hole Farm Ogden (now just foundations) the name was mispronounced over the years to raggle or raddle'].

Rastrick 1 (WRY). 1970s/F/FG., 16-10-19. 'I grew up in Rastrick near Brighouse. Definitely heard of and used the term. Hi, not rude at all, yep 1970s/1980s.'

Rastrick 2 (WRY). 1950s/M/FG., 17-10-19. 'My grandparents and great aunts/uncles used a fair bit of dialect but I never heard this word. The first time I came across it was as the Boggart Hole Clough Brewery when it ran the micro-pub in the Manchester Arndale Centre a few years ago. I lived in Rastrick in the 1950s and 1960s.'

Rastrick 3 (WRY). 1950s/M/FG., 18-10-19. 'When I was growing up in Rastrick in the late 1950s/early 1960s, we had a walk-in cupboard under the stairs, that we always called the boggard-'ole.'

Rossington 1 (WRY). 1940s/F/FG., 7-11-19. 'Born in late 1940s and grew up in Rossington. Bogeyman – yes. Boggart – no'.

Rossington 2 (WRY). 1950s/F/FG., 7-11-19. 'I grew up in Rossington near Doncaster in the late fifties, sixties and early seventies I have never ever heard of the Boggarts. Only one, Casablanca.'

Saddleworth 1 (WRY). 1990s/M/FG., 21-9-19. 'I grew up in the 1990s and heard the word in my house. Never understood it fully though as a child. And seemed to be the only one of my friends who ever knew it. So never looked into it fully. I'm from Saddleworth, mate. Diggle originally. But grew up in Springhead.'

Saddleworth 2 (WRY). 1970s/F/FG., 22-9-19. 'My dad regularly threatened us with the boggart in the 1970s. I likened it to the bogeyman. Similarly if we were a bit scruffy he would say "eeh, tha looks like a reet boggart." Funny thing is I knew exactly what he meant.'

Saddleworth 3 (WRY). 1950s/M/E., 8-8-19. 'I was born in 1948 and brought up in Saddleworth. During my childhood I spent a lot of time with my grandparents (b. 1880s) but I never heard them mention "boggarts" and I only learned about them by reading Ammon Wrigley. Was Ammon Wrigley's generation the last, I wonder, to have remembered these traditions from the old days of hillside farmers and domestic hand loom weavers?'

Saddleworth 4 (WRY). 1940s/M/E., 28-10-19. 'Do not know much about boggarts but here goes anyway. I was born in 1944 and have lived in Saddleworth all my life apart from three years. I remember school friends saying "the boggart will get you". Boggarts occasionally entered the conversation. My father told me that a man was on a cart at Lydgate, Saddleworth, which is at the top of a large hill. Something must have spooked the horse because "it took boggart" charged down the hill and the driver was injured.'

Scawthorpe 1 (WRY). 1960s/F/FG., 7-11-19. 'Yes. Born in 1963 Amersall Rd Scawthorpe. Terminology used when I was being disobedient 'Bogarts will be after you' like "Bogeymen". My Grandma from Watch House Lane and earlier Washington Grove Bentley used it. At the age of three we moved from Yorkshire. Definitely a phrase that older generations used.'

Selby 1 (WRY). ???/M/FG., 17-10-19. 'I come from Selby in Yorkshire. There was a bridge over a stream a mile out of town called "Boggart Bridge". There were tales of people being reluctant to cross it at night or being chased home by the Boggart.'

Sharneyford 1 (WRY). 1950s/M/E., 9-10-19. 'I grew up in the late 1950s in Sharneyford between Bacup and Todmorden. The village is little more than a semi-rural hamlet. At the time we had a cotton mill, a clay pit, a fired pipe works, two coal mines and a drop for a third mine. The farms were dairy or extensive sheep farming. By the early 1970s all the industry had gone. The boggarts were wraith like shadowy creatures. As children we were fearful of boggarts because we they lured children to their deaths. They lived in Boggart holes, dark, secret places and if children entered their lairs they would never come out alive! Living in Sharneyford with a number of accessible abandoned drift mine shafts, ventilation tunnels and quarry workings. The belief in the boggarts kept children safe in the days before health and safety made these sites safe. I certainly was not tempted, as I roamed about the moors and fields to go into old drift workings. Even in my sixties I can still feel the shadow of the Boggart around these places. Just a memory, don't know if it is relevant for your research. In my family we have an expression to describe someone running fast, or, out of breath after running, as "running at the boggart".'

Sheffield 1 (WRY). 1930s/M/E., 19-11-18. 'When I was a very small child [1935–1939, aged 0-4] we lived in what is now the suburb of Norton on the south-east side of Sheffield... When my mother was pushing me in a small pushchair along the road which led to our house on Norton Lane, she would suddenly start to walk quickly and break into a run when pushing me in the pram up a kind of arch of stone supporting the footpath, with trees overhanging the whole area. That place, called locally "Bunting Nook", was dark and gloomy… I asked her many years later why she did that, and she said she always felt afraid walking through there. She was very superstitious, and continued with superstitions inherited from her mother well into my late childhood… At least a partial answer to her fears of this location sprang out at me from Sidney Addy's *Sheffield Glossary*, which briefly describes the "Boggard of Bunting Nook".' [This was collected a year earlier than most of the memories given here.]

Sheffield 2 (WRY). 1940s/F/F., 26-9-19. 'I was born in Sheffield in 1943 and never heard any reference to this word from family members.'

Sheffield 3 (WRY). 1940s/M/FG., 27-9-19. 'I was born In Sheffield in the 1940s. Never heard of that'

Sheffield 4 (WRY). 1950s/F/FG., 26-9-19. 'Born Sheffield 1954 and sorry never heard of Boggarts.'

Sheffield 5 (WRY). 1950s/F/FG., 27-9-19. 'East end of Sheffield, 1950s and 1960s – no boggarts just bogeymen and Bobby Lick Lock would get naughty children!'

Sheffield 6 (WRY). 1950s/F/FG., 26-9-19. 'I grew up in Sheffield and I always believed there was a boggart that lived in Ecclesall woods. I was born 1958 and lived on High Storrs Road until I went to college in 1979. My Mum told me the boggart would get you if you misbehaved. I'm pretty sure all my friends heard the same story.'

Sheffield 7 (WRY). 1950s/F/FG., 26-9-19. 'When I was a Brownie Guide in Sheffield c.1960 I remember stories about the Brownies and the Boggarts. I'll email you if I can find any in my old books.'

Sheffield 8 (WRY). 1950s/M/FG., 26-9-19. 'I was born in 1957. My Sheffield family never mentioned bogarts but the term "bogey men" was often used which I think is derived from the word. Bogey men would "get you" if you went to certain places especially at night. My grandfather said as a child in Sheffield, he was told that they would grab your ankles if you stepped on cellar grates. The idea of bogey men was, and still is, generally used to frighten children into not doing dangerous things or straying too far. They haunt places where children shouldn't venture. Words are often adapted for children by putting a "y" or "ee" sound on the end. In my memory it was always said as a joke but it was still a little bit scary.'

Sheffield 9 (WRY). 1960s/M/FG., 26-9-19. 'My Dad used to say that the

Boggart will get you! [friend comments: 'And that would have been in the sixties! Did they live in those woods next to your house on Osgathorpe Road?'] Yes probably!'

Sheffield 10 (WRY). 1940s/F/FG., 27-9-19. 'I was born In Sheffield in the 1940s. Never heard of that [boggart].'

Sheffield 11 (WRY). 1960s/M/FG., 27-9-19. 'Yes... Sheffield born and bred (1964) my mum used to call me her little boggart when I was young, now she says I'm a "Hairy Boggart".'

Sheffield 12 (WRY). 1960s/M/FG., 27-9-19. 'Born in 1967. Remember the reference to the boggart monster in Rivelin Valley Woods. Scared me as a kid.'

Sheffield 13 (WRY). 1950s/F/FG., 27-9-19. 'No only bogeyman. Born Sheffield 1951.'

Sheffield 14 (WRY). 1940s/F/FG., 27-9-19. 'Born in 1949 and was always scared of the Bogyman as I was told by my Mother that he would get me. Never heard of the Boggart though and up to now have evaded the Bogyman too.'

Sheffield 15 (WRY). 1950s/F/FG., 27-9-19. 'Born in 1952. Never heard of it.'

Sheffield 16 (WRY). ???/F/E., 11-10-19. 'I don't know if this is useful but here goes: I'm not from the UK. I learned of boggarts from Susan Cooper's Young Adult novel set in Scotland which I read as a child. I live in Sheffield now, though, and there is a Boggard Lane in S6. While walking on it with my husband (thirty-five) and raised in Rotherham by Derbyshire parents. I asked if he knew about boggarts. He had never heard of them so I had to explain them to him.'

Sheffield 17 (WRY). 1950s/F/FG., 17-10-19. 'Born in 1958. Grew up in Heeley till I was seven, then Hillsborough. I've never heard of this [boggart].'

Sheffield 18 (WRY). 1940s/F/FG., 17-10-19. 'Born 1948, and lived in Gleadless until I was six. Never heard the word "boggart" there. I always thought it was Scottish to be honest. "Bogeyman" was the term my parents and grandparents used.'

Sheffield 19 (WRY). ??/F/FG., 17-10-19. 'Mother born shortly after WW1 and from just outside Sheffield referred to bogeyman, but not boggart. Partner's mother of similar age from very rural Peak Distrct Derbyshire was same. When child next door neighbour, who was born in similar area in early 1900s and moved to near Longshaw before WW1, was same too. Boggart seems to be referred to now but more in links to stories? Don't know why but a boggart to me brings up the idea of a large dog – but maybe from a story I've read.'

Sheffield 20 (WRY). 1950s/F/FG., 17-10-19. 'I'm born mid-1950s. My mother told me we had two bogey-men living in our house. In the cellar was Rammy Sammy, in the clothes closet lived Horace. I'd pictured Horace as a big man with swirling black cape and tall black top hat. My mother wished she'd kept her mouth shut when the panto villain called Horace appeared on stage dressed in black cloak and top-hat. I was aged three and screamed the theatre down. She apparently told me about the bogey-men so I wouldn't venture into said places unaccompanied as both were fraught with danger for a toddler. I just think she enjoyed scaring me to death with made up stories. On the positive side I think that's why I'm a writer!... Funny how I always write a happy ending?!'

Sheffield 21 (WRY). 1950s/M/FG., 17-10-19. 'I grew up in Sheffield in the 1950s, like XXX, I often heard the phrase "bogey-man", but not "boggart". I don't think I remember hearing of boggarts until possibly the 1970s.'

Sheffield 22 (WRY). 1960s/M/FG., 17-10-19. 'My husband and his mates used to go boggart hunting in Millhouses Park in the 1960s when they were at Abbeydale Boys School. He can't remember why!'

Sheffield 23 (WRY). 1970s/F/FG., 17-10-19. 'A boggart is a little shape shifter that changes shapes in the garden to eat the birds according to my other half. We always believed when we were kids, in the 1970s, that they lived in the ponds around Beauchief Abbey.'

Sheffield 24 (WRY). ???/M/E., 21-10-19. 'Our local boggart is at Bunting Nook in Norton, Sheffield. We have seen orbs there. I am a military historian and my wife a scientist. I'm from Sheffield.'

Shipley 1 (WRY). 1950s/F/F., 13-9-19. 'Always used the word "boggart", and still do. Friend also knew the word, something nasty that will get you! Baildon, 1950s, friend Shipley 1970s.' [This is a duplication of Baildon 1 (WRY)]

Shipley 2 (WRY). 1950s/M/FG., 7-11-19. 'The bogeyman will take you away if you don't behave. He'll put you in the bogeyhole where it's dark and cold. Shipley, Bradford 1950s. Maybe dialect changed "boggart" into "bogeyman".'

Siddal 1 (WRY). 1940s/M/F., 14-9-19. 'In our village we have a lane called Boggart Lane. Norland village heading down towards Sowerby Bridge. My hubby used to recite an old Yorkshire poem called "At' a' the'ere' Boggart?" meaning "Are you there Boggart?" I can't remember how it went now, does anyone else remember it? My hubby has said he can't remember it either but it was a poem/story his mum told him at bedtime. I've just asked him and he says he can't remember now all he remembers is the line "Atta' thee're

Boggart" in broad Yorkshire was said often throughout. No he didn't grow up in Norland his mother used to tell him this story when he was tiny in a village called Siddal near Halifax about two to three miles away from Norland. The words "Aatta thee're Boggart?" is the only bit of it he remembers. He emigrated to Canada when he was five and came back 1960 and moved into Norland where he found he lived close to Boggart Lane. When I met him every time we passed the Boggart Lane sign he would say "Att'a thee're Boggart?" It was always said in broad Yorkshire, so I think it must be something that was handed down. I tried to look myself last night as I Googled it but nothing fitted as the words were repeated several times. [Husband born in 1947, wife writes].'

Skellow 1 (WRY). F/1950s/FG., 7-11-19. 'I grew up in the 1950s and 1960s in Skellow Doncaster and have never heard this term used.'

Slaithwaite 1 (WRY). ???/M/FG., 18-10-19. 'My father used to say to me, "sit still you're up and down like a Boggat" so that must be what they (Boggats) do. 50/50 West Slawit.'

Slaithwaite 2 (WRY). ???/F/FG., 18-10-19. 'I grew up at Pole Moor by the masts and the track just below the school at Wilberlee going towards Merrydale was known as Boggart Lane. I always ran past so the Boggart couldn't get me! [Other Facebook user: 'yes that's right XXX, never liked walking past Boggart Lane in the dark on way up Heys, back in the day'.] As far as I know a Boggart is half badger and half fox! [Another Facebook user: The one just down from Wilberlee School!]'

Slaithwaite 3 (WRY). 1960s/F/FG., 18-10-19. 'I remember a Bogart being something/someone to avoid, someone tramp like, or a trickster. Slawit born and bred 1960s probably. Yes and I have Marsden descendants. Heard it a few times from my mum, or dad. It's only a vague memory now in a sentence. "He's a bit of a Bogart, better be on our toes".'

Slaithwaite 4 (WRY). 1950s/F/FG., 18-10-19. 'Some person/animal to be avoided at all costs. Slaithwaite born 1950s.'

Sowerby Bridge 1 (WRY). 1940s/F/FG., 18-10-19. 'I grew up in the Sowerby Bridge area in mid-1940s. Moved to Luddenden when married sixty-three years ago. When I first came here I was told that many of the woodland around here, quite a lot then was frequently visited by Oliver Cromwell to practice boar hunting. A house on the opposite hillside to our house was where he stayed and was called Boggard House. Sorry I don't know its name now and it would be somewhere between Sowerby and Mytholmroyd.'

Sough 1 (WRY). 1920s/F/FG., 7-10-19. 'I asked my mum she lived in Sough and Earby all her life born 1929. She has not heard of the term "Boggart"! Thanks.'

Southowram 1 (WRY). 1970s/F/FG., 14-10-19. 'Hi, house called Bogart House in Southowram, where I grew up in the 1970/80s. We used to run past it as we thought a bogart would come and chase us. I remember there was a skull in the window.'

Springhead 1 (WRY). 1950s/M/FG., 22-9-19. 'I would saying most kids in Springhead, Grotton and Lydgate in the 1950s knew what a boggart was. I don't remember any stories but recall at a young age, hearing of Boggart Hole Clough and wondering why a boggart would bother living in a hole.'

Springhead 2 (WRY). 1950s/M/FG., 22-9-19. 'My husband was born 1952, he lived in Springhead and so did his great, great aunts (the two sisters lived together). He was always told "Don't go over the 'Goatie' coz the Boggarts will get you". The Goatie is Ashbrook Valley, Springhead/Grotton/Less, farmers used to graze their goats there!'

Springhead 3 (WRY). 1980s/F/FG., 22-9-19. 'Our grandparents regularly told us boggart stories growing up in the 1980s. We know all kinds of boggarts! Springhead and Mossley.'

Stainforth 1 (WRY). ???/F/FG., 7-11-19. 'Little people lived in the bog also called bogtrotters. I'm a carer and gentleman from Stainforth said this what it is also word used if you saw a ghost on moors.'

Stocksbridge 1 (WRY). 1960s/F/FG., 27-9-19. 'Like XXX, above, I'd never heard the word [boggart] until I saw Boggard or Boggart Lane at Wadsley. (I'm from Stocksbridge).'

Sutton in Craven 1 (WRY). ???/F/FG., 7-10-19. 'I had a West Riding step great aunt from Sutton in Craven. She was a lovely Victorian lady. When she admonished me as a boy with a wave of her fist she would cry, "tanty boggarts al get thee".'

Swallownest 1 (WRY). 1950s/F/FG., 13-10-19. 'I grew up in Swallownest in the 1950s/1960s. I never heard the word "Boggarts" but remember Bogey man, if you went out in the dark or into a dark place, adults would say "the Bogey man will get you".'

Swallownest 2 (WRY). 1950s/F/FG., 13-10-19. 'We were told the bogey man would get us, I think they are probably the same thing. I grew up in Swallownest.'

Swallownest 3 (WRY). 1940s/F/FG., 13-10-19. 'I remember being told about the bogey man too. Although I can't remember the word "Boggarts". I was born in the late 1940s and grew up in Swallownest.'

Swallownest 4 (WRY). 1950s/F/FG., 13-10-19. 'I grew up in the 1950s in Swallownest, not heard of boggarts. Bogey man yes.'

Swallownest 5 (WRY). 1950s/F/FG., 16-10-19. 'Yes it was the bogey man, never heard boggarts. Grew up Aston/Swallownest 1950s.'

Tankersley 1 (WRY). 1940s/F/FG., 7-11-19. 'I was born in 1942. I never heard that word in Tankersley.'
Thackley 1 (WRY). 1950s/F/FG., 7-11-19. 'Born in the 1950s, Thackley. Other older people also used this expression, as I remember.'
Todmorden 1 (WRY). 1940s/M/FGH., 13-10-19. 'Born and brought up in Todmorden, dating from the 1940s! I do not recall ever hearing the word "boggart" used in Todmorden – until quite recently.'
Todmorden 2 (WRY). 1980s/M/FGH., 13-10-19. 'There are believed to be red haired boggarts up at Bungle's Mound, near Whirlaw in Todmorden. There used to be a rhyme that would get sung when I was little. 'Beware, beware the boggarts of Bungle's Mound/Red hair, red hair the boggarts of Bungle's Mound' [XXX adds: 'I remember this'.] It was when I was little so would have been the early to mid-1980s, though I'm guessing the rhyme is older.'
Todmorden 3 (WRY). 1940s/M/FGH., 13-10-19. 'I grew up in fifties and sixties whenever I set in a hurry my father would say I was off at boggled [*sic*]. Never any explanation of what a boggled was. The whole family was Todmorden born for about three generations.'
Todmorden 4 (WRY). 1940s/F/FGH., 13-10-19. 'I have lived in Todmorden all my life and naughty children were referred to as little boggarts in the forties and fifties.'
Todmorden 5 (WRY). 1980s/M/FGH., 14-10-19. 'When I was little, thirty years ago! there were always childhood rumours about them living in Bungle's Mound. I remember heading up there once. I was terrified of seeing one but, you know what, I never did.'
Todmorden 6 (WRY). ???/M/FGH., 14-10-19. 'I've recently heard that an old name for Whirlaw (the flat topped hill above Todmorden) was Bungle's Mound and there was a rhyme about the boggarts of Bungle's Mound. Having said that, nobody I know has ever heard of being called anything over than Whirlaw.'
Todmorden 7 (WRY). 1960s/M/FGH., 14-10-19. 'My friend XXX heard about them as a child in Todmorden, the early 1960s and they inhabited graveyards and they were horrible.'
Todmorden 8 (WRY). 1950s/F/FGH., 14-10-19. 'Grew up in Todmorden on the hillside of Higher Eastwood. My Dad had a phrase "going off like a boggart" who I knew as a sort of bogey man. I was born in 1952.'
Todmorden 9 (WRY). 1990s/M/FGH., 14-10-19. 'I heard the word growing up in the 1990s. One kid said to another kid "you look like a boggart" and we all said "what's a boggart?" to which he responded "No idea but he

looks like one". And it was true, this kid did somehow look like a boggart and the nickname stuck.'

Todmorden 10 (WRY). 1970s/F/FGH., 14-10-19. 'Kids' stuff really but I do remember a story about the white lady being seen near the monument. I think she belonged to a big house in the grounds. There were theories of her being murdered and dying of a broken heart so I don't really know what's true. We were told as kids if you stayed in the park late you would see the boggart but I never stayed long enough to find out, LOL. You'll probably find more info on Google. Late 1970s 1980s.'

Treeton 1 (WRY). 1960s/F/FG., 13-10-19. 'From Treeton, born in 1968, never heard of boggarts at all.'

Undercliffe 1 (WRY). 1950s/F/FG., 17-10-19. 'I grew up in Undercliffe in the 1950s, 1960s and didn't hear the word [boggart] locally, but my grandparents in Durham used it.'

Uppermill 1 (WRY). 1960s/F/FG., 22-9-19. 'I'm from Uppermill and the term was never used. But we were warned of a similar sounding being, "The Bogeyman". Good luck with your work.'

Uppermill 2 (WRY). 1960s/M/FG., 18-10-19. I'm very much on your page with this. I even believe I saw a beggar [*sic*] once up Pots and Pans. I live in Uppermill, was born in 1968 and am very Faery. My friend showed me your article in the newspaper saying it was right up my street so I am glad you have brought it to Facebook. When I worked away I believed the faeries were cleaning my flat but I know boggats can be a real nuisance. I've done a few odd things in my time on line with Faery belief and often go walking and looking around. I XXX tell many people though through them believing me completely mad.'

Wakefield 1 (WRY). ???/M/FG., 17-10-19. 'Not a memory but there were tales of a boggart that lived in a well in the grounds of Alverthorpe Hall where Flanshaw junior and infants school now stands. I don't know much more than that about it other than it was said to wander the grounds of the old hall.'

Wakefield 2 (WRY). 1950s/M/FG., 17-10-19. 'I grew up in the late 1950s and early 1960s. My grandfather used to tell me stories about a boggart that haunted the fields off Dewsbury Road in Wakefield, around the Flanshaw area. He said it was like a huge dog that had eyes the size of dinner plates. Within the last few years I heard about a Boggart haunting Kirkburton churchyard.'

Wakefield 3 (WRY). 1950s/F/FG., 17-10-19. 'I was born in Wakefield in 1950 and lived there for twenty-three years. "Boggart" was a word I had not heard of until recent years.'

Wakefield 4 (WRY). 1950s/M/FG., 17-10-19. 'Not a word I have ever heard. Born 1953 and left Wakefield in 1970s.'

Wakefield 5 (WRY). ???/M/FG., 18-10-19. 'Growing up in Wakefield (Portobello) we were made aware of a lunatic called Chip Harry who would hide in Many Gates Park or the unexcavated Sandal Castle, having heard lots of tales of his deeds we were scared shitless as night fell, we never saw him though.'

Wakefield 6 (WRY). ???/M/FG., 18-10-19. 'I grew upon Alverthorpe and I'm sure my parents wouldn't have told me tales about a ghost dog but somehow I knew about the Alverthorpe bogart. Sure, I confirmed it in Walker's *History of Wakefield*.'

Wakefield 7 (WRY). 1950s/M/FG., 18-10-19. 'I grew up on Keswick Drive born 1951 and moved away 1971. Not heard the term [boggart], then again my dad came from the Workington area and settled in Wakefield 1946/1947.'

Wakefield 8 (WRY). 1950s/M/FG., 18-10-19. 'Brought up in the Sandal and Portobello area. Never heard of "boggarts" – the term 'Bogeyman' was used, often as a threat. 1950s and early 1960s.'

Wakefield 9 (WRY). 1920s/F/FG., 7-11-19. 'My mum always refered to boggats as a bad person/thing. She was born in the 1920s near Wakefield.

Walsden 1 (WRY). 1890s/M/FG., 18-10-19. 'My grandmother was born 1897. She used the name "beggart" for me in the 1950s. She lived in Walsden. I thought everyone knew what bogarts were. I always thought of them being like elves. When I was a child if I was pestering my grandmother she told me I was worse then't bogarts. I asked what bogarts were and she said they were little people who played tricks on people and did mischief like turning milk sour. No one ever saw them.'

Wigglesworth 1 (WRY). 1960s/F/F., 7-9-19. 'My mother grew up in the Coal Clough Lane area of Burnley. She left home in 1933 to go over the border into Yorkshire to Wigglesworth. I was brought up around there and my godmother's family in Wigglesworth had a barn now demolished situated by the road side from Wigglesworth to Long Preston and that was called Boggart's Barn. My godmother and her sister weren't keen on going into that barn which they had to especially at hay time. The farm men had to go in the rest of the year to see to the cattle housed in there in winter etc. and they wouldn't let me go in at all. Said there was a mischievous sprite in there. They wouldn't say anything else. No not really. We used to visit my great great aunts on my mothers' side when I was little, before 1956. Their houses in Buck Street was demolished years ago [just off Coal Clough Lane.] They were staunch Catholics and had all sorts of religious pictures and ornaments.

Some of those pictures frightened me. But never heard them tell of any scary events. but there again they wouldn't in front of us children One of my great aunts on my mothers' paternal side married into the XXX family from Rough Lee. Apparently, he was a preacher at Gallows Top. So nothing there. And my brother helped to pull down what had been Dame Demdykes house near Blacko in the 1960s. Early 1970s. I don't know how he got to do that job or if there was anything. though I have read since of a mummified cat found there somewhere. But he never said anything about that. I must ask him and find out all about it. My ex sister in law lives in Burnley I'll ask her if she knows anything. Shame you are not asking about here in Keighley. The odd things that happened on night duty and at the old hospital in Keighley that I trained at and how we dreaded a full moon. And the ghost I saw in Haworth of someone I knew well. Mind I used to get "feelings" of something sinister at other places I knew well as a child. Ah well. Will get in touch with my sister-in-law and ask her if she knows of anything.'

Woodhouse 1 (WRY). ???/M/FG., 13-10-19. 'Brought up in Woodhouse. I remember the phrase "Hunt the Boggitt" used in my childhood. Not sure but I think it may have been related to asking for trouble.'

Woodhouse 2 (WRY). ???/F/FG., 13-10-19. 'Don't think I have heard of Boggarts. I was born on Falconer Lane and grew up with family from Fence and Woodhouse Mill.'

Woodlands 1 (WRY).1950s/F/FG., 7-11-19. 'Born in 1951 and lived in Woodlands Doncaster since 1953 and I have never heard the word "bogart".'

Wyke 1 (WRY). 1940s/F/FG., 7-11-19. 'Lived in Wyke from 1947 never heard that name!'

Yeadon 1 (WRY). ???/F/FG., 14-10-19. 'There's a dirt track known locally as Boggart Lane from end of Swaine Hill Terrace off Kirk Lane Yeadon which cuts through to Queensway along the bottom of Kirk Lane Park. I grew up round there and that track was always called "Boggart Lane". I don't remember if there were any stories, but that Lane was spooky as hell and you didn't want to warm [*sic*, walk?] there alone.'

Cheshire

Bredbury 1 (Ch). 1950s/F/FG., 18-10-19. 'I'm sure I'd heard of boggarts where I grew up in north-east Cheshire. At least the word was not unfamiliar to me when I moved here. As I left Cheshire when I was seven, and neither of my parents is alive, I can neither remember the context, nor ask them. I don't remember any references to boggarts in either Staffordshire or Buckinghamshire. I'm from Bredbury, just down the road from Hyde, and 1950s. I've asked my cousin's daughter, who lives there, but she's too young I suspect to have been warned of boggarts. I'll try asking her grandfather (my uncle) as he's far more likely to have been told of them by his grandparents.'

Edgeley 1 (Ch). 1930s/F/FG., 28-9-19. 'If you were naughty in the brownies (Edgeley) then you could be called a "boggart"! We felt ashamed to be called a boggart so we tried to be good and please the Brown Owl at all the meetings! I was a brownie in the early 1940s at St. Marks Church, Berlin Road Edgeley. I hadn't heard the word until I was a member of the pack and then found it was used by the Brown Owl to describe someone who was persistently naughty and didn't conform to the ideals that were instilled in us, i.e. loyalty, helpfulness, kindness etc. There is a road in Seacroft, Leeds called Boggart Hill road also!'

Hazel Grove 1 (Ch). 1960s/M/FG., 6-10-19. 'I'm in my sixties now and was brought up in Hazel Grove to parents from Leigh and Walkden in Lancashire. The main reason boggarts cropped up in conversation was if someone or something started behaving madly or irrationally. If the cat started racing round the walls or the washing machine was dancing about the kitchen floor, the verdict would be: "It's took boggarts!" i.e. he, she or it had been possessed by evil spirits.'

Hazel Grove 2 (Ch). 1950s/M/FG., 9-10-19. 'My hubby, born 1951, grew up in Hazel Grove. He knows of Boggarts but thinks of them being like trolls who live under bridges!'

Hazel Grove 3 (Ch). 1950s/M/FG., 17-10-19. '1950s never heard it said, Hazel Grove'.

Hazel Grove 4 (Ch). 1970s/F/FG., 18-10-19. 'I was born in 1971. I've got a vague recollection that this was why we had a horseshoe on the outside door. To keep the spirits away. Have you tried Blackley area in Manchester. I used to work near Boggart Clough. Must have been talked about around there. Good luck.'

Hazel Grove 5 (Ch). 1970s/F/FG., 21-10-19. 'I grew up knowing what a boggart was but not sure how/why I know. I went to the Brownies in the early 1970s in Hazel Grove. My six was the "gnomes" but [I] seem to remember the whole brownie thing was based on a boggart story. Maybe that was when I first heard it. My Parents are Mancunians and my dad's lot lived in North Manchester so maybe I heard it because of Boggart Hole Clough.'

Hyde 1 (Ch). 1970s/F/FG., 6-10-19. 'Hyde, 1970s never heard of them'.

Hyde 2 (Ch). 1970s/M/FG., 7-10-19. 'I seem to remember to watch out for the bogart in Bears Woods. My uncle XXX used to hunt rabbits and say "if the boggarts are about you've no chance". That was the 1970s and it was Hyde.'

Hyde 3 (Ch). 1950s/F/FG., 7-10-19. 'Born in Hyde 1951, never heard the word used.'

Hyde 4 (Ch). 1940s/F/FG., 7-10-19. 'Born in Hyde 1947. Never heard the word "Boggart". Mostly the Bogey Man. I think boggerts were mostly associated in Lancashire with Boggert Hole Clough.'

Hyde 5 (Ch). 1940s/F/FG., 7-10-19. 'Born in Hyde 1947 never heard the word "Boggart".'

Hyde 6 (Ch). 1940s/F/FG., 7-10-19. 'Born Hyde late 1940s. Although I knew the word it wasn't ever used where we lived.'

Hyde 7 (Ch). 1950s/M/FG., 7-10-19. 'Grew up in Hyde in the 1950s and only ever heard the phrase 'the bogey man will get you'.'

Hyde 8 (Ch). 1950s/F/E., 9-10-19. 'Have just read through your post in "Hyde Memories". I was born in Hyde in 1951 and grew up in Hyde and never heard the word "Boggart", as previous posts have stated, it was mainly bogey men. In the late 1960s and early 1970s I used to go to folk nights and followed the folk band from Oldham called the Oldham Tinkers. They mention Boggarts in some of their songs such as "Come Whoam to Thi Childer An' Me", which is a poem written by Edwin Waugh. One of their songs in particular is called "The Crime Lake Boggart". If you just type it into a search engine you find the song and more info. Crime Lake is in the Daisy Nook area between Ashton-under-Lyne and Oldham. I think someone has already stated there is a "Boggart Hole Clough".'

Hyde 9 (Ch). 1950s/M/FG., 7-10-19. 'Born 1952. In Gee Cross in my youth there was the story of the Boggart on the Low. It was supposed to be a Huge Black Dog around Cowlishaw. Aunty XXX was the source. As a teen I heard similar about Pipers Clough up to the Cenotaph. [FB user chips in: I heard it said about a huge dog on the Low but never heard it referred to as the boggart.] I knew about the Bogey man, but XXX definitely told me about the Boggart of the Low. Maybe she made it up? But then I also remember as a Scout (a very short duration), when we went on a night excursion to Pipers

Clough on the Low, being warned of “the boggart”. Again maybe the scout leader was from out of the area. I have no idea.’

Knutsford 1 (Ch). 1970s/F/FG., 29-9-19. ‘Hi. I was interested in your post. Not exactly what you are looking for, but I grew up on the dark edge of the heath and bogey men were known to live in the marshy heath! The heath certainly has a funny quality and it wasn’t somewhere to go at night alone. I am asking a few friends if they have any info too. Several of us worked in The Lord Eldon so there may be some boggart stories from there as it’s a very old pub with a lot of tales and encounters. It might be worth you contacting the Knutsford Heritage Centre. There used to be a local historian called Joan Leach. She has now passed away but the Heritage Centre may well have access to her notes and there may be something there. I’ll let you know if any friends have stories related to this. Best of luck with the research. Of course I’m happy for this to be included. I am very interested in folklore and sightings too, although this isn’t a sighting. I grew up on the very edge of the heath. I was born. In 1975 and I lived in that location from 1980 until leaving that area at seventeen. My family still live there. My parents talked about bogey men or the bogey man. My Dad is from Runcorn and his family have various phrases and words that I don’t hear where I live in the south now near Glastonbury so I expect the bogey man is from his side rather than my Welsh Mum’s side. My Mum has a lot of fairy stories in her family which are more ethereal whereas this is a more solid earthy feeling character if that makes sense! It does feel a very northern being to me in comparison to the stories I hear in the south or in Wales. The bogeyman for my sister and I growing up was and still is in my imagination a dark shadowy man in a long coat or cloak/ cape who lives in the marshy bits of the heath and was particularly an autumn and winter character who would be doing his thing in the mists. The heath still has some kind of force feeling around it that it’s a place of another realm at night and particularly in autumn or when it’s cool and misty. I still wouldn’t walk across there at night alone which I can probably trace back to this bogey man story. I’ve walked alone at night all over the world now but this is still a no go. But of course the images of childhood imagination are carried through life for many so it’s not unusual that this being has a power. You could also try putting an article in the local newspaper which because its a very small town is well read by many. It’s called *The Knutsford Guardian*. I’d be very interested to hear other stories about this so if it’s possible please could you let me know when the article or book comes out. Thankyou I’ve thought to that there are a few other places nearby it might be worth putting feelers out into… Mobberly, Lindow near Wilmslow, Alderley Edge.’

Macclesfield 1 (Ch). 1960s/F/E., 2-9-19. 'I may be slightly out of your boggart area, as I was born in Macclesfield – it's hard to tell from the map. My mother is from Salford but my late father was well out of the area because he was from Guildford. Anyway, in case this is useful… Boggart: an unspecified, but mildly malevolent, supernatural being that might be hiding under beds or in cupboards or coals-sheds. I think my mother might have done [used the word], and my Salford grandmother certainly did, though usually in the "Don't be silly, there are no boggarts in the shed" kind of way – she was a ferocious rationalist. I never knew my maternal grandfather, who was in any case a Londoner of Irish extraction (he moved to Salford to join the police, being too short for the Met). My paternal grandparents were Welsh and French and I can't recall either mentioning the subject. I'm sure both my children know what a boggart is from general knowledge, and in the case of my older one from an enthusiasm for folklore (he used to ask to be read *The Golden Bough* at bedtime), but I think their knowledge is entirely indirect, from books. My niece ditto. [Did you know any stories about boggarts or places especially associated with boggarts?] Apart from boggarts being the things that were definitely *not* hiding in the coal shed, I suspect only via fiction, from Andrew Lang to Alan Garner (a family friend). The main place I associated with boggarts was, accordingly, Alderley Edge. [Where did you grow up and in what decade?] Macclesfield until I went to university, and I was born in 1958.'

Marple 1 (Ch). 1950s/F/FG., 8-9-19. 'I think that boggarts were mentioned when I was at Brownies in around 1964-1966. This was the Marple area. I am sure that they were mentioned in a song that was sung in a circle, and the point was that they were enemies and we joined together to banish them. Hope that helps!'

Marple 2 (Ch). 1950s/F/FG., 10-10-19. 'A Boggart lived in my grandma's cellar on the ridge Marple… 1950s.'

Marple Bridge 1 (Ch). 1950s/F/FG., 11-10-19. 'I grew up in Marple Bridge my mum used to call ghosts "boggarts". She came from Stockport oh this was in the 1960s. I was born 1957. Just a few more memories: mum used to call me a "boggart" if I wouldn't keep still. On asking what a boggart was I was told it was a Lancashire ghost.'

Mottram 1 (Ch). 1950s/M/FG., 10-10-19. 'My husband grew up in Mottram in the 1950s, and his father used to say that he would believe in boggarts when he saw some "boggart biz"!'

Rixton-with-Glazebrook 1 (Ch). 1960s/F/FG., 27-9-19. 'I grew up in Glazebrook in the 1960s. My Mum would use the phrase of people who see boggarts where there aren't any, i.e. people who see a problem when there isn't one. Mum was originally from Shropshire (just in case it was a phrase imported from there) although was in Glazebrook from late 1950s.'

Stockport 1 (Ch). 1950s/M/C., mid-August 19. Didn't know the word.

Stockport 2 (Ch). ???/M/FG., 28-9-19. 'I grew up in Stockport, but the only time I've heard someone use the word "boggart" was an older family friend who was originally from near Preston.'

Stockport 3 (Ch). ???/M/FG., 28-9-19. 'As a kid was told about the bogey man, as a short form, he lived in Bogart Hole Clough. It was just the bogey man will come and get you, if you're bad, as a teen was told by someone in Moston, that he lived at Bogart Hole Clough. So it was obviously just one of those stories but known in Stockport and north Manchester.'

Stockport 4 (Ch). 1950s/M/FG., 28-9-19. 'My Granny use to describe our cat as "Having the boggars [*sic*]" if it ran around in a seemingly demented manner. 1950s and 1960s and earlier. I was brought up in Stockport in the 1950s and 1960s. My mother was born in Macclesfield, so I assume my Gran lived there in the early part of the century.'

Stockport 5 (Ch). ???/M/FG., 28-9-19. 'We have heard the word "BOGGART" IT'S SOMETHING THAT COMES UP FROM A BOG (a peat or marsh not toilet bog). A sinister blob that can SHAPE SHIFT INTO ANYTHING. My wife told me that she heard the term years ago If you go on GOOGLE SEARCH and type BOGGART IT WILL SHOW PHOTOS OF BOGGARTS.'

Stockport 6 (Ch). 1950s/F/FG., 30-9-19. 'Born Stockport 1953, at three moved to New Mills, never heard the word. Then. Know it now from books.'

Stockport 7 (Ch). 1930s/F/FG., 30-9-19. 'Born Stockport 1932, never heard the word but knew it from reading books. Actually, knew Boggart Hole Clough too as a placename. I'm sorry I really don't remember or the context either but I didn't know the actual meaning of the word, just a word I had come across. Maybe just as Boggart Hole Clough.'

Stockport 8 (Ch). 1920s/M/FG., 2-10-19. 'Boggart can mean anything that is awkward or difficult to handle. 1940s to present day among the "older end" rarely used by me because young ones wouldn't know the word. I think Boggart is close enough to B*gg*r. When used in family conversation. "That little Boggart has been at it again." Yes I am Stockport born and bred Yates St. by St. Paul's Portwood. 1929 to 1941 then Sth. Reddish and Heaton Chapel, Bredbury. Short stay on Lancashire Hill, Then High Lane and now in Hazel Grove since 1977. (I can never be a Grover though even if I have lived here all those years).'

Stockport 9 (Ch). 1950s/F/FG., 2-10-19. 'I lived in Woodley, Stockport during the 1950s and early 1960s. There were supposed to be boggarts in the canal long tunnel that started opposite the Navigation pub. As our garden was at the other end of the tunnel. I never worried because I didn't find it threatening. I also remember Boggart Hole Clough.'

Stockport 10 (Ch). 1950s/M/FG., 11-10-19. 'I would like an Irish input on that one [i.e. boggart], I suspect it may have come from that area, but would like a more informed opinion than mine. There ought to be references on a decent Search Engine to get an accurate view of that. I much preferred it in days gone by, when we were able to speak to someone who knew a bit about a subject, but was usually able to put one in touch with real experts. We had a cellar below our house when I was a youngster, the coal hole of course. No electric lighting down there, th'eld fella (He was in his twenties) was away at WW2 so no chance of improving the place until 1945. So candles were often used to light the way when the coal bucket needed filling. With candles you get black mobile shadows, no need to worry about an imaginary "Black Dog" (e.g. Winston Churchill). When you are around eight years of age, those shadows are real enough. The Bogey man was very real, especially if you have adults around you that suffered in a similar manner when they were kids. Bogey may be a regional variation of Boggart. [Someone else answers: we had torches in the 1950s and make shadows on the wall my dad it was the bogeyman and if my brothers and I were bad the bogeyman would get us, needless to say we were good and out went the torch]'

Stockport 11 (Ch). 1950s/F/FG., 6-10-19. 'I remember hearing "boggart" when a kid. It was a nasty entity that used to hide in the woods and get you. What it did after that I was too scared to ask!'

Wirral 1 (Ch). 1950s/F/F., 29-8-19. 'Back in the late 1950s, early 1960s my uncle decided to fill in a pond on his land on the Wirral. He had been offered a considerable sum from a builder to dump spoil from a nearby development, easy money! The pit/pond was said to be fathomless and the home of a "buggan", a local name for a boggart. My great-uncle warned him that no good would come of it but he had already spent the money many times over in his mind so it went ahead. The pond was not fathomless but it took all the spoil from the builder leaving a slight mound. Needless to say my uncle did suffer misfortune, to such an extent that he was forced to sell up not long after! It was over fifty years ago now and the land has changed hands many times. None of the other owners suffered any misfortune and now it has a shelter for llamas on it and they all appear healthy and happy! Thank you though for your kind thoughts about my uncle.'

Derbyshire

Barrow Hill 1 (De). 1940s/F/FG., 12-10-19. 'I was born and brought up in Barrow Hill and worked there had my children there, was in the brownies at there. Remember my friend and I were naughty and were sent out and were told we were "boggarts" so I guess it means naughty. I was born in Barrow Hill 1942 so it would be the late 1940s, 1950s. I am now seventy-seven years and I remember it well. My friend and I still talk about when [we] were made Hogwarts long time ago. XXX here have been in touch with my friend and yes we think it is folklore. [We] were in the brownies and were naughty so were made boggarts and could not go into the fairy ring. We went out and bought chips. Hope that this helps you.'

Barrow Hill 2 (De). 1940s/F/FG., 12-10-19. 'Never heard of them in my time at Barrow Hill from two to eighteen years old. 1940s, 1950s, 1960s.'

Buxton 1 (De). 1960s/M/FG., 16-10-19. 'I was born 1961 in Fairfield Buxton and never heard the word said. Still live there now.'

Buxworth 1 (De). 1960s/F/FG., 29-9-19. 'Locals in Bugsworth, near Chinley, now named Buxworth used to say: 'now then, surree, ast put boggart into boggart 'ole'. Translation: have you put the car in the garage! I imagine "boggart" meant car! Yes, 1962 to 67…'

Chesterfield 1 (De). 1950s/F/FG., 13-10-19. 'Although I come from north Derbyshire the first time I met boggarts (as a teacher) was in Scotland. Chesterfield, 1950s.'

Chisworth 1 (De). 1950s/F/FG., 6-10-19. 'Chisworth, 1950s heard of them [boggarts]. Nan used to tell us not to go in the woods on our own because of them and mum used to say there was one under the bridge.'

Cresswell 1 (De). 1980s/M/FM., 28-9-19. 'There was meant to be a boggart around where I grew up. It's north east Derbyshire rather than Glossop. But we were kids of the 1980s and knew about it – pretty sure me and my mates saw it once but we didn't hang around. Never shit myself so much. It was on the now called linear walk between Clowne and Cresswell villages in Derbyshire. My friend owned the farm at the end of the walk and we lived just around the corner from Hollin Hill. Think it was called Markham Grips back then. We used to walk over to my friends often after dark. We were told the stories of a boggart and if to see something then run. It was a white/blueish light. The national grid runs over the walk so you always used to hear noises, but we used to be always wary of lights on the track as there were non manmade. Would say maybe three or four times we believed we saw something. But it was thirty plus years ago. Just remember it being in the middle of the track in front of us then disappeared and then behind us. At this point [we] just ran for it. That was one occasion others we would see something in the middle of the fields at the side of the tracks. Tracks as it was an old disused train track ripped up. It's [boggarts] what our parents called them. When we told them what they were. Does it make a difference, my parents are from Sheffield and hers was from Ireland?'

Glossop 1 (De). ???/F/FG., 28-9-19. 'Simmondley school did a field trip looking for boggarts a few years ago and the children did a project on them, maybe ten years ago!'

Glossop 2 (De). 1970s/F/FG., 28-9-19. 'I've heard of "boggarts" (only recently) and was told they worked or could be found at the Printworks at Dinting Vale in Glossop.... Sorry you did mention the year. I have lived in Hadfield since 1972 and up until last year had never heard the name "boggarts".'

Glossop 3 (De). 1970s/M/FG., 10-10-19. 'In the 1970s a lady working at my husband's company in Glossop used to call him a Romiley Boggart!'

Glossopdale 1 (De). 1940s/M/FG., 17-10-19. 'There are lots of boggarts in this area of Glossop. My Parents and Grandparents warned me about the Boggart coming if I was naughty.'

Grindleford 1 (De). 1960s/F/FG., 16-10-19. 'I am from Derbyshire and we sang a song in school about a railway boggart, who used to clank chains and had lots of fun on railway trains.'

Hayfield 1 (De). 1950s/F/FG., 9-10-19. 'I'm originally from Hayfield in Derbyshire. Born in the 1950s. I have definitely heard of boggarts and thought of them as being evil and/or ghostly. I seem to recall, as young children, we used to call the road to Rowarth "Boggart Road" (it's actually Shiloh Road) as I was told it, and Shiloh Farm, were haunted. Mind you, that could have been my "big brothers" trying to frighten me! They also used to threaten me with the "bogeyman". Does anyone else have any recollections of calling Shiloh Road (the road down from the top of Mellor towards Rowarth) Boggart Road? Somewhere in the back of my mind we used to call it that because it was known to be haunted along there. Or, is my mind playing tricks? I'm going back over fifty years. [FB user wrote: the back lane going to the cross at Mellor is called Boggard Road] Ah, yes, so I see. That must be where I've got it from. Thank you for putting my mind at rest. Shiloh Road is opposite the end of Bogguard Road. So many different spellings though!'

Hayfield 2 (De). 1970s/M/FG., 12-10-19. 'I grew up in the 1970s in Hayfield and would call Highgate Hall the Boggart House by default and still do. Heard lots of older people referring to it as such. We (I) knew it as haunted more generally. It was only later that I looked up the word "boggart". I often visited a friend who lived practically next door. We never liked that stretch from Holly House to the Hallam's farm with Highgate Hall in the middle. I believe a good number of horses have spooked on this section.'

Hayfield 3 (De). 1960s/F/FG., 12-10-19. 'Our family also lived at Highgate Farm (1966 to 1976) and next door (Highgate Hall) was still known as Boggart House. I believe the story was that a peddler was murdered there by two sisters and he haunted the place. XXX was our postie and she said she would never walk up our road at night for fear of meeting it! I have to say it was a bit eerie at times up there, especially when the mists were swirling.'

Hayfield 4 (De). 1950s/F/FG., 12-10-19. 'There is a house on what was known as Donkey Street, now High Gate Road called the Boggart house and was supposed to be haunted (a Boggart being a ghost). So I heard it regular as a child in the 1950s. I and my family (XXX) have lived all our lives in Hayfield and my sister who likes to do a bit of writing wrote a very entertaining book (fiction but containing some facts) called the Boggart House.'

Hayfield 5 (De). 1960s/F/FG., 12-10-19. 'I regularly call my husband a "boggart", especially when he's just woken up. His family used the term all the time throughout his childhood in the 1960s and 1970s and beyond. They are a local family too. It's a great word.'

Hayfield 6 (De). ???/F/FG., 12-10-19. 'Heard the word "boggart" used many times when I was a child growing up. If there was a strange noise, and we wondered what is was my Mum (XXX) used to say "ooh it could be a boggart". I never really thought about what a boggart actually was, just that it was something a bit scary.'

Hayfield 7 (De). 1950s/F/FG., 12-10-19. 'I remember my Grandma talking about the boggart house. I grew up in the 1950s, 1960s.'

Hayfield 8 (De). 1970s/F/FG., 12-10-19. 'Highgate Hall. We called it boggart house, lived next door, my mum always claimed to have seen it, the boggart that is. [XXX chipped in: I'm [respondent]'s sister, we know the biggest house well, our mother worked as a cleaner there. She always maintained she had seen a figure passing the window and turned round to speak but there was no one there.] [age estimated from FB accounts]'

Hayfield 9 (De). 1950s/F/FG., 12-10-19. 'I had definitely heard this term when I was growing up in the 1950s and 1960s.'

Hayfield 10 (De). 1920s/F/FG., 12-10-19. 'My Mother who is ninety-five and still lives in Hayfield used the word "Boggart" a lot, as did my Grandma who was originally from Bugsworth. When someone was very pale or windswept hair they would say "she looks like a boggart".'

Kinder 1 (De). 1930s/M/E., 11-10-19. 'I have heard of boggarts. I was born in 1935 and lived in the Kinder valley until I was thirty. We lived at Upper House, a very old farm converted to a hunting lodge. The road to it passed through a large wood, which is where I learned to run! My father came from Scotland so he may have been the person who told me about boggarts and told ghost stories. But my wife, born 1944, in Cheshire also knows what a boggart is. In 1940 when I was five, I would have said it was a ghost. I know Boggart Hole Clough, Blackley, Fairy Hole, Greenfield and Mermaids Pool, Kinder. Have you heard Mr. Davies's accounts of happenings in Longdendale. He was a retired railway worker who lived in the railway cottage near Woodhead Reservoir embankment and the remains of Woodhead station. I last visited Fairy Hole in about 1965! It is a vertical hole in open moorland on Dick Hill. It is no longer on the OS Map but my guess is about SE0145 0532. Mr. Davies recorded his thoughts in the 1990s for Peter McGowan, Peak Park Ranger. A copy may be in Glossop Heritage Centre... He mentioned the large slimey creature on the A628 at Devil's Elbow and knocking on door of his railway house on anniversary of a serious railway accident at Woodhead tunnel. When I was going up to Kinder Reservoir in the 1980s I twice saw an old lady walking towards Hayfield from Bowden Bridge, Kinder. I moved from Kinder in 1966 having lived there for 30 years. Kinder residents told there were no old ladies living in the valley. "Young" XXX told me the name of the deceased resident! and I wonder if what I saw was just a childhood memory?'

New Mills 1 (De). 1940s/M/FG., 10-10-19. 'Not heard of it as I can remember. Over seventy-six years, lol'

New Mills 2 (De). ???/F/FG., 10-10-19. 'Bogart house up High Gate Road Hayfield, supposed to be haunted.'

New Mills 3 (De). 1950s/F/FG., 10-10-19. 'There was a boggart that lived in my next door neighbours coal cellar. Birch Vale in the 1950s.'

New Mills 4 (De). 1970s/F/FG., 10-10-19. 'I was born in New Mills 1970. I often heard the name "Boggart". My Grandparents lived on Bogguard Road in Mellor, my parents live there now. There was a cupboard under the stairs and we always called it the Boggart Hole.'

New Mills 5 (De). 1960s/F/FG., 10-10-19. 'I remember my mum used the word when someone was dashing about or restless – "He's up and down like a boggart!" I'm a child of the 1960s.'

New Mills 6 (De). 1960s/F/FG., 10-10-19. 'Born in New Mills, 1962. Mom born New Mills 1937. Dad RIP Born 1919. We left in 1966 to Canada. Always a Boggart about if you were naughty. Behave or the boggart will get you. Later was shortened to boggy or boggyman – the bogyman will get you. But always a reference to a ghost that would "get you if not nice". I don't use it with my grandkids. Not nice to scare children now unless it's Halloween.'

New Mills 7 (De). 1950s/M/FG., 11-10-19. 'I lived at Highgate Farm on Highgate Road, next door was Highgate Hall which was called the Boggart house. The Boggart was a traveller who stayed there on his travels, he was murdered by the two women who lived there for the trinkets he peddled. His body was thrown in the well. So the story goes he dances on Highgate Green between Highgate hall and Highgate Farm at night. The story is in a book about Derbyshire ghosts.'

New Mills 8 (De). 1970s/F/FG., 11-10-19. 'I was born in 1970. "Boggart" was used a lot by mum mostly telling me to sit down cos I'm like a bloody boggart, and I have to admit I called my dog Nelle 'a little boggart' as she doesn't keep still! I told you there was such a word, XXX.'

New Mills 9 (De). ???/F/FG., 11-10-19. 'When I was younger I was always on the go, and my mum used to say 'sit down and stop wandering like a Bogart'.'

New Mills 10 (De). 1930s/F/FG., 11-10-19. '1930s New Mills, anything untoward was "a bogart", a word used all the time. Don't think has ever died out, still say it...'

New Mills 11 (De). 1960s/F/FG., 11-10-19. 'Brought up in the 1960s. Both parents would use the word "boggart". Would say what are you wandering around for? You are like a boggart.'

New Mills 12 (De). 1960s/F/FG., 11-10-19. 'Highgate Road, Hayfield, The Boggart House. (We moved to Hayfield in 1966, but am originally from New Mills.) I remember being told, as a kid, in the late 1960s, that the house was haunted by the ghost of a woman, a housekeeper, I think. The story went that a beggar, or someone who was starving, anyway, called at the house and asked for food. The housekeeper was frying breakfast, and when she refused the man food, he poured the boiling contents of the pan down her throat, killing her. I'm sure there are many variations on this story!'

New Mills 13 (De). 1950s/M/FG., 11-10-19. 'There was always a bogart in the cupboard at our house if you were naughty. 1950s and 1960s in New Mills.'

New Mills 14 (De). 1970s/M/FG., 11-10-19. 'My mum used to say to me, "Look at the state of you, you look like a Boggart". Yes, in New Mills, early 1970s. Long hair just got out of bed, when I came in she today [*sic*] "eh up the Boggart returns". It never crossed my mind to wonder what a Boggart was. It wasn't til I saw this. It jogged my memory.'

New Mills 15 (De). 1960s/F/FG., 17-10-19. 'Up and down like a boggart!

Often said in our house if you couldn't keep still or was in and out a lot, or used when referring to someone when wondering what they were up to. He's been up and down like a boggart all day. Born New Mills, 1967.'

New Mills 16 (De). ???/M/FG., 17-10-19. 'I well remember being told that I looked like a boggart when I walked into the Royal Oak pub wearing a beanie hat, one night back in the 1970s, here in New Mills!'

New Mills 17 (De). 1950s/F/FG., 17-10-19. 'My wife XXX neé XXX grew up in Hague Bar in the 1950s and definitely knew all about the Bogarts in Shiloe Road and Farm. She tells me that when she was quite young a tramp resided in the basement of her house – Steephills, and for quite a time before they discovered him they used to hear noises – and her mum and dad used to say. "Ah, it's the Bogart".'

New Mills 18 (De). 1960s/F/FG., 17-10-19. 'Mum used to say "You look like a boggart, have you got a haunting job on" if we were sick and looking a bit pale. Hague Bar 1960s. [Other FB user: I can see your mum now. That was one of her favourite sayings about you and XXX]'

Strines 1 (De). ???/M/F., 29-9-19. 'I used to work in Strines and my friend used to come through the woods at five thirty in the morning. Sometimes he looked scared and he would say he could hear boggarts in the undergrowth. He was always going on about the boggarts. Probably 1980s or 1990s.'

Strines 2 (De). 1960s/M/FG., 9-10-19. 'Boggart to me was shortened to "bogey" as in the "bogeyman" and a word used to describe a scary man! So, if you didn't behave the "Bogeyman will get you". So, I grew up obviously in Strines, born 1963. But it was an expression my Grandma used (she lived in Buxton). A boggart was also someone who was not particularly nice, a trouble causer. They are my memories...'

Whaley Bridge 1 (De). 1950s/F/FG., 12-10-19. 'My dad used the word frequently until his premature death in 1984 at the age of 61. Born 1923 in Bugsworth then lived Whaley Bridge from 1934. He used to say "why are you boggarting about?" I grew up in WB from 1950.'

Lincolnshire

Belton 1 (Li). 1960s/F/E., 25-10-19. 'I grew up in Belton and Epworth in the 1960s and 1970s and didn't hear any talk of boggarts. As an adult I associate the word with the North East.'

Belton 2 (Li). 1930s/F/E., 25-10-19. 'My Mother grew up in Belton in the 1940s and 1950s and she says the same as me.' [i.e. no boggart]

Conesby 1 (Li). 1910s/F/FM., 11-9-19. 'I owe my love of folklore, particularly the macabre type, to my maternal grandma – a Lincolnshire girl born on a remote farm in this remote area in 1914, who had a love of these stories and heard them first-hand from country folk. My Grandma was born at a farm called Little Conesby (a lost medieval village, in olden days much larger) just to the north of Scunthorpe, in 1914. Look at a map of Lincolnshire and see how remote it is even now. Imagine life a century ago, without cars. She lived locally to that area all of her life. She very much had a love of the supernatural/fey and it [was] the belief in the family that she had second sight, there are many tales in the family of her prophetic dreams. It is from her I get my interest, though I am half Traveller (my father's side) and that plays a role in my "make up". I think she took a lot from her father who she said I reminded her of. I don't think my Grandma considered boggarts as fairies; I never heard her use that word in connection with them, she spoke of them more as we would ghosts or ghouls, and considered them a nuisance. I can remember her saying such and such a place "is haunted by a boggart" (Lodge Lane in Flixborough is in my mind), so she linked them with ghosts. She was very matter of fact about them, they were a part of life when and where she grew up. White Horse. She saw as a young woman during WW2 a well known (at the time) local ghost – a white horse as she cycled at night through a dip called Grange Beck on the road between Scunthorpe and Flixborough. This was during the blackout. You ask about other stories; do you class Shuck as a Boggart? Black dogs are/were common around here (I have a friend who was chased by one across the fields here) and I think grandma considered them as a type of Boggart, as she did what we could call poltergeists. If anything went missing she would ask for it back out aloud and leave the room, going back later she would find it returned most often. She taught me the same trick and I often use it – ask politely. Again we come to the idea of mischief and nuisance activities. I wonder if all those old stories of poltergeists would have been put down to boggarts by the country people who experienced them, like my

Grandma. This has been a not well thought out post. I would like to correspond further. You must be aware of the Tiddy Man of the Ancholme Valley; I live there, those tales fascinate me because of what they represent regards memories of older, perhaps genuine religious beliefs, surviving in folk memory and passed down mouth to ear over the centuries.'

Crowle 1 (Li). 1960s/F/FG., 7-11-19. 'There was a Tetley boggart or boggett as we called it when I was growing up. Lol cannot remember story though. Crowle, there is a Tetley Road next to north Ax school, [other user Yes Tetley boggitt (however you spell it) from Crowle North Lincolnshire I was born in 1972 and have always known about it growing up.] [message sent to XXX. No that is it. The tale was there's a tunnel that supposedly runs from Crowle Church to Tetley and they said a soldier died down there and constantly walked it! Only what we were told... dog in chains also mentioned but God knows] That's it. Knew you would remember. I remember standing one evening with XXX watching to see if we saw it [Other user: used to say there was a priest's tunnel from Tetley to the church. And the woods at the back of Tetley Hall was where the bogart was.]'

Wainfleet 1 (Li). 1940s/M/FG., 18-10-19. 'I lived "down the bank" in Wainfleet and on Queens Estate from 1948 to 1962 and can't recall the word at all.'

Wainfleet 2 (Li). ???/M/FG., 18-10-19. 'There's a Bogart buried under green hill. Woe betide anyone who digs him up. "King o the bogarts" at that can't remember. Probably grandparents' stories. Most people look at me gone out when I tell them about it. I think it's mentioned in the doomsday book or maybe some other old writings. I will try and find a reference to it.'

Wainfleet 3 (Li). 1960s/M/FG., 18-10-19. 'Never heard the word or name to do with Wainfleet during my childhood or since. The only Bogart I know of is Humphrey.'

Winteringham 1 (Li). 1930s/F/FG., 17-10-19. 'My mum was born in Winteringham in 1936, and she's never heard of it.'

Winteringham 2 (Li). 1950s/F/FG., 17-10-19. 'My wife grew up in Winteringham in the 1940s and 1950s and does not recall hearing the word.'

Winteringham 3 (Li). 1950s/M/E., 17-10-19. 'Not much help to you but a possibility to eliminate areas of the usage. Both my parents (like myself) were born and bred in Lincolnshire (Winterton, Barton Upon Humber and Winterton respectively). They in the 1920s and myself 1959. I have never heard of the term and am sure I would have had they used it on a regular occasion. Hope this "helps". That's an interesting map. I don't know if you are aware of the area but it looks like the eastern extremity of it just nudges into

North Lincolnshire. Wouldn't surprise me if the river Trent is it's natural border. West of the Trent is the Isle of Axholme and because of that Trent barrier they have a more Yorkshire accent than us yellow bellies. You probably need to be asking folk from Epworth, Belton, Westwoodside, Haxey etc.'

Winteringham 4 (Li). 1940s/F/FG., 18-10-19. 'As children we used to play on a triangle of grass at the junction of two roads and called it a boggart's green. That would be in the 1940s and 1950s. Mable Peacock says a boggart was a ghost or an apparition but to us it was a safe place to play.'

Winteringham 5 (Li). 1940s/F/FG., 18-10-19. 'Hi just to say I was brought up in Winteringham from 1941 to 1960. Yes, we knew about Boggarts, they used to be out at night according to my Dad, it was used I think to make you behave or the Boggart would get you. We had an attic in an old cottage where we lived that we weren't allowed to go into and one "lived" in there. My dad had a name for that one, it was "nut O nailer" and when we heard a noise at night Dad would say it was him. Thankfully we moved when I was eleven years and Boggarts were never mentioned again. Hope this is useful. My Dad came from an old Winteringham Family going back several hundred years. Strange that I saw someone else around my age had never heard of them but I know her father was not a local. Hope you get more feedback.'

Rhodesian, Scottish and Other Boggarts

Cyprus 1 (Oth). 1940s/F/FG., 7-11-19. 'I was born in 1948 and first came to Doncaster when I was seventeen, having lived on various RAF camps whilst growing up. I remember using the word "boggart" when I lived in Cyprus and was in the Brownies. Boggarts were the beings who would catch you if you weren't in your six corner when playing games!'

Colchester 1 (Oth). 1960s/F/E., 1-9-19. 'In a recent copy of *Fortean Times* you ran an article requesting information on a boggart in exchange for a boggart picture. I'm too young to have experienced boggarts in the usual folklore. However, I met someone recently on the bus and we got talking about local folklore, and I mentioned your article. I must admit, I was delighted by the idea of a creepy boggart picture, so I have been asking anyone who looks like they may be old enough to know something. I'm lucky I've got the gift of the gab, as my criteria for interviewing could have gotten me into hot water! The lady, who I shall call Kate, told me when she was at primary school at St Michael's in Hadleigh (Essex, up near Benfleet, not the one near Colchester), around fifty to fifty-five years ago, she learned a song about a railway boggart. I have located this online: if you Google railway boggart, there is a song which matches very closely what she could remember. The lyrics she mentioned were "he doesn't have chains, he just plays tricks on railway trains". Kate told me from what she could remember from St Michael's, boggarts were known as extremely unpleasant. Not quite malicious, but certainly not pleasant. A level above Gremlins, but below murderous activity. This is why the boggart on the railway train in the song was an exception. He played tricks on trains, so wasn't very dangerous. Because of the type of employment she has, she was not willing to tell me very much information herself so I'm not sure I could get her details for interview. However, I've got you a lead in St Michael's primary school in Hadleigh. They may even still have sheet music for the song.'

Gillingham 1 (Oth). 1960s/F/E., 13-7-19. 'In response to your *Fortean Times* column, I distinctly remember one occasion when I was a child and my mother was annoyed with me for some reason. Whilst giving me a scolding she snapped "you're not a Brownie, you're a Boggart." This would have been in the early 1970s and to be honest I thought she had called me a "yoghurt", not having heard the word "Boggart" before (or very often since, to be honest). This was in Gillingham, Kent, but may have had its origins in the fact that my mum was evacuated to family in Wantage in Berkshire during the early part of the war where she may well have encountered elderly relatives who remembered a more rural and superstitious age. If it would be useful I can ask her. I certainly grew up knowing of rites like washing my face in May day dew to avoid getting spots. [further email] I am pretty sure she was a Guide and went on to run a Guide company before I was born (I distinctly remember an occasion in my teens, when she stood in to take one of my Company meetings as a one-off because our Captain was away). Overall I seem to recall it being a fairly folk-lore aware childhood and nobody ever teased me for my own interest in such things.'

Kent 1 (Oth). 1970s/F/FG., 16-10-19. 'Boggart was used in Kent when I was growing up. Naughty sprites who liked playing tricks on walkers and travellers and occasionally on the farms and in graveyards. 1970s childhood.'

Kettering 1 (Oth). 1940s/F/F., 29-8-19. 'Me and my parents are originally from Northamptonshire and I recall dad calling me a "soggy boggart" when I had been out in the rain. My dad was born there but through his work we lived in different parts of the midlands. He would have called me this in the 1950s. I would think, then we lived in Stoke on Trent and Godmanchester near Huntingdon. Hope this is of some help, it could be he picked it up when he was in the army during the war where he would have mixed with people from all over the country. Sorry I forgot to add Kettering, Northants is where we are originally from. I lived there in the end of the 1940s but was only tiny when we left but I had grandparents there up till the 1960s and still have two cousins there. As I said moving around my dad could have picked it up from anywhere but I hope it helps you with your research.'

Kimberley 1 (Oth). 1950s/M/E., 27-9-19. 'Yesterday evening I asked my friend and neighbour XXX if he knew what a boggart was. At first, he said no, then after a lengthy pause said "Is it some sort of sprite?" But of course that is far too benign a term. He was born in 1959 and comes from Kimberley, a few miles north west of Nottingham, so not far from the Derbyshire border. The lack of knowledge is not a matter of lack of education: they are both Oxbridge graduates. XXX is particularly fascinated with the meaning of words, he is the head of XXX at Nottingham High School.'

King's Lynn 1 (Oth). 1940s/M/FG., 27-9-19. 'Born in King's Lynn of a mother from Sheffield and a father from London in 1948. Only ever knew of my mum's family and I have been aware of this word all my life, although it was seldom used.'

London 1 (Oth). 1950s/F/FG., 14-10-19. 'I had never heard of boggarts until I went to teacher training college in Retford. 1969. Not sure that it originated in Retford as we were from London, Nottingham, Newcastle, Doncaster, Birmingham and more. We had boggart hunts! The boggart dressed up and carried a mop and bucket. We had to find him (it was always a guy) usually in the local pub. It was an excuse for a pub crawl I guess.'

Northern Ireland 1 (Oth). 1950s/F/E., 15-9-19. 'I saw your post on the Discuss Littleborough Facebook site and thought I'd drop you a line. It's slightly off topic because I'm a blow in, and only moved to the area in 2007. However, I grew up in Northern Ireland and my Dad was very fond of stories about boggarts – I was born in 1976 and my Dad was born in 1947, so it would have been around the time that you were asking about that he would have learned the stories. By the time my siblings and I were hearing the stories the boggart was like a naughty creature who lived in our house, but whom we never saw – a bit like the modern day Elf on a Shelf. We even have a boggart box – a lidded metal box used for storing firelighters and kindling, which we still refer to as a boggart box to this day. Good luck with your research – it would be lovely to hear from you if you end up publishing anything about boggarts – I wasn't aware of the folklore that comes from my adopted home until you posted today, and I'm chuffed to learn that there's supposed to be a boggart hole near my house, on the other side of Shore Road!'

Nottingham 1 (Oth). 1990s/F/E., 11-10-19. 'Someone from my Morris side shared your census and I thought I'd drop you a quick note, just in case it's helpful. I was born in 1994, in Nottingham. My mum mostly spoke of Scottish folklore growing up but she knew it all. Selkies were our favourite. Boggarts were mentioned, but perhaps adapted for a child's fearful ears. They were playful and mischievous, but not at all malevolent. If they got into your house, they would probably make quite the mess of things, but they wouldn't cause harm. Nothing a Brownie couldn't fix anyway. I now live in Sheffield, where I dance with Boggart's Breakfast, a border morris side. We try to embody the spirit of the Peakland boggarts, who would lure people out into the dark moors with blue lights, never to be seen again. We wear all black, with sequins on our rag jackets, we have blue faces, and we wear blue lights on our hats when it's dark. At dance outs, one of us might wear the boggart mask and go out into the crowd. "The boggart" is energetic, and playful, and extremely mischievous. They might steal a hat from a Cotswold morris dancer, and place it upon the head of an audience member, silently cackling at the disruption they caused. The boggart may not speak or make sound, so all their movements are exaggerated. Past boggart mask wearers have taken it upon themselves to scare children, but these days the kids love playing with the "naughty boggart". There's a bit more about our lore and stuff on our website

– www.boggarts breakfast.org.uk so do have a look if you think it would be useful.'

Scotland 1 (Oth). 1940s/F/E., 22-11-19. 'Naughty, evil elf. I was a brownie leader and we had a boggart "six". This is the only place I've heard the word. My mother was a Brownie leader and she used the word.'

Shropshire 1 (Oth). 1970s/F/E., 15-9-19. 'I have just read your post on Warrington memories. Both of my parents were from Warrington and moved to live on a country estate in Cressage, Shropshire. My father was a gamekeeper. Our house was in the middle of a wood backing onto the river Severn. On one side of the house was a very steep incline which went around the side of the house. My parents always told my brother, sister and I, that we should never go near the incline as the boggarts lived there and they would kidnap us and we would never be seen again. The boggarts were huge monsters who lived in a lair at near the river. Shocking those boggarts! Their threats worked as we ventured all over that estate and had a wonderful childhood. We never went near the incline. I remember once being daring and went to look over the incline, straight away I could feel someone watching me and convinced my child self it was the boggarts. I never went there again. [Later email]. My Dad was born and raised in the Orford Parish and Mum the Latchford Parish. Those pesky boggarts came with them to Shropshire and haunted us for years. My parents married in 1968 and lived in the Wicklow mountains for two years. They then moved to Shropshire, lock, stock and boggart in 1970 with my sister who was born in Ireland. I was born in 1971 and my kid brother in 1972. We often laugh about them boggarts, but I'm actually convinced the sheer terror of being kidnapped by them saved us from serious harm. You could say it was a precursor of health and safety! I am so glad you received so many replies, have you discovered where they originated from? I spoke to my work colleagues, all around my age and all of them had various stories that there parents had terrified them with if they were to stray. The younger ones were horrified. But I guess in those days we were ill informed, social media hadn't been invented and we only had Charlie the cat and the green cross man to assist us! Just like any parent trying to keep our children safe we use whatever means available. Even a family of boggarts just waiting to kidnap a stray human child. I have just read your articles. Omg, my Father always said we should never go near the water of the duck pond as Jinny Greenteeth would get us and we would never be seen again. Are these tales built up to protect us or is there something more to these, what do you believe? As a child I would believe anything my parents told me. We weren't encouraged to question. My daughter is a post doc scientist currently working as XXX. From being a small child I have encouraged her to question everything, although as a little girl the fairies used to leave her letters in the tree at the bottom of our garden! So not matter how clever, there is always room for imagination!'

Southern England 1 (Oth). 1980s/F/FG., 27-9-19. 'I was born about a decade later than you are interested in and I've also only been in Glossop a few years (I'm a southerner)! Saying that I probably did know what a boggart was at ten as I have had a longstanding interest in folktales/legends. It may have remained in common usage around here because of Boggart's mill – part of Dinting Printworks which has some local legends attached to it http://www.glossopheritage.co.uk/potters.htm'.

Zimbabwe 1 (Oth). 1950s/M/E., 27-9-19. 'In a strange twist, my husband HAD heard of them. His little sister used to threaten him with "the Hairy Boggart will get you". So, I asked her where she got that from but, sadly, she really hasn't a clue. (XXX family are from Pulborough, West Sussex; prior to that they were 19C English landowners in County Cavan, Ireland, but John and his sister grew up in 1950s–1960s Rhodesia!). So it could have been via grandparents, parents, school pals. We'll probably never know.'

Addenda

Two pieces of information came in while this book was being prepared for press.

First, in 1950 Ernest Dewhurst, 'Belthorn Calling England', *Northern Daily Telegraph* (21 Apr 1950), 6, gave a possible boggart place-name (or at least a locution): 'I have even heard whispers that around Belthorn is "boggart's land", that a dragon used to maraud the district, and that even to-day womenfolk are not "over-anxious" to stir out of doors at night.'

Second, I would now add the following to the Boggart Census.

Derbyshire 1 (De): M/1950s/E., 31-10-21: 'My friend, the late Richard Scollins, who was a well-known Erewash Valley dialect expert and co-author of the *Ey Up Me Duck* books proposed that the derogatory term "bogger", applied to naughty children on the Notts/Derbyshire border, derived from "boggart" and not "bugger". "Tha's a little bogger", was a phrase I heard regularly during my childhood in the 1950s and formed a standard term for impish and mischievous behaviour amongst miners. The suggestion is given a little more credence, I think, by the reference in Elizabeth Mary Wright's book *Rustic Speech and Folklore* (1913) p. 194: "But whatever its origin, the name yet lives in proverbial sayings such as to roar like a barghest (Dur) and as a term of abuse (Yks, Not) e.g you noisy bargest, said to a child."'

Thanks to Barrie Whittamore for this consideration. I would, had it been possible, have added this to the discussion of 'Bugger' in Young, *The Boggart*, 30.

Appendix: Questions and Prompts

The following is my email questionnaire, which became the basis for most newspaper articles.

'In the past the word "boggart" was used a lot in XXX, but there is confusion about what it meant. We are hoping that you can help us with that. What does the word "boggart" mean to you? Did your parents and grandparents use the word? Do your children or nephews and nieces? Did you know any stories about boggarts or places especially associated with boggarts? Where did you grow up and in what decade? Do you know anyone else who could do this interview and help us with boggarts? How could I get in touch with them?'

I used versions of this for Facebook: 'My name is Simon Young and I'm a British folklorist finishing a book on boggarts (folk monsters). At present I'm looking for anyone from XXX or neighbouring communities who heard the word "boggart" in their homes growing up, say from around 1920 to circa 1970 (the period the word and the idea were dying out). I've managed, with a lot of huffing and puffing, to get some memories from throughout the north of boggarts and I'd like to get some more, particularly from your area. Negatives are interesting. So if you grew up in XXX in, say, the 1950s but never heard the word "boggart" I'd love to know. *Please write the decade you grew up in and which village/town/city.* BTW if anyone has memories but would prefer, for whatever reason, not to write here, my email is simonyoungfl AT gmail DOT com. I just need (i) the community you grew up in, (ii) the decade and (iii) what you heard about boggarts. I really appreciate you hosting this post and I hope this message isn't an imposition given that I'm an outsider!'